To Stephen

Acknowledgements

In loving memory of my mother, Edith, and my father, Jindi. This book could not have been written without the unswerving support of Stephen Brown, and my children Rivkah, Sarah and Dovid. Huge thanks are due to Jonathan Myerson, Louise Doughty and colleagues at City University, also to Kate Dunton, Leonie Sturge-Moore, Kate Worsley, Elizabeth Elford, Elizabeth Davidson, Hannah Michell. My friends and readers who helped me keep faith over the years include Sue Cohen, Sarah Cusk, Mikey Cuddihy, the much missed Fiona Freedland, Robin Oppenheim, Susannah Reichenstein, and Kath Libbert. Thanks to everybody at Honno, to my agent Veronique Baxter and publicist Emily Burns.

REPARATION

REPARATION

by
Gaby Koppel

HONNO MODERN FICTION

First published in 2019 by Honno Press,
'Ailsa Craig', Heol y Cawl, Dinas Powys,
Vale of Glamorgan, Wales, CF64 4AH
1 2 3 4 5 6 7 8 9 10
Copyright: Gaby Koppel © 2019

The Author would like to stress that this is a work of fiction and no
resemblance to any actual individual or institution is intended or implied. A
catalogue record for this book is available from the British Library.

A catalogue record for this book is available from the British Library.

Published with the financial support of the Welsh Books Council.

ISBN 978-1-909983-84-7 (paperback)
ISBN 978-1-909983-85-4 (ebook)

Cover design: Sue Race
Cover image: © Digalakis Photography/Shutterstock Inc.
Text design: Elaine Sharples
Printed in Great Britain by 4edge

Prologue

Budapest 1944

From the car she can make out the militia, rifles in hand and ragtag uniforms. Facing them, a huddled crowd of prisoners, faces white in the sharp air, some clutch whimpering children. One man with a cloth hat in his hands, wringing the life out of it. The commanding officer is the biggest brute of a brutal bunch, though hardly more than a boy. He strides up and down the shivering assembly, shouting, face contorted in anger.

– *Istenem, istenem*, mutters her mother. Oh God. Then louder, *Stop the car. Stop here.*

– *No! Too dangerous, Kovács Bacsi drive on.* And turning to her mother – *Sit down. Don't be a fool.*

Her mother is clutching the letter in trembling hands, and by now the foolscap is looking crumpled, the ink on the envelope is smeared. She prises it out of her mother's grip, opens her bag and slides the letter in, then closes the brass clasp with a loud click that reverberates in the tense air.

As the car passes the huddled mob, both women gaze out towards the river bank, scanning the detainees' faces one by one. It's all too quick, too distant. The motor bumps over the cobbled road. Is that him? No. Of course not. It's just another middle-aged businessman. A fat one, in a long coat with an astrakhan collar, who reminds her of a bank manager. *He* is altogether more charismatic. *He* would stand out from the crowd.

A little further along, *Kovács* manages to pull up, tucking the car into a side street. Her mother looks pale and frightened – as white and fragile as that precious letter. Aranca straightens the older woman's hat, and with her finger wipes off some stray lipstick. Checking the pavement in each direction, the two slip out of the vehicle and cross the road. By now, a small crowd has

1

gathered to watch the scene that is taking place beside the river. The dishevelled prisoners must know what's about to happen. The people watching certainly know.

There's a drop of three metres from the quay. It will take them a second or two to fall, she thinks, but for them time will slow right down from the instant the bullet leaves the barrel of the gun. They will know their last moments, millisecond by millisecond. Bang. She wonders whether you hear the gun going off when it's pointed at you. She's heard you don't. A burning, tearing pain in the guts. Momentum of the shot knocking you off your feet. The spinning whoosh as you fall through the sharp air. You can feel yourself hit the water, with a jarring splash. The half-iced hardness makes you gasp, as your body breaks through the surface and your stunned lungs pull at – nothing. The current drags you under. You are fighting for breath, every last desperate gasp. But the water is raging. The cold is paralysing and there's a roaring pain in your chest as your lungs search for air in the void. You are fighting to pull yourself to the surface, but as your lifeblood mixes with the murky water, strength ebbs, and blackness is all that is left.

She gazes, transfixed, at the surface of the river, thick with ice floes in a myriad different sizes, large white rafts surrounded by smaller pebbles, that are constantly moving and realigning themselves as they glide along, pushed by the merciless current.

He *is* there, she realises with a jolt. Standing slightly apart from the others. And yes, he does look distinguished. It won't help him now, his dignified air but the letter might, if only she could work out who she is supposed to give it to. The name on the envelope doesn't mean anything to her – she's trying to remember what they were told about Colonel Farkas. She feels a quivering hand grab her arm. Oh yes, her mother has noticed too. The older woman is gulping great mouthfuls of air, groaning. She's about to shout out. The word hovers around her lips. *Istenem* – Oh God – but no sound comes out. They know the forged papers in her pocket won't fool anyone. If they are going to save her father, they are going to have to break cover now, but her gut is warning her it is too risky by far.

She takes her mother's hand in her own, roles reversed – she's in charge despite her tender years. Seeing her now, few would guess she really ought to be in school. But that was another life, before a false step could cost everything. She squeezes her mother's trembling hand hard enough to hurt.

– *Shhh*, she says, looking her in the eye. *Don't draw attention. Not here, not now.* She's scanning the scene – where is he, this mysterious Colonel? Surely he's not the scrawny yob commanding the squad. She looks around for a more senior officer but can't see any, just the brute of a youth who is probably illiterate anyway, judging by the way he's going on. This wasn't how it was supposed to be. She stifles her own moan, pulls back on the tears so hard it makes her eyes hurt.

Her mother pulls at her arm.

– *The letter*, she rasps.

Heads in the crowd turn towards them. Aranca makes a face at her mother telling her to be quiet. There may be informers around to betray them. They can't just walk up to a bunch of militiamen and tell them to release her father because – because what? Because they have a letter from someone really important to somebody really important? They've got to leave before they are spotted. Keep on the move. But Mother doesn't budge, her feet have grown roots. She was always a stubborn woman, today is no different. On the quay, the prisoners are being tied together in threes.

The boy commander walks up to one, apparently at random. It's the bank manager in the coat with the astrakhan collar, which is now dragged off him. Underneath it, his double-breasted, pinstriped suit is crumpled and torn, and as he turns she can see that his face is bruised on one side. He looks terrified. The leader yanks him by the lapel, and coshes him over the head with a gun. As the man collapses with a yelp of pain, she can feel the crowd around her flinch. The commander shouts something at the man on the ground. In the crowd, hands go to mouths. Two soldiers take turns to kick the man on the floor, then jerk him to his feet. The leader looks at the distant crowd, grinning. *The bastard*, she thinks, *he's performing to an audience. He wants us to see this. This obscenity.* But she can't leave. Not now. He shouts out again, and his men grab two others. One is a working man with a grey moustache and shabby clothes, the other a slight young woman. Two militiamen bundle the two prisoners towards the edge of the quay and tie them up to the bank manager, so they make a ghastly trio. The commander screams at them, and all three remove their shoes. *Obedient*, she thinks, *why so obedient? They can't still be hoping.*

There is a moment's pause. She feels fast, hot breaths on the back of her neck, the person behind her inching forward to get a better view. The commander takes a pistol out of his belt, holds it to the bank manager's head and pulls the trigger. The crowd seem to shudder in unison as the shot reports along the quay, before the militiamen push his sagging body into the river. Pulling the other two with him. Makes the bullets go further. The crowd would get that. The soldiers' laughter cuts through the air. One of them kicks a stray shoe into the water. But he has missed its pair. Scuffed brown leather, worn at the heel and toe. It lies there on the quay, orphaned and accusing.

Her legs are about to buckle. She concentrates as hard as she can on keeping them rigid. Never before has she been so conscious of the muscles in her thighs and each side of her knees. She focuses on each one, pushing her mind between the sinews and counting *one–two–three–four–five*. Think of the numbers, she tells herself, the digits ascending with their

4

beautiful symmetry, think of them and nothing else. Clasping her mother's hand, she uses all her remaining strength to wrench her away towards the car. As they accelerate off, they hear muffled gunshots half-drowned by the sound of traffic.

And now the letter is in her hands though she doesn't remember taking it out. Hot tears drop onto the blue ink, the writing puckers and swirls, becoming fainter and fainter.

Chapter One

Cardiff, 1997

It's the middle of the night and my mother's gone AWOL in a field wearing patent leather loafers.

Two years after my father sells his business at a loss, Mutti has been despatched to Ibiza on a mysterious mission to do with their prized holiday flat but never gets any further than Rhoose, and is reported missing near the airport perimeter. It later turns out this isn't just another one of her little mishaps, it is the beginning of a whole new chapter in all our lives.

Dad's at home warming up the paprika chicken when the police ring to say she's been thrown off the flight. Sorry? At first it doesn't seem to make sense. The person at the airport end hesitates, and finally mutters something about excessive alcohol consumption. In plain language, my mother was drunk. When you reflect on the yobbish behaviour air crews actually do tolerate, for them to dump a sixty-something woman brought up to believe that 'we' always act like a lady however many gins we may have sunk, she must really have been giving it some. But Dad doesn't waste time thinking about that as he rushes down there, and to his credit he does manage to manhandle her into the car. But just as they are driving off, she leaps out of the door and disappears into the dark.

So here I am now, sitting in the passenger seat of Dad's decrepit Datsun as we cruise the airport approach road. The midnight pips sound on Radio 4. By the time we glide past the terminal, a newsreader is intoning the details of Tony Blair's new cabinet in prayer-like cadences. The fifth time I've heard it today. I jab the off button and the whole complex begins to recede behind us. I gaze vainly into the gloom, but there's no sign of a woman in a car coat with a handbag over her arm, who might happen to be ambling about in the bushes, giving the wildlife the fright of their lives.

"We've definitely been along this road before," I protest.

"*Nein*, looks the same, but was coming from other side. Porthkerry Road," says Dad, crunching the gears as we cross the A4226.

"Honestly, we have been here before. An hour ago."

"So, in an hour she can go a long way."

"She can barely walk from the car to the supermarket. She's just not up to walking a mile in the dark."

"What zatt?" He stops the car.

"What?"

"See, over there."

I jump out, stride across the verge and peer over the fence. The mulchy grass sucks in my boots. I can't imagine her lasting long here in patent leather heels. I lean over the fence, and stare into the gloom. Away from the streetlights, everything looks grey. On the charcoal expanse, there's an ashen shape moving about. It could be a person lying on the ground, writhing in pain. Why on earth didn't I bring the torch? Then, as my eyes adjust, I make out a pile of bin liners disgorging their half-digested contents onto the grass, the empty bags flailing in the wind. We retreat to the car. At least Mutti's not dead in this field. We drive onward.

I phone the airport police again. Straight through to voicemail. "I can't go on like this," mutters my father. "I will, I will…" I think his lip trembles, or is it a streetlamp passing over the car? "…I will take a powder." It's probably the wrong moment to point out that the powder thing doesn't actually work in English, unless you are talking about Beecham's but that's not what he means and it's irritating. I'm thinking for God's sake you've been here long enough to learn the language now, get the idioms right for once. Of course I don't actually say anything, but grind my teeth. However grim things have been before, I've never heard my father threaten suicide. That's her style not his.

"Don't be silly," I say, trying not to snap. "We'll get her home, and by tomorrow morning, you'll feel a whole lot better."

"Tomorrow I feel better, *ja*, but then it happens again, and again. I am too old for all this," he rasps. "You don't know what it's like. I finish it now." He jerks to a halt in the middle of the road, and starts banging his head against the steering wheel. His white mane shudders with each thump. If he carries on, he's going to concuss himself. I lean over and wrap my arms around him.

My parents have long given the impression to outsiders of having perfectly matched eccentricities. People think of them as sweet but slightly dotty European émigrés. It's a smokescreen.

"Why don't you get help?" I ask, as he subdues.

"We've had help. What do you think she was doing *schlepping* to London for years and years to see Dr Hellman? Cost a fortune."

What a complete waste of money that was. Lies of omission. I bet my last fiver there was never a word about booze in all the hundreds of hours on the couch. Darling Ilse may well have been best mates with Anna Freud, but she was into therapy, not telepathy. There's a price for being so economical with the truth.

"That was years ago. You need help now."

"You take her. You try. She won't listen to me."

"How bad is it?"

"You've seen her."

"What about your doctor, can't he help?"

"She doesn't like him."

"And?"

"It's not the same since Ernest retired. He's just a run-of-the-mill GP." He screws up his face.

"So she's right."

"To be honest he's a complete *arschloch*."

The thunder of an airplane taking off directly above us cuts our conversation. If I can get him over this, then everything will be back to normal. A few rounds of bridge and some *Sachertorte* could do wonders to restore their sense of equilibrium.

"Why don't we go back to the airport?" I suggest. "At least we can get a cup of coffee, and talk to the police again – maybe they've heard something." I don't want to be the person that finds her in a ditch. Whatever mess she's dragged us through, she deserves better than that.

"The airport?" He's shouting again now. "Why should she go back there?"

"Because there's nowhere else to go," I shout back at him. "Unless she asks the nearest sheep to do her a favour and run her down to the Savoy for a spot of dinner!"

At the terminal, I trip over a familiar looking shoe. Patent leather slip-on with two-inch heels and decorative gold buckles. It stands alone, on the granite floor, orphaned. A few feet away, my *Mutti* is sleeping with her mouth open, on a row of chairs near to the police desk. She's bathed in the pale green glow of fluorescent light, her suitcase and handbag propped next to her. As I lean over, the smell of sweetly decaying booze breath swills over me. The Madame Rochas she's wearing is no match for it, and has thrown in the towel.

* * * * *

The following day, I wake in my old bed with the alarm going off. I force myself up. I can't afford to be too late for work, and there's a hundred and sixty miles of M4 motorway between me and Shepherd's Bush. I pull on my jeans and stumble down to the kitchen. Mutti's sitting at the table, cleaning the sticky black nicotine goo out of her cigarette holders with little torn-up twists of tissue, reading glasses pushed down her nose. She's smoking while she does it, poring over the congealed tar. The bitter smell of nicotine and fresh smoke mingles in the air with the acrid aroma of mocha. A long, quilted dressing-gown of stained rose-patterned fabric is gaping over her round belly. Next to the ashtray full of brown-stained tissue twists lies a pile of crosswords cut out of the *Daily Telegraph*, and a pencil, which she picks up now and then to write in an answer.

"Good morning," she says with a bright smile. If she's got a hangover, she's hiding it well.

"Morning," I mumble.

"What do you want for breakfast?"

"Just coffee."

"Go on – I make you an eggy."

A peace offering. For my mother, food has always been love on a plate. She brought me up on *streuselkuchen* with *schlagsahne* and when I was fifteen told me I was half a stone overweight. Her. The one in the Crimplene tent. I etched my anger in blood red ink into my diary. I stopped eating. I thought that'll show her. She can do her thousand calorie a day diet from now until Christmas, but I'll drop half a stone before she's even opened that can of Weight Watchers soup. So what if my periods stop. Then she hoiks me off to the doctor, and it turns out they all think I'm pregnant. As if.

I look at her puppy pleading eyes. "No, honestly," I say, "I'll have something later. But I'll have some of that fresh coffee."

I want to scream at her for forcing Dad and me to patrol the airport in the early hours, for making me late for work, and then pretending nothing happened. But I find myself submitting to her forced warmth. It's easier. She puts the kettle on, and clucks around tidying things away and wiping green patterned splash-back tiles with a damp J-cloth. My father comes down the stairs.

I wait to see whether he says anything about the ordeal she's put us through. But he just makes himself a cup of lemon tea and pads off into the other room to watch the headlines on breakfast television, stopping only to give my mother a reassuring pat on the bum. I realise that it's always been like this.

The following day Mutti gets on a flight to Ibiza. She's called Customer Services at the charter company to complain about the outrageous way she was treated. After all, she's been a loyal customer for many years. With profuse apologies, she's been put on the next convenient flight out. She phones me, triumphant, to announce her victory. I wish her *bon voyage* and am left sitting in the office. She gets away with it every single time.

When I next visit my parents they seem more united than ever, and there's something new going on – they are strangely secretive. I notice their eyes meeting when they think I'm not watching. As usual there's nothing much to pass the time, apart from shopping. My mother loves the supermarket. She parks in the disabled parking bay, though there's nothing whatever wrong with her. "They can't give you a ticket," she points out.

"What about the genuinely disabled people who come to the supermarket and discover you've taken their space?"

"I come here at least three times a week, and there are always spaces. Ridiculous, the number of disabled spaces. It would take an epidemic of polio to put so many people in wheelchairs."

"Just because you can get away with it, doesn't make it right."

"What is wrong, is they make too many disabled spaces."

"There are plenty of others."

"But they are further away."

"Being lazy is not a recognised disability. Anyway you need a bit of exercise, it would do you good." I become stern, "And it would stop you becoming disabled in the future."

"Ha!" says Mutti, letting go of her trolley and putting up her two index fingers. "I must do my exercises, exercises, exercises," she chants, bending and straightening her fingers up and then pointing them towards each other in unison. It's an old joke. She uses it to divert attention from the argument, laughing and looking at me coquettishly, as though she was twenty-five instead of nearly seventy.

Although she has hobbled through the revolving doors leaning heavily on her trolley, once we are inside the supermarket Mutti scampers along the aisles with the playful energy of a Labrador puppy chasing a roll of toilet paper. She compares similar products, hunts for unusual ingredients, and examines new lines with great interest. It's an endless, amusing game. Items can be substituted for one another or combined in different ways. She is particularly pleased to discover that there is a promotion for a new type of cheese. A pretty girl in a bright green sweatshirt is offering samples on a tray. Mutti helps herself to two, then does a circuit round the tinned vegetable section and has another couple. I study the contents of our trolley in a desperate bid to avoid eye contact with the promotions girl. And pray she has a memory impairment.

The numerous choices available in the savoury cracker section seem to hold an improbable fascination for my mother, and I think she could write a doctorate on the multiple uses of tinned tuna. At the fresh fish counter, Mutti asks for some mackerel. The shop assistant has difficulty understanding, and asks her to repeat her order three times. Mutti's now getting irritated by having to repeat herself to a girl who speaks one language badly, when she herself speaks four fluently and two others well enough to make small talk over the bridge table. The girl tries to make up for it by being apologetic to the point of servility. She's got that right, anyway. Mutti pulls herself up to her full imposing height and gives a benign smile. As the girl is wrapping the fish, she says to my mother,

"Where to you from then, sweets?" There's a frozen moment. Mutti's expression, which was beginning to thaw, now drops to minus fifty. She seizes the package and throws it into her trolley.

"Rhiwbina," she barks, and stomps off leaving the girl looking baffled.

Her favourite section of the shop is refrigerated goods. She is lingering there, studying the ingredients of a type of fruit yoghurt that I am certain she has never bought. Then she replaces it, and starts scrutinising some pots of salad. I know that she would not consider buying shop-bought coleslaw, when it is "so easy", and "so much cheaper and better" to make your own, and therefore it's puzzling that she is so interested in these products. And now I really want to get out of here.

"Do you really want that, then?" I ask. "If we get back in time I'll be able to go for a swim before lunch."

"Wait a minute, won't be long now," she says looking at her watch.

"What won't be long?"

"You'll see."

After a while, a shop employee arrives with a ticket gun and a clipboard. He starts going through the chilled section, marking down prices. Now a small crowd of jostling pensioners has collected around him. Mutti's tactics have put her in pole position. She loads the trolley with low-fat soft cheese, wafer-thin sliced ham and hummus, all reduced to a fraction of their original price. Then, as she is bearing down on a carton of marinaded olives, they are lifted from the fridge by a white-haired woman with a walking stick. I see a tiny flicker of annoyance pass over Mutti's face. She eyes the frail-looking woman with all the concentration of a sniper taking aim. Then her trolley suddenly lurches forward, apparently out of control. It misses the old lady, but flips the walking stick out of her grasp, knocking her off balance. As she clutches on to the edge of the fridge for support, she lets go of the olives. Mutti manoeuvres the package into her own trolley, while simultaneously putting her hand out to "help" the old lady.

She bends over nimbly to pick up the walking stick and places it in the lady's hand with a solicitous pat. As she takes it, the old dear makes a point of saying how rare it is these days to come across people with "good manners". She has no idea. Satisfied with her haul, Mutti pushes on to the checkout.

"Is it really worth it?" I ask, while we are waiting in the queue.

"Is what worth it?"

"All that faffing around just to save a few pennies."

"*Ja*, you know darling. Things are not easy, I do what I can."

"What do you mean?"

"Ach, you know, since Daddy sold the business, we have to be a bit more careful," she says.

She starts emptying her trolley onto the conveyor belt. I look at what she's chosen, and realise how meagre it is. Of course, she used to feed a family of four plus my grandmother and a constant stream of other guests. Now it's just her and my father. But even taking this into account, the lavish excesses of the past have evaporated. Seeing that she has been reduced to scavenging for cut-price bargains silences me.

But then I notice that there are a couple of bottles of vodka in the trolley – I didn't see those going in. Of course. Mutti "forgot" the mayonnaise, and asked me to pop back. I wonder if she really believes I won't notice what she's done while I was gone. She must think I'm really stupid. What is the point of indulging in that ridiculous rigmarole for a few cut price items from the delicatessen when she's going to pour twenty times the amount she's saved right down her throat? I'm ready to explode with indignation, but the evident desperation as she stands stooped next to the trolley pulls the rug right out from under my fury. I don't ask any more questions.

On the way home, Mutti breaks the silence. "Daddy spoke to *Onkel* Bernhard yesterday."

"Oh yeah?" I know what's coming next. She might as well be jabbing me with a size six darning needle.

"Apparently Hanni is engaged."

"To a nice Jewish boy, no doubt." I snap. If she picks up on my irritation, she pretends not to.

"Apparently he's a lawyer."

Lawyer is code for a decent income and prospects for the future. My parents would so love me to get engaged to a nice lawyer, doctor or accountant. In this respect they are traditional. Unemployed photographer is not on their list. But they are eternal optimists. "How is David?" she asks.

"Good, good. Dave's good," I reply. That's code for we are still together. And he's still not Jewish.

Chapter 2

On Monday morning, London is flat and grey, but at least I'm not responsible for anybody else's emotional well-being. In the hope of repairing my own, I stumble out of the flat while Dave's still comatose and head to the gym for a sweaty workout. After that, I feel I've earned a full fat latte, "extra hot, extra shot", to keep me going through what promises to be a long production meeting. This proves to be a sound investment. There's a tedious discussion about whether the new police liaison team is paying off. I suck the warm, milky drink through the hole in the lid. The phones went hot after the item about attacks on elderly women.

I finger the cardboard jacket around my cup. Nobody attacked my mother while she was lying comatose in the airport lounge. And then I suddenly think there was something odd about the whole incident. I want to call Dad right now, but can't leave till the end of the meeting. I take another swig of coffee.

"So, Elizabeth, what have you got for us?"

Just as I have put the cup to my mouth, all faces in the room turn to me. I swallow the coffee too quickly, some of it goes down the wrong way, and I start a coughing fit. As I'm coughing and rifling through my files, coffee foam gets smeared all over my printouts. The sheets now stick together, making it even more difficult to find the right one.

"Yes, I've got a great story here, it's here somewhere... It's..." While I'm trying to sort out the mess, Sarah's looking at me with a caustic expression I think must surely be on the Oxbridge curriculum.

"Don't worry, Elizabeth, we've got all day." A theatrical sigh followed by low level laughter rippling round the room. "While we're waiting, let's move on. Andrew?" I'm still dabbing the coffee with a damp tissue and hunting for my missing sheets, so I miss his opening line. But I catch on soon enough.

"...the thing about these uni dorms is that security is pretty slack, and the poor girls are sitting ducks for some bastard who gets in during the night." That gets me sitting up all right. Feeling my face redden, I strain to see what Andrew is reading from. But even he wouldn't be stupid enough to take my actual notes.

"It looks as though the rapist is somebody who knows the building, just from the confident way he finds his way around," he continues. "He knows where all the exits are and how all the corridors connect." There's no way he could have known that kind of detail because it comes from a conversation I had with the DI on the case, who made it very clear that they weren't going to make a general release about it until he heard back from me. It was mine, that was clear.

There's an earnest discussion. This story – *my* story – appears destined to be the lead story in the next programme. Andrew avoids my gaze. Sarah never says "fabulous", "excellent" or "well done". That's not her style. She just looks at him as though he's her favourite nephew. They probably went to the same college or something. Then she turns back to me and I've stopped fumbling through my paperwork because I know it's pointless.

"Ready?" I'm holding a scrap I've ripped in haste from a newspaper, but haven't had time to follow up. It's all I've got left.

"Erm, a little girl was murdered..." The coffee-stained cutting feels inadequate in my hand. I scan the details in desperation. "Nine years old, no – er – ten," I say. Out of the corner of my eye I can now see Andrew smirking.

"So this dead girl was either nine or ten, which was it?" Sarah, snaps. "Come on Elizabeth." Her frown has worn a deep groove between her eyes.

"She was ten, yes ten."

"And I take it from the fact that you are reading from a cutting that means you have yet to speak to the police force or the family concerned. What's the story?"

"The little girl disappeared from a party which was being held at her home. Nobody noticed she had gone, until the guests left."

"A ten-year-old girl was murdered in London, and somehow it wasn't headline news in every national paper in the country? You've got to be kidding me." Sarah glared at Elizabeth as if it was her fault. "How on earth did that happen?"

"Don't know, really – the election?" The explanation felt lame. "Maybe the family didn't want the publicity? – But anyway, it was in one paper."

"Where it was somehow overlooked by your razor-sharp colleagues."

I didn't take the bait. After all, Sarah would sneer at anybody. It's her default. That enviable hauteur must be genetic. My inheritance has come via the *shtetl* and suburban Cardiff. Subservience. I scan the rest of the cutting as fast as I can.

"She wasn't missing that long. Her body was found... about a mile away the following day. In Stamford Hill – North East London. Does that qualify as the East End? It's in Hackney, anyway. Near Stoke Newington. Nobody's quite sure what happened. They think maybe somebody gate-crashed the party, and took the little girl away with them. Or it's possible that the suspect is one of the guests, a friend of the family. Maybe the kid just wandered off and was picked up off the street by somebody."

"So, as usual, PC Plod and his gang haven't got a clue. A little girl is murdered in broad daylight, and they haven't even worked out the most likely chain of events. Where on earth is Inspector Morse when you need him?"

I'm now itching to phone my father. I need to ask him what's going on. Everybody in the room is laughing. Of course, the boss has made a joke. I smile weakly, and far too late. Sarah glares at me. Numpty.

"Family?"

"Er... a single mum, big family – seven kids. The little girl was pretty much in the middle."

"Sounds interesting. OK, call the Met, and see if they'll put us in touch with the local police in Hackney. Who's the contact for North London? Andrew? OK will you two get together on this – let's make the approach through someone we already know if at all possible."

I keep on thinking about the airport, my parents, those secretive looks. What were they hiding? There's something going on that they haven't told me about and it's not just about being hard up.

"Elizabeth, I want to know what we could do on this one by tomorrow. Is there enough of a story to build up a reconstruction?

19

Will the mum do an interview? Can the officer in charge of the case string together a sentence and if not can we interview the deputy?"

As the meeting breaks up, I'm about to switch my mobile back on, when Sarah calls me over.

"The Manchester canal rape."

"Yes?" For half a moment I think she's going to say well done, that was a tough story and you delivered. Your hard work paid off in viewing figures and phone-in numbers. I let a smile edge its way onto my face far too soon.

"I don't want to hear any more about you pushing your luck. I spent half an hour in hospitality after the programme, having my ear bent by a pissed Chief Superintendent."

"Point taken."

"If you fancy yourself as some kind of gumshoe, join the Met. This isn't the place for it."

"Yuh, OK."

"I'm going to keep you on Bill's team. Watch him, if you know what's good for you. He's the business."

"Cool."

"And the police will be OK if you stick to your remit. Don't tell them how to do their jobs. Buy them a drink and tell them how wonderful they are," she winks. "Remember, they're only men." She must think that's really clever because I've heard her say it before.

Forcing my mouth into a conspiratorial smile, I run an eye over her emerald green power suit and stilettos. They say fuck me or promote me, preferably both at the same time. It seems to work. And if she can do it, why not me? Well, however much I tell myself I'm worth it, subconsciously yours truly is forever the comprehensive school kid lurking at the back of the class, trying to avoid teacher's eye.

Andrew's diction was *not* moulded at his local comp. "Stoke

Newington police," he says in a theatrical aside as he flicks through the card index thing on his anally tidy desk. "Actually, I can't seem to find it."

"Yeah, but you seemed to find my story easily enough. What happened? Did it just jump off my desk into your hands?" The office suddenly seems to go quiet while everybody pretends to be busy.

"Don't flatter yourself," he retorts. "That had been round the block a few times, every DC in London seemed to know about it."

"But somehow you didn't manage to find anything better yourself," I say.

It's hardly worth putting up a fight. He knows he's won. "Now hand over the contact details for Stoke Newington," I spit. "I know you've got them."

"Let me see..."

"Andrew, for God's sake, you're not in the dorm any more playing pranks." A deep red patch is gnawing its way up his neck, towards his bumfluffy chin. He takes out a card and reads out the name of a detective inspector at Stoke Newington police headquarters, then adds, "He's a jobsworth. You'll be wasting your time."

As I walk away, Susannah points at Andrew and mouths the word "wanker" to me. But the truth is, I need this story to come good after my idiotic performance just now. When I get to my desk, my notes are there, lying on top of a pile of old newspapers and looking a lot grubbier than last time I saw them. Six stories with all the relevant crime details, meticulous lists of witnesses and contacts for police officers in charge of each case. And, not leaving anything to chance, a list of any previous contact the programme has had with them. I crumple the sheets into a ball and hurl it at Andrew's empty desk. But it falls short and skids across the carpet tiles.

Before I phone Hackney Police, I call my father.

"Dad, there's something I need to ask you."

"*Ja*. What is it?"

"You know the other day, when Mutti went missing at the airport?"

"Mmmm." He doesn't want to talk about it.

"It's not about that. Why on earth was she going to Ibiza by herself anyway?"

There's a silence on the other end of the line. I can hear paper being moved around, and computer keys being pecked at. He sighs.

"We are selling the flat."

"What?"

Their little piece of paradise, they called it, immune to the concept of cliché in any language. It was their sanctuary in the sun, a two-hour charter flight away from strangulating, foreigner-phobic, England. I remember when they bought it, long before the island became the ultimate clubbing destination. Up at the back of San Antonio, on the quiet streets where the town starts to rise into the hills. It was second home perfection; two beds and a balcony on the Med. A little bit of their beloved Continent that was going to be forever theirs. And the subtext – unspoken of course – somewhere to run if the fascists ever emerge from the political margins. Gone.

They must be desperate for cash if they've sold up. So, how bad are things? Are we talking bailiffs? I picture their house in Rhiwbina as it was when I last visited. The house I grew up in, all its teak and leather furniture was still be there. I think. I can't convey any of this to my Dad. It's unsayable. He would feel more relaxed about dropping his trousers in public than discussing his finances with me. I whisper, "Oh." I want to ask how bad things are. Tell me honestly. Except it just won't come out like that.

22

"But where will you go?"

"Holidays we won't have for a while. Not necessary."

He makes it sound like a minor detail of a business deal. Which makes me suddenly feel very tender towards him. I click down the receiver cradle, and when I hear the dialling tone, punch in the number for Stoke Newington Police.

Chapter 3

The following weekend, my folks come down to London for a family party. In preparation for their arrival, I've poured away that half bottle of Rioja we had left over. If Mutti just happens across a stash of drink, the weekend will be wiped out while she's snoring on the sofa. So, out of consideration for my father, the rest of what we like to call "the wine cellar" has been stuffed in the wardrobe. Côtes du Rhône with my sexiest lingerie and two very nice Pinot Grigios nestling in the murky depths of my Russell & Bromley boots.

We've agreed that we'll meet at Dave's place, but I'm running late. At six o'clock I'm still in the office waiting for a phone call from the officer in charge of the Stamford Hill murder. I've spoken to him every day, and he still hasn't agreed to put me in touch with the dead girl's family. Now he's "locked into a meeting" again, and I'm phoning every five minutes to make sure he hasn't left for the day. Pestering it may be, but I don't dare to face Sarah tomorrow without a result.

I call Dave. Of course my parents arrived as Big Ben chimed six, their Germanic instinct for punctuality overriding not just the build-up of weekend traffic on the M4, but also a three car pile-up on the Cromwell Road. Dave's playing host. Even though we've been going out for two years, I've managed to keep them apart pretty successfully until now.

"Don't worry," he says, "I'll look after them."

"Are you sure?" My parents will take a dim view of my poor timekeeping. No business deal or important meeting ever stood in the way of my father getting home *pünktlich* each evening at seven. By now he will be pacing up and down the bare floorboards, while my mother's looking round the loft and wondering out loud why Dave doesn't have fitted carpet. Then she'll ask (again) why we aren't living together.

Mutti loves to advertise her liberal credentials, and that includes actively encouraging me to do what was once called *living in sin*. She's so keen to be modern or as she would say "with-it", that she doesn't realise the only person she's liberating is herself. I spent my adolescence dodging her chummy one-to-one chats about periods. I didn't want to discuss sex with her when I was sixteen, any more than I want to discuss why I'm not living with Dave now.

"It's cool," says Dave. "I've taken the lemon vodka we bought in Moscow out of the freezer. We're having a few shots before dinner to celebrate. We can tell them our news then."

I don't hear the last part of that because I feel as though someone's just put a bullet through my chest. My mother is downing "a few shots" with Dave. Will she go AWOL in Islington, and be found asleep on a park bench with her handbag round her neck? Dave doesn't get it about my mother and drink. Yes, I have moaned to him about her antics, but he insists on seeing this all as the eccentric yet harmless behaviour of a colourful Hungarian émigré. Somehow it's never been quite the right moment to spell it out to the man you want to marry that you are the daughter of a dangerous drunk. But surely he could have cottoned on by now?

I know what he'd say – a few bevvies, what's the harm in that? He'll be shocked when he finds out. He's not had my years of training. I am Coping Strategies Central, and my bleeper is going off right now. I'll have to put off my pursuit of Inspector Jenkins till tomorrow, even if it means facing a bollocking from Sarah. I race down to the basement car park and drive off, jerking my way through the gears. The Westway is four lanes of solid, stationary hot metal suspended over Notting Hill, and I'm trapped in my baking car, with raw sulphuric acid burning a hole in my stomach lining.

By the time I get to Dalston High Road, my blouse is glued to the centre of my back. I stand in the street and look up. What will the folks have made of this, I wonder? It's hardly the red brick, three-bed semi that is their concept of residential bliss. It isn't even a house, or really a flat in the accepted sense. It's a vast, crumbling loft, rented out at a subsidised rent for use as a workshop-cum-studio, on the explicit understanding that no one lives there. I ring the bell. There's a pause, and the sound of Doc Martens on stone stairs before Dave answers, beaming.

"Is everything OK?" I whisper.

"Yes sure, why not? Why are you whispering?"

"Well, giving her neat vodka could be a bit like..."

"She's not like anything. You exaggerate. Let the poor woman have a couple of drinks, for God's sake. I gave them a guided tour of my palatial studio facilities and a look through my portfolio." He winks.

The entrance to the studio is guarded by a life-size illuminated plastic statue of Madonna and child. My parents will have been startled to see that as they arrived. They may think they are sophisticated Europeans, but irony's been deleted from their list of functions. It's only a matter of time before they start wondering out loud whether Dave attends Mass.

We wind our way between the freestanding clothes racks that serve as a wardrobe, and a medley of second-hand furniture that's been artfully arranged to form rooms. The effect is charming/a complete mess – delete as appropriate depending on your own personal taste in interior design. And I know what my folks would think of it. Pretty much the same as they think of Dave.

As I peer through the forest of paraphernalia heading for the part of it which serves as a kitchen, I see that Dave has misjudged the situation. The shot glasses are scattered all over the table. Two of the mannequins have fallen over and are skewiff on the floor on top of each other, their pith helmets scattered around, still rocking. They look as though someone's tried to mock up a sex scene using dummies, like some weird pornographic art installation. My father looks preoccupied as I kiss him hello. Mutti is red in the face, her polyester knit top askew, dark sweat patches creeping outwards from the armpits. I brace myself as she gets up to greet me, but after a cursory hug, she turns back to Dave.

"Come on, we aren't finished."

I scan the room, looking for the bottle of vodka. Surely they haven't drunk the lot? Dave takes off his denim jacket and sits down at the kitchen table opposite Mutti. I see her registering the tatts. They'll only confirm her view of him as a bit of a yob, but she cans that one for later. Now it's time to get down to business. They fix eye contact with each other, alpha male against alpha female, put opposing elbows on the table, then lock hands. She was never much of a one for small talk so instead she'll challenge a bloke of any age to beat her at arm wrestling.

There's a lot of heaving and huffing. As a much younger man, he should win easily, but bulk is in her favour. She may look all very genteel, but lurking behind that triple string of pearls is a pair of shoulders built by years as a swimming champ, tennis player and all-round athlete. Maybe one of the reasons she survived years of privation is that she's got the constitution of an ox, and though she barely lifts a finger these days, she's still incredibly strong. It's infuriating. By the time we get to the Italian trattoria in Islington, she's beaten him by four rounds to three and they are buddies.

Though we order some more wine with the meal, Mutti's on her best behaviour. In fact, both my parents are on top form, telling all their best anecdotes about being a foreigner in Britain after the war. The absence of civilisation broken only by the blessed relief of having German-speaking shop assistants at Woolworths in Swiss Cottage and the ancient story about my uncle in the Home Guard, lost on manoeuvres near Merthyr – a fat man on a bicycle wearing a British army uniform and speaking with a thick German accent. This and more is brushed down and whirled out for Dave's benefit.

The good thing is that it means there's very little time left for my parents to probe Dave's professional activities and finances. What a relief. They'd never understand how many years it can take to get one's work seen by the right people. Eking out an existence on the dole while he draws together his portfolio is unlikely to impress.

My efforts to steer the conversation away from those delicate areas pays off. My parents have forgiven Dave for not being a Jewish lawyer. After all, he laughs at their jokes and has a healthy appetite, and that's nearly as good. But they think he is just another in a long line of boyfriends. Possibly because I made it known several years ago that I was "never getting married". I did that to stop my uncles and aunts asking every single man I ever brought home whether he was going to "make an honest woman" of me, as though I was a career criminal not a television researcher.

As the dessert arrives, everyone is relaxed. Too relaxed.

"So, David, what are you doing with these photographs?"

"I'm sorry?"

"Are you selling them? Putting in a magazine?"

Dave laughs, as though Mutti has cracked an amusing joke.

"When the portfolio is complete, they will go into an exhibition, in one of the good galleries," I say. Dave looks surprised, but nods. "Somewhere like the Photographers' Gallery, or IKON," I add.

"That would be great, of course," he says, sounding mystified. It can only be a matter of time before Mutti asks him how much he earns. You have to be born British to understand just how impossible that question is.

"And at this exhibition, you sell the pictures?" I see this question for what it is. A warm-up to the main act.

"Actually," says Dave, "that's not really the point." Now it's my parents' turn to look baffled. "You see, the point is to create work with integrity and meaning like any other artist would. I don't think Degas or Van Gogh or Picasso set out thinking 'how much can I earn from a painting'." There's a lot of nodding round the table, and I'm pretty certain Mutti is checking out Dave's ears, to make sure they are well attached to his head. Dad is probably thinking well, at least Picasso made a few bob.

"So," says Mutti, "how much would you charge for one?"

"Well..."

"Two hundred pounds," I say, trying to sound blasé.

"That would be very nice..." says Dave.

"Or guineas?" suggests Mutti.

"You are getting it mixed up with Sotheby's," I say, with a touch more acid than I'd intended.

"Very good," says Dad. "Two hundred for just a photograph. A snap. Maybe I should sell some of the ones I took in Ibiza. Ha ha. And how many do you think you would sell in one show?" This is offensive to Dave's artistic sensibilities in so many different ways.

"It's not really about the money, Dad," I say.

"No?"

"As Dave said, it's art."

"But a photograph isn't a work of art like a painting. We can all take a photo. Click, there you are."

28

"Er, not quite as simple as that. I thought Dave showed you his studio and dark room?"

"But painters spend years, they learn the technique, perspective, colour, all this."

"And Dave spent two years at the Royal College of Art." He nods. Anything with Royal in it works for my parents. However dubious they may be about this country and its impenetrable Establishment, their belief in the royal family and everything associated with it remains inviolate. But my darling father is not above calculating the pecuniary value of Palace associations.

"So, this means you can charge more for a picture? Good. How many do you think you sell from this exhibition?" Any moment now, and he'll be asking for the date.

"How about some coffee?" I ask, waving my hand over-enthusiastically at the waiter, to create a diversion. I make a big production number out of the relative merits of cappuccino and filter coffee, and a pantomime of considering an Irish coffee, even though I know that none of us are really interested in anything other than a double espresso. Then I excuse myself from the table, stopping only to whisper in Dave's ear.

"I'm just going to the loo. Can you come out there in a moment, I want to tell you something." He makes a face at me, but a few minutes later we are squeezed together in a corridor.

"I don't think we should tell them tonight," I say.

"Why not? I've got them eating out of my hand."

"My folks can be – unpredictable." He looks worried, so I add, "They do like you, that's absolutely true. They think you are great." I kiss him. "But maybe we should talk about it just once more before we go ahead and share it with them."

"We've got to tell them some time. Preferably before the wedding." He's beginning to get annoyed.

"All I'm saying is it doesn't have to be right now."

"I don't know what you're so worried about. They'll be thrilled, believe me."

Dave returns to the table while I go to splash cold water on my wrists and brush translucent powder on my shiny nose. When I get back they're all grinning at me, and the waiter is opening a bottle of sparkling wine. The cat is out of the Louis Vuitton handbag.

"*Mazel tov*, darling," says Mutti as I sit down at the table.

"Are you sure you are OK about this?" I whisper to her.

"What do you mean? You are engaged aren't you?" There's a worrying note of desperation here. Maybe after waiting so long for me to get hitched she's lowered her standards.

Many years ago I raised her hopes when I told her that my first serious boyfriend's father ran a soft furnishings shop in Golders' Green. She was half way to booking the caterer by the time she realised that he was the only non-Jewish trader in a mile–long stretch of the Finchley Road. A public school background and baffling enthusiasms for cricket and jazz, meant that First Serious Boyfriend was holed under the water. Even without the beard. My mother is single-minded in her disapproval of facial hair.

And tennis is the only sport she acknowledges. Back in the day, she adored Rod Laver and Jimmy Connors, who therefore paved the way for general acceptance of Indian tennis professional boyfriend, and his impeccable door-opening-for-ladies manners. My parents tried to put the most favourable possible gloss on the situation by emphasising how much Indian people are like Jews. They have, my father repeated many times, the same family values. The thing is, they are *like* Jews. But they're not. Our parents met, on a single excruciating occasion, when his mother described in loving detail, a journey over the Him-aa-lia mountains. My parents nodded. But I could tell they were mystified about this exotic location.

By the time Dave comes along, most of my cousins are married, the bottom drawer Mutti has been putting by for me is now full of moth-eaten treasures. A compromise is on the cards. I pull her away from the table, and towards the cloakroom.

"Well, you know Dave's not..." I glance round at him, but he's sharing a joke with my father.

Mutti seems oblivious. Grinning, she whispers, "I can't wait to tell Auntie Miriam. If I swear her to secrecy, it will be all over Cardiff by the next day."

"But you aren't worried about the fact that Dave's not – you know." She looks at me, blank.

"Not?"

"*Not Jewish*. It's always seemed such a big problem before."

"He can convert." Yeah sure. Just don't mention the circumcision.

Chapter 4

On Sunday, my parents and are invited to a dreary party at Uncle Bernhard's house in Hampstead Garden Suburb. I was invited too, but I've made it clear that my weekends are too precious to waste munching kosher canapés with a load of wealthy businessmen and their dragon-skinned wives. Dave's got us tickets to a lunchtime pub gig where some of his friends are playing.

I'm woken at an unreasonable time in the morning by the clank of pans and the open-and-shutting of drawers in the kitchen of my flat. It's my parents trying to be quiet. I emerge from the bedroom to find they've taken in the *Guardian* and spread its sections all over the table. What's left of the toast is cold.

"So," says Mutti, scrutinising the jeans I've pulled on, "what are you going to wear?" I help myself to some lukewarm coffee. The skin which has formed on the milk hurls itself into my cup with gloopy abandon, and breaks into bits which bob on the surface.

"Just a tee shirt and a jumper over this," I say. "We're only going to the pub."

"But I've told Bernie you are coming to the party."

"Why did you do that?"

"Because you should."

"But I've already said that I don't want to. I'm not coming. I've got other plans."

"Hanni will be there, with her fiancé."

"And – let me guess – you want me to be there with mine. It wouldn't do to be outplayed by Uncle Bernie, would it?"

"It's nothing to do with—"

"Look, Lisbet," Dad interrupts. "Mutti and I would like you to come. It's a family event."

"So you want Dave to come too?" They look at each other. I detect the merest frisson of panic. They don't have to say anything. I get it. However happy they appeared to be last night, he's a second class type of fiancé. A temporary face-saver while they scour Britain for the Jewish Prince of their dreams. Fine. "Why should I leave Dave in the lurch? He's already got the tickets." Mutti stands up.

"I am going to get ready now, and when we are ready to go, I expect you to be ready too." She behaves as though I'm still a spotty schoolgirl ready to do her bidding, on pain of being grounded.

I retreat into my bedroom, and try to wake Dave. He's still rubbing his eyes as I explain what's happened.

"I don't get it," he says. "Last night we were all best friends. I was welcomed into the bosom of the family. Now we are doing battle over ownership of you. What's happened?"

"It wasn't a welcome," I say, "It was a tactical surrender as she prepared to do battle on another front."

"So are you coming with me, or going with them?"

Bernhard lives on a wide street, lined with fat detached houses, and the pavement is now jammed with Jags and Mercedes. Dad squeezes his battered Datsun in between a red convertible and a gleaming XJ6. Through the window, I can see waitresses in white aprons handing round drinks. The guests look like the kind of rich people who brag about golfing handicaps and compare the vital statistics of speed boat performance.

Our host embraces my father in a giant bear hug, kissing him on both cheeks, in a great show of affection, which Dad reciprocates without enthusiasm. As I'm standing next in line, I move towards my uncle and put out my hand, poised to kiss and be kissed. To my surprise, Bernhard jumps back, as though he's been stung.

"Sorry, no, not with ladies."

"But I'm family," I say as the realisation begins to dawn on me. I notice that his beard is shaggier than it ever was before, like an overstuffed teddy bear sitting on top of his bulging stomach. He's wearing a skullcap with Hebrew letters crocheted into it, which can only mean one thing. He's got religion hence the no-touchy business. My non-Jewish friends think that being Jewish means no bacon. They have no idea how much further it can go. My parents look weary.

There are so many conversational no-go areas that for some considerable time, none of us utters a word. We all stand there smiling at each other and nodding, as if we've challenged each other to see who can stay *schtumm* for longest. I crack first.

"So, Uncle Bernie, how have you been?"

He says something which sounds like "*B'ruch ha shem, b'ruch ha shem*," and is presumably Hebrew for something. The expression on his face suggests a positive meaning, so I smile and nod. I'm floating in ignorance because I've been reared by Jewish atheists. Their faith is based entirely on a love of chicken soup and appreciation of the Marx Brothers. Let's not bother too much about the troublesome spiritual bit because we are rational people, is the general idea. My dad's an engineer, so he applies the fifth law of thermodynamics to religion and decides it's rubbish. Oddly enough, that doesn't seem to impact on their entrenched view of themselves as the rightful descendants of Moses. When we're standing in a crowd of Jews like today, we feel as though we belong. The problem is that my intimate knowledge of chicken soup and all its variations and accompaniments doesn't help much when Bernhard starts quoting the Bible in its original Hebrew.

I turn to my parents for a bit of support, just in time to see them wave at somebody they have recognised on the other side of the room. It's time to admit that I may not exactly been gracious about coming here in the first place, now they pay me back by beetling off into the crowd and I'm left standing there with my uncle the religious zealot.

I scan the room, for support. Faces in the melee of guests look familiar. But it's just the type I recognise, not the individual. Gold jewellery on wrinkled brown necks, English with a genteel trace of accent. They share a puzzled expression, as if they are wondering where the bridge tables have been hidden. In the distance I see a waitress offering my parents a drink. O God, if you do exist, could you make sure the buck's fizz is mainly orange juice?

Uncle Bernhard steers me across the room toward a young woman, whom I now recognise as the little girl I last saw when we played in the paddling pool in our back garden.

"Hanni, here's someone you haven't seen for a long time," he exclaims. Looking at her, I don't think it's not a coincidence that the words "*frum*" meaning religious and "*frumpy*" are so similar. They probably share the same etymological roots – a Yiddish word meaning a sack with a belt. I'm sure her outfit is all terribly correct. It certainly covers the forbidden knobbly bits, lest the merest suggestion of a curve underneath all that fabric should set torrid imaginations on fire.

Next to Hanni is a bearded young man in a dark suit. She kisses me on both cheeks.

"Elizabeth, it's been so long," she says, clocking my Lycra top, pencil skirt and suede stilettos with a wary expression.

"This is Moshe Chaim, my fiancé."

"Hello, you must be the famous lawyer". He shrugs, unsmiling. Either diffident or humourless, it's impossible to tell. I turn back to Hanni.

"You've changed since I saw you last." I don't mention the paddling pool in case the merest suggestion of semi-nudity in the distant past will trigger the collapse of the Wailing Wall. She smiles.

"I hear you are getting married too."

"My goodness," I say, "the bush telegraph is working very fast these days."

She looks puzzled.

"So, your fiancé... is from?"

"Luton."

"Sorry?"

"You know, Luton, just north of London. Known for its car plant."

I suddenly see that I'm talking to someone with a selective understanding of the geography of the UK. I try to imagine a map of Britain rearranged to reflect only how many Jewish people live in each place.

"It's about an hour from Golders Green, in the direction of Prestwich."

"Aha." She looks embarrassed. Good.

"So, is there a Jewish community in – Luton?"

"He's not—"

"I see." Awkward moment. I enjoy her discomfort and wait for her to change the subject. But there is no other subject.

"And you aren't worried about marrying out?"

"Why should I worry?"

"It's a risk. You might regret it, later on."

"Marriage is a gamble for everybody, isn't it?"

"It's less of a gamble if you marry someone like you."

"But," I say, "someone doesn't have to be Jewish to be like me. He can be like me in other ways. Like sharing the same brand of toothpaste. Let's face it," I shrug, "I'm not exactly all that Jewish."

She looks at me as if I am a small child. "You are most definitely Jewish, as your children will be." And then, "Don't your parents mind?"

"They haven't said anything." Well, it's almost true.

"These things come out, Elizabeth."

It's a merciful relief that Bernhard now announces lunch.

We shuffle into the spacious dining room, and find our places on five large round tables. When everybody has found their place, he stands.

"Welcome to you all, and thank you for joining me on this very special day," he says. "Now, some of you will be familiar with the concept of *gematria* – each letter of the Hebrew alphabet has a numerical value. And today it seems especially apt that the Hebrew words for wine, mystery and knowledge, all have a value of seventy." There are smiles and nodding, while Bernhard gives a short discourse on the inner essence of Torah, and the knowledge of the seventy elders.

As he sits down, beaming, there is a round of applause. Two of Bernhard's closest friends reply, telling funny anecdotes about their holidays together in Jerusalem, and adding their own biblical homilies.

Now I notice with horror that my mother has risen to her feet, and is standing there. And there's one thing I know with complete certainty. She's had far too much buck's fizz. While she struggles to find her words, people start fiddling with their cutlery.

"Dear... Bernie." This took a huge effort, and she now seems lost for words again. A pause of the right length can make a speech. It adds drama and tension, bouncing the reader from one thought to the next. Mutti's pause starts like that, but as is lengthens and crumbles, its drama shifts into something darker. The audience begins to worry about the speaker, and whether she'll make it to the other side of the pause. As if she's jumped across a ravine and missed her footing. She catches onto the edge with the tips of his fingers and struggles to pull herself up on the other side. The odds are against her, but she does it.

"You have been... my brother-in-law for forty years..." Uncontroversial. There's another long pause during which I bite my lip. I take a gulp of wine, it stings. What on earth could she say next? I brace myself. The matron opposite me puts a hand up to the heavy gold chain around her neck. She plays with it, and looks thoughtful.

"I would just (pause) like to say (pause) we are very (pause) fond of you. I will never forget that many years ago you helped me to (very long pause) come into Britain from Budapest at a very difficult time." Though her words are slurred, this sentiment seems appropriate, even moving, and there is a murmur of agreement from the room. For a moment, Mutti seems lost in her own memories of those difficult times. Then she adds, "But I must (pause) say (pause)." Her eyes are closed now, and it looks as though she is asleep on her feet. I hope she manages to sit back down on her chair and thank God that she has stopped speaking. She hasn't.

"But why all the *religion* now, Bernie? You got a message from God? Maybe he told you to stop eating the ham and cream cheese sandwiches. And stop *schtupping* the cleaning lady while your wonderful wife is dying from cancer. Or is all this piety now all about guilt?"

Shit. Jaws go limp. Hands clench. "Some of us have long memories, you know."

She starts swaying precariously from one side to another. At any moment, she will lose her balance and topple over. Bernhard is sitting next to her. If he cannot touch Mutti, even to stop her falling, she will crash to the floor. Anger and indecision are fighting it out on his face.

Everybody in the room is watching him sitting there rigid as an ice sculpture. And just as intently, he is watching her. She shudders and open her eyes, and we all breathe a sigh of relief. But just as soon as she regained awareness, she's gone again. Like a great tree that has been cut away at its base, she is floating on the wind for an elastic moment in time, before the inevitable collapse. Just when that moment cannot stretch any further, Bernie leaps to his feet and holds her steady, until my father has time to come round from the other side of the table and take her arm.

Dad tries to guide her out of the room, but she's like a bumper car. They collide with several tables and chairs, sending Bernhard's biblical beverages spilling onto the pale carpet. One of the women at my table raises an eyebrow. "She meant well. Yes, she meant well."

I glare at her meaningfully, then gather myself with as much dignity as I can scrape together, and go upstairs to find Mutti on the guest bed. A three-quarters empty bottle of vodka is peeping out of her bag. She's out cold. My father is sitting next to her looking resigned. I want to shake her awake to tell her what I think of her for putting us through this. But when I touch her, she jolts in her sleep, like a troubled child having a nightmare, and I end up stroking her cheek.

"What shall we do?" I ask.

"Let her sleep."

"Are you OK?"

"*Ja, ja.*" He shrugs. We go back downstairs, where waitresses are serving plates of poached salmon and potato salad. I sit back down in my chair, and discover that my dining companions are still carrying on an analysis of my mother's performance, like the panel on Radio 4 dissecting an avant-garde play.

"Is OK to say a few words," says the gold chain woman through her jutting chin. "But one should think it through first. Or make some notes on a card." I try to convey my disapproval with an icy stare. The woman smiles back at me.

"Really, Gretchen..." says her neighbour, shaking her head. Her aggressive, gold perm doesn't budge as her head moves. "I don't think she was in any state to make notes." In a stage whisper loud enough for us all to hear, she says, "Too much to drink!" And just in case any of us hadn't quite understood, she makes a gesture with her hand as if tipping a glass into her throat. I want to kick her under the table, and leave. But out of the corner of my eye, I can see my father engrossed in conversation with an academic looking man in a bow tie. There's an old-fashioned air of courtesy about the way they nod to each other in response to each point. It wouldn't be fair to march him out just when he's finally enjoying himself.

"Maybe she's taking some medicine on prescription, then after just one glass you get knocked out. Even one sip."

"I think she is Bernie's *schwägerin*. She is a lady with – problems." I can feel my bones tingling under the flesh, as I listen to these two wealthy, spoilt women talking about my mother. But what is most unbearable of all is the thought that Bernie has been sitting round with a gaggle of his smug friends picking apart my parents' lives.

I stand up. "That poor, pathetic woman – the lady who has drunk too much," I mime the drinking gesture, in an exaggerated way, "is my mother." Now the whole room is looking at me.

"How dare you wrinkle your noses up at her for daring to show her weakness in public. It's such hypocrisy. You are all the same as her, but she dares to show her scars. That's the only difference."

I look round at them, shaking. "You integrate, assimilate and God forbid that you, or you, or you," I jab my finger in the air, "should just for one moment show the world what's underneath the surface. Yes, you go along to your meetings of the Anne Frank Trust, once a year you shed a tear for the victims, praise the courage of survivors, and light a candle for the dead.

"It's all very dignified. Then you pack it all away until the next time. Let's make sure we never have to look at the mess underneath." At the end of the sentence my throat tightens, making my voice quiver away to nothing. I look round the room at the pinched eyes and wobbling double chins. My face goes hot, as if fifty red spotlights are trained on me. The rims of my eyes prickle. I can't bear the thought of this bunch seeing me cry, so I grab my bag and lurch out. Turning right out of the doorway I crash straight into a young man in a dramatic purple silk shirt, banging into his violin. I push him aside without bothering to apologise and bolt towards the door.

Then I'm out, and heading somewhere along the spotless pavements. I don't know where. Just away. I don't hear any footsteps coming up behind me, probably because I'm sobbing. A familiar handkerchief is pushed into my hand, and Dad falls into step besides me.

"What about Mutti?" I say. "What if she wakes up?"

"Someone will look after her."

"Like they are all her best friends after what she said."

"Doesn't matter. She'll be out for hours." Actually, she could wake at any time. I know that, and he knows that. But we're so desperate to escape that we pretend it's not true. Dad marches along the pavement, breathing deeply. As we get further away from the house, I can see the lines on his face relax under the afternoon sun. We find ourselves by the car, though we weren't looking for it. "Let's go up to the Heath," I say.

With an almost supernatural degree of forethought, I'd left a pair of trainers in the car, otherwise the gravel at South End Green would have ruined my shoes before we'd even left the car park. And I'm thinking what if she does wake up, anyway? I'd like Bernie to squirm just a bit more before the end of the afternoon. Maybe Mutti will stagger downstairs half-undressed. Serve him right for being such a pompous prat.

"Are you OK?" I ask. Not that I really expect him to admit anything. My Dad. I just wish he'd just fight back sometimes.

"*Ja*, you know what she's like. She finds it difficult, such events. She gets nervous. Of the other people. She thinks they are judging her."

"She's right", I say, "They are."

"They've all had… difficult experiences."

"They just seem to behave as though it never happened."

"Everybody got their own way of dealing with it."

"They hate it when people dare to emote. It's like they all made a smooth segue from German formality to the stiff upper lip."

"So you think they should be more like your mother?"

"Of course not. But I admire her in a way. At least she tries to be honest. Even if it all goes tits up in the end." We pass the pond. Children and parents are feeding the ducks, as the sun bounces off the water.

"Yes," he says. "The situation we are facing now is difficult for her."

"How *are* things?" I can feel him flinch. He's strayed into difficult terrain, now he's looking for a way out.

41

"Tight."

I'm thinking how tight? Are the bailiffs outside the front door yet?

"Our agent in Ibiza has found somebody who wants to buy the flat. I told Aranca this morning. Was stupid of me to tell her before the party. These kind of changes are destabilising."

"And if you sell, will that buy you a bit of time?" He pauses to catch his breath as the path begins to slope steeply uphill.

"Will last us for about six months, if we are careful." I'm trying to work out how much that is, and how much of it Mutti will smoke and drink her way through.

We climb in silence for a few minutes. As Parliament Hill comes into view, we can see kites skidding about on the clouds above us.

"Now she's got this idea."

"What kind of idea?"

"She thinks she can get money."

"Not quite with you – what money?"

"Compensation."

"What for?"

"For the war. She thinks she can get compensation for what happened. From the Hungarian government. Some kind of new scheme."

"So. Why not?"

"Just another bit of madness. Will be very little money. A token. Not worth it. A mountain of paperwork, lawyers' fees, and God knows what else. And you know what your mother is like. It's too difficult for her, this digging up the past. The price is too high." He turns to me. "You need to help me, Lisbet. We must stop her going on with this *meshugas*."

It's like I'm the only thing standing between my parents and the void. What can I offer them? Not money, that's for sure. I barely earn enough to maintain myself. I'm engaged to a bloke who just about scrapes together enough to keep himself in dark room equipment. Let's not even think about a wedding.

"So," I say, "She needs something to do, why not that? She might surprise you." He shakes his head.

"Nothing good can come of it. It will kill us, this stupid scheme."

He doesn't look like a desperate man. Striding up the hill, as we talk, he's all energy, the snowy hair setting off his tanned skin. Like a Saga advert for iron tablets. My friend Jane has always said he is her most perfect looking dad. Almost handsome, if it wasn't for the too-long nose and the too-small chin. Jane says nobody wants their dad to be too good looking, so his imperfections just add to his perfect dad-ness.

But the weak mouth is a giveaway – he hides behind a German engineer's approach to problems. When I was a teenager in pieces after splitting up with my boyfriend, he said let's get out a piece of paper and write the pros on one side, the cons on the other, and decide on the best course of action. The only course of action I was capable of was throwing myself on the ground and screaming my head off. But his ridiculous logic was soothing, if maddening too.

We carry on climbing up to the top of Parliament Hill in silence. The grass is worn away at the top, where people stand to look at the view. We stand there now, London stretching away at our feet. Towards the city, the Heath unfolds its undulating greens – a civilised, rationalised form of nature, framing the horizon. In the distance you can just about make out St Paul's Cathedral.

"I used to come here after the war when I was at university", says Dad. "I loved the feeling of being on top of the city." The trees waver in a warm May breeze.

"Nowadays it is fashionable to criticise the British for not letting in enough Jews. But I felt they treated us very reasonably."

43

"Even when they locked you up?"

"*Ja*, what could they do?"

"So did you sit in your prison on the Isle of Man, and think – the Brits, how fair-minded and reasonable they are? And did you really think that when they sent you to Canada? One torpedo and you'd have been at the bottom of the Atlantic."

I've seen the picture of my teenage father sitting round the camp-fire in the forest with lots of other confused looking men and boys. And the scratchy little notes he sent his mother asking her for parcels with *shockolate*. The first ones are in German, then later in English, very badly spelt. He was a boy running for his life, so they locked him up. And made a German boy write to his German mother in English so that his sad requests for home comforts and warm trousers could be read by the censor.

And though he still speaks strongly accented English, he's absorbed something much more profoundly British – he's horribly reasonable. "Yes actually it was fair enough," he insists. "They were right, I could have been a spy."

"You were seventeen!"

He shrugs. "You know, Lisbet, other people were not so lucky." That shuts me up. As we make our way back down the hill in silence, I'm wondering how to stop Mutti driving my fair-minded, reasonable dad crazy with a hopeless compensation claim.

At Bernhard's house, the waiting staff are washing glasses and stacking chairs. There's no sign of Mutti. Bernie is sitting with a few remaining guests, taking coffee with petit fours. He doesn't invite us to join them, which is hardly surprising given the unscheduled floorshow we put on.

"Er, my mother?" I venture. They barely turn their heads.

"I'm not a babysitter for the feeble-minded," spits Bernie without turning his head. "Can't you control her? It can't be that difficult to keep her off the booze. Or just leave her at home next time."

In the silence that follows, one of the guests picks up a petit four from the tray and examines it closely before biting it in half. "She went for a walk," he says, from the corner of a mouth half-full of oozing marzipan. The remark is directed at Dad rather than me.

"A walk?" asks my father. "Aranca? Are you sure?" We look at each other.

"I'm sure she wanted to clear her head. Probably just gone round the block."

"Yes, you are probably right. We'll catch up with her." He's rubbish at lying, but no one seems to notice. Bernie ushers us out into the hallway for a farewell that manages to be both unnecessarily elaborate and arctic in its coldness. It takes the form of a lecture on the subject of respect. My father nods, patiently.

His reward is another of Bernie's ceremonial bear hugs, though there seems little true affection in the embrace. And I am treated to an obscure and improving religious *bon mot*. Dad is halfway up the garden path before I manage to extricate myself. As I turn to join him, I feel a sharp sting on my backside, but I'm on the doorstep before I can work out what it was. I've been pinched on the bottom. I turn my head just in time to see teeth glinting through facial hair as the door slams shut.

We get into the Datsun, and start cruising round Hendon. It's looking as though the evening is about to turn into a repeat of our airport adventure, when the mobile rings. It's the head waiter at the Cosmo restaurant in Swiss Cottage. A lady customer seems to have lost her bearings, he says.

When we get there, Mutti is tucking into the restaurant's signature dish – *Wiener schnitzel* and mixed salad, with a large glass of iced soda water. I slide into the upholstered bench next to her, and she gives me a terse nod without looking up from her plate.

Dad and I order coffees, but none of us say anything much. When Mutti has finished her meal, Dad pays the bill, and says, "Come on then, old girl."

She puts her head on one side, and lights a cigarette. "Is not the same here any more."

I look around. The restaurant is half full of elderly Mittel Europeans just like my parents. It's busier in the café beyond a half-wall. The espresso machine is going non-stop, and plates and plates of apple strudel are doing the rounds below a canopy of smoke.

She shakes her head. "I stay here."

"You can't stay here. They shut at ten-thirty."

"Not here in the restaurant. With Elizabeth."

"What?"

"Cardiff is not a civilised place."

"Bit late to decide that now. You can't stay with me."

"Your spare room will be most comfortable, thank you."

"But what will you do all day, when I'm working?"

"I have – business interests."

"What business interests?" As long as I can remember my mother has been a *hausfrau* plus. The only business interests she's been cultivating are investments in mayonnaise futures, given the number of jars she's got stashed away in the larder.

"You will see."

"Is this something to do the compensation thing?" My father winces and she gives him one of her blackest looks.

"*Confidential* business interests," she glares. It's a stand-off. She refuses to get into the car with Dad, and by now we are the only people left in the restaurant. The waiter keeps asking if we want anything else and looking at his watch.

As Mutti puts on her jacket with elaborate slowness, I'm desperately trying to work out a strategy to get us out of the stalemate. He's standing there, his best suit now looking crumpled, fiddling despondently with the car keys. Surely the poor man deserves a bit of a break. Nobody ever thinks what all this is doing to him.

Ten minutes later, I watch the Datsun disappear up the Finchley Road towards the North Circular heading for the M4 and the uncivilised lands beyond, while I set off for the tube station, Mutti two paces behind me. Dave'll be staying at his place. If I didn't know better, I'd say she was doing her best to keep us apart.

It's only when we get home that I really understand what I've agreed to. My new flatmate is an elderly alcoholic and nicotine addict who's got me in a psychological half nelson. It sounds like a script by Roman Polanski. Let's just hope neither of us meets a sticky end by way of the rear balcony. Long after she's hit the sack, I'm sitting up with a large glass of red, asking myself how I let it happen.

Chapter 5

For my tenth birthday my parents gave me a typewriter. Not a toy one like some of my friends had, but a proper Olivetti Lettera 32 portable, in a dashing shade of turquoise with a same-colour carrying case. By then I'd already shown some flair for writing, and Mutti was determined to encourage me. Ten was double figures, she reasoned, which meant I was virtually an adult. That meant I needed to be equipped for the job.

But the transition from childhood also needed to be marked in some appropriate manner, and not just with gifts however lavish. Of course there was a three-course dinner at Sully House, but that's how we had celebrated all my birthdays since I could remember. It was a family tradition and the only difference this time was that I was permitted to sip the Piesporter Michelsberg. No, Mutti declared, this year I would have a grand party.

In retrospect, maybe she was feeling guilty because I'd never had a birthday party before and she wanted to make it up to me with one big world-beating bash. She didn't realise that I'd deliberately avoided the ghastly indignity of bringing my parents and my school friends face to face. Actually, calling them "friends" is a vast exaggeration – acquaintances would be more accurate. They were a pallid lot of Susans and Carolines, who looked like they belonged to a different species to me – blonde and blue-eyed, with squeaky little voices.

Their mummies were like grown-up versions of themselves, with Alice bands on their blonde manes, and neat little skirts. None of them ever spoke to Mutti at the school gate. Her booming Hungarian vowels formed a ten metre exclusion zone. You could see them looking at her rolling red locks and billowing cigarette smoke as they might have regarded a African tribesman wearing nothing but neck rings and a horn over his penis.

When it came to the party, I must have got carried away with a combination of Mutti's florid fantasy and my own pre-adolescent hormonal ferment. She'd been a debutante herself in Budapest, and been courted by scores of young men bearing bouquets to her door. So at least she had some experience of romance, and that must have convinced me.

We had inevitable differences about the style of the event. The whole Beatles thing had passed Mutti by, so she envisaged ball-gowns and cups of fruit punch followed by Coronation Chicken to the strains of a big band in what passed for a smart local hotel. I was aiming more for mini-skirts and Coca Cola, with cheese and pineapple chunks on cocktail sticks stuck into half a grapefruit, while "Yeah Yeah Yeah" blasted out of the Dansette in our front room. To my great surprise, she gave way on everything apart from the menu. She even got her dressmaker to knock me up a dress just like one Mary Quant was wearing in a picture I cut out of a magazine.

On the day, I watched with trepidation as the butcher and greengrocer delivered, and Mutti set to in the kitchen. Thirty minutes before the appointed hour, Mutti was still up to her elbows in coleslaw.

Mercifully, she managed to get upstairs by the time the first few guests were smoothing down their velvet pinafore frocks as their coats were whisked away by "the help". I'd put on a long playing record. Shy girls were making stilted conversation with spotty boys while their parents admired our collection of delft china figurines. Then, out of the corner of my eye, I noticed that Mutti had come back downstairs wearing an outsize version of the style of dress that Jackie Kennedy went for. Her love of patent leather must have started around then and she was wearing a nice pair of shiny black court shoes. The whole ensemble would have looked terrific, if only she'd managed to get her lipstick on straight.

I became aware that she had pounced onto an unwary trio of parents, and was regaling them with her opinion of the music, which was poor. By the time we approached the buffet, she was far from steady on her feet. At some point in the evening, a lot of food ended up on the floor and angry words were exchanged. I was hiding in the downstairs toilet; when I came out most of the guests had disappeared. So by the time we got to Uncle Bernhard's reception in Hampstead Garden Suburb Mutti had form in the party department, and I shouldn't have been surprised by what happened.

The Grand Ball proved to be a bit of a watershed in all our lives. Together with the typewriter it signalled the official start of my adulthood, but not in the way Mutti intended. Though she must have been drinking for years by then, I don't remember it affecting anything much. Afterwards it affected everything.

The first day of high school I found myself having to explain why I wasn't wearing the uniform tie. I wasn't brave enough to tell the truth. That my mother had taken me out, heading with all good intentions to the department store to get the necessary. She'd become confused halfway through the day and came home without half the kit. After writing out "I must remember ALL my school uniform" one hundred times, I went home and helped myself to enough money from her purse to get a tie the following morning. So I got another hundred lines for being late.

When she didn't turn up for parents' evening at school, it was apparently because I'd failed to tell her about it. Meissen china plates smashed because I was clumsy. And when she crashed the car under the influence, I was hastily swapped into the driver's seat and had lost my no claims bonus before my eighteenth birthday.

I tried my best to get on with being an ordinary teenager, albeit one without much of a social life. But in the frequent periods when Mutti's drinking got out of hand, I was also handbag carrier, clearer up and fixer. Dad was at work and didn't see that I'd made the dinner and ordered the groceries. I also negotiated with irate tradesmen, smoothed out relations with the neighbours and even on one terrible occasion kept the police off our backs. I spent many lonely nights yearning for a mummy with a velvet Alice band, even if she was holding a chip pan in her hand. But at least I had my Olivetti for company.

Chapter 6

The focal point in our office is a white board fixed to the wall, divided by thick, black grid lines. Current stories are listed down the left, and progress charted in a series of squares, culminating in transmission date. Next to my case, there's a large question mark, then blank, blank, blank and blank. The production meeting is tomorrow. I turn towards my desk, with a knot in my stomach, and catch Andrew's eye. He winks. Bastard.

I've left Mutti at home with strict instructions. No smoking in my flat. No cooking. Don't ring me at work unless it's an emergency. She's got a copy of *The Times*, twenty pounds, a tube map and directions to the British Museum.

I finally get through to DI Mike Jenkins at Stoke Newington. I need to get him onside without sounding bothered. Play it cool. Unfortunately, goes on DI Jenkins, there are "massive" local sensitivities around the whole incident. The orthodox Jewish community are wary of the media. He would love to work with us, natch, but he very much doubts the family will want it.

I bet he hasn't even asked them. I put my pen down, and move one step up from nonchalant. I run through our case solved stats. A single film can generate so many calls. Sway local sympathies. What about justice for the little girl? And what about the risk of the perpetrator offending again?

"Do you really want the death of another child on your conscience?" I ask. There's a silence from the other end and I swear I can hear DI Jenkins rolling his eyes. Click, whirr, dialling tone. He is, it seems, far cooler than me.

I pick up my car keys. "If anybody wants me, I'll be in N16." Andrew doesn't respond. Which is probably a good thing. He'll only be on to Sarah and the next thing I know it's another lecture on our partnership with the police. That partnership works like a pair of standard issue handcuffs.

It's a damp, humid afternoon as I inch my way through the Islington logjam and fork right down Essex Road. Just before the traffic lights at the end, I've reached the edge of known territory. I stop to get out the *A-Z*. If I turn right here, I could stop at Dave's and spend a lazy hour together without anybody being any the wiser. I hold that thought, and drive on. I work my way forward, past a scraggy green. You can tell you've crossed the border into Hackney because litter begins to pile up on the pavements and it's now raining. The main road becomes narrow and winding, forcing the buses to push past each other between the tottering terraces. The road ends in front of a shabby, thirties-built civic building.

I turn right, splashing through puddles, into a narrow street lined with shops and cafes. It's all got an air of down-at-heel hippie chic. Multi-coloured macramé shopping baskets and babies in slings. On men.

Round the one-way system, the Bohemian vibe gives way to Turkish grocery shops and pound stores. I kick aside a sodden fried chicken carton as I double lock the car. Using my copy of the local paper as an umbrella, I make a dash for the less ghastly of two ethnic greasy-spoon caffs. The cappuccino is watery and bitter. I stir in two heaped spoons of sugar, but that just makes it worse.

It's on the front page of the now soggy paper. In a crime-ridden borough, this is one that stands out.

I go through the article, looking for clues about exactly where the family of Bruchi Friedmann lives. From my dreary years as a cub reporter, I know it must be here, the name of the road. Local people want that kind of information. They want to know which of their friends lives in the same road as the dead person.

Next stop is three doors up, a scrappy looking estate agent's. There's only one person in the office, an acne-faced young man who introduces himself as Tim. He's wearing red braces as though the yuppie dream never died.

"I'm looking for something in St Kilda's Road," I say.

"Rent or buy?" I take a punt on what's going to net him more.

"Buy." He raises an eyebrow.

"They're pretty big. Is it just for you?"

"Sorry, didn't I say? I'm looking for a flat."

"How much did you have in mind?"

"It depends…" He's beginning to suspect I'm wasting his time. Which of course, I am.

"I'm not getting much. To be honest, we don't get too many in that area. They tend to go privately."

"Meaning?"

"No agents. They keep things close."

"When you say 'they'?" He stops tapping and looks straight at me.

"You do know that in St Kilda's virtually every house is umm, Jewish?"

"Well…"

"You have been down there, haven't you?"

"I knew there were Jewish people living there. I just didn't realise it was so…"

"Then you aren't…?" He stops himself, looking embarrassed. "I sort of assumed that you must be – somehow – though you don't look, quite…" He makes a hand gesture towards my jeans and leather jacket.

"I'm Jew-ish," I say.

"OK, cool. Sorry, it's easy to say the wrong thing. Fall foul of the political correctness police, and all that, you know."

He starts tapping again. There's a rattling sound from behind me as the door opens and a gust of damp air wafts through, blowing the papers around his desk. A man in rain-splattered overalls walks in. He shoves a piece of paper onto the desk with dirty hands.

"As you can see, I'm just with a client, Germaine," says Tim, scribbling a signature. The man seems oblivious to the reprimand.

"Them's the ones I've done. 'Av' you got any more for me?" The estate agent shoots me an apologetic grin and mouths

"Sorry," at me. He swivels round on his chair, picking up a large hard-backed notebook from the desk behind.

"Have you done the new ones in Durley, East Bank and Holmleigh Road?"

"Yep."

"And how about putting the 'sold' notices on Cranwich and Heathland?"

"I've run out. Got three For Sale left, no Sold."

"They're out the back. And do me a favour mate, use the back door when you leave." Germaine stomps out, and Tim resumes at his computer, rolling his eyes for my benefit.

"Hold on, we've got a couple of things here. A two-bedroom flat in Paget Road – for one hundred and fifty thousand, leasehold. You'll love this one. It's packed with original features, and another one in St Andrew's Grove for one five five – lease is shared between four flats – any good?"

"Yeah, can I see the details?" I wait until the printer is chuntering until I say, "That little girl. Killed last week. That was round here, wasn't it?"

"Yep. Ghastly. It was in St Kilda's, actually."

"Oh?" I say. Tap tap tap of his fingers on the keyboard.

"But I think you knew that, already." He looks straight at me and I blush, waving my newspaper. "It was in the *Gazette*."

"That's not why you want to live there?" He must think I'm a bit of a weirdo.

"Oh God no. But it makes you think, doesn't it?" He takes the copies from the printer and hands them to me. "Nice fireplace," I muse. "But the kitchen needs a bit of work."

I spend some time going through the descriptions line by line, to reinforce the impression that I am a genuine flat hunter. But I decline the offer of a viewing, saying I need to show the details to my boyfriend first. As I get up to leave, Tim hands me his card.

"Thanks," I say. "I don't suppose you know what number that little girl lived at, the murder?"

He smiles a resigned smile, "Eighty-eight." As I'm turning to open the door, he adds, "You know, if that's all you wanted, you could have just come in and asked." The door clicks shut behind me.

Back in the car and up the road. Past the one-way system it broadens out to four lanes, and then quite suddenly everything changes. Men on the pavements are dressed in the full kit. Big black hats, with curling earlocks and long black coats. Long white socks. Dave should see this. He'd realise how easy he's got it with my parents.

Most of the women are pushing prams. Not buggies, but big old-fashioned perambulators that most other people junked years ago. You can't even buy those any more. The children with long earlocks blowing in the breeze, and the women and kids are all dressed in a strangely old fashioned way you don't see anywhere else. I can't quite put my finger on what seems so out of time until I see that some of the women are wearing plastic rain bonnets. My grandmother used to wear those in the 1960s to protect her shampoo and set.

As I'm cruising along what looks like the main shopping street, a news bulletin comes on the radio. The cause of death of the girl has been established – it's definitely a murder then. At least the poor mother hasn't been left in the dark for weeks wondering what exactly happened.

I pass a busy parade of shops and pull up just long enough to look around – none of them are chains apart from the incongruous betting shop in the middle. Some of the signs are in Hebrew, all of them seem to be selling exotic stuff you don't get elsewhere. This, I realise, is a whole different world, and though it's next door to normal London, it's as though there's an invisible wall sealing off a little network of a few streets.

It's easy to find St Kilda's because it's the one cordoned off with police tape. And on the pavement just beyond, there they are. It's like a horde of alien invaders in this little world – a whole crowd of people dressed in their own uniform of combats and parkas, with a lot of Nikons slung round their necks looking like hi-tech jewellery. It had to be only a matter of time before the tabloids cottoned on. We're going to lose this if we don't move fast.

Where to go though? I'm not getting anything here. I'm back in the car and heading up the main road, across the junction then I take a right and park. There's an old-fashioned red telephone box a few yards along. I walk towards it, open the door, and am greeted by the familiar smell. Pee and damp paper. Above the phone, the usual selection of prostitutes' calling cards offering "Full French", and inviting me to "Be Naughtie with Norma". To the right, there's a full set of telephone directories, hanging by their spines in a metal holder. I twist one up towards me, S–Z. The covers are torn, and some of the pages are missing. I leaf through, looking for "synagogue", and when I find the place there are quite a few. I run my finger down the list. There it is. Egerton Road N16. "Synagogue, The New".

I walk to the end of the road. Above the Post Office is a sign telling me this is Egerton Road. I'm here already. So where's the synagogue? There's a makeshift fruit stall, and a large house with a doctor's brass plate, then the waste land and the row of houses.

As I'm sauntering along, I call my home number, but there's no reply. Maybe Mutti is out improving herself, with the help of the Elgin Marbles. And then, there it is. Must have been splendid once, presiding over its street corner in its cathedral-like way. Grand stairs leading up to four big columns beneath a double dome. And a sign:

UNITED SYNAGOGUE

NEW SYNAGOGUE
ORIGINALLY FOUNDED IN LEADENHALL STREET 5520 – 1760
RE-ERECTED IN Gt St HELEN'S 5598 – 1838
REBUILT ON THIS SITE 5675 – 1915

ARCHITECTS
JOSEPH & SMITHEM

I knock on the enormous front door, turning to survey the scruffy frontage as I wait. Tufts of grass, and cracked paving stones, strewn with a light scattering of used cans and crisp wrappers.

"Yes?"

I turn back to see a small, elderly man with a moustache and a cross expression holding the door half open. He's wearing an ancient hand-knitted jumper under a jacket. Round his neck is a black cab driver's licence number.

"Umm." I'm fed up of lying. I flash my researcher identity pass. "I work for a television programme, and I wondered if somebody here would have the time to tell me a bit about the area?"

"Hmph."

"It's just er... a documentary about the community. Sort of." On reflection, one can have too much truth.

"You want to come in or not?"

As he shuts the door behind me, clanging reverberates through the empty building. I follow the old man through a foyer and up some dusty stairs covered with threadbare carpet, and reeking of a dusty gloom. He leads me into a small office that smells of mothballs. Behind the desk is second elderly man, bent over a ledger.

"Sidney, the young lady works for the television. She wants to know about the area. What can we tell her?" He looks up from his book keeping.

"What's that, Morrie? Television? Is she going to put us on the television?"

"Don't get your hopes up, Sidney. You're too old."

"I'm younger than Magnus Magnusson."

"You were born too old." Sidney frowns and puts down his pencil. They both turn to look at me.

"I'm interested in the Jewish community," I say.

"What can we tell her?" asks Morrie again, as if I wasn't in the room.

"Well", says Sidney, folding his arms, "It's all changed now. It's all the *frummers*. Not that there's anything wrong with them, of course. We get on very well. But it's not like it was."

"Frummers? Do you mean orthodox – religious?"

"Bit more than that, dear. The Hasidic people. In Israel they call them *Haredi*. The guys with the black hats."

"So, you're not Jewish, then?" says Morrie. "We could do with a few new members. The old ones are dropping like flies."

"Mmmm, like flies," repeats Sidney.

I think it's wiser to skip my religious credentials. "I'm interested in the little girl who was killed recently – St Kilda's Road."

"We could make you a nice *shidduch*," says Morrie.

"Yes," says Sidney, "I'm still single."

"It's a bit late to start thinking about that, Sid. You spent too long as a mummy's boy." He turns to me. "Would you believe he lived with his late mother until she died at ninety-one?"

"St Kilda's Road," I repeat, beginning to feel exasperated. "The little girl."

"Tragic."

"The murder of the little girl?"

"No, Sidney and his mother."

"But what about the murder in St Kilda's?"

"Terrible business that," says Sidney.

"Terrible," agrees Morrie.

"I want to get them to agree to a reconstruction of the crime on television. So we can catch the killer."

"Good idea. So what's the problem?"

"The police won't let me speak to the family. Can you help me find some other way around?" The two men look at each other. Sidney picks up his pencil and turns it around in his hands.

"You know anything about the Friedmann family, Sid?" asks Morrie. Sidney nods.

"Well?"

"What d'you think, Morrie? I'm not sure."

"What you mean you're not sure?"

Sidney says something in something that sounds like a garbled form of German and I assume is Yiddish, a language I feel I should know but have actually never heard before. Yes, my parents' conversation is spattered with slang like *meshuge* and *broiges* and *tuchus*, but they can't actually string it together in sentences. Not that they'd want to, of course. It's for the peasants, as Mutti would say with a shudder, as if her normal mode of communication was some kind of elevated Platonic discourse instead of a bastardised hybrid of kitchen German crossed with English. But, in her private linguistic hierarchy, Yiddish represents the lower orders, and when her snobby friends come round to tea they converse in terrible French, under the illusion that it makes them sound elegant.

What I hear now is something she'd dismiss as the language of the *shtetl*. Though the cadences are familiar, identifying separate words is like trying to pull fish out of a fast-flowing stream. I manage to catch "*weyss nicht*", and "*rebbe*", the rest is a current of verbiage. After a minute or two, Morrie says to me,

"You really think it will help to catch the person who did this?"

"I'm afraid there are no guarantees. But would you rather put your faith in Stoke Newington police?" They shake their heads in mournful unison.

"The family belong to the Veltz community", says Morrie. If you like, I can introduce you to Rabbi Stern.

"That would be fantastic. Do you think I can speak to him today?" He arches a grizzled eyebrow at me.

"You think I got so many other important things to do?"

Rabbi Stern's house is a large, brooding, thirties-built semi. As we are approaching, Morrie takes a skullcap out of his pocket and arranges it on his head. A little girl answers the bell. He says something to her, the only bit I catch is "*Reb Stern*". She runs back into the house, calling out, "*Tateh, Tateh*."

When the Rabbi emerges, he's a dead ringer for Tevye in *Fiddler on the Roof*. It may be the biggest cliché on the planet but this man really *is* Topol. And what makes him come over all earthy and Eastern European is that over his shirt he's wearing one of those cream vest-like garments with fringes and black stripes at either end, just like in the film. Morrie and the Rabbi shake hands. They talk for some time in an undertone, Morrie gesturing towards me while I try to look respectful, and the rabbi throws the occasional glance my way but never seems to look straight at me – he's hitting a spot about two feet to my right. The two men become very excited. I wonder if they are having an argument. Finally, they shake hands and the rabbi goes back into his house.

"Sorry, my dear," says Morrie. "No movie."

"It sounded as though you put my case pretty forcefully, Morrie. But I would have loved to have a go at persuading him myself."

"Wouldn't have helped."

"Why?"

"Why d'you think? Some things you just have to accept."

"There's a killer at large, doesn't he feel in any way moved to *do* something?"

"He doesn't think it's right for his community to enter the spotlight. He says, once you say yes, then it's open season, and you are in the public eye forever. That's not how they want to live."

"So he goes for the Pandora's Box theory of public relations, as opposed to Andy Warhol's famous for fifteen minutes idea?"

"Absolutely."

"He's pretty switched on, then."

"Don't be taken in by the get-up." Sidney walks me back to the car and says goodbye with a regretful sigh. I thank him, and drive off.

But I've no intention of leaving the *shtetl*. Round the corner, I stop and wait. Then I drive back to the Rabbi's house and ring the bell again. He doesn't seem surprised to see me.

"Rabbi, I'm sorry to intrude on you, but I would like you to reconsider your decision." He nods, says nothing and I suddenly realise that I haven't heard him speaking English, and I imagine there is every chance he doesn't.

"Please put yourself in the position of the mother," I say, speaking slowly and enunciating each word. "Can any of us imagine how it must be to lose a child – let alone like this? For her sake and the sake of the community, please reconsider your decision."

He looks at me, and holds his arm out, inviting me to enter the house. It's taken thirty seconds for me to get further with this than Morrie managed. A polished parquet floor sweeps along the hallway and into the front room. Along one wall is an ornate glass cabinet, full of ceremonial silver cups, plates and candlesticks. The Rabbi calls something up the stairs, and after a few moments a girl of about nineteen appears, book in hand. She sits on a chair in the corner and starts reading, without even looking at me.

The Rabbi gestures to a chair, so I sit. He remains on his feet, the tip of his beard level with the top of my head.

"Thank you for agreeing to talk to me," I say. I still haven't heard him utter a word of English, so I back pedal on the language, trying to select basic vocabulary. "If – you – will – think – again – about – letting – us – make – a – film, I am – sure – you – will – not – " I scrub the word regret " – be sorry." He looks at me, still silent, so I add, "Television – is – a – very – powerful – er, medium." OK, medium breaks the simple vocab rule, but I can't think of an easier alternative. Rabbi Stern takes a few paces along the room with his head down, as if thinking, then turns towards me.

"OK, young lady, let's make one thing absolutely clear." His accent is as New York as pastrami on rye. "We don't need any lectures about the efficacy of TV. Believe me, we know all about TV and all the great wonders it has to offer."

"Then," I say, "you will realise that it may be your best bet for finding the guy who killed Bruchi Friedmann."

"And of course, you have no vested interest whatsoever in suggesting that?"

"If you want to see figures for clear-up rates, following appeals on *The Crime Programme*, I can bring them over."

"You prove any damn thing you like with statistics. And you are making one hell of a big assumption anyway. Finding the guy who did it may not be my top priority. We've already got some of your colleagues from the nation's least attractive publications crawling round the area, and that is more than enough."

"Statistically speaking, there's always the risk he'll offend again."

"Here? In the same place?"

"Not necessarily."

"So why should I care?"

"Don't you?"

"I look after my community. If I wanted to represent the nation, I'd stand for prime minister."

"How about justice for the Friedmann family? Isn't that a Jewish principle?"

"Look, one of the most loathsome clichés about Jewish justice is all that 'an eye for an eye' stuff. People think we're a load of religious fanatics hell bent on revenge. Sorry to disappoint."

"So you'd rather a dangerous man stay out there?"

"You talk as though there's nobody else out there fighting the forces of evil. As a law-abiding citizen of this country, which I have been for twenty years, it may surprise you to know I am willing to trust the Metropolitan Police to do their best on our behalf."

Chapter 7

It's six o'clock by the time I leave Stamford Hill. I've achieved nothing and can't bear to think what's waiting for me at home. Outside the flat, I sit in the car listening to the end of the *Six O'Clock News*. I shuffle around the jumbled mess inside my handbag, looking for my keys but find my phone instead. As it comes back on, the voicemail icon flashes at me. One message.

"Hi Liz, it's Millie here. Sarah's wondering where you are. You know you were supposed to be here for a meeting with her and Bill about your story at four o'clock. It's four thirty. And I think you should know that Sarah's – umm – a bit—" Beep. It cuts out. Fill in the gap. Now let me guess. Sarah's a bit –

delighted? Thrilled? I'm in the shit again, empty-handed and way too tired to handle the bollocking she's lining up for me. As I'm going into the flat, I quick-dial through to Dave.

"Hi," I say. "What are you doing?"

"Keeping a low profile so that I don't upset your darling Mutti while she's adjusting to the trauma of me joining the family."

"You don't have to, you know. You could come round."

"Mmm. Yeah, or I could stay here reading a medical text book. Then next time I bump into your parents I could pretend the photography thing's just a hobby. I'm actually a doctor. I could even perform circumcision on myself, in a hopeless bid to convince her I'm the son-in-law of her dreams."

"Very funny."

"I'm a changeling – a Jewish boy brought up by unwitting Christian parents. A kind of Moses for *nos jours*, just trying to liberate my inner medic."

"I'm glad you find it funny."

"But Elizabeth, I'm pining for you. What about abandoning your precious Mutti tonight? Pop round here for an illicit bacon sandwich."

"As it happens, my mother would have no objections to a bacon sandwich, so strictly speaking, it wouldn't be illicit."

"So I'm less acceptable to your Jewish parents than a bacon sandwich."

"Welcome to the family. I'll call you tomorrow."

"Babe, take pity on me. Pop round here for a *licit* bacon sandwich with your *illicit* boyfriend."

"Fiancé, you mean."

"How could I forget, my gorgeous bride?"

"Love you, speak tomorrow, byeee." I open the door of the flat, bracing myself for the stink of cigarette smoke. I sniff. I take a deep breath through the nose. The only unusual smell I can detect is floral.

And then I see why. My black lacquer dining table has been covered by a lacy cloth of man-made fibre. In its centre is a cut-glass vase containing a bunch of carnations and dahlias in violent, unnatural shades of pink, yellow and blue. The mantlepiece has been adorned with a selection of what I can only call modernist bric-a-brac, and the back and arms of my leather sofa are sporting jolly, crocheted white antimacassars which Mutti wouldn't dream of having in her own home, so she must think my taste in decor calls for desperate measures. The minimalist front room has been transformed.

Mutti comes out of the kitchen, wearing a frilly gingham apron and a look of supreme self-satisfaction. She is polishing a wine glass.

"Good day at work, *dahhlink*?" she says.

"Could have been better," I reply. "And it looks as though we've had a visit from the *Changing Rooms* team. Don't tell me – Carol Smillie's hiding in the bedroom."

"Is better, though?"

"More – colourful, certainly," I concede.

In the kitchen there are dishes everywhere – a starter of Russian eggs, a vat of goulash, a pan of parsley potatoes glistening with butter, a technicolour salad, and a massive gateau. My mother's food obsession covers every spare bit of surface. In a flash the fat child and anorexic teenager inside me are doing battle, one clingy and the other desperate to escape. The mean-spirited adolescent wins. Though I can see Mutti's desperate for me to ooh and ahh over her ridiculous creations, I say: "I'm going to have a shower," and turn my back.

The steaming jet of water feels as if it's scouring out the resentment. Mutti's trying very hard to please me. I towel myself dry with more than the usual vigour, as if I can pummel my fury into gratitude. That doesn't work, but as I'm pulling on some clean jeans I realise I haven't eaten all day. I'm starving. On the pretext of admiring the spread, I stand near to Mutti and sniff her breath. She's sober. Relief and affection well up inside me.

When she serves dinner I eat as I used to do before I began hating her. The starter is a familiar concoction of diced vegetables laced together with lashings of mayonnaise and served with boiled eggs. As if there's not nearly enough saturated fat in it already, the yolks have been removed, and mashed up with butter. The yellow paste has then been piped back into the halved whites, with a pinch of paprika powder on top for decoration. The effect is baroque, and maybe it was aesthetics that made this one of my grandmother's most beloved dishes. I thought I'd reached my lifetime limit of Russian eggs after forcing them down every Sunday for fifteen years. Until now. I hoover my plate and look round for the next course.

British people think they know what goulash is. It's a stew seasoned with a teaspoon of paprika and served with rice. Serious foodies give a knowing smile at such lack of sophistication. Of course, they say, everybody knows that the "*gulyás*" is actually a soup. It is the staple of the Magyar tribesmen, who have inhabited the plains of the *Puszta* for centuries. My mother's goulash is no soup.

Like so many other bourgeois refugees who grew up with a household full of servants, she and my grandmother had to teach themselves to recreate their most beloved Magyar dishes in chilly Britain. Back then it took resourcefulness to find the key ingredients in a small provincial town like Cardiff. You might as well have asked for frankincense and myrrh at the local grocers as requesting paprika powder and sour cream. But these were women who had survived the Nazis, and 'not available' just wasn't part of their lexicon.

By now, Mutti has had time to refine the dish to the point of perfection. Hearty chunks of pork and slices of smoked sausage have been steeped in a dense, meaty broth, thickened with flour and seasoned with a generous amount of paprika. A handful of caraway seeds give another, lighter dimension to the symphony of flavours that is building. A large jar of sauerkraut is stirred into the rich, red sauce. By itself, sauerkraut is a sad thing. Limp, acidic cabbage, lacking in soul. But it gives heart to my mother's *Szegedin Goulash*, soaking up the juices and melting them together. The final ingredient and the most magical is the sour cream. It transforms something prosaic into poetry, endowed with an exquisite soft sharpness.

This is the food I'll dream of when I'm dying. A yielding, flavoursome plateful. As full of contradictions and complexities as my mother herself. I don't compliment the food, as I know I should. But my clean plate and full stomach speak for themselves. Mutti is beaming.

"I hope you don't mind," she says as we put our plates away, "but I've invited my old friend Liesl for *kaffee und kuchen* after dinner. I nod. By now I've eaten so much that I'm past caring.

At eight o'clock on the dot the bell rings. Mutti goes to the door and I hear the smack of hearty Mittel European kissing, and exclamations of, "*Darhhlink*, how are you?" Liesl is a grande dame of Viennese provenance, her hair a golden dome fortified with a whole can of Elnett. She sweeps into the room, followed by her son, a gawky young man in a sports jacket, with trousers that stop two inches above his shoes. I've eaten so much that I believe her when she says *he* has come because *she's* afraid of driving in the dark.

Something strange happens when you indulge yourself with rich food. Instead of satisfying your craving, you want more and more. The Hungarian half of my subconscious will not be content until the final part of the meal has been served. I've seen a cake in the kitchen, stacked with creamy layers of chocolate cream. I'm so desperate for it I am even willing to overlook the ridiculous silver paper doily that it's sitting on.

As I come back into the room, there's a pause in the conversation. I hand round generous slices, each topped with a mountain peak of *schlagsahne*.

"So, Elizabett, your mother tells me that you verk in television."

"Yes," I say, "and what do you do, Michael?" He stares at the carpet and mutters something. "Sorry," I say, "I didn't quite catch that." Michael's eyes bore into the carpet with such intent that I wonder if he's spotted a stain.

"I work in a pathology lab."

"Oh that must be interesting. What exactly do you do there?" He nods at the carpet, and a blotchy redness starts spreading up his neck.

"We analyse slides, for signs of malignancy."

"And do you have to train a long time for that kind of thing?"

"Just the usual six years."

"Six years, goodness, that's the same as a..."

"Yes?" I look at my mother. She looks back, a picture of innocence.

"So, you are a fully qualified, *medical* doctor?"

"Oh yes, sorry, didn't I make that clear?"

"I understand. I understand everything."

"Oh really, have you worked in a lab?"

"Only the laboratory of life." I pause. "And let me guess, Michael, you are probably *single*?"

When the cake has eaten and our visitors are making their way back to Stanmore, I turn to Mutti.

"I know you aren't that mad about Dave, but it's too late to start introducing me to eligible bachelors."

"Why ever not?"

"What do you mean why not? Because I am engaged to be married."

"So?"

"You know perfectly well that one fiancé is the maximum number one can have. There is no vacancy."

"There's nothing wrong with having two fiancés. I had two for a considerable period. It was very chic."

"Did the two men involved know what was going on?"

"Of course not. A woman should have secrets. It adds to her mystique."

"But that's wrong. It may not be illegal, but it's deceitful and immoral. It's verging on bigamy."

"A young girl is permitted to be fickle. You use your charm later to extricate yourself."

"I'm not a young girl. I'll be forty in a few years. And anyway, if I was prepared to two-time Dave, it wouldn't be in favour of an autistic mummy's boy in a tweed jacket. Even if he is legally entitled to carry a stethoscope."

"You are right, he wasn't at all suitable. Difficult to believe this *klutz* is actually a doctor. I'm sure Valentina will find somebody more appropriate."

"I've already got somebody more appropriate." I glare at her. She looks suitably apologetic. I get up to clear the plates when I realise.

"And who, may I ask, is Valentina?"

"She's – a businesswoman."

"I get it. What did you say her name was?"

I find my handbag and pull out the now very crumpled copy of the *Jewish News*. In the small ads at the back, under Social and Personal, there it is: Valentina Fink Introductions.

"This Valentina?"

Mutti nods.

"And how much does Valentina charge for these 'Introductions'?"

"It wasn't that much, considering."

"*Wasn't*? You mean you've already paid this charlatan some

69

money? What will Daddy think? You're broke as it is, and now you are wasting money you don't have on a hopeless attempt to get me hitched to what you imagine is a nice Jewish boy."

"*Dahhlink*, I'm just trying to give you options."

Chapter 8

When I wake up the following day, my stomach is still aching as though it's gone five rounds with Barry McGuigan. Stumbling towards the kitchen, I see the spare room door is open, the bed has been made. No sign of Mutti, but the Italian espresso pot is on the hob, and it's hot. Clean dishes are piled up on the work surface. While I'm waiting for the kettle to boil, I look into the lounge. No sign. I take my mug into the hallway, and open the front door. There she is, smoking a cigarette, drinking coffee, watching the traffic go past. A shaft of early morning sunshine catches the steps.

Leaving the front door on the latch, I tuck my dressing gown under me and sit on the top stair.

"So, what are you planning to do today, then?"

"Oh I don't know."

"I'm sure the Bar Council would welcome a visit. You could always pretend you need a lawyer, then go through the list of members, looking for suitable sounding names like Cohen, Levy and anything ending in 'stein."

She flicks her head to the side, tapping ash into the wind. "I'm just trying to help. You know I only want you to be happy."

"It would make me happy if you could accept Dave, and realise that he is the right man for me. What makes me unhappy are the constant suggestions of disapproval."

"OK, OK."

"And what are you going to do about Valentina? You know

I'm not going to meet any of her eligible bachelors. Can you get the money back?"

"I don't know."

"So what are you really doing today?"

"I think the Victoria and Albert."

Ah yes. The costumes, the Ming vases, and the whole edifice a tribute to a happy, fruitful marriage, which I seem to recall involved a controlling mama somewhere along the line. So, why don't I believe her?

When I get to the office, it's almost empty, the only person around is Sarah's assistant Millie, guarding the entrance to the boss's office.

"Where is everybody?" I ask her.

"It's studio day."

"Oh Christ. So it is." That's a near miss. I'm supposed to be on phones. "I suppose Sarah wants to see me?"

"Yeah. You may not want to see her though. She was ready to eat you alive yesterday."

"Oh Jeez. What can I say to make it better?"

"I think you'll need to prostrate yourself on the ground uttering repentances. Sacrificing some kind of small animal as an act of contrition might also help."

When I get there, the rehearsal is in full swing. I creep into the back of the darkened gallery, trying to pretend I've been there for ever. I can see the presenter's image refracted across a bank of monitors, showing him from five different angles. Down in the studio he's perched on a desk with a wad of scripts in his hand. As the camera cuts, he looks up, and explains about a disturbing series of stranger rapes in different Dorset towns. On his last word, the director cues in the video, but stops it after thirty seconds.

"OK everyone, from the top. Bit static on the read, Jim darling. Can we try making it a walk?" There's a lot of business on the studio floor. A spark uses a big pole to adjust some of the lamps, and as he does so, Sarah swivels round in her chair next to the director, and gives me one of her most cutting looks.

"Thanks for gracing our humble premises today, Elizabeth," she spits. "I was beginning to think that the attractions of London N16 were so overwhelming that you were going to open a satellite office over there."

"I'm sorry I missed the meeting," I mumble.

"Missing a meeting is not the problem. A bit of notice would be nice. I believe that in some circles it is even considered polite to send one's apologies."

"I'm really sorry. I got, kind of, caught up."

"So I hear."

"You did?"

"Look. Your failure to keep us in the loop with what the hell you are up to – that would be enough in its own right to make me question your judgement."

"Yes."

"But that you have absolutely disregarded a clear instruction I gave you."

"Sorry."

"Have you got amnesia?" I say nothing. "Well, have you?"

"No."

"Did I or did I not tell you that you are *not* an amateur sleuth? You work with the police, alongside them at all times. We rely on them for everything. We don't go freelance, off-piste, as the whim takes us." The whole gallery is now looking at me. The vision mixer has stopped mixing. The sound ops have taken off their cans. The director is looking at me with undisguised pity.

"Hello folks, is anybody listening. How's this?" It's Jim, from the studio floor. He's suddenly realised that he's not the centre of attention any more. The gallery crew re-focuses, except for Sarah who is still glaring at me. How does she know I went to Stamford Hill yesterday?

"Look, I'm really sorry. But whose toes did I step on?"

"Does the name –" she looks puts on her glasses and looks down at a yellow sticky attached to her notebook, "– Rabbi Stern – mean anything to you?"

"Ahh—"

"Because his description of you was uncannily accurate." Tevye. Seems that the principal tradition he's brought over from the *shtetl* involves grassing me up to the police.

"I met some guys in the area who introduced me. It all seemed very – above board."

"Don't be so fucking innocent, Elizabeth. These guys may dress like they are still living three hundred years ago the backwoods of Poland, but that doesn't mean they rely on a man on horseback to pass a message. Your pal Stern was on the phone to DI Jenkins before you'd even got back through his garden gate. There's been a snowstorm of electronic messaging. You might as well have put up a Wanted poster with your photograph on every billboard in Stoke Newington."

After the programme I get home late to discover where Mutti's been, and surprise, surprise, it isn't the Victoria and Albert. She's been hunting round Kilburn for information to kick-start her compensation claim. Her source is the owner of a small grocery shop that serves the needs of London's émigré Hungarian community. As a consequence we've now got enough salami to open our own Magyar deli. But when I try to find out what she's actually learned from Mr Gabor, it's disappointing in its vagueness. His friend applied for compensation, and got something. No names, dates or other details. Just a lot of salami. Despite the lateness of the hour, I call Dave.

"Call me old fashioned," I say, "but isn't the mother of the bride supposed to take a teeny bit of interest in our forthcoming nuptials? Instead of which she's obsessed by two other things – finding me an alternative groom, and spending the limited wedding budget on this hopeless quest for compensation."

"Can't you interest her in something else?"

"Like what?"

"I don't know. How about the Women's Institute or voluntary work in a charity shop?"

"Mmm, I don't think you've quite got the hang of my mother."

"How about knitting booties for the gorgeous grandchildren we're going to produce?"

"Even she's not *that* optimistic."

"Optimistic is the word if she thinks there's any real chance of getting money out of the Hungarian government. And to be honest why should she after all this time?"

"Well," I say slowly, "I think there is a *moral* case for it. When you think of what her parents went through. How much they lost."

"Don't forget, people in this country suffered too in the Blitz and all that. My grandparents gave free board and lodging to Land Girls for years. But they aren't about to start asking for back rent forty years later. It's perverse, as your father would agree."

"What's my father got to do with it?" I pause, "And how on earth do you know what my father thinks about it?"

"We spoke on the telephone. Is there some kind of unwritten rule that we can't?"

"No. No, of course not. So what *exactly* is it that you and my father agree on in your cosy tête-à-têtes?"

"Calm down, we're not forging some kind of pact behind your back. The matter in hand is the compensation claim. And the one thing we can agree on is that it's a waste of time and money. You've got to stop your mother obsessing about it."

"Really?" OK, I know he's right, but it's none of his business. I bang the phone down, and go back to Mutti and the salami mountain. It's well past midnight now, but she's still up and at it. I sit down at the dining room table facing her.

"Look, if you want to pursue this compensation thing, you need to take it seriously. Treat it as you would a proper business interest." She looks like a schoolgirl who is about to get told off for not doing her homework.

"Don't put on that face. It's serious. We need to put together a case. Trying to corner the market in salami may be a bit of a distraction." I get a cardboard file out of my room, and write COMPENSATION CLAIM on it in black marker pen. Mutti looks very satisfied with this, even though we haven't got anything to put in it yet. Except a leaflet advertising the Hungarian salami shop, and some kind of émigré news sheet. Well, it's a start.

In the office the following day I'm on menial tasks with a work experience girl whose Daddy is a Labour MP. She's Tony this and Cherie that all afternoon and at four o'clock I snap and tell her that unless she's got a hotline to Number Ten, can she just shut up and get on with it.

I get home to find the flat spotless. And empty. There's a smell of multi-purpose spray everywhere, with a note of bleach in the bathroom and a hint of lavender in the bedrooms. Mutti's never gone as far as commenting on my levels of household cleanliness, but as soon as she's feeling at home, she's whipped out the Marigolds.

And, leaning against a vase of fuchsias in the middle of the dining table is – the card from Valentina's dating agency. That's straight for the bin. But then half a glass later, I fish it out again and have another look.

At nine o'clock Dad phones to say he's picked Mutti up from the station. They've kissed and made up, and everything is getting back to normal. I wonder how long that can last.

Not long at all. By the following day when I talk to Mutti, she's focusing on the Hungarian compensation claim with renewed vigour. And I can tell it's starting to wind Daddy up. Over the next week, she's revving the engine. She's been to the library and got a pile of books about Hungary. She's dug up a file of old papers, and a lot more old photographs. The dossier is beginning to fill up. Every time I talk to her, she sounds more and more excited, rattling on about how many people her father's factory employed, how big it was; how large the apartment, and how near to the river, how lavishly it was furnished and decorated.

She's been to the travel agent's to get prices for flights to Budapest, and has come back with a detailed itinerary for a two-week trip. My father calls. He sounds like a man being pulled along by a big, bouncy dog. The lead is pulling his arm off.

"Really Lisbet, I would have thought you'd know better."

"About what?"

"Encouraging your mother to pursue this fantasy about compensation."

"I didn't encourage her."

"Then how do you explain this – this dossier? She's obsessed with it. And we can't move for salami."

"I'm innocent of anything to do with sausage acquisition."

"I think you've been egging her on. How come she suddenly knows so much about it?"

"Look, we talked it over a bit..."

"Ja, *genau*. Exactly. You have to watch what you say. She thinks you are serious. Now I hear you've hired some kind of specialist, a hot shot lawyer."

"*Whaaat?*"

76

"I don't know where she thinks we'll get the money for this, Lisbet. I'm ticking over with the translating work now. But it's not enough to pay for a trip to Hungary yet, let alone the deluxe tour your mother is planning."

The following day Mutti calls, with an excited rundown of the capsule travel wardrobe she has acquired. It's all in practical, drip-dry, manmade fabrics. Did I know that these can be hand washed and need no ironing at all?

I give her one of my lectures. I tell her to stop pushing her luck. Does she know how lucky she is to have Dad? If she doesn't want to push him over the edge, she's to stop her spending right now, and get back to the bridge table. There is silence from her end of the line. And sniffing.

Saturday night. Dave and I haven't seen each other all week because I've been busy with Mutti. It's his turn to choose, so we see a three-hour Iranian film about incest, shot in black and white. The father is forging a dangerous alliance with his daughter's fiancé, and after that a tragic ending seems inevitable. It's all a bit too arty for me. Not that I'm pushing for a romcom with Hugh Grant, but I'd love some popcorn. Apparently my crunching would ruin his appreciation of a subtle (slow) and nuanced (boring) film, because it would detract from the essential auteur/director's vision.

In the gloom, I sneak an occasional sidelong glance at Dave, but he's absorbed in the movie. Let's not even think about holding hands. By the end, there's a lot of grinding sex on the banks of a river and far too much masochistic self-harm including the leading male castrating himself with a saw. To look on the bright side, this is probably better viewed in monochrome. As we're coming out, I venture,

"So, what did you think?"

"Mmm."

"Did you like the film?"

"I can't come out with pat answers straight after the end credits. I'm still digesting it."

"OK," I say. "He could have cut out at least half of that wedding scene, it went on for ages. But it looked fabulous. Apart from the, er, you know."

"I said it's too early to discuss. I'm not going to play Radio 4 with you, like some fatuous, so-called intellectual with an opinion ready at the drop of a microphone."

"So you mean that you'd rather go to the cinema by yourself."

"That's not what I said." He puts his arms around me. "Don't be so touchy, will you? Not everybody moves at your frenetic pace."

"OK, what do you want to do now? I'm hungry. If we go out to eat will you insist on separate tables and refuse to discuss whether the food's delicious or not?" There's just a moment when I think he doesn't get the joke. He looks at me all angry and misunderstood before the smile breaks through.

We go for a pizza. But the conversation is halting. It looks as though all the people at the other tables are having a better time than us. After a night out, we usually end up at Dave's place. I'm getting bored of having to choose. God forbid he'd give up living in that draughty studio. Fitted carpet may be a hideous middle class indulgence, but it's also very soft on the feet.

As we get out of the car, I'm thinking through the script for making my excuses. But I can't get it right. There's no way of saying I don't want to spend the night with you that doesn't sound like the beginning of the end of a relationship.

Once we are home, Dave puts on the TV. He opens a bottle of red wine, even though we didn't finish the Chianti at the restaurant. He pushes a glass towards me, and I take a gulp. It tastes sour. He puts on *Match of the Day* and sits down next to me on the sofa. Without taking his eyes off the television, Dave reaches for my hand and raises it to his lips. I slide closer to him, but whatever feeling moved him has evaporated. He's still holding my hand, but it might as well be a football rattle. I could read the match with my eyes shut.

"I'll get ready for bed," I announce, and he nods, without taking his eyes off the screen. Though it's late, I have a shower. A few months ago I treated myself to some expensive body lotion. It's still there in his cupboard. I unwrap the towel on the bed and massage some of the rich cream into my freshly shaved legs, making them sleek and soft. My nightie is vintage Victorian lace, picked up from a stall in Camden Market. It feels crisp and clean as slip it over my head and do up the pearl buttons, leaving the top two open. His bed hasn't been made, and is covered in this morning's toast crumbs so I pull everything off and give it a shake. The sheet gets stretched flat and anchored with hospital corners. On top I arrange the bedding like they do for magazine shoots, artfully plumping the pillows, and folding down the edge of the duvet. And the finishing touch, a dove grey mohair blanket across the foot of the bed. With both sidelights casting a warm glow, it's bed perfection. I slide into my side, trying my best not to disturb the covers.

I must drift off over my book, because the next thing I know is that Dave's weight is on top of me and his hands are pushing in between my legs. He's coming on all strong and sultry, and though this is exactly what I've been waiting for, suddenly I just want to escape. I untangle myself from his arms, ignoring his protests and make for the bathroom, where I sit on the lid of the toilet for what seems ages, trying to work out what to do next.

When I creep back, Dave is dozing. I find my clothes, in a neat pile where I left them on a wicker chair. I'm dressed in seconds, dumping the nightie on the floor and with one last backward glance at my snoring man, I grab my bag, and shut the door behind me. It's past two in the morning when I get home. Comfort is a clean pair of old-fashioned men's striped pyjamas and a milky drink. Sitting on the sofa, I pick up my copy of *Vogue*. A card falls out of it onto my lap. Valentina's card. A line-drawing of a man and a woman, with the strapline, "Out there, someone is looking for you." Yuk. I think about Dave and what's just happened. It's hardly the first time we've had a bad night, of course. But after all this time I'm beginning to suspect my parents are right about him.

For all their faults, and despite all appearances to the contrary, they are trying to accept Dave, and I can see what it's costing them. I try to imagine the conversation they've had about him. About us. "He's not Jewish – so what?" would almost certainly be Dad's line. "As long as he makes her happy," would be Mutti's, trying to deny both gut instinct and fundamental beliefs. Experience, upbringing and everything they know has taught them that it matters, nothing to do with religion and everything to do with who you are at heart. Money would play a big part of their thinking – and watching their struggles now I can see why. But she would definitely be on the lookout for something else. I don't know a word for it in English, but I think hers would be *"gemütlichkeit"*. And her surprisingly accurate powers of perception would be telling her it isn't there between him and me. And the Jewish thing is a kind of proxy. It's all about the quality of connection.

Maybe Mutti's right. Maybe she's been right all along, and I'm just too stubborn to admit it. How many more bad nights do I have to endure before I throw in the cards with Dave? We're engaged to be married, for Christ's sake. It's not a game any more. Sure, I know the predictable crap about why I chose him. The *goyishe* boyfriend so perfectly calculated to wind up my folks, as described in a thousand self-help books. My parents are above that knee-jerk response, I think they do want the best for me, but I can't just give him up because that's the *sensible* thing to do. As if I knew what that was, anyway. We aren't in the realms of the rational here. Question: How do you know when a relationship is worth pursuing?

Chapter 9

When I next phone home, my mother gives me the usual catalogue of unremarkable recent domestic purchases and tedious social events. It sounds *über* dull, suspiciously so.

"Is everything OK?" I ask.

"*Ja*, fine, fine," she replies. I can hear her teeth clacking down as she bites onto her cigarette holder.

"Are you sure?"

"Mmm, well Daddy is being not very nice really."

"What do you mean?"

"He won't talk to me." Well I never.

"At all? Or just about – certain topics?"

"Weeell, *ich weiss nicht*, Lisbet. He is being *Ekelhaft. Wirklich wahr.*" Surely not.

"Do you want me to talk to him?"

"*Nein, nein.* You don't have to." She sighs. I can see her sitting in the usual place by the kitchen table, with her pile of cigarette filters, crosswords and well-thumbed address book. And no doubt the "COMPENSATION CLAIM" file isn't far away, getting fatter by the day. He's in the next room, watching *Panorama*. I put the phone down and go to the gym.

As the week winds on, the tension is building. She's getting more and more excited about Hungary and he's getting more fed up with it. They take turns to call me – him from the office, her from the kitchen. The frequency is building. It's clear that though both of them are speaking to me, they aren't speaking to each other. So there's only one thing for it.

I join thousands of other people sitting in a tailback on the Chiswick flyover. I'm thinking about Dave and that awful night. All week my default mode has been a hopeless attempt to evaluate our relationship, as though there's some kind of magic formula for balancing the nights of passion against the clangers. I relive the Sussex summer when we made love in the sea at dusk, and by the time I hit the M4 proper, I'm flying along the overtaking lane, feeling the sensual excitement of the waves and his body besides mine. Easing off the accelerator, I find myself once again trying to work out whether I want Dave, or need him or – is it love?

But thinking doesn't work, and feelings are unreliable. They don't account for the way we've grown together, helping each other over life's all too frequent disappointments, sharing aspirations, battling with the outside world and making a bid far too late in life to finally grow up, together. But when you grow up you move on. And what about the crap nights when we can't connect – do they matter? Maybe they are a sign that it's just not working any more. Risking a major road accident, I fumble around in my bag one-handedly for some gum and instead pull out Valentina's now rather crumpled appointment card. The whole idea of a dating agency seems outrageously simplistic, reducing the thousand facets of any personality to GSOH and taste in music.

I've been trying not to notice that Dave's been texting me and phoning me all week. But I don't trust myself enough to return his calls. And now I'm driving away from him at 90 mph. Outside it's dark and *Any Questions* has finished long before I hit the Severn Bridge. It always feels downhill to Cardiff from here, I'm freewheeling home past Newport, powered by a spike of adrenalin as I peel off the motorway and weave my way through the country lanes that stretch into the back of Rhiwbina. At the house Mutti greets me rather formally. From her air of unsteadiness, and my father's defeated demeanour, I understand the situation. It's my adolescence all over again. She's going to wobble around with overcooked food and stinking of alcohol while we sit there looking sheepish. Well, it's time to break the habit of a lifetime.

"I'm fed up." I say. "Not just because I've spent three hours on the motorway to get up here. But because when I finally do, you are pissed."

"Ach Lisbet, it's OK," protests my father. "You don't have to."

"No it's not bloody OK." I hiss. "It's been going on for too long and nobody ever says anything."

"You really – don't know what you are talking about," says Mutti, with a steely expression.

"Yes I do. I've grown up with it, remember. People rolling their eyes sympathetically at me. What about that ghastly mess at Bernie's party? Are we supposed to pretend it didn't happen?" There's a shocked silence at this. I've stepped over an invisible line. And now there's no stopping me.

Between the dining room and the kitchen there's a wall of cupboards that opens on both sides. Clean plates can be put in on one side, and taken out from the other. I march up to it, slide open the centre right drawer, and take out a bottle of scotch, and a bottle of vodka. Both are half full.

"How do you think I knew these would be here? Do you think I'm deaf or something?" For as long as I can remember, Mutti has had a habit of sidling out of a room half way through a sentence. A subdued clink of bottles, and a glugging sound. Then she re-emerges, to complete her sentence. And she thinks I haven't even noticed. Me, the ever-so-clever A grade pupil/graduate/television researcher. Am I really so daft that I don't notice she's walked out of a room in mid-flow, and come back stinking of spirits. "The really stupid thing is the fact we've all put up with it for so long."

Dad is looking uncomfortable. Mutti re-loads her cigarette holder. "Maybe there are reasons we don't talk about these things always," he says. He puts a hand on Mutti's.

"But it's been going on for so long. What's the big secret? Surely, it's healthier to talk about it. To get it out into the open."

"Lisbet, we will talk about these things. When the time is right." I look from him to her, and back again. They think if we don't talk about it, it'll just go away. That never worked before. Mutti speaks.

"You want to talk now? OK, we talk. About the past. We've done our best. You wanted something – you got it. Clothes, holidays, parties. We gave you everything we knew how. So we're not perfect. No, but who is perfect?"

"I'm not asking for perfection. All I'm saying is why didn't you just throw away the fucking booze?" There's a kind of air pocket. My parents don't swear and I don't do it in front of them. We've broken through the sound barrier.

"You show me another parent who tried harder to get it right," screams Mutti. "You were my precious baby. My chance to start again, after all the shit I went through. I wanted everything the best for you. I wanted to start again, to make things new, to make them right. We done our best, maybe that's not good enough. We spoilt you."

"That's great, just have a go at me. I'm the spoilt brat only child."

"It's true. You took everything and turned on us. Now we have no more to give. Ungrateful bloodsucker."

"It's so much easier to make me the problem."

"I think we made your life too easy."

"That's right. You gave me everything and it wasn't enough.

Nothing's good enough for me, and that includes you, my goddamn parents. You try to pretend the past hasn't happened. And the booze is just another way of obliterating it. But it's just trauma in a different guise." It looks as though she's about to yell back at me when a baffled look comes over her face, as though I've just said something in Swahili. "Why won't you talk about the drink?" I yell at the top of my voice. She suddenly looks crumpled and forlorn.

"I go to find my lighter," Mutti mutters as she ambles out of the room. We can hear her rummaging around in the kitchen.

"She had a phone call," says Dad.

"Yes?" Mutti lives on the phone, so this is unsurprising.

"From America."

"Yes?"

"You remember Mutti's cousin Vonni?"

"Sure, how could I forget?"

"He died."

"Right. And now I'm the insensitive bastard. You could have mentioned it."

"You didn't give me a chance."

So even though it's barely nine o'clock I go to bed, and just sit there with anxiety knotted in my stomach. I can't concentrate on my book, and the sound of the newspapers crumpling drives me mad, so I throw them on the floor and rearrange the covers. Lying down with my eyes shut doesn't work because it's way too early to sleep, even with yoga breathing and relaxation exercises. So I get out and stretch. My phone's lying on the dressing table. I pick it up and start scrolling through all the Dave's texts and his missed calls that I've ignored. There were quite a few on Sunday, and a spasmodic pattern during the week. Surely he must know something's wrong by now, even if he didn't appear to grasp it on Saturday night.

The need to call him is now physical in its intensity. Because that's what I do. And every time it happens, he manages to make me laugh about my parents instead of wanting to scream, which means I can face them again in the morning.

I'd have to apologise first and have some kind of unnecessary discussion about our relationship, which I really can't face.

I hear the stairs creaking, which can't possibly mean my night owl parents are going to bed. Instead there's a horrible possibility that one of them is coming up to build bridges. I click on Dave's number, press call and blast out "Hi it's me," while the phone on the other end is still ringing. So when he does pick up the phone all he hears is silence and heavy breathing.

"Yes?" He says. "Who's there? Elizabeth?"

"Yes, I'm at my parents'."

"Are you OK?"

"As I said, I'm at my parents."

"Why are you shouting?"

"I've just had an argument with them," I say, trying to find a normal speaking register.

"I can't remember a time when you went to your parents and didn't have one." The fact that he's right doesn't make it any less annoying. There's a sound of dripping in the background. He must be in the darkroom.

"Not that good on Saturday, was it?" It's more a statement than a question.

"I wondered if you'd noticed," I reply, trying to sound dry but ending up more like pathetic.

"I think it's insensitive of you to suggest I'm so insensitive."

"Is that a joke?"

"Hardly." Drip, drip, drip.

"What are you processing?" It's a simple enough question, but the answer is one long pause. Eventually he says, "Faces."

"After a ten-year obsession with still life, you've suddenly gone into portraits? You'll be doing weddings and barmitzvahs next."

He doesn't laugh, doesn't even really react to what was admittedly an extremely weak joke. That's the thing about Dave, he's steady. He carries on calmly talking about his work.

"You'll like these. I think you'll like them quite a lot."

"You're making it sound very mysterious."

"There's no mystery. I'll show you soon enough. And Elizabeth..."

"Yes?"

"Don't worry about it. Don't angst. You over-think. Make up with your parents. They aren't as bad as you make out. Especially your mum, give her a break."

"That's what I try to do, all the time. The arguments just seem to come out of nowhere. She ambushes me."

"Just keep trying. And one more thing..."

"Mmmm?"

"Remember this. One bad night doesn't mean the end of a relationship." After I put the phone down, I sit there trying to work out my own feelings. Of course he's right, one bad night doesn't mean the end of a relationship, I can't argue with that. But it sounds so pat, like something you find in the agony columns of the clever newspapers. I'm caught between my parents and Dave, and it's going to be some kind of eternal stand-off. I can't keep using him as a comfort blanket and human shield, and however much I think I love him, there's only one way of finding out what life would be like without him. I've got to make myself walk away, to find out if I can live without him.

I've been carrying Valentina's card around in my bag for days. I take it out and have another look at it. It is heavy and unyielding in my hand. Feeling treacherous, I dial the number.

The answering machine clicks in. Of course it's night-time and weekend, what was I thinking? I leave a message.

The following morning I wake early. The divan gives way under my weight. It must be twenty years old, so the springs have given up. A comfortable sitting position doesn't work. When I lean back, the whole thing rolls away, so I slide down in the gap between the bed and the wall.

I open the fitted wardrobe, looking for something to wedge behind the castors. Half the wardrobe is taken up with some old dresses from the 1950s. Mutti's. I flick through them – nice fabrics, fine cottons mainly. At a time when lots of women made their own clothes, she did too. When I was a kid her old treadle sewing machine was parked in the spare room, abandoned, but these frocks testify to its heyday. I lay out the dresses on the bed, look at the hems, the seams. She was good in those days. Before things started getting to her. At the bottom of the cupboard is a pile of old handbags, some of which would fetch a fair price in a vintage clothing store. While I am wondering if Mutti would mind me having them, I find some other stuff, pushed to the back of the closet. A bag of my old baby clothes, and then a large plastic bag containing something lumpy. I open it to find a pile of dusty photograph albums.

I spread them out on the carpet, and open one, taking care lest the worn binding comes apart in my hands. It has a red velvet cover adorned with gold embroidery and a jewel-encrusted clasp, broken. On the first page, there's one rather magnificent sepia print, a family group, very formal. It's fixed on the page by cardboard corners. The mother is wearing a dark dress with a high-necked white lace collar. A sombre young man at the far right is wearing an army uniform for – what? Probably the Great War. His left hand is resting on the crook of what looks like a long walking stick propped between his legs, but may be a sword. The younger children wear sailor suits, and two older girls are in identical silk blouses and tall lace-up boots that would still look good today. The rest of the book has smaller snaps of groups and individuals taken around the same time, and some shots of a 1920s wedding. The bride and groom are dressed like silent movie stars but the expression on their faces is exceptionally grim. And then, over the page are some pictures of an elegant but ugly woman, and a sharp young man with oiled black hair.

Most striking of all is a series of pictures of a beautiful girl. There are several of her in ballet costumes, posing on her toes. In one she is arched over backwards so far that she is touching the floor by her feet. Here she is skating, one leg held up high behind her, way above her head. Big, shiny smile, like a model. There she is a bit older, playing the violin in a ruby silk dress. This is the record of the life of a family. I recognise some of the faces. But most of all I know the ballet girl is my mother.

The door opens, and she is standing there, looking at me looking at the albums. The smile is drifting from her face, a waft of cigarette smoke dissolving in the air between us.

"Put them away," she says in a flat voice. She stands there wearing an impassive expression until the cupboard is shut. Then she turns and walks away.

After I've dressed, things are still chilly. This is no moment to raise something as contentious as the compensation claim, so instead I wave the white flag by suggesting a visit to the supermarket. And this time I maintain a diplomatic silence over the disabled parking.

We are delighted to find some red plums marked down. We put a large number of punnets in our trolley to make a cake for the afternoon, and amble the aisles discussing the relative merits of different recipes. Should it be a buttery *gleichgewichtskuchen* – a rich sponge slab, studded with soft fruit? Or maybe we'll stew the plums first, and layer it between a good almond pastry, like the one my grandmother used to make.

As we debating the relative merits of whipping cream and crème fraîche, Mutti says, "Ach, the plum season was marvellous."

"The plum season?"

"You didn't have deep freezes or any of this," she waves her arm around the store, its shelves heaving with tins and jars.

"At the plum harvest, we used to make preserves, jams, schnapps. The smell was fantastic. Everybody got involved in picking the fruit into huge baskets, the maids, the cook. My cousin *István* and I were allowed to help too. Cleaning, cutting, stewing. For days there were piles and baskets of fruit all round the kitchen.

"We ate so many plums we got belly ache. But it had been months, you see."

"What had been months?"

"Since we had seen plums. You made your preserves and then lived off them, until they ran out. We had a larder with rows and rows of huge jars filled with different fruits and vegetables. But they never lasted the whole winter, so by the time spring came you were desperate for something fresh.

"I loved the plums most of all. They were the type that turns bright red when cooked. They brought life back to us after a long winter."

"You never talk about your childhood. This is the first time I've heard any of this stuff about cooking plums."

She examines some camembert cheese, taking off the lid of the thin wooden box and prodding it.

"*Ach*, you know. Nobody is interested."

"Really?" We turn a corner. "What about the albums?"

"They came from Omi's house when she died."

"You were angry that I'd found them." We walk along an aisle of cleaning materials.

"No," she says. I look at her, doubtful, but she doesn't seem to need to explain her reaction.

"You know, if you are serious about pursuing this compensation thing, you are going to have to get used to the idea of talking about Hungary, the past. And not just about how fantastic the plums were."

She nods, and we continue shopping in silence.

After dinner, when we have emptied the cafetiere and eaten as much plum *kuchen* with *schlagsahne* as we can manage, she tells me a story. About a girl who grew up in another country, at another time. In a lavish apartment, furnished with velvets and brocades. It was a strict life, but full of music and parties. She didn't realise how happy she was. Until her father ended face down in the Danube river, with a bullet in his head, while his family hid and starved.

Mutti draws strongly on the cigarette in her holder, fortifying herself against the memories. With her eyes fixed on the tablecloth, she says,

"They got away with it. You know, they got away with it."

Chapter 10

The bar is done up like an ersatz front room, with stripped floorboards, battered brown leather sofas, and piles of logs near the open fire. It looks like a place where couples come to read the Sunday papers over a pint. Established couples, not a first date. I wander through a series of linked rooms with similar furnishings and strategically placed cosy corners, looking round for single men. Nope. Maybe he's in the loo. If he's as nervous as I am.

I can't quite believe I've let things escalate to this level, but I wasn't prepared for the force field that is Valentina. Red lipstick and shark-like teeth. Before I knew what was happening, she'd bitten off some part of me. The part that knows how to say "No".

So where is he? I get myself a glass of wine, pick up a magazine and plonk myself down on one of the sofas. I'd love a packet of crisps, but I don't want to be licking the salt off my fingers just as Mr Right turns up. Do we shake hands? Too formal. Kiss cheeks? Too intimate. There's a whole quagmire of etiquette to negotiate, so let's just hope he's not some kind of Jewish Mr Bean or I'll end up with a broken arm. The sofa stuffing creaks as I settle down. What kind of man would choose this location for a first meeting? I know. One who has been here before with a steady girlfriend. They split up and he's too busy to do anything about it, because he's obsessed by his *shmattes* company/Harley Street practice/accounting firm – delete as appropriate. So he signs up for Valentina's dating service. And she matches him with me, poor *schnook*.

"Elizabeth?"

I get to my feet and grin like an idiot. "Yes, hi, er, Jonathan." He puts out a hand to shake mine, and then puts his left hand on top so that he's squeezing my hand between both of his, Bill Clinton style. He's taken my hand prisoner, and I don't know the procedure for getting early release. So I giggle. He smiles, letting go of me. Phew. I was wrong about one thing, there's no sign of nerves. On the contrary, he is calm to a preternatural degree.

"Jon," he says. "Only my mother is allowed to call me Jonathan." Fine. We are less than one minute into the date and the Jewish stereotype has put in its first appearance.

Jon, known only and exclusively to his *yiddishe mamma* as Jonathan, heads to the bar to get himself a drink, having checked out whether I need one too. And I worry that it may seem a bit forward of me to already be drinking. I should have waited, or at the very least ordered mineral water.

At least that gives me a chance for a good look at him. Chinos and loafers with those tassel things. Close cropped dark hair, revealing a receding hairline. The chinos are ironed into a knife-edge crease that suggests a man who is a bit OCD about his clothes. The warning lights go on. There should be something a bit careless about the way men dress, or at least they should cultivate the appearance of carelessness.

Like Dave in jeans and distressed leather. Style by James Dean by way of Paul Smith. Quirky touches like mauve suede brogues. Unselfconscious chic. This guy's a pedestrian in the sartorial stakes. Conventional preppie stuff, straight off the shelf. His conversation's going to have to be pretty smart to overcome the first impression.

It's only when he gets back to the table that I realise I was staring at him, and now he's followed my gaze. There's an embarrassed hiatus.

"Tell you what," I say. "Let's not say what we do for a living. That way we'll be thinking about ourselves, and not whether our mothers would approve." Jon looks aghast, which is not surprising because I am trying to block his only conversational avenue and judgemental yardstick. He laughs.

"Great joke."

"It's not a joke. It's a way for us to be honest with each other, without having to lean on the usual boring platitudes. We can talk about who we really are and what we like, not how we support ourselves financially. And it will stop us jumping to judgement. For example, if you said you were a lawyer, I would make certain assumptions about what kind of person you are and how much you earn. And those things may be irrelevant to whether you are a nice person or not."

"O...K", he says, separating out the two vowels, as if he's playing for time while the cogs of his brain process what I've lobbed at him. But then he catches up pretty fast and lobs one back. "Any other no-go areas? If you like, we could put a cordon round anything like, which *schul* we do or don't go to, whether we eat bacon, do we drive on a Saturday."

"Cool," I say. "Great idea."

"And one last thing," he says. "Parents. Let's not talk about them, or even mention them again."

"Genius. Let's not even think about them."

"So, we know the ground rules," he says sounding very much like a lawyer. "As I'm a bit new to the concept of the conversational no-go area, you start. I wouldn't like to make a *faux pas* straight away and land a penalty point." Smart Alec.

"OK, but it might be easier if you asked me a question."

"Let me think – where did you go on your last holiday?"

"Ibiza."

"Alone?"

"With, er, with a friend. A female friend."

"Great, so where did you stay?"

"My p— Er, an apartment."

"And did you hit the bars and clubs?"

"Yes, though to be honest we spent most of the time by the pool and in the restaurants."

"OK, we won't discuss whether or not you indulge in forbidden varieties of seafood. Bit of shopping?"

"Yeah, though I wouldn't like to make out that I'm a total JAP."

"One nil to me – you mentioned the 'J' word."

"That's a bit pedantic. I said 'JAP'."

"Which stands for?"

"OK, I concede." Definitely a lawyer. "So, your turn. Where did you go on your last holiday?"

"Safari in the KwaZulu National Park, in South Africa. I went out with a group of mates and we stayed in a game lodge."

"How brilliant," I say, thinking high end holiday and friends to match so maybe he's an accountant. Which doesn't have to mean boring. Well, actually it does. "The wildlife must be amazing out there."

"Yeah, and the shooting is superb."

"Shooting?" I'm not seriously considering a night out with a man who shoots fluffy creatures for fun?

"You should try it some time."

"Is it legal?"

"As long as you don't take a pot shot at any of the protected species. It's fine."

"So, tell me about a day's hunting in the KwaZulu, Jon." I wonder whether the apparent indifference to the sight of blood is the tell-tale sign of a doctor at play. Or merely a psychopath.

Jon tells me quite a lot about hanging out with his buddies, driving across Table Mountain, and eating what sounds like a whole herd of non-kosher animals. And about skiing at Lech, swimming in Lake Maggiore and snorkelling in Eilat.

By now it's apparent that whatever I've done he has done better. His record collection is second to none, and he's been at more astonishing, ear-drum breaking and historic gigs than I have. He's been to everything from Live Aid to the Isle of Wight, which by my calculations must have been when he was still at primary school. I'm not altogether sure where the conversation goes after that, and I think we may have broken the rules we set ourselves at the outset. We decide go for a bite. At his suggestion we go in his car, and I agree, not because I've downed two large glasses of wine, but because I want to see what he drives. A red Mercedes 500 SEL. Convertible. Shit. It's massive. We eat *mezze* at a Greek restaurant somewhere in Camden.

"So," he says, peeling the shell of an enormous, butter and garlic soaked prawn, "what brought you to Valentina's? Or is that on the list of forbidden subjects?"

"Umm, you tell first."

"Married for ten years. Childhood sweetheart, no kids. We were both concentrating on our profession. Not mentioning what it is, of course, but we were in the same one. Very competitive. Her not me. Long hours, then she had an affair and we split up. Now you."

So I pour myself another glass of retsina and tell him about Dave, and without mentioning my mother so much as once, outline the kind of dilemma I am facing.

"Are you over this Dave? Sounds as though you've had a bit of a lover's tiff to me, then you rush out to play the field."

I shrug.

After coffee Jon says he's taking me back to my place. Not in that way. I've drunk more than him. And though I know I'm fine to drive, I agree.

So then there's that moment when I think it's a first date and I don't even like the guy that much. I think he's formal and conventional and not my type. I'm careful not to suggest a coffee, but somehow he still ends up seeing me in. At which point I begin to realise I'm not feeling too well. Maybe it was the kebabs or the retsina, but I'm throwing up in a way which is definitely inappropriate for a first date. And Oh God Jon's still there. What must he think? He's astonishingly cool about it, which may indicate medical training. Whatever. He even holds my forehead as I am chucking my guts into the loo.

I wash my face and throw myself onto the bed. Later I hear the front door click shut, and think he's gone, thank goodness I never have to see him again. But when I wake in the morning with a throbbing head, the guy's still there fully clothed and asleep on my sofa. What's going on? What if Dave turns up right now? My aching brain is creaky as I join the dots. Not good. But for some reason I don't feel guilty. Worried about being found out, yes. But not guilty.

On the other hand, I don't *think* I've had sex with him. Maybe there's nothing to feel guilty for. I creep out to brush my teeth, and bring a couple of cups of tea and some paracetamol tablets back to bed. He stirs.

"I'm really sorry," I say. "Maybe I ate something that wasn't quite right."

"Mmm", he says. "I ate the same as you." He sits up and takes a sip of tea.

"Yeah. Maybe a stomach bug." I shoot a nervous glance towards the door.

"Yuh, lot of it around." He looks lost in thought for a moment, then we both become aware that he is holding my hand. And just as I think he's about to let go, embarrassed at the evidence of intimacy, he strokes it. He kisses it. I feel his warm, soft lips moving up my arm, then on my mouth. His kiss has an urgency that pulls me in. I can feel his stubble grazing my chin, I push my face against it enjoying the rough texture, like a cat nuzzling up against the leg of a chair. Now his arms are around me, my head on his shoulder. The fuzz in my brain is beginning to clear. We lie there for a moment. His arms feel strong, around me, his hands rubbing the small of my back.

I'm still wearing my tee shirt from last night, lacy knickers and worst of all, socks.

"I must look ridiculous," I say, trying to push my hair away from my face.

"Absolutely," he says.

"You aren't supposed to agree with me," I protest.

"I don't care. What is it with you and rules? Ever since we met you've been busy constructing this mesh of regulations about what we are allowed to say and do. Are you so scared of letting go? Well, hello, I'm breaking the rules. Yes, you do look ridiculous. And cute."

"I suppose you are a psychiatrist, then?" He ignores my last comment, instead pushing up my tee shirt and running his hand over my stomach. "Oh I get it, psych*ologist*." There's a flutter of pleasure further down. I guide his hand up under my tee shirt, to my breast, and feel the nipple harden as he caresses it. I undo his shirt, one button at a time

And then I undo his zip. OK, yes, it's all a bit Mills & Boon. And when I wake up again at lunchtime, he's gone.

The feeling of pleasantness soon evaporates. This time I know for sure. I've had sex with a conventional, rather arrogant Jewish man. Who wears loafers with tassels. Dave's bound to find out. He'll smell it on me. That's if I don't just blurt it out. And I know nothing about him except the fact that he shoots cuddly animals for fun. I have only myself to blame. Whatever possessed me? And what will he be thinking about me this morning? Why didn't he just leave me to wallow in my own misery?

I groan at the thought of anybody seeing me like that, remembering that he held my forehead as I threw up. What a bastard. What right did he have to take advantage of me when I was in that state? I wish there was someone I could talk to about the whole ghastly thing, but the only person I can talk to like that is Dave. What a mess. I blame my mother.

I go for a cleansing run round the park, and settle down to read the Sunday papers when the phone rings. It's Dave.

"Do you fancy brunch in Hampstead and a walk on the Heath? And you can tell me all about the latest developments in the story of the Mueller missing millions." He sounds so breezy. I don't reply. I've gone through a whole chapter of my life since we last saw each other.

"I'd love to," I say. "I miss you so much."

"But you saw me on Friday."

"Y–yes, I mean, it *seems* so long." What I really mean is that

I can't believe that he's believed the feeble excuses I made about last night. We always go out on Saturday nights. All couples do, unless they've got kids, don't they? Why isn't he more curious? I suppose I should be grateful. I just want to get back to normal and forget the whole sordid business, just airbrush Valentina and everything connected with her out of my life.

As I'm getting ready, the phone rings again. I think it's Dave changing the arrangements, so I rush to the phone. But it's not Dave.

"Hi."

"Hello Jonathan, er Jon. Thanks for the other night. Sorry I was a bit – er, indisposed."

"You seemed to make a good recovery. Pulse and blood pressure seemed normal by the time I left." So he is a doctor. "Will you meet me for coffee this afternoon?"

"Um, that's a nice idea." OK, maybe he's not that arrogant. And he looked after me when thousands of others would have walked away. He's confident and clear about what he wants and though this really shouldn't matter, he does seem to be earning a decent living. Life would be so much simpler.

"To be honest, Jon, I'm not feeling that... Actually, I'm going to be straight with you about this. Dave called me. I don't think it's over between us yet." There is a taut pause.

"The semi-unemployed photographer?"

"Yes."

"I think you are making a mistake."

"But it's not really your business to make that judgement."

"Well I can make this one – you are supposed to fuck the Goy and marry the Jew, not the other way round. Think about it." There's a click and the line goes dead.

Chapter 11

Monday morning I'm back in the office and still serving my penance for crimes against journalism. Sarah is doing her utmost to make sure I remember to play by her rules in the future.

And it's not just work, either. Walking round Hampstead Heath with Dave was supposed to be cleansing, but it felt as though I was dragging round a ball and chain labelled *guilt* each step of the way. He was full of the joys of nature while I was terrified that we'd turn a corner to find Jon bounding towards us.

So I've messed up at work and now I've sabotaged my home life, the only crumb of comfort is that at the moment my relationship with Mutti is having a harmonious moment, however brief it may turn out to be. I suppose that's something to soothe me while I trawl my way through a stack of newsprint piled as high as my desk. The *Westmorland Gazette*, the *Blackpool and District Messenger* and the *Hounslow News* are waiting for my attention. Then there's a list of fifty senior police officers to call. And if I do unearth any journalistic gems, they'll go straight over to Andrew, who will get all the credit. At least there's no trace of the work experience girl with the Jennifer Aniston haircut. Maybe she's gone to help out Tony and Cherie as a media advisor.

The day stretches out in front of me. I'm planning a latte at eleven. For lunch I'm thinking of an avocado wrap. If I find more than ten possible leads, I'm allowed a KitKat at four. And to burn that lot off, I'll go to the gym on the way home. To forget about my own duplicity, if nothing else. I get the keys to the stationery cupboard. There's nothing like a new notebook and some fresh pens to renew one's appetite for a task. I help myself to a packet of Day-Glo highlighters, a roll of Sellotape and a shiny pair of scissors. Then I add a whole packet of HB pencils, some staples and a large ring-bound lever arch file. With some of those plastic document holders that clip inside them. I organise all my booty on my desk, and look at it. This is the infrastructure for my new role.

Andrew swivels round in his chair to get a better look at what I'm doing.

"Marvellous to see you really getting to grips with your new assignment," he says. "I've got a new toy as well. But it hasn't come from the stationery cupboard." There's a bag on his desk, from one of those hi-tech shops on Tottenham Court Road.

"Really," I say, loading the new staples into my stapler. "Let me guess. It's a Rubik's Cube to keep yourself amused on all those long train journeys to the fabulous locations you'll be visiting. No sorry, it'll be a new pair of Raybans because the sun in Doncaster is so intense at this time of year."

He smiles, taking a box out of the bag. Inside is a shiny device that looks like a bit that's fallen off a camera. I'm reluctant to give him the satisfaction of seeing my curiosity, but I can't help myself.

"What is it?" I ask

"A director's viewfinder. You use it for sussing out the good shots in a location before the cameraman gets there. Three hundred pounds. Worth it, though."

"So you've borrowed it from a director, then?"

"No it's mine."

"Talk about ideas above your station. I bet you're A-level results haven't even come through yet. Bit early to indulge in expensive toys."

"As it happens, Sarah's asked me to direct second unit."

It's like a biff in the solar plexus, that is. But I just say, "Oh yes, are you going to film Mummy changing your nappy?" then turn back to the *Westmorland Gazette*, mentally adding a packet of gourmet vegetable crisps to my lunch order. I console myself with the thought of Andrew looking like a complete plonker. What kind of twerp arrives to shoot a couple of GVs with a stupid director's widget, as though he's Ridley Scott?

At eleven I'm just leaving for the cafe when my phone rings. It's Mutti.

"Do you remember Mrs Schein?" she asks.

"How could I forget. The lady with a massive bosom and a mole on her chin?"

"That is very unkind. Mrs Schein suffers a great deal from her husband's diabetes."

"And he suffers a great deal from her opinions, as I recall. They are as numerous as the stars in the firmament. And your point is?"

"Mrs Schein has given us the details of a lawyer who specialises in these kind of claims. And you'll never guess what?"

"Well, if I'll never guess you'd better tell me."

"He speaks Hungarian."

"But you can make yourself understood fairly well in English these days."

"No, silly, this is marvellous because he can read all the Hungarian contracts and legal papers."

"That's – actually very useful. And how much is he going to charge us?"

"Mrs Schein says he is very reasonable."

"And that could be because Mrs Schein's husband made absolute squillions out of his chocolate biscuit factory so a few hundred quid here or there doesn't make a lot of difference to her."

"Don't be silly. Anyway. He will see us tomorrow lunchtime."

"When you say 'we'..."

"Daddy will only agree to the appointment if you come too."

I see, he wants to make sure Mutti's outnumbered.

"Look, I'm working. It's not as though I can slip away without anybody noticing."

"They don't allow you out for lunch? What kind of job is this?" I don't have the energy to argue, and anyway I'm going to need a break from the *Westmorland Gazette* by this time tomorrow.

"OK, I'll work something out." The phone rings again, and I'm just about to tell Mutti not to keep bothering me at work, as I have many important local newspapers queuing up for my attention. But it's the switchboard operator.

"Do you know a Mr Maurice Cohen?" I shuffle through my mental Rolodex.

"I don't think so. What's it about?"

"I don't know, but he's calling from Staffordshire."

"I've never been to Staffordshire. It must be a mistake."

"We're not allowed to put members of the public through unless they're known to you."

"Sorry." I put the phone down, and go back to the papers. The phone rings again, and it's the switchboard operator once more.

"I'm sorry, but this caller is very persistent. He's saying something about a synagogue, in Staffordshire."

"Stamford Hill, not Staffordshire! It's Morrie! Put him through."

"Hello?"

"Hi Morrie, is that you?"

"Could I speak to Miss Mueller, please?"

"Yes, speaking. Call me Elizabeth."

"You are the young lady who came to see us at the *shul*?"

"Yes that's right. How can I help you?"

"I hope you don't mind me calling. I heard your last visit didn't turn out too well. For you."

"Gosh, word travels fast."

"I'm sorry. Please don't think we wanted to get you into trouble."

"It's OK. I'm over it."

"Good. You see, it's happened again."

"Another television researcher has turned up at the synagogue?"

"No, another little girl."

"Killed?"

"Well, not exactly the same. Someone tried. *B'ruch ha shem* they didn't get away with it."

"But what can I do about it? Surely it's a matter for the police."

"The police don't know."

I inhale, but don't say anything. It's an exclusive, and it's been put in my lap. I could sell it to the tabloids and make a killing. In another life.

"I think it would be a good idea to tell them."

"The community leaders don't want to."

"But why not?"

"They are worried about the impact this would have. The publicity. They've seen what happens once. The police, newspaper people, television, radio. It was a madhouse here. People felt like they were in a zoo, being stared at all the time. If word gets out that it's more than one, you can just see the headlines. CRAZED NAZI MADMAN ATTACKS JEWISH CHILDREN. Stamford Hill will be overrun."

"Yes but don't you think they are running a huge risk by not telling the police? What if he does it again?"

"The *frumm* community believe they can pull together."

"Er – that didn't seem to be quite the line Reb Stern was taking with me, when we were – when we met. He seemed ready to completely put his trust in the police."

"Things change. It's not just him, there are others."

"So he got overruled? Either way, that's a big risk to take with the lives of their children. So, why the phone call? I'm afraid I do work for a television production company, so maybe I'm the wrong person to talk to right now if you are intent on avoiding publicity."

"Look, my dear. Rabbi Stern has asked me to apologise if he seemed – abrupt. It's nothing to do with you. You are obviously a nice girl."

"I appreciate the compliment, but Reb Stern has an odd way of showing his appreciation of my finer qualities."

"That was unfortunate."

"I'm not bearing grudges. But I don't quite understand what I can do for you."

"You asked about a film. You wanted to – act out – what happened to the little Friedmann girl. To help catch the person who did it. Reb Stern thinks it would be a good idea to do this now."

"So he's changed his mind now he realises it may not be a one-off? I can talk to my boss about it, and it's brilliant that he wants to go ahead. But Morrie, I don't think I'll be allowed to work on it, however nice a girl I may be. I'm kinda confined to base. I'll have to hand it over to my colleagues."

"Because of us, you are punished?"

"Sort of. Well, to be fair, there's more to it."

"Well I'm sure we all feel bad that we get you into trouble. And now we would like to make up for it. Maybe you have an idea?" There's a terrible twinkle in his voice.

"Crikey, well – er – I mean just how bad do you feel? If you'd be prepared to say..." Listening, I whisper, "Yes?" just in case anybody else in the office is listening to me. "Gosh, Morrie, it does sound a little bit dishonest."

"Even if nobody is harmed? Go on, tell me."

"Well maybe you could say that *I* need to be part of the

filming. Because you trust me, since we already met and discussed it – "

"Well *of course* we trust you. You're Jewish, aren't you?"

"Umm I'm not sure that line is going to carry much weight with my boss. And maybe I'm not all that Jewish, anyway."

"You know my dear, I've been around long enough to recognise a *Yiddishe Maydel* when I see one and it matters, here in Stamford Hill it definitely matters. After all, what do we know from these other people?" He chuckles. "I'm sure Reb Stern will agree with me on this."

"Tell you what, Morrie, you're a *mensch*."

Sarah's busy in a meeting, which runs on past lunchtime. Through the glass of her goldfish-bowl office, I can see a group of people poring over scripts. They watch a clip of a tape, then rewind it and play again. And again. I loiter outside for so long that I'm starting to get on her PA's nerves. She suggests I take a lunch break. She'll call me when the meeting's through. I slink off, but my appetite's gone and I make do with a polystyrene cup of lukewarm mushroom soup.

Sarah takes a bit of persuading. But, like a shark scenting blood, her instincts get the better of her. She makes me wait while she calls Reb Stern to confirm my version of events. She nods a lot, and as she puts the phone down gives me a look which is half grimace, half smile. There's to be a strict protocol in place. Every step I take will be under police supervision. That makes me wince. Whatever Reb Stern and his friends think of the cops, we can't afford to work behind their backs. So that's another hurdle for yours truly – I'm going to have to explain the rules of engagement to the man with the big beard. But at least by mid-morning, my shackles are cut, and just after lunch I'm meeting DI Jenkins at Stoke Newington Police station.

He leads me into a small interview room and sits me down,

as if I'm the suspect in a crime. His lengthy briefing about the Stamford Hill Hasidic community tells me far less than I learnt in twenty minutes with Morrie and Sidney. But I nod respectfully, and make copious notes.

"There's one other thing," he says as we are leaving the room. "You are dealing with a group of people who don't watch television. They have never heard of *Coronation Street*, let alone *The Crime Programme*." He shuts the door behind me and locks it. "So don't make any assumptions about how much they understand."

Together we get into his unmarked police car and drive towards Stamford Hill in silence. Down at St Kilda's, the incident tape has been removed from the end of the road, but the huddle of paparazzi is still there. The uniformed officer on duty outside the house nods at DI Jenkins. In the garden, weeds threaten to strangle the few shrubs, which are evidence of some long passed fit of optimism. A kid's bike has been abandoned on the path. I wonder if it belonged to the dead girl.

Paint is peeling from the window frames, but as Mrs Friedmann answers the door she seems too preoccupied to notice the state of her surroundings, or the dank smell of boiling fish which fills every corner. Going through the hallway, I feel my soles sticking to the carpet. Its few remaining fibres have been smothered by dirt and the residue of old cooking oil.

Mrs Friedmann wears a floor length garment which is a throwback to my sixties childhood. Known as a 'housecoat', its overriding characteristic is a complete lack of shape. On her head is a black turban thing made out of stretch fabric. She dispenses orders to the older children, comforting the tinies and cuddling the baby. As she turns to deal with us, she's like a mournful entertainer, setting just one more plate to spin.

It's a front room, but not as we know it. Instead of sofas, it's been set out with a huge dining table and at least fifteen mismatched chairs. There are a few bookcases filled with books, I scrutinise the spines and the ones I can make out are all in Hebrew. Some of the volumes have been pulled out, and are scattered around. There are a few dishevelled toys and a broken cassette player. But, as DI Jenkins predicted, no sign of a television. It's the scene of chaotic family life, and could have looked quite wholesome had it not been frozen by the glare of the fluorescent lighting tube.

As we are deciding where to sit, there's another ring on the doorbell. One of the children shows a bulky figure into the front room. As he enters, I see it is the Topol lookalike himself, Reb Stern. He gives a curt nod in my direction and shakes hands with DI Jenkins. The men sit on one side of the table, opposite Mrs Friedmann, me, and a uniformed female police officer. I hadn't noticed her before, though she was there all along. She is introduced as a family liaison officer, Sergeant Evans.

"I'm sorry for your loss, Mrs Friedmann," I start. "It's very good of you to see me about this." She nods. "If it's OK with you, I'd like to go through all the events of the day in question. That will help us work out what we can show." She nods.

"Just take your time, and go through it step by step."

Mrs Friedmann looks at Sergeant Evans, who gives an encouraging nod. But she's scanning me, looking down at my bag. I know I need to say something warm and reassuring, but it's difficult to come up with anything when she's radiating pure apprehension.

"I'm really sorry," I say, "but are you worried about something?"

She blinks. "You are not recording this now? Not filming?"

I don't react to this. It's critical that nobody in the room suspects me of sneering at her naivety. I'll have to take it straight and very slow.

"I don't have a camera or microphone, Mrs Friedmann. I'm

not trying to catch you out with secret recording." I unbutton my leather jacket, and put it on the back of the chair, to show that I'm not hiding anything – and then suddenly feel very exposed in my short sleeved tee shirt when everybody else is completely covered up despite the clammy heat in the room.

"It's not that kind of thing. We are on your side, believe me."

I'm desperate to inject some warmth into the solemn proceedings to comfort the poor woman. But with the combined police and rabbinical presence in the room, it's clear there's a significant risk of appearing too frivolous if I do so much as smile. I take her hand and look her straight in the eye. "We want to catch the killer of your little girl, believe me."

She nods, seeming embarrassed. "Sorry, I'm worried to do the wrong thing." I shake my head.

"There is no wrong thing. I understand why you are wary of me when you've got a bunch of paparazzi camped on your doorstep. We aren't like that. I want you to trust us. What might help is if I give DI Jenkins some tapes of the programme."

She looks at me. To misery has been added something else – bafflement – embarrassment – or a mixture of the two.

"Tapes?"

"You don't know anybody at all who has a TV? Or a VHS player – maybe?"

She shakes her head. I haven't forgotten what Jenkins said about this being a community without TV, but I just hadn't thought it through. To be honest, I'm slightly nonplussed, and not just because I work in it. No television, a complete world without it. That's a first for me and I've seen a lot of the awfulness that comes from having no money. I've seen rampant damp and boarded up windows, rat droppings and filth, people sleeping and eating on top of each other in squalor with rank, repulsive bedding you wouldn't want to touch let alone lie in. And I have to admit, this place is right up there. The whole house seems to sag and crumble with despair, from its grimy carpet and tatty mismatched jumble of decrepit bits of furniture. But no telly, I suddenly realise that I've never, ever been to a home that's too poor for a box.

I look round the table. From the expressions on everybody's faces, there's something going on that I don't get, and everybody else does. Like the girl in the playground who has had a sticker attached to her back saying "I AM STUPID".

"In our community," says Reb Stern, "we don't tend to have televisions. We have other – diversions."

"Of course. I'm sorry."

I realise how stupid I must have sounded, and how ignorant about the people I am offering to help. Of course tapes are no use if you live in a world where nobody has a TV. "Er, maybe D I Jenkins could play them for you at the police station?" He nods.

"Thank you. That would be good." Mrs Friedmann looks across to Rabbi Stern, and he also nods approval.

"Now, I'm really sorry to make you do this, but let's go back to the day when it happened." She sits there thinking for a few seconds. She has a nervous way of pulling down her turban, then pushing it back on her head.

"It was Wednesday, we were making an *upsherin* for my Yakov Chaim. It was a drop-in, there was a buffet. Open invitation to all our friends, the whole *kehillah*." Her English is accented, but I can't place it. There's a hint of German, or maybe Hebrew.

"Sounds lovely, but I'm afraid you might have to explain some of the terminology to me."

"Yes?"

"What was the occasion you mentioned?" She looks at me, uncomprehending.

"The reason for the party?"

"It was Yakov Chaim's *upsherin*, I already said this."

"I'm really sorry, but I don't know what that is."

"They say you are Jewish, no?"

"Yes, I am Jewish. But not very – er..." She nods, she gets where I am on this.

"Is hair cutting. For three year boy. We don't cut the hair until he is three."

"Really? So little boys have long hair?"

"A pony tail." She shrugs. "Keeps hair out of his eyes."

"I see, so what happens at this event?"

"Boy sits on chair, everybody takes turns to cut off a little bit. Then barber makes nice afterwards."

"Maybe," interrupts Sergeant Evans, you could explain to Miss Mueller why the *upsherin* is important."

Mrs Friedmann looks at me. "Little boy now have *payes* and *kippah*," she mimes earlocks and skullcap. "And he will go to school. No more playtime, is beginning of child's education. Very beautiful. He lick honey off a letter, a Hebrew letter. Shows learning is sweet, you see?"

"Sounds wonderful. And you said you invited all your friends, but who were the closest, the most involved in the hair cutting?"

"My ex-husband Yisroel Friedmann, Rabbi Stern has come, my brothers Pinni, Avram, Dovid, and all my sisters. And their children. And few other friends, neighbours, members of our *kehillah*."

"So there was quite a crowd. And it took place in which room?"

"In here." She nods, looking around as though she can see the excited crowd of people in the room once more.

"And when did you notice that Bruchi was missing?" She stares into space with a helpless look on her face. And utter exhaustion.

111

Sergeant Evans puts a reassuring hand on her arm. "According to the statement we've taken, which we can give you, the smaller children were playing inside for a while. The they went outside, where they were riding around on some bikes and a scooter. Then, when it was time for the hair cutting—"

"I looked out of the window and called them," interrupts Mrs Friedmann. "They had on their *Shabbes* clothes, I didn't want them get dirty."

"And they all came in?"

"I don't know."

"You don't remember seeing Bruchi come back in with the others?"

"There was Channi and Chaye Sorah, Yankel and Rivki."

"And they are all yours?"

"Yes, but also their cousins were there."

"So can I be clear about this one thing? Did she come in with the others when you called?" Mrs Friedman shrugs, an expression laden with hopelessness.

"OK, so she may not have come in then. Do we know if anybody else saw her after that point?" She shakes her head. I turn to DI Jenkins.

"We've spoken to several of the guests," he says. "The accounts are – confusing. One person says this, another that. We are finding it almost impossible to work out a clear timeline."

"Other witnesses? Outside the house?"

"There are a couple of neighbours, and we've managed to trace a young woman who was pushing her buggy down the road while the party was in full swing, and there's also been some mention of a white minibus or van."

"For the reconstruction, we normally get a full set of all the statements. And the key thing is the appeal points – what are we asking the public for information about? You mentioned the white van. Did anybody see the driver? Can we put together an e-fit?"

"Maybe that's something we need to discuss back at the station."

Before we leave, I explain to Mrs Friedmann how we will put together the film. Everything should be based on known facts, taken from witness statements. We won't speculate or make anything up. And to Rabbi Stern I say that we will need his help to reconstruct the party. We can't afford hundreds of extras or the wardrobe full of black suits, hats and wigs. He'll need to help us with the background action.

"And just one other thing, before I go," I say to Mrs Friedmann. "Bruchi's an unusual name outside the Jewish community. What does it mean, exactly?"

"Is short for Barucha. Blessing."

I nod. Mrs Friedmann nods. There's nothing left to say because it all feels so horribly trite and inadequate, and I've said the only useful things I can. I hope she understands that.

Before heading home, I cruise around Stamford Hill. School must have just finished for the day, because the pavements are chocker with kids. The girls all seem to opt for the same neat, long-sleeved checked blouses and navy skirts, with thick navy tights, as though they forgot it was the middle of June when they got up this morning. The little boys' faces are framed by ringleted ear-locks, which makes them look more like girls. But there's one thing that worries me more than that. Some of the children look very young to be walking home by themselves. Girls who look no more than six years old are leading even younger ones by the hand, not a parent in sight.

I'm now stuck behind a rusty minibus. It stops in the middle of a narrow road to disgorge a consignment of tiny girls. The driver doesn't bother to park, even though spaces are available on both sides. Instead, he jolts to a halt, and opens the side door by twisting his right arm round behind him, allowing three tiny little tots to help each other down the steep stairs and over to the pavement. I'm in no hurry, but the three cars behind me sound their horns, and edge to the middle of the road. Then at last the door of the minibus slams shut, the driver honking as he drives on, and the little girls have disappeared.

The pent-up clog of cars steams forward, only to stop a few yards down the road as our minibus gets stuck head-to-head with another rusting, overladen van. There's an impasse while the two drivers work out which one of them knows how to use the reverse gear. And so it goes on. For parking, the centre of the road seems to be just as popular as the curb. Near some shops on Dunsmure Road, I have to negotiate a litter of double-parked Volvo estates, all of which have seen better days.

The pedestrians appear to know the rules of this game, weaving their way down the middle of a road, adults flanked by handfuls of small children while simultaneously pushing heaped-up buggies. The concept of road safety seems alien, both to the wild-eyed drivers of the minibuses, and to the walking roadkill that seems to regard pavements as an optional extra. I'm astonished that fatalities aren't a daily occurrence.

Not far from the shops three little heads dart out from between two cars. I stamp on the brakes, juddering to a halt, just as they retreat nervously. I want to lean out of the car and yell at them, "Where are your parents?" They ought to make sure they can look after shedloads of kids before they bring them into the world. My hands are trembling on the wheel. Is it even possible to be a good parent to ten children, if you can't keep your eye on them?

Then I see myself. I walked to school by myself, too, couldn't have been more than six years old when I started. Yes, sure it was the sixties and the provinces, so there was no traffic and paedophiles hadn't been invented yet by the tabloid press. But the risks were just as real. Where was *my* mother? When I got home she was usually out cold on the sofa (fully clothed), or in bed (naked as a baby), with an empty glass and her beloved soda siphon next to her. And she only had one child to care for. Did that make her a bad mother?

When she wasn't unconscious, I spent a lot of my time trailing after her. Always just far enough behind to catch the disdainful looks on the faces of shopkeepers as she slurred and stumbled her way around. It was only later that I heard some of my aunties had taken my father aside to warn him that she was driving me around "under the influence".

How much gossiping must have gone on behind our backs to get to that point. All the "Should we tell him?", and "Is it our responsibility?" Anyway, there was a scene. Mutti threatened to top herself if they pursued it, and the whole matter was quietly dropped.

Chapter 12

The following day there's news – the second missing child has been found, and somewhere on Stamford Hill a family has been spared the torment Mrs Friedmann is going through. I try to be happy about this, but the truth is I'm worried that yesterday will now turn out to be wasted effort and we are back to square one. But no, it seems the change of heart has stuck and I need to get down to setting up the film. We've got just under two weeks to sort out locations, props, crew, script and cast. It doesn't seem like the best time to mention that I need a couple of hours off to take my parents to the lawyer's. I put it off until mid-morning when the witness statements arrive on a bike from Stoke Newington nick. The job has been assigned to Bill, one of our most experienced directors and I'm hoping that now he's got all the information, he'll be busy writing his script all afternoon. I've phoned the casting agency to set up auditions for later in the week, faxed over a full list of the principal roles, got the contact details for the best available crews, and sorted out the car hire.

Then, as Bill is bent over his computer, I tap him on the shoulder.

"I just need to – um – pop out for a while. Is that OK?" He looks at me as though I'm talking a foreign language.

"Things are red hot right now, kiddo. I can't really spare you."

"I need to meet someone – for lunch."

"You can pop down and grab a couple of sandwiches for both of us. And a packet of crisps as a reward for good behaviour. That's all the lunch either of us are going to get today, kid." There's no way round it. I go across the road and get two lots of cheese and pickle on wholemeal. My parents are going to be arriving at Paddington station any time now, and I won't be there. I've failed them again.

I put Bill's sandwich on the edge of his desk, and while he's eating, I run through the list of what I've done, and what's left. He seems pretty impressed by my efficiency, but just as I'm thinking he's going to let me slide off, he starts with another long catalogue of things that need doing by the end of the afternoon.

I've just got started when my phone goes. It's Dad from a payphone at Paddington.

"Look," I say, "I can't really get away at the moment. You might have to get in a cab and go round to the lawyer's without me."

There's a bleep bleep bleep, followed by some shuffling and the sound of coins being loaded. "What you mean? This won't take long. Surely they can spare you." It's always been a bit difficult to get Dad to take my work seriously, mainly because I'm not an engineer. On some level he still thinks I'm in some kind of nice job for a girl to do until she gets married. He thinks I'm "helping out" with a bit of filing.

"Well, actually they can't," I snap. Silence, more bleeping, scuffling and coins being loaded, and then the murmur of my parents talking to each other. Mutti comes on the line.

"Darling. Please come, we appreciate it." Wheedling.

"Look," I say, "If you really think I am essential to this meeting, then just have a coffee and hold on. I'll do my best to get away." Even as I say it, I think why am I bothering? We'll be here until ten tonight, at the very least.

As I put the phone down I look over at Bill. He looks up at me, and I make like I'm terribly busy doing lists and things. Shit. For once, just cut loose. Do your work, I say to myself, do your very important work. Let them get on with their thing, you do yours. Ha. I can't even concentrate. Then the brainwave.

"I'll have to see this bloke about the suits for the actors," I say to Bill. "It's not the kind of thing you can do on the phone." He looks pretty distracted by now, and hardly takes his eyes off the computer, scrolling up and down the script he's writing.

"Sure, kiddo," is all that he says. And I'm pretty sure he winks at me.

Tottenham is only a few miles up the road from my flat, but I never go there. It's a place I pass through on the way to somewhere else, moving on as fast as the traffic allows. Until now. I've managed to scoop up my parents and get them in the hatchback, and now we're edging up the High Road, a confused litter of fried chicken joints and emporia devoted to hair products for black people. This is the land the high street chains forgot, but it doesn't care, surviving on its own brand of visceral energy, and dominated by a huge police station.

After we park, my parents walk along the pavement clinging to each other, with the uncertain look of people who think the borders of civilisation stop at Swiss Cottage. Above a shop selling roast nuts appears to be the office of the legal practice of Mr L Zoltán.

This is not a solicitor's office as we know it. There's no brass plaque, or coiffed receptionist, just a stained stair carpet and wood chip wallpaper painted cream a very long time ago.

A mismatched, collapsing set of filing cabinets is spewing out its contents. There are files on the desk, piled up on the floor, pushed against the wall in great heaps. There is nowhere to sit because there are files on every chair. An inappropriate tasselled lampshade in scarlet dangles above, casting a boudoir tinge over proceedings.

Mr Zoltán greets us with theatrical formality, kissing my mother's hand in an exaggerated display of Austro-Hungarian etiquette and uttering an elaborate multilingual torrent starting with "*Gnädige Frau*". He shakes hands with me and Dad, adding something which is I think is supposed to be English. The accent is thick as the legendary cherry soup at the *Gay Hussar* restaurant in Soho.

As we are now looking round for somewhere to sit down, Mr Zoltán moves files off some of the chairs. There is a lot of puffing involved, because he is a large man well into middle age, bursting out of his clothes, as though they are unable to contain his exuberant personage. He sits down, mopping perspiration from his face with a crimson handkerchief, which clashes violently with the rust-coloured locks of hair, draped in Bohemian fashion over his right eye. He addresses my mother.

"So, my dear lady, where shall vee begin?" Dad is nodding encouragement at me, so I butt in.

"As I think you know from your phone conversation with my mother," I nod towards her, "she would like to find out about the possibility of – would like to know whether she can make a claim for compensation from the Hungarian government." Zoltán nods gravely, as I add, "For things that happened to her and her family, during the war."

"Yes, yes, many tragic events swept our homeland during these difficult years," he says grandly, and Mum looks at him with an expression of extreme respect. He sweeps onward.

"This is a subject vizz vitch I am very much conversant. I, László Zoltán, am a very rare professional – fully qualified in legal practice of both British and Hongarian jurisdictions, and of course bilingual. You vill find that I am at the forefront of legal developments in this specialist field, and I am fully up-to-date vizz all the very latest *letchislation*."

He surveys his domain with a regal demeanour, and our gaze followed his around the room. The ramshackle surroundings did not appear to reflect well upon his bilingual legal expertise.

"Do not be deceived by the appearance. Zoltán is at this moment residing in a temporary premise, while new office being refurbished. In Finsbury Park," he says with a flourish as if the aforementioned location was anything other than a public toilet *en route* to Arsenal football ground.

"Mr Zoltán," I say in my best business manner, "could you please summarise the legal situation, as it currently stands, and give us some examples of cases which you have successfully concluded?

"Of course, of course, young lady, no problem. But first let us talk about the dear lady's case. Excuse me, but vill be best if I discuss the matter in our mother tongue." He turns to Mutti and addresses her in rapid fire Hungarian. She looks ready to dissolve with gratitude. I have not heard her speak what is supposed to be her first language since my grandmother died twenty years ago and it doesn't seem to come easily. She is struggling for words, responding to Zoltán's questions in hesitant, stuttering phrases. He prompts her benignly at intervals.

After ten minutes she seems to have got the hang of it, and is making up for lost time. I am beginning to feel at a loose end. What exactly are they talking about? Now he seems to be expounding at more and more length. I catch a few Latin phrases amid Zoltán's billowing Hungarian. She is saying less and less, listening reverentially to his dramatic declamations.

"Mutti – could you tell us what's going on?" I say.

"Wait a moment, I tell you in a minute."

She and Zoltán are getting more and more animated. At one point she sheds a ladylike tear, and he proffers the red handkerchief to her, which she takes despite her usual concerns for cleanliness. But the sadness does not last. Minutes later, they are both roaring with laughter, and then again expressing surprise and shaking hands vigorously.

"Is good, is good," exclaims Zoltán to Dad and me. "Vee vill have a great victory – Hongarian government will pay for the terrible crimes committed against your family." How this victory is to be achieved remains vague, as after we leave Mutti seems unable to fully explain the legal advice Zoltán gave her. Despite this, she maintains a high opinion of him. And best of all, I manage to slip back to the office by way of Stamford Hill, dropping off measurements and selecting fabric, but still get back into the office just at Bill is writing the final scene. Job done.

That evening, I'm hanging round at Dave's, my parents having retreated back across the Welsh border to my overwhelming relief. We're in the dark room, immersed in the blue glow of the safety lamp as he processes a roll of film. I've given him the rundown of today's legal encounter, but now he's concentrating on his pictures. The conversation has petered out amid the sloshing of liquids. As I watch him, my last phone call with Jon is still washing around in my head. What was it he said?

"Fuck the goy and marry the Jew." How bloody cynical is that, anyway. Does that mean I should marry a pig-headed, arrogant, self-centred guy just because he's Jewish? With stupid tassels on his shoes?

"This Zoltán character sounds like a complete chancer," says Dave, immersing some photographic paper into a tray of liquid and jolting me back to the here and now.

"Sorry? Oh yeah, aside from the accent and the overly dramatic manner, he's probably OK," I say, pulling myself back to the present. "Anyway, he's the best hope we've got so far."

"Don't defend him, you just said yourself he was untrustworthy."

"I didn't say that. I said that we need to check out his credentials. Is he as well qualified as he says?" Dave picks a dripping sheet, holds it up for a moment and then slides it into the next tray. "By the way," I add, "Zak's given me the contact details for a picture editor at an interiors magazine who might, apparently, be interested in your work."

"Really? Are you sure the picture editor at this glossy doesn't just want to keep his star photographer happy? And if it means he has to spend half an hour flicking through a portfolio he has absolutely no interest in, then it's a price worth paying."

"It's a she, and does it matter? Once she sees your work, then she'll be won over. Don't worry about how you got there."

"She won't like my work. I've been there so many times before. It'll be too dark, too moody, too this or that. Like they think I couldn't do chic interiors too if I really wanted to."

"Go and see her, or at least put in a call."

"Look, Elizabeth, if you want to marry someone with a fabulous career, why don't you do what Mutti wants, and find yourself a nice doctor?" I look at Dave. He glares back. There's some kind of other meaning there in the narrowing of his eyes. Oh Christ, does he know? How on earth did I manage to give myself away?

I shut my mouth tight, sifting through what I've said for the fatal clue. Down in the tray of chemicals, an image is resolving itself onto a sheet of photographic paper. From the opposite side of the table, I'm looking at everything upside down and blurry from the rippling liquid. Even so, as it begins to take shape, I realise what I'm looking at. Dave lifts it out and dunks it in the next tray along.

I come round to his side, to see a photograph of a Hasid in full kit and fur hat hoisted out of the liquid and pegged up on a line. Chin out, barrel chest, full lips one stop short of a sneer, he's radiating attitude into the lens. Reb Stern.

"I know that guy," I stutter.

"They don't all look the same, Liz. You've met a few of them, doesn't make you the big expert on Stamford Hill."

"No, they don't all look the same. That's Stern, the guy who stopped me from filming. I told you. Now my best buddy and filming contact."

"The so-called Tevye?"

"The very guy. How did you get to meet him?"

"I didn't exactly meet him, I went up there with a camera."

"It's a great photo. You are so good, I just wish you weren't so fucking temperamental about it. What made you go there?"

"Well..." He's dunked another photograph in the bath now. It's a group of women in headscarves with overloaded double buggies, stopping to chat. I recognise the spot, near the supermarket at the crossroads. One woman is laughing, another is looking down, blushing. There's a kind of relaxed intimacy, very unselfconscious.

I suppose I should be thrilled, but it's such a sudden change I'm still trying to get my head around it.

"Come on. You've never been interested in reportage since I've known you."

"It was just when you were talking about the people... I dunno. Curiosity or something." The line starts filling with pictures now. People shopping, picking up children, carrying those velvet embroidered bags I've seen them all with, women perched on the front step of terraced houses. That sitting on the stoop is so old world but it really captures the atmosphere of Stamford Hill, a place that seems decades behind the rest of London. Elsewhere most people just go home and watch television, but here there's real life out on the streets. He's captured the feel of the place in a handful of shots.

"You drive me mad, sometimes, you know."

He puts his arms round me, and kisses my neck. "I know. But Elizabeth?"

"Yeah?"

"Can I have Tevye's phone number?"

And I feel as though I've been dipped in developing fluid myself, the image of who I am and who I want to be is coming into sharper focus as I stand there in the dark. I'm watching Dave dipping and dunking and looking and I'm thinking *How can I have been so stupid?* I just want to expunge any memory of Jon and that awful night. I kiss Dave on the cheek and leave him sorting out his chemicals.

Chapter 13

Three days later, we receive a letter from our legal friend Zoltán setting out his plans for the case. According to legislation introduced by the Hungarian government only this year, surviving relatives are entitled to the grand sum of one hundred and fifty US dollars for a parent killed during the Holocaust, and seventy dollars for each sibling. In Mutti's case, that means she might be eligible to receive one hundred and fifty. By coincidence, Zoltán's fee for obtaining this compensation comes to one hundred sterling, which is almost exactly the same amount. I phone home for a long distance council of war.

"One hundred and fifty paltry US for a life – it's derisory, it's an insult, it's…" I have to stop myself, for the second time this week there just are no words.

Mutti defends Zoltán to the hilt. It is not his fault that the Hungarian government has introduced what turns out to be a derisory piece of legislation, Yes, she can see it is intended to offer symbolic value rather than true compensation. But symbolism is important too. The Magyars are a warrior nation, she reminds me. It is a matter of national pride and tribal honour.

"You are not a Magyar," I point out. "Around the time the Magyars were settling in the Danube plain, your tribe were tending their herds on the banks of the Jordan, which is thousands of miles away. And I think it was dishonest of Zoltán to lead us up the garden path like that, making grand speeches about putting right the evil that has been done to our family. What rubbish!"

In the squashed silence that follows, I regret being quite so vehement. There's a crackling noise on the line before Dad intervenes. "You have to admit," he says, "that a hundred and fifty dollars to compensate for the death of a parent is inadequate, whether or not it is intended to be symbolic. Frankly, it's an insult." There's a rustling, clicking noise which I recognise as Mutti fiddling with her cigarette holders near the speakerphone. I can just imagine the miffed look on her face, so I put on a more conciliatory tone.

"Do you really want to spend a lot of time and energy on this application, when almost all the money simply ends up in your friend Zoltán's pocket? And what if his fee goes up, and we are left paying him money you need to live on?"

For a moment, all I can hear on the line is heavy breathing. I start wondering what's happening up there, but actually I realise I can probably work it out. It goes like this – he squeezes her hand, they look into each other's eyes, and she nods reluctant but finally submissive.

And just as I think this little drama should be coming to a conclusion I hear her say, "*Ja, ja*, okay. You are right." Bingo.

The following day we are auditioning actors for the reconstruction. We've called four for the role of Mrs Friedmann and five little girls to play the murder victim, ten-year-old Bruchi. They are spread out through the day, which means I'm up and down the lifts, shepherding people in and out. I have to deal with their train fares and get them all hot drinks and sandwiches or orange juice and biscuits. But between all the running about, I'm going to have to call Zoltán. The third try-out for Mrs Friedmann looks hopeless. She's wooden and far too pretty. This is going nowhere, so halfway through her audition I slip out.

If there is supposed to be a secretary in his office she must be on a day off, because Zoltán answers the phone himself. I tell him that my mother does not deserve to have her hopes toyed with like this.

"My dear young lady," he protests. "The nature of the compensation is out of my hands, I have not determined amount available."

"Mr Zoltán," I retort, "You gave the impression that the compensation we were entitled to was an – appropriate amount. How on earth can a few dollars compensate my mother for any of the things which her family endured during the war and after. It's an insult."

"My dear young lady, do not be naïve," retorts Zoltán. "This is not compensation for what happened. Believe me, I know vott happened." He has dropped his mannerly language. "This scheme created for von thing and von thing only. To prepare vay for Hongary enter European Community.

"So are you telling me it's nothing to do with genuine regret? The whole thing is a piece of political public relations that has been cooked up as a matter of expediency."

"So now you get it! Miss Elizabett, welcome to real world." Zoltán snorts. "I see your parents have done good job – they bring you up to believe in British way of doing things, no doubt. Fair play, justice, and other such ideals. Hah!

"And if you got thousand dollars instead of hundred fifty, would it make one bit difference? Would compensate your mother for loss of her loved ones? It would not! Or hundred thousand? No. Will you feel better about loss if compensation so great it bring about collapse of Hongarian economy? What happen then? More crimes, more cruelty, and more compensation. Compensation without end.

"Money cannot compensate for such losses, so really does not matter how much. All equally worthless." I wasn't prepared for this foray into philosophy.

"Mr Zoltán," I say, "you are getting carried away. We just want to find out if there is more than one option for us. Or is this scheme and the one hundred and fifty dollars all that we can hope for. Because if so, we might as well stop now."

But Zoltán is on a roll, and carries on, disregarding what I have said. "And what about your motives and mother's motives for applying for this money? If money cannot compensate you, then why apply? What good it do? Maybe you need money now – so you exploit name of late grandfather in order to solve problems of your own making. Nothing to do with respected grandfather. And nothing to do with war. Is *you* who is being cynical, no? If you feel bereaved by this loss, your family has suffered a terrible injustice, yes. But how can money put that right fifty years later?"

He's right, of course, I have no answer for this. But just as I am about to put down the phone he seems to swing round and take the opposite tack again, as if he'd just been playing with ideas, "You take my advice, Miss Elizabett, you think of dear mother. She carries huge burden. She grieves for the life she could have had." I'm feeling a bit dizzy but I also think I have underestimated Zoltán. He has assessed my mother's state of mind with surprising lucidity.

"Never mind. You apply for this. If you don't, you give strength to people who say nothing happened here."

"What do you mean?"

"There are people, you must know this. People who say there was no Holocaust, no camps. No one applies for compensation, so then these will say, see! Are no relatives, because no one was killed here."

"So now we are all that stands in the way of Holocaust deniers?"

"Think about it." I no longer know whether he is manipulating me, and if so what he is trying to achieve.

"As for my fee, you go to big West End legal firms, they will charge you same amount for five minute consultation. More. And they will engage translators, work with lawyer in Hongary. All at extra, extra, extra."

He's probably right about the cost of a big legal firm but the language is beginning to get over-excited once more. So I say goodbye.

"One other thing."

"Yes?"

"There may be better way for you to get justice on behalf of late grandfather. No," he corrects himself, "for dear mother."

"Really?"

"Elizabeth!" Bill's stuck his head out of the door and is yelling at me.

"Hold on a second, Mr Zoltán. Yes?"

"Shelley is waiting for you to take her back to reception," fumes Bill. "And Amelia Smith is here with her chaperone. They've been waiting for twenty minutes, because your phone has been engaged. This really isn't the time for personal calls."

"Gosh, look I'm really sorry. I'm on it. I'll be there in a tick." He gives me a furious look and slams the door.

"Sorry," I say to Zoltán. "I'm going to have to go. But what's this other justice thing? What thing?"

"Weeeell," says Zoltán, as if he's deliberately taking his time. "She say her family owned property in Budapest. If you can prove they owned apartment, say, or industrial buildings, and this was stolen by Nazis, or nationalised by the communists, then maybe you regain that property for use of your family, now that I-ron Curtain has fallen."

"But, but that could be worth thousands."

"Maybe."

"So why haven't you mentioned that before?"

"Goes beyond my professional expertise," he says. "But Miss Elizabeth, is always risk of disappointment. Is she strong enough for this?"

I'm still pondering the answer to that as I push my shoulder against the door and prepare to grovel to Shelley for keeping her waiting.

Chapter 14

On the weekend, Dave and I drive out to Broxbourne, leave the car in a pub car park and walk along the River Lee. I'm not a great one for nature and I don't know the names of trees or wild flowers, but there's lots of them and it's pretty. I never realised there were so many different shades of green. There's a field on one side, with some horses. The ducks swim along the river in straggly little families, fluffing their feathers in the sunshine. We hold hands, ambling along the towpath. And it's like we've turned the clock on our relationship back to how it used to be. That's when he says it.

"I've got some news."

"*Good* news?"

"Remember that friend of Zak's you wanted me to phone?"

"How could I forget? It's OK, you don't have to. Carry on with the Hasidic portraits."

"I called her."

"You don't have to, honestly. I understand. No compromises with commercial crap."

"I wanted to. You're right, I need to start thinking a bit more practically. Raise some funds."

"Really?"

"I've been to see her. Big woman, red hair, garish dress sense."

"This is Zizi?"

"I think her mother named her Susan."

"And?"

"Says she'll try me out for a magazine shoot."

"What's the subject?"

"Sort-of home and garden type of stuff." He's half looking away from me, and half muttering it.

"That's just the kind of thing you've always loathed. Are you sure you really want to do that?"

"Oh you know, the pay's surprisingly good."

"But what happened to art?"

"That's bullshit and you know it. Showing off." I look at him, but he's still avoiding eye contact.

"Look at me and say that again."

"No pain, no gain, kiddo," he says in his Clint Eastwood voice.

"It's not a joke." His face drops.

"No it's not. If we're serious about getting hitched – and I bloody well am – both of us need to be earning some dough. I don't think your parents or mine are going to fork out for much of a do."

The mention of our marriage brings a lump to my throat. I know we've announced it to my parents which means it's real and does exist, but somewhere deep inside I don't really believe in it. Even forgetting my night of idiocy with Jon, the fact that I'm actually engaged to be married seems like something theoretical and distant, not practical and immediate. It's an idea that's still taking shape. I smile in a way that I hope is sphynx-like and mysterious but suspect is more like an uncomfortable grimace. Thankfully Dave doesn't seem to notice, he's still on photography.

"So?"

"So, be happy. But not too happy because it hasn't happened yet."

We have a pint and a cheese sandwich to celebrate, sitting on the lawn outside the pub.

On the way home, driving along a country lane, Dave suddenly tells me to pull in. Up ahead of us is a picturesque little church. I don't worry much about this, because it's what he does. In London, he's always pointing out interesting bits of architecture and historical whatnots, though he favours industrial features, mostly Victorian. This church is older than that, with ivy growing up one side. All around it, ancient gravestones peep out of the grass at odd angles, like a set of bad teeth.

"This is really cool," he says. "Come and have a look inside."

According to the inscription on a brass plate, there's been a church on this site for hundreds of years, though the present building is Georgian. Sunbeams pierce the stained glass windows, reflecting on the airborne motes of dust. He gets his camera out to run off a few shots of the carved ceiling and simple altarpiece. Then he takes my hand.

"Do you fancy getting married here?" Suddenly the whole marriage thing is terribly real. Dave is taking it seriously in a way I didn't expect him to. Worse than that, it's all going off in the wrong direction. I should love the fact he's thought so carefully about it, that he's taking it seriously for God's sake, that he wants it to be utterly beautiful. Unfortunately there's just one thing I can't stop myself saying.

"But it's a church."

"Yes. And I believe it is common practice for people to get married in places of worship."

"Hold on a second," I say. "I know we're not going for the big Jewish thing, with the canopy, stamping on the glass and people shouting '*Mazel tov*'. But getting married in a *church* is something else completely."

"Think of it as a location. We don't want to get married in a register office, do we? A church is the only cool kind of place to get married."

"I don't think my parents will be happy about coming to a church to see me married."

"But these days a church has no religious implications at all," he insists. "It's neutral but pretty. Rural, in an inner city kind of way. Romantic in an English kind of way. There's no such thing as a nice register office. However much they try, there's always the depressing air of bureaucracy."

"It's still a church, though. That means a vicar, hymns, Lord's Prayer and all that."

"Nobody takes it seriously. What else is there?"

"A lot of people have a humanist service. We choose prayers that we like, or readings, or poems."

"That's a bit *Blue Peter* isn't it?" In the pause before he answers, it hits me. This walk in the countryside was his idea. He must have known this church was here. Now the conversation about work strikes me as horribly calculated. He's played me, priming me to feel good about him, by throwing me a carrot. He'll drop the artistic pretentions to pay for the wedding. And while I'm feeling grateful to him, he slides in the church business and expects me to fall for it.

"If you think it will be easier," he says, "let's talk to the vicar about bringing in some Jewish stuff. Let's see if we can put together something tailored to our needs but based on the traditional service. With lots of flowers. Ranunculus and gerbera if you like. Bold colours."

"Hold on a second, not so fast." My heart is banging in my chest. I should walk out now and tell him the whole thing's off. He can't just expect me to go along with this.

"Elizabeth, you are always telling me that you aren't that religious. You haven't set foot in a synagogue since we met, and that's two years ago."

"We do Passover, w-we always have a Seder – you know that!"

"So once a year, you and your folks sit down for some chicken soup and matzo balls. That doesn't strike me as reflecting a deep religious commitment, any more than Christmas lunch makes the rest of the country into devout Christians. And if I remember correctly, you trotted home for turkey and all the trimmings with your parents in December – you're already halfway there."

"Yes, but it's a long way from that to getting married in a church."

"It's one way of showing your parents that you are your own, separate person. You have to decide, are you going to put them before me?"

"Of course not, but they are dubious about the whole project as it is."

"Whatever gave you that idea?"

"I just know."

"And there was me thinking they were warming up. Silly old me."

"They do like you. You are perfect in every possible way. Except one."

"Now let me guess – would it be something to do with the kind of toothpaste I use? No, of course, they don't like my record collection. They are into Acid House, and can't understand what I see in Wham." I try not to laugh, and fail. "Elizabeth, you want to marry me, I want to marry you. Can't we leave your parents out of it? You're old enough to make your own decisions."

"I'm terrified they might be right." I say, looking away. "What if they really do know something about me that I don't understand myself yet?"

"All they are saying is that they don't feel entirely happy and relaxed with me, because I'm not like them. I'm not a middle-aged, middle European businessman. Terribly sorry, my dear, but I'm not marrying them, I'm marrying you."

"I feel like a fraud getting married at all, it's not for people like me. It's for girls who believe in the redemptive power of a designer wedding dress and the sanctity of the perfect table setting."

"There's no rule that weddings have to come out of a 'Brides to Be' catalogue. It will be special in the way that we want it to be." He puts his hands on my shoulders and turns me round so that I am looking directly at him. "Not the way our parents want it to be. It's about what makes us happy – wearing fur loincloths in a cave if we like."

133

"Being married and being happy are not the same thing. Look at my parents."

"Now who is falling for the glossy magazine view of marriage? Believe me, your parents are happy. That's what happy looks like. They have loved and supported each other for nearly fifty years. It doesn't get much better than that."

"Apart from the times when they want to kill each other, or themselves."

"For better or for worse, remember?" I'm about to snap back that "better or worse", far from being universal, comes from the Christian wedding service. But I think better of it.

We look at each other across the sunny, dust-glinting haze of light. And, somehow, I realise that I've pretty much agreed to the church. After the ceremony, a liberal minded rabbi will come to the reception to bless our union, but I doubt that will impress my side very much.

Chapter 15

As it turns out, we have to call on the rabbi earlier than expected because my father dies of a heart attack during a minor operation to remove piles. Just over a week has passed since we agreed on the wedding venue but we haven't quite got round to sharing that with my folks when the phone rings and I think it must be Mutti. But it's a nurse and I think she's made a terrible mistake. It's a wrong number. No, she insists. She is very, very sorry. The silent moment stretches out. It's like when you cut yourself, at first you can't feel anything but you can see the blood leaching out of your finger and you know that the pain will come.

The nurse is talking to me but I don't hear her. I'm watching myself holding the receiver to my ear, but I don't know what the conversation is about. Then, like a television that has come off standby, I re-start. The nurse is concerned about my mother, who is unable to come to the telephone. I'm gripped by a terrible fear about what kind of craziness grief will lead Mutti to, all alone there in the hospital, with no company but the corpse of her husband. Dave takes over. He puts me in the car and drives me down the M4. I am still waiting for the pain when we arrive, and furious with myself for being grateful that this has happened on a weekend. God forbid my father's death should interfere with my work schedule.

We find Mutti stranded on a taupe sofa, marooned in a sea of fitted carpet, lost in the atrium of what looks like a business hotel. It is actually a private hospital. We discover that Dad decided to rush ahead with the op before his health insurance ran out. He's been killed by an irrational fear of the NHS and desire for an ensuite room with a la carte menu options. He didn't even tell me it was happening. When it came to discussing his bottom, he'd turned out to be surprisingly English.

Behind her dark glasses, Aranca looks like a burst balloon that is being kept upright on a stick. I put my arms round her, she doesn't respond, though I can feel her trembling for a moment before she pulls away. It's not clear exactly how long she's been waiting here. She sits back down on the sofa again, and rocks slowly back and forth, like an orphaned child.

When we get home, Mutti goes into her room and shuts the door, leaving us to arrange the funeral. Uncle Bernhard calls. His sympathy soon evaporates. Cremation is not permitted for Jews, he bellows down the phone. I remind him that his brother had very strong views about burial, which he regarded as both primitive and environmentally unsound.

Bernie calls several more times, and gets some of his rabbinical friends to call us too, to dissuade us from the sacrilegious incineration. I tell them it is not a question of whether it is correct in Jewish law to cremate my father, but it is what he wished. They all say that is irrelevant. If his ashes are scattered, where will I go to pay my respects? Where will I say *kaddish*? I tell them that I don't know how to say *kaddish*, I wasn't planning to start now.

And finally, the predictable, "You are finishing the job that Hitler started."

"I didn't kill my father."

"No, but you'll shove him in an oven, just like the Nazis."

On the day of the funeral, flowers are delivered early in the morning, from one of my father's oldest business associates. Mutti accepts them with an expression of disbelief, then leaves them on the hallway table as if she thinks she can stop death entering the house, if she keeps its floral tributes outside. Soon after, the hearse arrives, followed by a large, shiny black limousine. I see the two vehicles gliding up the road towards us, and drawing to a halt next to the raised flowerbed. A man wearing a fraying black top hat and tailcoat gets out. He processes towards the front door. My mother, who has been subdued for several days, sees all this from the upstairs landing, and starts screaming "*O mein Gott*, it's a cortège. Why? *Warum?* A cortège, a cortège!"

"I'm really sorry", I scream back at her. "It's a funeral. What were you expecting? A carnival float?" She looks at me with disdain.

"Not a cortège. Never."

"But, Mutti," I say, trying to reason, "it's what happens."

"I will not have a dead body at my house," she shouts. "This is disgusting."

So I've broken her taboo on the paraphernalia of death. It's here now and banging at the front door. My mother screams and screams. And once we are in the limousine, the stream of bile is unending, as the despicable cortège moves off at walking pace. With us in it.

"You, I blame you for this!" she repeats, and "A cortège, o *nein*, a cortège", over and over again on a loop. "Ach *nein, nein, nein*, I will never forgive you for this, never, never."

The man in the top hat is marching ceremonial style in front of the hearse, holding a silver-topped black cane to his chest. I'm beginning to panic, wondering if he's going to process all the way to Thornhill. It's not that far, but at this pace it will feel like a lifetime. At the end of the road, the convoy halts for the man to step into the passenger seat, continuing on through Rhiwbina village at a dignified speed, calculated to allow people on the pavements to turn and show their respect. They can have no idea what is going on inside the limo. Dave looks desperate.

"Hey", he says to the driver. "Step on it, will you." At the roundabout, the limo shoots forward, overtakes the hearse and carries on at breakneck speed past the Deri and up Thornhill Road. We arrive at the crematorium fifteen minutes early so we carry on past and pull up in a layby, for Dave and me to get out and walk along the road for a few minutes clasping hands. It's a brief respite from Mutti's onslaught, but as it turns out there is far worse to come.

The crematorium is a squat, eyeless building, brooding on a landscaped plot of regular lawns and symmetrical hedges. As we approach, my eye climbs its industrial-looking chimney. Thank God Bernhard and his *frumm* friends can't see this. Sacrilege would be the last thing on their pedantic bloody minds. The place is like a cross between the Auschwitz garden centre and Treblinka town hall. Soon my father will waft up in a big puff of smoke because I was too blinkered to see how wrong it was. Talk about dysfunctional, we can't even get death right.

Outside the building, several small groups dressed in black huddle together, each waiting their turn on the production line. Familiar faces look towards me, uncertain whether it's a breach of funeral etiquette to smile. I get out of the car first, to start shaking hands, and turn to see Dave giving Mutti a hand out of the back seat. Her foot catches on the ledge, and she tumbles head first towards the driveway. The chauffeur comes round just in time to catch her by the shoulders. He yanks her up so hard that she stumbles onto her knees with an ungainly crash. Ladders zigzag up her tights in three places.

It's left to the rabbi to try to maintain decorum while Mutti heckles from the pews, in between the few moments of religious observance. It wasn't supposed to be like this. My mother should have gone first. She's the one who does all the drinking and smoking. Why isn't she paying the price? Dad would have been fine. A bit sad, in a dignified kind of way, but that would pass, with consoling visits to the bridge club. We'd go together to the Science Museum, to discuss the common bonds of technology between Britain and Germany over model engines. He'd bemoan the low status of engineering in this country. In Germany, which he always still thought of as home, he'd be *Herr Doktor Inginieur Mueller*.

"In this country engineer is nothing. Someone who clears up shit is a 'sewage engineer'. Same word. The British only know from bankers or barristers. Who respects an engineer?" And the rest of it, about how the word culture is misused nowadays to embrace anything from salt beef to steel drums. How *Kultur* means Mozart and Goethe. Maybe he'd have a lady friend. And it would have been cool. As long as he didn't come over with too much information about their sex lives.

He'd take an interest in my work. And of course by then I'd be a fully-fledged producer filming abroad for a documentary series on Channel 4. So he'd feel proud of me, as parents are supposed to be. Not worried about his *nebbich* daughter and her *goyishe* boyfriend.

But her without him, that is not possible. Who's the sewage engineer now? I'm standing here with the frigging mop in my hands. I look at the coffin, resting on the platform at the front of the chapel. He's finally escaped without having to go to the trouble of taking his stupid powder. Thanks to him, I'll be looking after Mutti as she gets madder by the day, while my career and marriage plans rot in hell.

By the end of the service, Dave has taken the prayer book from my limp hands. The coffin starts moving towards the end of the dais, as if it can't get out of there fast enough. Mutti watches, with a sudden expression of lucidity. Just before the coffin disappears behind the curtain, she gets to her feet. Behind her, some of the other mourners stand too, in respect. Her shoulders heave, her face crumples, and she bellows at the top of her voice, "You old bastard. I hate you." There's a shocked silence, as Dave takes her arm in his and marches her out of the chapel, as fast as decency will allow.

We have invited everybody back to the house for a cup of tea and a piece of cake. Not the mouth-watering plum *kuchen*, but a less delicious chocolate marble loaf cake, made by me for the occasion. Although I have followed her recipe to the letter, I cannot replicate the soft, delicate texture of my mother's baking. She's not there to criticise it though, as she has taken refuge in unconsciousness. Leaving me to make small talk with the rabbi.

I'm just beginning to wish Mutti would wake up and challenge him to an arm-wrestling contest when Dave steps in. He manages a convincing impression of being interested in Hebrew forms of prayer. I do the rounds with a large teapot, dispensing its soothing brown linctus like the perfect housewife my mother once hoped I would become. But then I leave them to it and go upstairs to phone Bill. Compassionate leave is all very well, but we're shooting in four days' time.

Chapter 16

The following day I drop Dave off at Cardiff Central Station to get the train back to London, leaving me alone with Mutti. She's subdued. Her anger seems to have dissipated, though she doesn't actually apologise for her performance at the crematorium. She sits at the kitchen table, flaccid and purposeless. A weak sun straggles through the blinds, but falters before it reaches her corner. She always sits in the same place, an alcove by the larder, where the kitchen table nestles against a small fitted bench built into the wall, its seat covered with green velvet upholstery. Next to her hangs a small notice board, with a raffia basket attached to it – the kind of thing you find in gift shops at stately homes. She pins appointment cards and invitations to it, and uses the basket to store her pencils, crosswords, and spare cigarette holders. This is her niche, she sits there now with a cold cup of coffee and a full ashtray.

I don't really want to, but I put my head on her shoulder. What I want most is to get back to work, but decency suggests I should stay for a couple of days at least. I wonder how she's going to fill her days without my father to look after. Everything she used to do was for his benefit. She cooked to his tastes, and to a timetable dictated by his work. She cleaned and organised the house, and planned their social calendar with his wishes and needs in mind. Every bed she changed, every load of laundry she put in the machine was in some way determined by his needs, his schedule, his preferences.

Will it be like this for me and Dave? Torturing each other for years then abandoned and bereft? Mutti doesn't want to cook or shop. For the first time in over thirty years her fridge is empty. The larder is still full of tins and jars, but we can't live on morello cherries and horseradish sauce, so I take her to the supermarket. Today she blanks the special offers with a blind, robotic gaze. She's standing there looking helpless, so it's left to me to put a few things I think she would like into the trolley. Some fresh bread, unsalted butter, sliced Emmenthal cheese and garlic salami. They sit there on the cold metal mesh, looking stranded. Then we retreat to her house to contemplate the rest of the empty day.

Even though Dave only left a few hours ago, I'm overwhelmed by wanting and missing him. I want to marry as soon as possible, before we start hating each other, and end up like my parents. I resolve to set a date as soon as Mutti can be restored to some sort of normality.

My normality is work. I decide to make a base in the office, so that I can keep in touch with Bill. The fax machine is creaking with age, and the computer doesn't have anything as newfangled as an internet connection, but I can do most things on the phone. As I settle into the swivelling chair, it feels odd being here without my father. I've usurped his place. I reach for the receiver, but shrink away with the realisation that the last hand that touched it was his. Am I imagining that the seat's still warm? I can almost feel his shape at the desk around me, the familiar jerky movement of his pen, ancient slide rule never far off along with the silver propelling pencil he used for technical drawings. The instruments of his profession peep out from the letters and invoices scattered around the desk, as though he's just gone to make a coffee. I hastily gather everything up into a neat pile and put it on the window sill next to his creaky old wireless set.

Press the button. Clanging chords. Of course it's preset to Radio 3, the soundtrack to his day, and right now it's playing some kind of modernist symphony. I switch it off again, but the silence is worse. I force myself to get on with my list of chores – update the casting agency, get the contracts sent out, book chaperones for the children.

As I type out their names and addresses, it occurs to me for the first time really how tricky a thing we will be asking of these kids. It's like this – you are going to play the part of a little girl just like you who has been brutally murdered not long ago and right here. It's like a horrific game of make believe. Bring on the bogeyman. The only surprising thing is that none of them have ever been too spooked to do it. Not as far as I know, anyway.

The photo of Bruchi we've been using for casting was taken at a wedding where she was a bridesmaid. I take it out of the folder. Usual kind of thing – big skirt in shiny material and a row of silk flowers on an Alice band. The high neckline and long sleeves make it look severe and unrelaxed, but her smile manages to cut through the overwhelming layers of taffeta. She was a pretty girl, sweet looking in an intense kind of way. That smile is odd. It's a few degrees short of radiant. Is it a mystical Hasidic quality or just some kind of profound disconnectedness with everyday life? I think it is that, some quality of unworldliness, as though they're not in touch with other people's reality. What tosh. Actually, it's nothing spiritual at all, just comes down to an intense distrust of outsiders. Probably they've been told lots of weird stuff about women in short skirts who eat bacon. I'm contaminated by the evil world of television and God forbid I may reveal something of it to them. I wonder what it's like to grow up in a world so full of prohibitions. There are so many things they aren't allowed to do. Or to know. Maybe that's the look they share, the fear of breaking a thousand and one rules.

What do they really think will happen if a morsel of bacon was to pass their kosher lips? Will they wake up a Christian in the morning? They inhabit a world of fear as much as love, that's for certain. Either way, would that have made Bruchi more or less likely to go with a stranger? Maybe she'd have been too terrified to refuse.

From the kitchen I can hear cupboard doors opening and closing, as Mutti drifts about in her purposeless way. A blanket of snow has descended and wrapped her in its icy folds. She's become a living ghost, just like Mrs Friedmann. One woman grieving for a child, another for her husband. They've both got the same hunched posture and blank eyes. But a mother's grief comes from the reversal of natural order. What about partners? One of them has to go first, barring accidents or suicide pacts. As you get older I guess you expect that one awful day you might lose your soulmate.

But Mutti's an innocent too in a way. Frozen in childhood. I don't think it ever occurred to her that one ghastly day she and Dad would be separated. Of course he'd never have left her while he was still alive. They were joined by some demonic force that was bigger than both of them. Love, need, terror of being apart, a shared knowledge of the unspeakable past.

The post arrives. Bill has sent me the scripts, which means I can finish the call sheets and transmit them back to London. While I'm waiting for him to approve them, I decide to clear out Dad's paperwork. We have to notify all his business contacts about what's happened. There will be outstanding accounts to settle. All the letters that have been delivered since he went to hospital are stacked up in a haphazard pile. I open a bank statement. It's not good news, but this hardly seems like the right time to talk to Mutti about her medium term financial strategy and whether or not it means she'll have to sell the house. (She will.)

I take comfort in a stroll around Roath Park Lake, which conjures up heaving nostalgia for my childhood. The day when we hired a rowing boat and I managed to drop the oars, and Dad shouted at me before collapsing in hopeless giggles. The lollies and the playground, the Scott memorial lighthouse, the grassy bank we used to roll down, and the rose garden where my grandmother enjoyed a stroll are all there, just the same as they used to be.

When I get back to the house, I notice the old photograph albums have been taken out of the wardrobe and piled up on the study bookshelf. I take them into the kitchen, and lay them on the table. Mutti puts down her cigarette, regarding the books with a look of suspicion, as though she's expecting a column of poison ants to emerge from their covers.

I busy myself with my paperwork back in the study. When I come back, I find her looking at a familiar picture of herself looking elegant way beyond her years and absorbed, as she holds the violin in a dramatic pose. Though lifelike, it's actually a small format oil painting copied from a photograph, the black and white snap is pasted onto the opposite page and shows what a good job the artist did. Adding colour breathes life into the image, with the sumptuous folds of fabric and thoughtful Mutti holding up her bow as if in mid-note. The dress is magnificent. It's fastened at the front by sweep of tiny buttons, each covered in the same red fabric. The high collar is turned up at the back, sleeves long and tight along the forearm, with another sweep of the same buttons. From the elbow, the fabric balloons out into glossy folds. Her auburn hair is swept up into a formal chignon. The whole effect is very Hollywood.

"You never play any more," I say. She nods, turning the pages this way and that.

"I haven't got a violin."

"I thought it was upstairs."

"We sold it."

"But you brought it with you when you left Hungary."

She nods. "It was made by a student of Stradivarius."

"I remember you playing it when I was little – what was that?" I sing, *"Debrecenbe kene neni..."* I know the words only in a phonetic way. The syllables and their tune, but not what it means.

She smiles, and picks up with *"Puy ko ko kosh kene venni."*

We laugh, at the lisping melody. "What is it?"

"It's a nursery rhyme. All Hungarian children know it."

"What does it mean?"

"Come, come to Debrecen everyone, come."

"But I never heard you play anything else."

A pause, a remnant of her childhood stammer. "I didn't. After I married, I played in an orchestra for a few years. Amateur, but good standard. Before you were born."

The story of my life. It's all near misses and things that weren't quite said. So maybe it's apt that I grew up with the next best thing to a Strad in the cupboard, and all I ever heard it play was a squeaky kiddie song. However much my parents claimed to revere *Kultur*, the only evidence of music in our home was a battered, upright piano that hid in the spare bedroom. And a walnut veneer radiogram I wasn't allowed to touch. Yet I had a musical mother, concert standard, trained by legendary teachers. She fingers the page. "Because I hated it."

"You can't have." She shrugs.

"My parents were – not that easy to please."

"But you were concert level, Liszt Academy, worthy of a valuable instrument. How much pleasing did they expect?"

"Ja, ja. I know, sounds – I don't know. Really I don't." She has turned back to the ballet pictures. In one picture, she is wearing a peasant costume and tap shoes.

"It started with this. My mother was an ambitious woman, she wanted me to be a – what is it? A prodigy, is that the word? So I learnt to dance." She points to a picture in which she is dressed as a balletic chicken, with a costume made of coloured ribbons, and a headdress. She is standing *en pointe*. "How old do you think I was there? Five? Six? Too young to stand on my toes. I wasn't ready."

I look closely. She's right. The shoes with their reinforced toes look too big for the little-girl legs, rippling with babyish curves.

"When I was about ten, I started getting these terrible headaches. Migraines, I suppose, but we didn't know that word. My mother took me to one doctor and then another, finally the specialist paediatrician. He said no more ballet. My mother was furious. She had invested everything in this prodigy and now I'd let her down. So she said OK, no more ballet. We will have violin."

"But you were obviously good at it. You were good at ballet, you were good at the violin. Your mother must have got the message that you were clever and talented?"

"People didn't think like that in those days. Now, we've all read the psychology books. Listen to your child, find out what makes the child tick. They tell you to praise, praise, praise. If your child coughs then you praise her for making such a nice cough.

"Those days it was different. If I didn't practise, I was beaten. If the teacher said I could do better, I got beaten. My mother would shriek at me. Then he'd come in and take off his belt." She pauses, eyes swimming.

"When I had my own children, I always said I would do the opposite."

Looking exhausted, she shuts the album, and puts a cigarette into her holder. It's as though she has emptied herself, and has nothing else to give.

"What's the opposite, exactly?" I ask. "What does it mean?" She doesn't answer.

In the London office, Millie's putting together script packs. She calls me towards the end of the afternoon.

"Elizabeth, just one thing. I can't see a booking for a white van."

"What white van?"

"If you look at the script, on page ten, it calls for a rusty white mini bus or minivan, which one of the witnesses saw pass the house around the time of the crime. It's an appeal point. Have you booked it?"

I rummage through my copy of the script. How could I have missed that?

"Oh God, no. What's the driver supposed to be wearing?"

"Mmmm, male Caucasian driver, black clothes. Quite vague." I look at the script again. The white minivan is observed by Passer By One, a local mum with a kid in a buggy. It's not a brilliant appeal point. There are hundreds of crummy white minibuses in Stamford Hill. There must be a farm where they breed them.

"Can we get one for Monday?" I ask.

"I've got a handful of companies to try," says Millie. Let's hope it's not too late."

I put in last-minute calls to DI Jenkins and the police liaison officer. I'm sitting at Dad's desk, and by now I'm relaxed about being here because though I can actually feel him in the room, I don't mind. Actually his presence is quite soothing. I'm finally showing him that this is how I do my job, and allowing him to see that despite appearances to the contrary, I'm actually quite competent. It's a good thing Mutti doesn't actually come in, because I'm talking to him out loud, having the conversation I always wanted to have. As dusk is settling on the semi-detached houses that hunker down around a grassy square, I have a last rundown through my checklist for the shoot. Mrs Friedmann and her family are expecting us. As is Reb Stern. Of course.

Under the circular glow of the anglepoise, I tap all the documents into a neat wad and push it back into its file. The photograph of Bruchi as a bridesmaid falls out onto the teak desktop, and I have to wedge it in on top, the formal pose and reserved smile peeking out as I close the cardboard flap over her. I suppose her mother must have looked like that once, all girlish innocence instead of borne-down by exhaustion and grief. Even before this happened, I imagine Mrs Friedmann always wore an expression that reflected the pains of life, not its joys. She's like a sponge that absorbs unhappiness from the world around her. Probably not even forty yet, just a few years older than me, but she moves like a biblical ancient, *criching* around that forlorn looking house with its oily carpets and torn wallpaper. I suppose there's no escape for her. It's like a filthy prison. She's still got six kids, no husband and no money to speak of, just an unending round of praying and the relentless cycle of joyless Jewish festivals. And that's her reward for marrying a nice Jewish boy.

I'm clearing a space on the desk to sort out my paperwork, when I find a plastic folder containing paperwork from the hospital. It's worth checking that the insurers have been told to stop taking my father's premiums. A spare sheet is stapled to the back of the insurance document. It's headed in thick capital letters "STOP. DNR", and on the next line "Do Not Resuscitate". In the body of the text, my eye catches the lines "… has directed that life-prolonging procedures be withheld or withdrawn in the event of cardiac or respiratory arrest." So, this was his parting shot. No electric shocks, no cardiac massage. No scenes from *Casualty*. He wanted out, that much is clear. I'm just the collateral damage.

Later on I decide to show Mutti the document. But when I

go into the kitchen, she's sitting in her usual place, swaying gently like an abandoned child. I groan at the all too familiar sweet smell of spirits on her breath.

Over the next days, Mutti potters around the house aimlessly. She doesn't say much, barely responds to my feeble efforts to engage her in a bit of low level cooking, but spends long hours sitting in the kitchen smoking, with daytime telly on in the corner. It's a relief that I have to leave on Sunday night. She hardly seems to register that I'm saying goodbye and when I call to say I've arrived home, she sounds listless. I ask her what she's doing.

"Nothing."

"What about tomorrow? You can't just do nothing all the time."

"Well, actually..."

"Yes?"

"Mrs Breslauer phoned to ask if I like to go round for coffee."

"Sounds good. "

"Maybe I take round a poppy seed cake. Oma's recipe."

"Ideal. I can't think of anything better. How about a game of bridge while you're there? Very therapeutic."

I don't tell her that I'm at Dave's. I need a bit of his nonchalant, understated supportiveness. But I can't even really explain to myself why I should need to conceal this.

Chapter 17

A black people carrier with tinted windows is parked outside the Friedmann house, passenger door open. The cameraman Roger and sound recordist Ernie are on the pavement, taking a digi camera out of a silver case. They set it onto a tripod, watched by a dozen boys in skullcaps and earlocks. As Bill gets out of his GTI, and crosses the road towards them, the gaggle of kids doesn't move. They are crowding into the crew's personal space, staring unembarrassed with open mouths as Bill shakes hands all round.

It's my job to introduce Sandra to Mrs Friedmann. She's the actress who will play the dead girl's mother in the film. And I suddenly realise this is the least OK thing I've ever had to do. Mrs F will be there for sure, from the moment Bill shouts "action!". We're asking a mother to re-live the moment she lost a child, which is like pressing broken glass into an open wound. To cover up the awfulness of it, we talk like bereavement counsellors.

Maybe that's a way of making ourselves feel better about what we do, to anaesthetise ourselves just a little from the rather brutal hypocrisies we dance through to get the job done. We sort of pretend that we are just doing this to solve a crime, to bring a murderer to justice, and hence it's all coming from a noble place, really it is. But nobody goes into programme-making purely to do good in the world. We aren't police officers or charity workers, so what we are really driven by is ego. If we had to choose between catching a killer and winning a BAFTA for a film that failed to do that, which would we choose? Most of us wouldn't have to pause for one moment thinking about that one.

Though Sandra and Mrs Friedmann have been cast in part for physical resemblance, when they are standing together the similarity is slight. It's puzzling that two women of similar height and weight should occupy their space so differently. The actor floats in a white trench coat of light fabric, worn over white jeans and strappy, high heeled sandals. Mrs Friedmann labours on drainpipe legs in a navy suit and comfortable shoes that throw her bulging varicose veins into sharp relief. She moves with effort, shoulders creaking with the burden of each step. Today she seems to have abandoned her black turban in favour of a bulky brunette wig.

We follow her heaving form upstairs. We've got a navy dress and cardigan ready for Sandra, and a wig. She'll change in the bedroom, with guidance from Mrs Friedmann. I leave them to it.

Downstairs they are recreating the moment of the *upsherin*. In the front room, the sideboard has been set with platters of little rolls, fishballs and miniature Danish pastries. Bill is briefing the crowd of family and friends with the help of a Yiddish interpreter who may not have been strictly necessary, but there were a lot of notes from Sarah about cultural sensitivity and that seemed to tick a box. The children jostle to have a look through the viewfinder and even the adults nudge each other, grinning.

Mid-morning, I call Mutti. She still sounds pretty lugubrious, but I can hear the grinding of the electric food mixer in the background, which gives me hope. I end the call and look around. I've wandered down the road, away from the house with its noisy crowd of kids. And now my eye catches a familiar figure in a brown wig loping into the distance. I shout as loud as I can,

"Mrs Friedmann!" No response. I walk towards her, calling. Then I break into a trot, and a moment later I'm running as fast as I can. As I catch up with her, she whirls around. There's an ecstatic expression on her face.

"I saw her."

"Saw who?"

"Bruchi."

"Mrs Friedmann," I say. "You can't have." She puts a hand on each of my arms, and shakes me.

"I did, I did! I saw the children in the front garden, and there she was, just like before. She's come back. I saw her. Her shiny hair, so lovely her hair. We washed it this morning, you know."

"Maybe you saw Chloe out there – the little girl who has come to play Bruchi in the film?"

"No, no, it was her. You think I don't know my own child? It's a miracle, *b'ruch ha shem*. Come on, we find her now." She tugs at my sleeve, in excitement, pulling me along.

"Where are we going?" I ask.

"I come out to get her, and she disappears." She points into the distance.

"She's gone – that way."

"Are you sure?"

"Yes, come on, we can find her." Surely a mother can't mistake her own daughter? Mrs Friedmann starts striding towards the crossroads, and I follow. At the junction she looks both ways, hesitating, then goes straight across. She's picked up so much speed now, even with her uneven gait, that I have difficulty keeping up. We take a left at the main road and then another left at some traffic lights. I think we've done a circle around St Kilda's, and now she's gone through a gate and up a pathway with a wall on one side and a fence on the other.

The path ends in a small park. It's divided into separate plots – we pass a mini obstacle course of bridges and beams built out of wood, a wilderness, and play areas for toddlers and older children. Then, in a clearing behind a line of trees, a rope has been slung between two posts. There's short piece of cable hooked over it, with a pulley on one end and a rubber disc on the other, it's a primitive sort of zip wire, and none too safe-looking. A mismatched group of children are there now, taking turns to take rides. In turn, they grab the rope and run uphill to the end post with it, then jump up and wrap their legs round the rope, sitting on the rubber disc, as they hurtle downhill, screaming and laughing as they go.

Two of the boys are sporting skullcaps and earlocks, one girl of about twelve is in leggings, wellies and a dress that might just be a long jumper. An older boy is wearing a woolly hat in Rastafarian colours. But there's no sign of an orthodox girl of ten with long, strawberry blonde hair. Mrs Friedmann looks bewildered. There's a dirty mark on her face. A tear is wobbling just inside her eye, she wipes it away.

"She's gone."

"Maybe," I say, "it was someone else." Mrs Friedmann puts her face into her hands.

"No, no, no, no. She's out there somewhere." Her voice falters.

"So who was the child that was buried?" I ask and immediately feel like a monster. But if I've said something horrible, it's barely registered. She's in a daze. I rub her arm. "Mrs Friedmann?" My gentlest voice is not gentle enough. She jolts as if she's waking up, then gives me a desperate, terrified smile. I look around the park, at the children sliding round on the rope and pulley next to the railway embankment. Bruchi's not here, that's certain. But the person who killed her may be. My skin tingles.

Mrs Friedmann comes towards me and puts her head on my shoulder. I can feel her trembling. When the tears subside, we trail back to the house, her hand hooked round my arm.

Bill is talking to a ten-year-old girl with long, strawberry blonde hair. Mrs Friedmann starts as she sees her, looking bewildered.

"You have met Chloe haven't you, Mrs Friedmann?" I say cautiously. "You remember we chose a dress for her to wear?" She nods, staring intently at the girl, as if trying to make sense of what she's seen.

"Oh yes. I'm sorry. You said... You must think I'm so stupid."

"Nobody thinks you are stupid, believe me." She gives a doubtful nod.

"Thank you."

Next scene is outside – filming the witnesses known to have passed the house at the time Bruchi disappeared. After that, we're supposed to interview Mrs Friedmann, but I wonder whether she will be able to go ahead with it. While I'm talking to Bill, I see her going upstairs with a tall, slim woman who I don't recognise.

Half an hour later, we're filming an actress in jeans pushing a buggy down St Kilda's. As she reaches the end of the road, a red Ford Ka is supposed to drive past at speed in the opposite direction. It takes a long time to get the actress and the car passing each other at the right place. We are on take four when Mrs Friedmann and the other woman come out of the house to join the huddle of people watching.

"This is my sister, Leah," she says. Leah is wearing a darker brown wig, but while Mrs Friedmann's looks bedraggled, this woman could be modelling for a shampoo commercial. The hair is long, layered bob, and so realistic that I find myself staring at her hairline to see the joins. Leah conforms to all the complicated rules of the Orthodox Jewish dress code. But while her sister is squashed by it, she exudes an air of sexy sophistication.

"How do you feel about doing the interview?" I ask Mrs Friedmann.

Leah puts an arm round her sister, "She'll be fine, won't you?"

"Yes," she replies, "What could be wrong?" It's as though the earlier incident never happened.

And that's how she is when we come to do it. She listens as I explain how we will operate. Bill will ask the questions, she's to look at him, not at the camera. We can stop at any time, and repeat any question or answer she's not happy with. But all my careful briefing seems unnecessary. Mrs Friedmann faces the camera with unswerving gaze. She smiles a broken smile, sighs, looks thoughtful, and when asked to go back over an answer, repeats her previous response, word for word. She's like a pro. At just the right moment, her lip trembles, and a solitary tear tumbles down her cheek. It's made of glass.

When we've wrapped, I wish her goodbye, and look for the woman who cried on my shoulder in the park. She's not there.

"Thank you for looking after us," says Leah.

"Oh, I haven't done anything above and beyond the call of duty," I say. It's the kind of automatic thing I say at moments like these to cover up the joins and make people feel OK. In that moment I understand perfectly that it's a trite cliché, a phrase taken off the shelf, a bit of social sticking plaster. But there's something about this woman that tells me she's not taking it, that she disapproves of the self-negating message I'm broadcasting. The "Oh, little me?" suggested in the innocuous phrase rings round my head and she gives me an odd look, a kind of "C'mon, girl what are you saying?" that makes me feel embarrassed. I'm actually going red, and I can't believe I'm taking unspoken lessons in self-belief and even feminism by a woman who wears a wig because her natural given hair might render the men in her community completely overwhelmed with sexual desire.

"I think you have," she says. "You've done a lot." And before I can demur, she says, "Come to *Shabbes* lunch, and we'll talk about it. Maybe you'll find out there's more to us than wigs and black hats."

"OK," I say, "you name the date. But only if I can bring my heathen fiancé."

"Don't worry, we'll have him in a black hat before you can say the *Shema*."

As I drive home, I'm making a mental list of the stuff I've still got to do for the second day of the shoot. When I get in to the flat, the red light is flashing on the answering machine. The

LED announces three messages. I'm expecting a call about some new curtains I ordered six weeks ago in what seems like another life. And if things are getting anywhere near back to normal, Mutti will have phoned at least once. Make that twice. With any luck, she'll have important news on key developments in the continental coffee circle, as if I'm gagging for the latest on Mrs Breslauer's varicose veins.

I flop down at my desk to rattle though a list of contributors for tomorrow. There are calls to the man with the scruffy white minibus and to the cab company to confirm cars for the actors. I'm in the kitchen preparing dinner when I remember the messages. While some eggs are boiling and green beans steaming for my salad, I go out to the hallway and press play.

"Hello, its Jane here from JL Brown and Co. Your curtains are ready, could you come in and collect them, please." Bleep. Silence. Bleep. Someone coughing. Bleep. "Hi Babes, it's me. Do you want to go to a private view at White Cube on Friday night? Gimme a call." Bleep. "Hello, this is South Wales Police, my name is Sergeant Andrew Evans. Could you please contact me urgently on the following number." Come again? Is this something to do with work? I fear not. So what on earth has Mutti been up to this time? I rummage round for a pencil. Let's hope she hasn't been arrested for illegally parking in the disabled bay while under the influence. I scribble down the number and call as quickly as I can. The sergeant answers straight away.

"I am sorry to worry you. It's about your mother Mrs Aranca Mueller. She's in Heath hospital."

"What happened?"

"We had a call from a Mrs Morris of 6 Lansdowne Square at eleven this morning, reporting that your mother's milk had not been taken in. We entered the house and found Mrs Mueller collapsed."

"From what?"

"Bit early to tell. Looks like an overdose." I thought she was getting there. I thought – I was wrong. Evidently.

"Miss Mueller?"

"Yes?"

"Maybe you should get up to the hospital."

"Oh yes. Yes of course."

"As soon as you can."

I have already driven halfway down the road when I remember that I've left the eggs and beans on the cooker. By the time I get back, the pan has dried up and its contents started to burn, I stand there with helpless tears stinging my cheeks. I try to tidy up, but I'm shaking too much, so I dump everything in the sink and head for the endless, monotonous motorway. I drive in silence because the smug radio presenters jag my nerves. More to the point, I need to work out what I'm going to do about tomorrow. I've got the cash float and the list of contributors. I'm stage manager, assistant director and head of catering. And now I'm driving at ninety miles an hour away from the location.

It's after midnight when I get to the hospital, not the private glass and steel affair with the atrium and tasteful carpet but the sprawling University Hospital of Wales locals know as the Heath. I find Mutti still unconscious in intensive care, hooked up to a monitor and a drip. Her hair is pushed up away from her face, revealing white roots. She looks old and shrunken, a fairy tale witch with bad teeth and claws for nails. There's a yellow tinge on her face, sagging lines laid bare under the clinical light. I know this isn't the first time she's tried to kill herself, but it's the first time I've had to clear up afterwards. I imagine Dad sitting here in my place, as he must have done so many times. Though his long nose gave his face a perpetual look of mournfulness, he never seemed to despair of finding a rational solution to an emotional problem. It's so lonely being here without him.

I fall asleep in the chair next to the bed, holding Mutti's inert hand, and wake with backache. An exhausted looking adolescent with an oversized doctor's coat appears. She says Mutti's taken a lot of sleeping pills washed down with most of a bottle of vodka. It's still touch and go. Too soon to tell whether there's any brain damage. I gulp down some black coffee, and go outside to call Bill and explain what's happened.

"I'm sure you can manage without me today," I say.

A meaningful silence fills the chasm between us.

"Please, Bill, I'll ask the office to send out their best workie with another float, and a copy of the call sheet. And I will personally brief them in exacting detail about what needs to be done."

"Look, kid, I understand. Of course. The cavalry are coming in the form of some posh teenager with a few quid in an envelope. Don't worry, we'll manage somehow."

In the end, Mutti comes round just after midnight. When she opens her mouth her teeth are still black from the charcoal they have given her to neutralise the sleeping pills. Now the witch is a monster too. I stay with her for a while, but still she says nothing. She's furious to be alive, and the burden of keeping her that way is all mine.

Chapter 18

It's the early hours when I let myself into my mother's empty house that stinks of cigarettes and despair. I'm not sleepy, sensible television is finished, and it's too late to call Dave, so I go into the study. Rummaging through my father's in-tray, I find an invoice from the legal practice of L Zoltán. Mutti has paid him £100 plus VAT to submit a claim for compensation to the Hungarian government. And then there's something else. It's been pushed to the bottom, but there's no disguising what it is. A letter from the building society, headed in giant red letters: "Mortgage arrears – notice of default".

Is this what did it, then? The thing that pushed Mutti over the edge? She's run out of cash. At an age when most sensible people have paid for their home, Dad and her were still living on the edge. Borrowing was the way they coped with life's ups and downs, and now she thinks there's no way out. I imagine her sitting there in her kitchen niche with the vodka and pills lined up, brooding over the letter. But you don't kill yourself because you can't afford to go on living. Not these days. Any more than they sling you into debtors' prison along with the ghost of Mr Micawber.

The one thing she'd never consider is just calling the building society to discuss the problem with a member of staff. Too easy. The concept of an affordable payment schedule wouldn't appeal to her sense of drama. No, in a crisis she's reverted to her national stereotype. However little I know about Hungary, one thing I have managed to grasp is that suicide is pretty much a participation sport over there. It's not the last resort at all. It's lucky I didn't come in to find her swinging from the crystal chandelier that her mother *schlepped* out of Budapest.

I try to work out whether I've got enough spare cash to pay Mutti's mortgage for a while. My account dips into overdraft at the end of each month, and surfaces into black after I've been paid, like a diver coming up for air. I'll have to put in a call tomorrow and plead for a few days' grace.

I take a shower, but I haven't brought any fresh clothes, let alone anything to wear in bed and I feel grimy in every way, so I pop into Mutti's bedroom to spray myself with some of her

Madame Rochas and look for anything approximating to a nightie.

Then I notice. My father's clothes are arranged on his bed, as though he's the one taking a shower. Shirt, jacket, silk tie. Even underwear. I look in the wardrobe. A row of suits and jackets on wire dry cleaner's hangers, with tickets stapled to the plastic film covers. I check the dates. She's carried on having his clothes cleaned ever since he died. The waste of money is the least worrying thing about it.

As I brush my teeth, I'm thinking what on earth I can do to stop the madness and keep Mutti in the real world. In bed, I try to still the tornado of thoughts and breathe in. I run through a relaxation exercise that never fails to get me to sleep. Tonight it flops. Everything irritates. Even the air in here feels scratchy on my throat. I sniff. What is it? It's the bedding. The sheets reek as they've been steeped in the contents of Mutti's cigarette filters. It's *Air de Tabac*. I try the spare bedroom, but it's just the same. The acrid aroma of nicotine pervades the whole house. Breathing through my mouth doesn't seem to help either. When I shut my eyes, I'm choking – suits and mortgage arrears jump around in my head. Madness and money, money and madness, swirling in puffs of cigarette smoke. I massage my forehead, but my fingertips feel as though they've been rubbed in ash.

I go down to the study, to choose something to read from my parents' eclectic collection. I've grown up with these books. Worn leather volumes of Heine's *Gesammelte Werke* and Ernest Jones's two volume biography of Freud nestle side by side with a load of Agatha Christies and Dirk Bogarde's autobiography. And, of course, the slim volumes of humorist George Mikes, my mother's favourite Hungarian ex-pat. Then, pushed to the back of the shelf I find a tattered paperback. Unfamiliar, even though it's been well read if the battered pages are anything to go by. The cover image is a collage of sepia photographs featuring a woman and a little girl with a teddy, overlaid on a map and a hand written letter. It's some kind of memoir of a family who left Budapest for London. Something about it intrigues me.

I take it back up to bed, and start turning the yellowing pages. There are bits underlined here and there in a familiar looking soft pencil. The kind Mutti uses for her crosswords. Now and then there's a bunch of exclamation marks.

It's the story of a mother and daughter from a comfortable family of assimilated Budapest Jews, as they fight for survival against the tormented background of the war and its aftermath. It's about a café society that turned rancid then murderous, about loathing and self-loathing, and terror. There's lots of terror on every page, brutality and horror layered upon horror. It's about all kind of things my mother never mentioned, and as I read it I understand why. There's much here that I never knew before and plenty that one really should know about one's mother.

Feeling sick and sweaty, I read on and on. Of course the book isn't about Mutti's family, but surely it must come jolly close. That's what the scribbling is. She's made it hers, because she feels it is about her.

And the stupid thing is that I've never tried to find out any of this before. I've avoided the facts, squashed my own curiosity. Even though the outcome was smacking me in the face every day of my life. Sure, everything was tied up in emotional knots. But that seems like a crappy excuse for wilful ignorance. It's morning by the time I look up. I feel ashamed.

Light is breaking over the swaying birch trees at the back of the house. I stuff the book into my bag and leave the house.

When I get back to the hospital, Mutti's still out cold. The nurse says she came to a while ago but it seems now she's refusing to talk to me, as though I'm responsible for her misery. She lies there with her eyes clamped shut. I want to tell her I understand, or at least I'm beginning to.

So I sit in one of those awful green piss-proof upholstered hospital chairs, hoping to grab a few minutes with a doctor who has actually completed his training. He's at the next bed but one, discussing the patient's continence problems in a voice loud enough for everybody else in the ward to hear what size pads are required.

I'm clasping my scripts and call sheets just in case there's a technical query about a piece of equipment, or some niggling actor's agent gets on the phone. The crew will be meeting up around now for day two of the shoot. Everything connected with the film has begun to seem trivial beyond belief, but I still pop out and call Bill to make sure he's OK.

When I get back to the ward, the doctor's just leaving Mutti, so the gravity of her condition can't have merited more than the briefest consideration.

"Excuse me," I call, flapping towards him as he puts his hand up to pull back the curtain around the next bed.

"Yes?"

"My mother, Mrs Mueller."

"Yes?"

"Is it possible to discuss her – er – condition with you?" He turns to look at me, with a face that says I have no business to interrupt his busy schedule.

"Sure. What do you want to know?"

"Well, nobody's actually said what the outlook is. Or, er, anything."

"She took a quantity of sleeping tablets which would have killed most ordinary mortals. Which means she's got an extraordinary constitution. That and the fact that we pumped her stomach means she lived to tell the tale. What kind of questions do you have?"

"Will there be any after-effects?"

"The short answer to that is no. But there's evidence of long-term alcohol damage. If she keeps on drinking the way I suspect she does, it will have the same effect in the long run."

"Sorry?"

"She's killing herself the slow way, drink by drink."

"OK, what treatment is there?"

"I would recommend a psychiatry referral, which is standard. But Mrs Mueller was adamant that she does not want that."

"She was awake then?"

"Oh yes, she was surprisingly lucid." He opens the curtains of the cubicle and as he is disappearing, he turns his head towards me. "Maybe you should talk to her." He jerks the curtains closed behind himself.

Talk to her. Does he think I haven't tried? I want to yell back at him. And yet it all seems so pointless. A psychiatry referral, even if Mutti would accept it, now seems like so much sticking plaster for a broken leg. An aspirin for an amputation. But that doesn't change anything. Especially as Mutti continues to lie with her eyes shut, her capacity for stubbornness apparently unaffected by the overdose.

I stroke her hand, saying her name over and over again. Then she opens her eyes a smidgeon and looks at me. The fug of confusion and fear is still there, whatever the consultant says. But there is far more. I read her disapproval and her anger, with me. Then she closes her eyes again. The eternal barrier between us is still there, solid as the Berlin Wall once was.

As the hours tick by, I watch the nurses check her vitals. I go down to get some breakfast from the tea bar and call Dave to tell him what's happened. He offers to come down by train, and that makes me cry. I snuffle through my blocked nose that there's no point because I won't be staying long, I've got work to do and she's asleep and cross with me anyway. She hasn't spoken yet but words are not needed, I know how things stand. I'm somehow in the wrong again. But it's difficult to drag myself away. Time creeps on, Mutti moans and moves her legs as though she's trying to run away from a nightmare.

At noon, I reluctantly decide I can't do any good here, she's out of the woods so I leave Cardiff once more and head for home. With my call sheets wedged between my legs, I storm down the M4. Just past the Severn Bridge, I'm still stuck on the intractable problem of Mutti's death wish and her money crisis when the mobile goes off. It's the workie. I slide into the inside lane, slow down to sixty and tuck the phone under my chin. It turns out she wants to know where should she get the crew's lunch from.

When I get home, a package of VHS tapes from the first day's shoot is sitting with the letters on the communal hallway table. In my flat, the beans and eggs are still in the sink, smelling burnt and rotten at the same time. Everything else is just as I left it, the television on standby, my raincoat and briefcase thrown onto the table. It's a touch after four, which means they'll still be shooting for a couple of hours, but sod it. I decide to stay here and get on with Bill's shot list.

I put a cup of tea down by the video player, slide a tape into the machine, and set up my laptop. But it's difficult to focus. I'm pursued by images of Mutti with a black mouth, and marauding gangs of fascist thugs shooting Jews on the banks of the freezing Danube. Of course she should get compensation. It's the least the bastard Hungarians should do for her. I'm as guilty as anybody. I've been using the whole claim thing as a distraction, to keep her off my back, like a toy you dangle in front of a cat.

And maybe it is the one thing which might distract her from her death wish. Of course, when she discovers it's hopeless I'll be back to square one. What if it isn't hopeless, though? Not that I really expected Zoltán to come up with anything. Maybe it's time to get stuck in myself.

Bill has used some exterior shots of Stamford Hill to build the atmosphere, with gaggles of black-hatted men standing on street corners, women pushing prams. Shop signs in Hebrew. He's caught the mood with more charm than it has in reality, avoiding the boarded-up shops and illegal roof extensions that look as though they're about to tumble onto the pavements. I work on in the stuffy room as it becomes dark outside. Just as I'm sliding the eighth tape into the machine, it comes to me. It's not a solution, but a next step.

Chapter 19

I sleep badly, and wake at five-thirty. With a couple of hours to kill, I tidy the flat, put on a wash, and finish the shot list before jumping into the car and heading east. At this time in the morning, there's barely any traffic. I get to Stamford Hill in ten minutes. While the rest of London is still asleep, Egerton Road is bustling. Buses rumble out of the garage, Hasidic men are streaming into the *shtiebl* opposite. There's something majestic about the sweeping black coats. But it's sadly undermined by the supermarket bags they wear on their heads to protect their expensive hats from the drizzle.

Pushing open a side door of the synagogue, I can hear the sing-song intonation of prayer – part chant, part mutter. It's coming from somewhere behind the big hall. I follow the sound along a damp, echoing corridor which smells of public toilet. A door. I take a deep breath and push it open. I'm in a small, shabby room with peeling cream paintwork and threadbare chairs. About a dozen elderly men are standing, facing the opposing wall, wearing oversized cream prayer shawls. They have thick leather straps around one arm, and on their heads the small black boxes held in position by more leather straps. As they pray they rock backwards and forwards on their feet. The group has an intense unity as they hum and bob. Then suddenly it's over. They open their eyes, take off the leather straps, and fold their prayer shawls into neat squares. Two of them go into the corner of the room where I now notice a kettle and some crockery. They make hot drinks and hand out bagels from a plastic bag.

I recognise Sidney from my last visit. He's looking sideways at me as he busies himself with the beverages, but it's Morrie who comes over to speak.

"Very nice to see you my dear."

"Thank you. How are you?"

"Oh *b'ruch ha shem*, my dear. All the better for seeing you. It's not often we get ladies to our early morning gatherings. How did your filming go? I heard they brought the cameras up to the Hill."

"Very well, thanks, I was just looking at some of the shots – they look great."

"Well, we pray that it will help to catch the evil person responsible."

"Oh, yes. Of course."

"Will you join us for a coffee?" He gestures over to the corner. "We indulge in a morning ritual of a light breakfast."

"Thank you very much, but I have to admit I've come to get some help. Something else, this time."

"Aha, well maybe I should have guessed. I didn't think you'd had a sudden rush of religious fervour." He smiles. I feel myself go red.

"Don't worry, it's OK. We don't mind. What can we do you for?"

"I don't suppose I mentioned this at the time, but my mother is a Hungarian refugee. She wants to make a claim for compensation from the Hungarian government. Have you got any idea who might help us with that?"

"Well, that's a poser." He turns to the men who are now chewing the bagels. "Sidney, Norman, Ira, who can help the young lady with a claim for compensation from the Hungarian government?"

"Hungarian? Does she know Johnny Lukács?"

"Compensation for what?"

"Those Hungarians are a load of *schnorrers*. They won't give you a penny dear."

"Tell that *schmock* Lukács I'll see him in court."

"A load of pig farmers, they are."

"Shut up you guys. A bit of respect for the young lady." The man who has just spoken is smartly dressed, wearing a checked sports jacket, slacks, and a trilby hat. He has a small, grey moustache, which he rubs with quick movements of his index finger.

"Now hold on a minute. There was something in the *Jewish News* recently. It may have been this week." He scuttles over to the pile of coats on the table at the side of the room, rummages around, locates a briefcase, and gets out a battered newspaper.

"Forget the newspaper." It's a bulky, shaven-headed man. He's folded his arms over his sleeveless V-necked sweater, and is resting his head on one hand. "It's the JRO you need," he growls. "Hendon – the Jewish Refugees' Organisation. They have a whole department to deal with compensation claims. But don't get your hopes up. A friend of mine tried it, and he didn't get a penny. So many boxes to tick and loopholes, they've got six million ways to get out of paying you. Lost his entire family, thirteen brothers and sisters he had. Not one survived. Bastards."

"Yes here it is. He's right," says trilby man. There's a loud snort from the bald guy.

"Of course I'm right. What do you think I am, some kind of *shlemiel*?" The bald guy stomps off to the corner, and starts making himself another cup of coffee. I'm looking at a newspaper article about something called the Claims Conference. It's a report about a development involving the European Community. I scribble the details into my notebook, and wonder if it has anything to do with the $150 Zoltán told us about.

"Take it," says trilby man. "I've finished with it. Don't worry about Ira. He's never been the same since he lost his wife. Now he can't be grumpy with her any more, he's grumpy with us."

"Yeah," adds Morrie. "Luckily, we love him nearly as much as she did."

"But unfortunately," says trilby man, "we aren't nearly so good in bed." They all laugh, and then look at me expectantly.

I drive straight into work, calling the hospital while I'm stuck in a traffic jam on the Westway. Mutti's awake, and wants to speak to me. I can tell her what I've found out at the synagogue. But she gets in first.

"I'm going home."

"Er, has the doctor agreed to that?"

"I don't care. This place is filthy."

"Just hold on."

"I don't think you understand. It's disgusting here."

"What exactly is so bad?"

"It's," stage whisper, "the people. Filthy."

"I understand that you would prefer a private room."

"Is not possible," she sniffs, "I have asked." I swerve, to avoid crashing into a lorry.

"Look, next time you take an overdose, just leave a note telling the ambulance which private hospital you want to be taken to. Then you won't have to put up with the humiliation of the public sector."

That's not what I meant to say at all. It just came out. Before she can reply I add a hasty, "OK, how are you going to get home?"

But it's too late. I've said it. A pause. "I call a cab." Dialling tone.

At work, there are two people eating breakfast at their desks in an otherwise deserted office. A red light is flashing on my phone. One message, left at seven-thirty this morning.

"Hi, it's Mike Jenkins. Just thought you might like to know there's been a breakthrough on Stamford Hill. I wanted you to tell you before you see it on the news. Give us a call." I put the phone down and switch the nearest TV monitor onto the main breakfast programme. The main story is about the new government's legislation programme. Then a short report on the arrest of Pavel Wiśniewski, a Polish builder living in Barking. He's been charged with murder. They show a few ancient shots of Stamford Hill somebody's dug out of the library, clumps of Hasidic men visible in the distance. That's all.

Oh shit. That's all I can think. Oh shit. Of course it's great news. Justice will be done and all that, but I'm so fucked. The film which was about to save my career is about to hit the dustbin of history. If somebody has been arrested, then there is obviously no need for an appeals film, and apart from anything else, it's now legally impossible to show it, on the grounds that it would prejudice a future jury. All that hard work – and now the film will never be seen. Bugger justice, what about my future? And what's worse is I'm going to have to pretend I'm really happy about it. I call Mrs Friedmann.

"Have you heard?"

"Yes." Her voice is muffled, squeezing out each word. "Detective Jenkins called earlier. And the family liaison officer is here now." She sniffs, but I can't work out whether she's crying. "There are photographers and television people outside the house still. What do they want, these people?"

"They want you to say you are pleased that an arrest has been made, I guess."

"Let someone else say it."

"If he is the right man, then you must feel some satisfaction. The police have done their job."

"I am... relieved. But there are others."

"Other – murderers?"

"Polish."

"Sorry – you are worried about other Polish people? But not all Poles are murderers."

"You think?"

"Poles, Czech, Slovak, Russians, Serbs. They are all the same."

I wonder where this is leading. "People who come over here to work from Eastern Europe aren't all murderers."

"What did they do during the war?"

"Most of them are in their twenties, they weren't even born during the war. Not even their parents were born during the war."

"So their grandparents. And their parents and their parents and theirs. What did they do to the Jews in Poland? Millions killed in the death camps. Who was punished for it? And before that the pogroms."

"So, Mrs Friedmann, are you trying to tell me that you think there's a link between the builder who's been arrested for Bruchi's murder and centuries of Polish anti-Semitism?"

"Do you?"

I open my mouth to say no, of course not, don't be silly. Then

I shut it again. I think about my mother, and what happened in Hungary. Rational doesn't come into it.

"Just because one man has been arrested for one murder," I say carefully, "it doesn't make all Polish people guilty. That's just the same as anti-Semitism – making huge generalisations about a group of people. And what if he turns out to be innocent? Are they all off the hook?"

I regret sounding so self-righteous, I have no other response to offer. But I wonder what about the white minibus? That was supposed to be such a major appeal point. What happened to that? I call Jenkins again, to see if I can prise any more information out of him. He sighs.

"I didn't tell you this, right, but Wiśniewski is picked up every day from the corner of St Kilda's to go to work. By a white minibus."

"Could be a coincidence. Stamford Hill is overrun by white minibuses."

"And a lot of Polish builders too. But the evidence points..." He trails off.

"OK."

It all feels a bit unreal, unsatisfactory. Like a balloon that's burst – something that looked so substantial reduced to a few shrivelled bits of rubber. And not just because our film is wasted, binned, thrown on the cutting room floor. It's shitty, of course, but this is different. Yet again, Bruchi's mother. I don't know how I expected her to react, but not like that.

I go for a commiserative coffee with Bill, and resist the urge to get the hell out of the office. The film Andrew's working on for the next programme can be fast tracked in time to replace it. I'm sure he won't waste the opportunity to rub my face in the reversal of our fortunes.

All that's left to do is go back to the cuttings file to see if I can find another story. I wasn't aware of actually putting my boots up on the desk until I hear the sharp click of stiletto heels, and Sarah materialises by my desk. Oh God, I think, she must have noticed my extensive absences. Or Andrew's been telling tales. I should have called in, kept in touch with the office. I'm in trouble again.

"In my office," she says. She's not smiling. Come to think of it, she doesn't smile much. That idiotic thing about women needing people to like them doesn't seem to apply in her case. But I still think she's just loading her guns.

Here it comes. Heads turn as we pass. They're probably having a good laugh about the bollocking I'm going to get. Ahead of me is a black pencil skirt and the tailored jacket. Sexy power suit. You probably need a licence to wear one. She sits at her desk with a very straight back. I try not to flinch.

"Bad news about Stamford Hill," she says.

"Look, I'm really sorry," I'm preparing to grovel.

"Why are you sorry?"

"Because, because of the arrest. We can't use – "

"Not your fault, darling. That's my problem. Time to move on."

"Really?"

"Well, there is one thing." Of course, there would be one. Put on the flak jackets. "You were bloody lucky to get away with it after playing so fast and loose. You bloody nearly lost the story."

"Point taken."

"But if it's fucked now, that's hardly your fault. So, why are you wasting your talent?"

"Sorry?"

"You should have been a producer years ago, and for some reason I really just don't get you are pissing it all away." It's the T word. Talent. Nobody has ever thrown that at me before. They're usually too busy telling me what an idiot I've been. A fucking idiot, usually.

"What do you mean?"

"You're a real self-starter. You've got flair and imagination. But you sometimes give the impression that life and everything else is getting on top of you. You turn up late for work, or don't turn up at all. You look knackered and disengaged." It's impossible to deny the truth of this. I look at my hands. Broken nails and chipped varnish.

"Let's not even mention your infantile war of attrition with Andrew – just block him, OK? I see you making the same stupid mistakes time and time again, yet somehow in the midst of that, you still manage to deliver. I just wonder what you could come up with if you were giving a hundred per cent."

"I've never actually been, sort of flavour of the month."

"I'm not here to be your best friend, Elizabeth. You need to grow up a bit and drop the pointless paranoia. What's your current project?"

"Well I haven't – exactly – well, I'm..."

"Yes?"

"Well I was thinking we should follow up that off-licence robbery in Leicester. The cashier got shot in the arm. There are other similar robberies, probably the same perpetrators." She nods to herself. Then picks up a piles of paperwork from her desk, and starts flicking through them as if she's looking for something.

"You sent me some notes, I think."

"Yes, three sides—"

"With your customary thoroughness."

"I didn't think you'd noticed."

"Give me a bit of credit, will you?"

"Gosh, sorry, no I didn't mean..."

"Yuh, here they are." She pulls three stapled sheets out of the pile and puts them in front of her, leaning forward and drumming her oval red nails on the desk as she reads. Then she looks up.

"Well, here's the deal. I'm going to let you direct the film."

"What?"

"It's time for you to step up to the mark, sweetheart, or you are going to be running round for other people all your life."

"You're kidding me."

"For God's sake, Elizabeth. What are you doing here? You should be beating a path to my office every day, begging me to give you a chance. Like some others I could mention."

"Well..."

"Unless I've somehow got it wrong and you are nurturing an ambition to be a researcher for the rest of your life?"

"Of course not."

"Thank Christ for that. Now, do me a favour and get yourself focused. Your work is good when you concentrate, just locate your aspiration. And get used to the idea that I'm prepared to take a risk on you."

"But it's an armed robbery. That means guns and cars. I've never even had to book an armourer before, and now you're saying I'm actually going to be in charge of the whole shebang?" The slash of red lipstick opens to reveal even, very white teeth.

"An armourer isn't that big a deal, he just looks after the guns so you don't have to. I'll make sure Bill's there to hold your hand."

"I don't know what to say."

"'Thank you' would be acceptable. And, given the circumstances 'I'll do my best not to let you down,' uttered with sincerity, would be appropriate."

"Of course, thank you. Thank you so much." I get up to leave, feeling dizzy as I get out of the chair.

I'm halfway to the door when she says, "Do me a favour. Don't fuck it up."

Andrew raises his eyes as I come out of Sarah's office. I must look shell-shocked.

"Had a tongue lashing from her highness, have you?"

"Yeah. I'm going to sit here and cry about it. Hope you've got a big box of hankies for me."

It's impossible to concentrate, because I'm shaking. Someone's blown a dandelion clock in my stomach, and all the little fluffy bits are going round and round. I wish my Dad was still alive so that he could be the first to know about my big break. Instead I call Mutti. She can't have got round to phoning that cab yet because she's still there on the ward. The nurse keeps me on hold for ages while she's making her way to the phone. She seems to listen intently enough as I explain what it means, responding now and then with a "*Ja*", or a "*Wirklich?* Marvellous!" But it sounds flat. She's still preoccupied with the need to escape the hospital, and to be fair she's recently had a narrow brush with death so my latest career moves must seem bordering on trivial. On the other hand, she is my mother, but I'd forgotten that relationship plays two ways.

"I hope I haven't caught something nasty," she sniffs. "I don't suppose you can come to take me home?" Her voice has taken on a wheedling tone.

"What happened to the cab?"

"Nice if you could come. I would appreciate it." The depth of understanding I have acquired of my mother's tortured history is beginning to wear a bit thin on lack of sleep.

"I'm at work," I snap. "Trying to catch up on stuff I've missed."

"Later?" There's a genuine note of desperation.

"Can you wait till tonight?" She sounds so beaten down. It's only a few hours on the motorway. In the light midweek traffic, maybe I can get there by eight.

I call Dave to ask what he thinks, explaining about the ghastly doctor, the filming, the book, the workie, and the amazing opportunity that seems to have fallen in my lap, but it all gets tangled up in a knot. I try to explain how all the things are somehow connected, even if they aren't. I'm not making any sense, and now he's getting annoyed with me.

"But I've got to get Mutti from hospital."

"You are *not* driving up there to get her. I forbid it. Don't be ridiculous. You sound shattered."

Dave's right, of course. It's true that I am my mother's main source of emotional support right now but even she can't expect me to drop everything and steam down to Cardiff to give her a lift home. And anyway, she'd be happy if she knew what I was doing instead. It's all for her.

I'm planning to slip out this afternoon. Just for an hour or so, nobody in the office will notice. Really. My new assignment isn't on the urgent pile, and I have a burning need to find the next piece in the compensation jigsaw. The offices of the Jewish Refugees' Association are tucked behind Hendon Central tube station.

Inside it's all orderly furnishing in muted colours. People speak in whispers. I'm led into a small interview room. After a few moments, a young woman enters. She shakes my hand, with a flat smile. She looks like a sixth-former dressed up in her mother's clothes. Probably reminds her clients of their grandchildren, but it turns out that she is the hottest thing in town when it comes to this very particular bit of international law.

"Restitution of property is possible in theory," she explains, "but to be perfectly honest we haven't had that much success with it so far."

"So are you saying that in truth it's all window dressing?"

"Let's just start with the facts. Since Hungary started its application to the European Community, it has introduced a limited law on compensation."

"You mean the hundred and fifty dollars my mother can get for the death of her father?"

176

She wrinkles her nose. "Yes, I know it's a bit of an insult. But you should make a claim, if only to make the point."

"I think my parents have done that," I say nodding. "But what about reclaiming actual property?"

"That's trickier. What you need to do is establish that your grandparents owned certain assets, and of course that may be hard to do. Maybe it's not there anymore. Maybe it's been knocked down for re-development, or destroyed during the war." I tell her about my grandfather's factory and about the family's apartment. She nods, and I detect a note of weariness alongside the efficient manner. She must have heard the same story so many times.

"You have to search the official records, to establish ownership in 1939, and find out what happened after that. The records are held in Budapest, but are open to the public. You may need to engage a Hungarian lawyer to make a claim."

"But what happens to the person who owns the property now, or thinks they own it. Presumably I can't just get them thrown out onto the street because I prove that the place now belongs to me? Or can I?"

"It's all a bit new, I'm afraid. Nobody really knows what happens."

"How many successful claims have there been so far? She shuffles the file in front of her, thoughtfully, then looks up at me.

"Look, we are in uncharted waters. Since the Iron Curtain came down, there have been a lot of changes, but the bureaucracy is still struggling to catch up. We're talking about something which exists more in theory than practice."

"So the answer is none. Zero." She looks at me straight in the eyes, and then nods. "So we are talking about a huge battle, uncharted territory, a lot of legal unknowns?"

"Absolutely."

"And apart from that my mother is – can be – emotionally – she finds it difficult to handle these things."

"Of course – that is true with many of the people who come to us. It's hardly surprising. They've been through such a lot, and now they are getting on in life."

"So what should we do?"

"That's up to you. I can only advise on how to go about it. And I'm really not an expert on the emotional side of things. That really is something the family have to think about because it is not going to be an easy road to go down."

She gives me some forms and written information to take home. The response is low key, but I think what she's trying to say is that we may have a case. If we can face the battle – and that's a hell of a big if.

It's mid-afternoon by the time I get back to the office. I've just been gone for a few hours and nobody seems to have noticed my absence, so I get stuck into setting up the off-licence robbery film, making up for lost time. It's early evening before I realise with a shock that I forgot to tell Mutti I'm not coming to pick her up from hospital. I phone the ward. I can imagine her sitting there with her coat and suitcase, fiddling with a packet of cigarettes, doing the crossword and watching the clock.

"...look, I'm really sorry. I've got a lot on."

"*Ja*, so I see."

"Don't be like that. I've got something important to—"

"I expect you tomorrow, then."

"I can't do tomorrow either. But I wanted to tell you something. You'll be really pleased about it."

"Since when are you working on the weekend?"

"It's not work."

"I see." Those two words say a lot. They say you don't care about me in the way you should. If you can't give me grandchildren or earn decent money to look after me in my old age, then you could at least give me a lift home from the bloody hospital.

"Look, I'll book you a cab and pay for it from here."

"Hmph." There's not much else I can say. To make things worse, no cab firm in Cardiff will take my booking because I haven't got an account. So I do the only thing I can. I get the transport book from Millie's desk, and use the programme number for my next film to book a cab to pick up Mutti from the hospital. I'll sort it out with Millie on Monday and pay her the cash.

I don't think Mutti's speaking to me anymore, so I call the hospital back and tell the nurse what I've done. She says she'll get Mrs Mueller to pack her bag for ten in the morning.

I work late that night, writing up my notes and trying to make up for the time I lost in the afternoon. But when I stop to re-read what I've written, I find my eyes slithering over the words. I go back to the beginning and start again, but I can't seem to find a purchase on the text. I find myself gazing out of the plate glass windows, at the dark city skyline picked out in lights. As I stare at them, they go out of focus and re-form themselves into an image of Mutti lying there on the bed, looking yellow and witchy.

There's a lump in my throat which doesn't clear when I cough, and a burning pain in my stomach. It takes me a moment to realise that I'm angry. Angry with my mother, of course. But most of all, I'm angry with my Dad for dumping me like this. *He* should be there in the hospital with her right now. And of course then I feel guilty for missing him in the *wrong* way. I drive back to Dave's needing the comfort of another body next to me. Past midnight I clamber into bed where he's fast asleep in crumpled sheets, and the heat off his body is like balm. I roll the edge of the duvet around me and fall asleep with my head on his shoulder.

Chapter 20

In the morning, I check with Red Dragon taxis that Mutti has been picked up from the hospital and dropped off at home as per. She's still cross with me, but lets slip the fact that she's already been on the phone to Auntie Miriam. Word of my "promotion" is spreading round South Wales. By the time it gets to Freddie and Frances in Cyncoed, I'll be chief executive and director general rolled into one.

I've kept that paperback I found at her house, and carry it around in my bag, growing more and more dog-eared. I read it surreptitiously over coffee. At home, I worry away at it, reading and re-reading about the shootings by the river, the hiding, starvation and constant fear.

Just after noon on Saturday, sun is warming the streets of Stamford Hill, and the men are out in their fur hats. Big brimmed ones like hairy frisbees, others towering up like chocolate Swiss rolls balanced on their ends. I hate to think how much sweat is being produced under those things. But they just carry on, like it's totally normal to be wearing a massive furry hat on a midsummer's day. Hot, me? Don't be silly. Family groups are strolling in both directions on the road, each set of kids dressed in matching outfits, like strange *Sound of Music* tribute bands. And yet again, the girls are all wearing thick navy tights and cardigans over their summer frocks. They must be so itchy in all that knit.

We pass St Kilda's where the Friedmann family live. A police patrol car is still parked discreetly at the end of the road, and the remnants of crime scene tape flutters from the garden gate looking forlorn. A For Sale board has now been planted in the front garden of the family's house. Though it's secured against the fence, it's listing in the gentle breeze.

A couple of streets along, we find the house and knock on the door. A boy answers the door. There's nothing to suggest that he's expecting us. I stand there for a moment transfixed by his perfectly curled earlocks and wondering whether they are permed.

He doesn't even say anything to us, just stands there staring.

"Mrs Schlesinger?" I ask.

He just walks away leaving the door open, and allowing us to find our own way into the kitchen. On the way, we pass two teenage girls carrying dishes of food. Neither of them acknowledges us. Through the orderly hallway, Dave takes my hand and pulls me into the kitchen, where we find a cheerful Leah chopping pickled cucumbers into slices and putting them into small bowls.

"Hello, hello!" she cries. "Welcome. The others aren't back from *shul* yet. It's very hot, isn't it? Do you want a cold drink?" She's wearing one of those long house-coat garments, with a turquoise-stretch turban covering her head.

As she opens the fridge, I say, "I thought the community didn't go in for estate agents."

"Sorry?"

"Your sister's house – it's for sale." A frown. She pours some red coloured cordial into a jug, and fills it with water. The whooshing sound of the tap fills the room.

"She's moving to be near our other sister's in Gateshead." Her eyes flicker away from my gaze, and there's a moment's uncertainty on her face. But she pushes it aside, just as there's a loud rat-a-tat knock, a man and two boys arrive. They fill the house with noise and energy, slamming doors and shouting *Good Shabbes*.

Leah's husband Moshe introduces himself, pronouncing it 'Moishy', and before I know it is greeting Dave like an old friend. It's all hearty handshakes and backslapping, real familiar stuff. And of course, I'm wondering what on earth is going on.

181

"Hi," says Moshe. "Nice to see you again. I didn't recognise you without the camera."

"Do you two know each other?"

"I came down to take some photos. You know, the portraits. You gave me Reb Stern's number." Of course, that's why he looks familiar. I've seen him hanging in Dave's studio.

The older boys join the little ones, who are playing on the floor with some building blocks. Leah disappears upstairs, and while she's gone a man comes into the room, ignoring us. He has a sallow complexion behind the beard.

"My brother Nachmann," explains Moshe. Nachmann nods nervously, avoiding eye contact, as though he's afraid he could catch something nasty from meeting our gaze. He sits down in the corner, opens a pocket-sized prayer book, and reads it with intent concentration, moving his lips as he goes and rocking. Everybody else seems to just ignore him – they carry on playing or laying the table.

Leah sweeps into the room. She's changed into a dress and replaced the turban with a wig. It's brilliant, you really would never know that those gorgeous tresses were anything other than her own hair. It's impossible to stop myself staring.

"It's late, let's eat," she says, leading us to the dining room where a long table has been laid out with a starched white table cloth. That is pretty much what I expected, but the surprise is that the table is covered with a large plastic decorator's dust sheet. There's no sign of the best china, all the plates and cutlery are plastic disposables. My idea of the Jewish Sabbath table has been trashed. Moshe picks up the one real piece of tableware, a silver goblet full of wine, and starts intoning a blessing.

Then it's all out to the kitchen, where the children line up at the sink. There's a big mug with two handles. I watch the children fill it with cold water then wash each hand alternately, muttering a prayer under their breath as they do so, then turn to pass the towel along the row. Looks like I'm expected to do the same.

Dave's in front of me. There's a look of intense concentration on his face as he mutters something under his breath while washing his hands alternately, just as the boys did. Then he takes the towel from Leah, and as I'm about to ask him what's going on, he puts his finger to his lips meaningfully. I stare at him, a questions swirling round in my head. Since when has he been an expert in Jewish prayer?

Now it's my turn, I'm still not sure what is going on. It's like some strange game and I'm the only one who doesn't know the rules. "Do you want to say the prayer for washing hands?" Asks Leah. There's no other way round it. I nod. "I'll say it, you copy me."

"*Baruch ata* ..." I feel myself going red. Two of the children are peeping round the door, giggling, and I can see why.

It may be the hottest day in the year so far, but the lunch menu makes no concessions to a heatwave. It starts with chicken soup, and goes on and on. *Gefilte fish*, bowls heaving with salads, heavy stew with beans. I think wistfully of the gym and its juice bar, where I'd normally be hanging out on a Saturday.

By the time a platter of cold meats comes round, I've lost track of whether this is the third or fourth course. As I'm helping myself to the smallest piece of chicken I can find, one of the older girls pipes up, "Do you work for television?"

"Yes," I reply. "I work on a programme about crime. We made the film about the attack on your cousin." The room goes quiet. The children stare into their laps, their parents look uneasy. Nachmann gets up with a jerk, spilling a beaker of drink onto the table, and leaves the room without even trying to clear it up. In the silence, the pink liquid starts pooling on the plastic decorator's sheet that's doing service as a table cloth. The juice runs towards the edge of the table, and is about to drip onto the carpet.

"Have you ever met anybody famous?" One of the girls is looking at me with big eyes and a cheeky grin.

"Yes, have you ever met anybody famous?" chimes in one of the younger girls, and a row of faces is turned towards me. At least I've got the right answer to this one.

"Let me see," I roll my eyes dramatically. "I've met Charlton Heston and Tony Blair." A row of blank faces is staring back at me. "You know, Tony Blair the Prime Minister of Great Britain? Our prime minister, now the leader of our country." They shake their heads.

"Charlton Heston, legendary movie star?" They shake their heads again. "You know, *Ben Hur*?" Then, with fresh inspiration, "*The Ten Commandments?*" Surely you know there's a film about the ten commandments – Charlton Heston as Moses! No. Maybe it was a long time ago. Perhaps politicians and aging Hollywood stars aren't the best way to engage young children. So I try again.

"Nelson Mandela?" No. Maybe not.

Disappointment is beginning to creep in. I'm a let-down. I sift through my CV very quickly.

"The Spice Girls?" Blank faces.

"Paul McCartney?" No.

"Paul McCartney is the biggest name in popular music. You must have heard of Paul McCartney? The Beatles? 'She Loves You, Yeah, Yeah, Yeah'?" There's a glimmer. They look at each other, quizzical. Then shake their heads.

Leah is laughing at my desperation. "Our kids don't know about any of your celebrities." She says something to them in Yiddish. The children look at me, excited.

"The *Rebbe*, you've really met Rebbe Avrahamson?" asks the oldest.

"Good try," I say to Leah. "No, I have to admit I have never, ever met the *Rebbe*. I've never even heard of him."

"You've never heard of the *Rebbe*?" Chaye-Sorah is aghast. In her world he's Charlton Heston. He's bigger than Charlton Heston. After all, Charlton Heston was only pretending to be Moses.

"Where exactly does he hang out?" I ask.

"Crown Heights, New York," says Leah.

"I'll remember to drop in on him next time I'm there," I say, grinning. The children exchange giggling glances, as though I've said something very funny. There's a rustling and bumbling that suggests a certain amount of kicking under the table.

"He's dead."

"Well that sort of rules him out, then." I say. While they're laughing, I sneak a sideways glance at Dave, who seems surprisingly at home and relaxed in what should be an alien environment. Something about that annoys me. And how come he knew the words of the prayer?

"I tell you what," I say to the children, "I have got one you'll know. Prince Charles, the Prince of Wales. Oldest son of Her Majesty the Queen."

"You've met the Queen?"

"Not quite. Her son."

"A real prince. You've met a real prince?"

"Yes," I say, triumphant. At last, the children are almost impressed. "I have met a real, genuine prince." There's a lot of nodding and smiling, then one of the children says something in Yiddish, and Moshe shakes his head as he replies. He turns to me.

"Chaim wants to know whether, when you met the prince, you said the blessing for meeting a member of the royal family."

"If I had known there was such a blessing, I would most certainly have said it," I say. "And I will definitely say it next time." I try to imagine the expression on the royal household

185

flunkeys as I am introduced to His Royal Highness and just as I am about to drop the standard curtsey, I start declaiming "*Baruch ata...*"

I'm trying to catch Dave's eye. I want to tell him it's time to go. I'm desperate. But he's involved in a long conversation about arranged marriages. Moshe and Leah met just once before they got engaged. It hardly seems decent to mention that Dave and I have been dithering around for the best part of three years.

"What about your brother Nachmann," I ask. "Is he married – or has he been?" Leah sighs.

"His parents tried. But he is a bit – different." I nod.

"When you have people who are a bit – unusual – isn't that where arranged marriage is supposed to come into its own?"

"In theory," says Leah. "It's not always that easy." I'm waiting for her to explain what she means, but from her silence I understand that's as far as she's willing to go.

It's late afternoon by the time we manage to escape. I wait until the house is receding behind us before I peel off my clammy cardigan. We don't speak, but our hands find each other as the heat of the day sweats itself out. We're approaching the tube when I break the silence.

"That went on a bit."

"Mmmm."

"Thanks for coming. Sorry it took so long." He shrugs.

"It's cool," he says. "She's an amazing woman."

"Really? I suppose if you think having trillions of kids and the perfect wig is the thing to aim for." Gathering momentum at the stairs down into the station, we separate on either side of the handrail.

"Why do you always have to sneer at things that go beyond your narrow world view?"

186

"I'm sorry?" We push through the ticket barriers. Dave gets on to the escalator first. As we descend, he turns to face me.

"You see something that's different. Values you don't aspire to, a lifestyle that's not quite the same as yours, and your response is to say it's crap."

"But it's creepy. You never know what's really going on. Why are you so keen to defend it?"

"I'm not defending anybody. I'm just saying, be a bit more broad-minded."

"Why should we be broad-minded about them when they aren't about us? They wouldn't put on jeans to come for dinner at our place." Dave glares at me. I get it. "You like it."

"What?"

"The Hasidic thing. Big families, rigid lifestyle. That's not you at all."

"We're all allowed to change our minds, aren't we?" He looks at me with an intensity I've never noticed before. "I wouldn't even say I've changed my mind – it's not something I've ever really thought about. It's not as though you run into Hasidic families every day of the week."

"I'm surprised, that's all, it's just..." and I peter out before I finish the sentence because what I want to say is *Where is the cool guy I thought you were*? But then, I don't suppose we've ever really discussed child rearing. Maybe I just didn't know him as well as I thought.

"You can call it rigid, or just structured," he says. "They offer the children firm boundaries, give a clear message about what's right and wrong. That's surely what kids need. We are always being told lack of structure is at the root of youth crime and all the other ills of society. Yet here is a social group who do offer their kids a warm, loving, strong family, and the rest of the world can't wait to have a go at them – you included!"

"But it's deeply odd that they don't want to discuss Bruchi.

Didn't you see how they all clammed up at the merest mention of her name? What are they hiding?"

"That is hardly surprising. Elizabeth, for Christ's sake have a little bit more sensitivity. I worry about you sometimes. And don't expect grief to come in neat little parcels. You're so distracted by your own agenda that you forget the most important thing. You were born with this amazing heritage, and you dismiss it all the time. At your father's funeral, you were obsessing about your mother and her behaviour, which to be frank was perfectly understandable."

"She abused me all the way to the crematorium."

"She had good reason to be upset."

"I thought you were on my side."

"It's not about sides. By obsessing about your poor mother, you totally missed the fact that the service itself was very moving. You undervalue the most important thing your parents have given you."

"Next you'll be telling me next that the Torah is the word of God, given to Moses at the top of Mount Sinai, every word written by him and handed down the generations unchanged. Get real."

The train arrives. We sit next to each other, staring straight ahead in red hot silence. I get off the tube at Caledonian Road. Alone. Well, at least I've found out one thing anyway. They are permed. The earlocks.

I get home to find the answering machine flashing like a Belisha beacon. Back to normal, then. Mutti uses the telephone like it's some kind of therapeutic device, freely associating into it even if there's nobody on the other end. I wipe all her messages and call her to find out if there's anything critical to tell. It rings for a long time. I count seven, eight, nine.

"Hallo?"

"Are you all right?"

"Sure, why not?" You'd think she'd just got back from a spot of over-energetic shopping instead of coming out of hospital after a near fatal overdose. She's reluctant to speak, probably because I'm dragging her away from an unmissable re-run of *Columbo*. So I ring off. But sure enough, later that night she calls back. I don't trust myself to answer. At night I screen my calls, listening to the machine click on and trot out my message. Then her voice cuts in, slurring and stumbling away. Something about the claim, her father's factory, her mother's jewels. None of it makes much sense.

My hand hovers over the phone. Then falters. If I speak to her in this state I'll just get an earful, she'll just end up abusing me. I've tried sympathy in the past, I've tried being stern. I've spent hours on the phone with her at night, trying to unravel her incomprehensible anger about some encounter with a bureaucrat or something a neighbour said to her. But she's never, ever allowed me anywhere near what's underneath, and if I try to find out she doesn't listen. Instead, she turns her anger on me and the random alcoholic meanderings morph into blame. She knows how to scent out my weaknesses. I wonder where she learnt to do that.

Dad's death hasn't really changed anything. The phone stops ringing, it's quiet again in the flat. She's sitting up there in the smoke-filled kitchen, unable to face a cold bed without him. I play back her rambling message. Once, twice, and a third time. I go to bed.

Chapter 21

In the end, Pavel Wiśniewski, is released without charge after twenty-four hours. I don't imagine that expunges the guilt of the entire Polish nation in the mind of Mrs Friedmann and her community. But it means the film can go out. Bill and I celebrate with a cold lunchtime beer.

A week later I meet Mrs Friedmann and DI Jenkins in reception. She's brought her sister along. One crumpled, one glam, they look like the "before" and "after" contributors in a makeover programme. The copper is accompanied by a junior officer, whom he introduces as DC Rogers and addresses as Ben.

"We're just rehearsing at the moment," I explain.

"Where are we in the running order?" asks DI Jenkins, with the air of an old TV pro. I flick through the thick script.

"About halfway. Item eight."

We enter the studio and hover at the edge of the set. An assistant floor manager signals us to wait while the rehearsal is in progress. Cameras wheel around the studio floor in a silent dance.

"What's the..." begins Mrs Friedmann. All over the studio floor, angry eyes swivel towards us.

"Shhhh," I whisper, putting my finger to my lips.

"Three minutes twenty-five on VT," announces the floor manager. Loud rock music and the squeal of tyres followed by heavy footsteps and shouting. I use the pause in proceedings on the studio floor to usher my guests up the spiral staircase.

At the control desk, Sarah is sitting next to the director. Without turning round, she waves us towards the back of the gallery, where we can watch the rehearsal, squeezed up against the wall. I can tell from the back of her head that today she's wearing her charming face, not the angry one she usually saves for me, even now.

"Coming to VT in five–four–three–two–one," chants the girl sitting next to Peter, clicking one of three stopwatches in front of her.

Mrs Friedmann is scripted for a live interview after the film has been shown. Sarah seems to reckon an appeal direct from the mother is our strongest card. I'm not so sure, but it's my job to make sure she can deliver.

"OK studio," says Peter. Let's take a fifteen minute break." Sarah turns round.

"While we're paused, why don't you show your guests round?" she says, which is what I should be doing anyway. I know that, so heaven knows why I need to wait for her to tell me. We retrace our steps down to the now empty studio. I let the two women stand in the presenters' places, try out the autocue, and walk along the banks of phones. They giggle girlishly, and it lightens the moment.

Where the foyers of three studios meet, there's a tea bar. It's now buzzing with technicians on their breaks. I switch my phone on to check my messages. There are three, all from Mutti. She'll have to wait. The sisters won't consume anything that doesn't carry the seal of approval from an approved rabbinical authority, which means they can have – two bottles of water. I grab some coffees for the rest of us, and we pull up some chairs round a formica table.

"So what will happen?" asks Mrs Friedmann..

"You mean from beginning to end?" She nods.

"Well, as I said, we are item eight in the running order."

"Why not item one? A robbery is so much more important than a child's death?"

"Well, item one is the pre-title tease – a sort of taster for what's in the show. It mentions the most important stories we are covering and shows little clips from the films – and yours is included in that. And item two is the opening titles."

"And item three? This film about Bruchi, it should be three – you must tell them. Inspector Jenkins, please, tell them this is right."

"When you are building a show," I explain, "you don't always put the best, I mean most –umm – compelling – item first –

you need to make sure that there's something later on to keep the viewers hooked. The point of the pre-title tease is to make them want to hang on for something really good." I can see something's bothering her. "Er when I say 'good' you know I mean worth watching, interesting, moving." Mrs Friedmann gives a grudging nod. "So your story is trailed both in the tease, and once more at the beginning of the show."

"Good," says Leah, giving an encouraging smile.

"And when we come to item eight, the presenter will read the introduction, which is here in the script." Another nod.

"Then we play in the film that Bill made when we came up to Stamford Hill. After that, Susan will interview Mrs Friedmann," I try a tentative smile, "and you will appeal to anybody who saw anything to call the studio number." She nods, looking as uncertain as I feel.

As we come back into the studio, I point out the phone desks at the rear of the set again.

"All these seats here are filled by police officers and researchers. The phones flash red instead of ringing, and they write down any details that callers can give." Mrs Friedmann picks up a phone and puts it to her ear.

"Is not working."

"No, they only switch them through just before the programme."

"But who will call, why should they call?"

"Lots of reasons. Maybe they were on the street just before or after a crime and they saw something suspicious. The film may have jogged their memory. Maybe someone they know has been acting oddly."

"And do you really think anyone will call?" Mrs Friedmann looks at me with her child's eyes.

"We don't know. All we can say is that a very young girl is involved, which makes it emotive. But every case is different."

"I think no. People will not call for us."

"Why not?"

"Because we are not like them. For an English girl in jeans they will call, but not for a *frumm* girl in a modest dress." Leah puts an arm around her.

"People don't think like that, really they don't," I say.

"No? I see the way they look at us in the supermarket, on the street. You pass another woman pushing her buggy, and she's blank, as though I don't exist."

DI Jenkins catches my eye. He thinks she's right.

"We wouldn't have made this film if we thought it was pointless," I say. "A child's death is always upsetting, and nobody is going to judge you for being who you are. If anything, they will watch Bill's film and realise that family is the most important thing in your lives."

There's a silence. DI Jenkins turns away to talk to his junior, and the two women speak Yiddish to each other in an urgent undertone. It's a total disconnect, of course. These people who think television is the work of the Evil One and have never heard of Paul McCartney being here in the middle of a massive, live studio show.

I'm trying to break them in gently, but we're on a tight schedule. Before we're needed for the rehearsal again, I take the sisters into an empty dressing room where I've had a television set up, so they can view a VHS tape of the film. There's a lot of nodding, and Mrs Friedmann gets out her hankie. I put a hand on hers.

I start the tape, and watch the two sisters watching it. They seem astonished at all the detail we've managed to get right, thank God, there are nods of recognition and once or twice they ask me to stop the tape to tell me how real it seems. But then, they burst into laughter.

"Have we got something wrong?" I ask, starting to panic. A recut is possible, just about, but at this stage it would be nerve jangling. I count the time between now and transmission, to see what the window would be. The two women try to explain to me just what the problem is, and as we wind the tape back and forward to isolate the shot they are worried about, I realise that only a couple of hundred people in Stamford Hill would notice this and none of them has a television. I start the tape again, and as the storyline develops, the tears start. When the video finishes, Mrs Friedmann buries her face in her hands, rocking back and forth. I put my hand on her shoulder.

"Are you OK? Bit of a shock, seeing it?" She nods, and wipes the tears away. And then I can't help noticing that she seems to catch her sister's eye. "It must be strange seeing yourself on telly," I say. She looks at the dirty, crumpled hankie in her hands, and nods again, but there's no suggestion she's going to explain what passed between them.

Instead the two of them rattle along in Yiddish to each other once more. I smile, my blank, uncomprehending smile and ask if they want to visit the ladies' loo before we go back into to the studio. But something weird has happened and I haven't let them in on it. I've started to tune into the Yiddish, a language I have no real knowledge of. When I first met Morrie and Sidney it just seemed like a blur of 'ach' and 'vatt'. But then, you learn to kind of tune in to it, and it's like fast, flattened form of German, which I do understand because at home that was the language my parents used when they spoke to each other and all their Mittel European friends.

And though they were careful to rear me as an English-speaking girl, the other language rubbed off. It's there, in my soul. And I'm pretty certain I've just heard Mrs Friedmann say something that sounded an awful lot like it meant "Did you see Nachmann on the film?" Nachmann. That rather odd, unmarried older brother. Now, why would she be interested in him? There were loads of brothers on the film. And brothers-

194

in-law, uncles, cousins, nephews. What is it about Nachmann being on the film that worries them?

Those two are hiding something behind that innocent, ever-so-naïve exterior. Maybe it's all just an act. I remember how worldly their mate Reb Stern was when he needed to be. So, those big eyes and Oh-my-goodness in the face of TV's latest technology. Really?

It's time to rehearse Mrs Friedmann's interview. As people fuss around adjusting a lapel mic and dusting her with translucent powder, there's a panicky look in her eyes. I give her arm a little squeeze before handing her over to the floor manager and beetling back up to the gallery.

As we come to the end of Bill's film, Susan turns to Mrs Friedmann.

"So, tell us a little bit more about Bruchi."

"Well, I – she is little girl. I – what should I say? A good girl. Reads nicely from her *siddur*, and knows her *davening*. Normal little girl. She had lovely hair."

"Stop – stop." It's Sarah in the gallery. She turns to me. "Elizabeth, I think you need to brief Mrs Friedmann more. She needs to try to stick to conversational English if that's at all possible." I run down the stairs.

"I'm sorry," she blurts, white-faced despite the make-up department's efforts. "I get it wrong. Please tell them not to be cross with me." I'm squatting by her chair, rubbing her hand. It's damp and trembling.

"Nobody is cross with you. Don't worry about that. If anything, it's our fault, always wanting things to be done in a particular way. It's just we have to think about an audience who don't know anything much about the Jewish community, and don't understand any Yiddish or Hebrew words. Can we try it once more?" I stay on the studio floor this time, hovering behind the cameras in case any more reassurance is needed.

Take two and Mrs Friedmann tells us what a lovely girl Bruchi was, she could read her Hebrew prayer book and knew all the important prayers by heart. And she had strawberry blonde hair that shone in the sun.

"So," says Susan, "What would you like to say if somebody out there knows what happened to her?" Mrs Friedmann's lip trembles as though she's trying to open her mouth, but it's glued shut. Is it the thought of the person out there who knows something? Or is it the fact that she knows something herself? A battle is being waged across her face, and it dislodges a tear. When she manages to say something it's, "I–I–I–I, I miss her so much." She's shaking and crying, hand on mouth, blubbing uncontrollably. I've stayed on the studio floor this time, so I go over to put an arm around Mrs Friedmann, just as the floor manager calls out, "Cut, cut..."

"It's OK," I say. "Not your problem. Honestly." The studio floor has gone silent. Sarah declares it'll be better if DI Jenkins does the interview. Can't we see that Mrs Friedmann is too fragile for such a role? Er, yes. I think I did say that. But then there's a tugging at my top.

"I will do it. I can do it."

DI Jenkins is put into position next to Mrs Friedmann and the rehearsal kicks off again.

The programme is due to go on air in just fifteen minutes. In the break, I put in a call to Mutti. Since coming back from hospital, she's been in touch with the bridge circle, there's even been talk of a poppy seed cake. She doesn't know that I know. But I am cautiously optimistic.

"How are you?" She ignores this question, and gets straight down to business.

"I have decided there's only one solution."

"For what?"

"The compensation." OK, deep breath.

"And that is?"

"I need to go to Hungary."

"Well, yes. I think we will need to go to Hungary. I'm on to it, honestly. But you're not long out of hospital. How about a few rounds of bridge? If you feel up to it."

"I'm going to Budapest next week. I've just been to the travel agent."

"You're broke, have you forgotten?"

"Bit savings. Was keeping in case."

"Hang on to it." The assistant floor manager has put her head round the studio floor, and is beckoning at me. Oh shit, I'm the last one in. I put up my hand and spread out the fingers to signal "Give me five."

"I need – evidence," Mutti is saying. Since when did she deal in evidence? I've never heard her utter the word before. She trades in emotion. "It's there, not here. I found lovely hotel. Very cheap. And I will have coffee at the Gerbeaud, swim on the Margaretteninsel, walk along the Danube."

"I don't think the Café Gerbeaud is where they keep the evidence. And anyway, you can barely walk round the supermarket. How are you going to stroll along the Danube?"

"I will manage."

"I really don't think it's a good idea."

"Why ever not?"

Mental instability, physical infirmity and problems with alcohol all spring to mind as good reasons why Mutti should not go to Budapest. Alone. And that's before she tried to kill herself.

"You'll get lost."

"It's where I was brought up. I don't think it has changed that much. And I believe they do have maps. Why are you are so keen to stop me going?"

It's impossible to explain to my calm, rational and sober mother that she's not always like this. While her diabolic alter ego is cowering in the wings. The way she's presenting it now, her wish to go back to Budapest seems reasonable. It's me who's got it wrong.

"It's just a really bad idea. You shouldn't go alone."

"So come with me."

"I can't just drop everything and waltz off to Budapest with you. I've got work. But I will come, honestly. We will go together, once we've done all the ground work properly and put together a case."

"What is more important, work or your family?"

"That's not fair. You are talking about my future, and it's my livelihood. One of us has to earn some money!"

"They don't allow you to take holiday? What kind of job is this? Really..." I don't hear the rest of it because I've cut off the call and switched off the phone.

It's dark by the time I slip into the studio, the programme is going to go live on air any second and I'm breaking all sorts of rules by coming through that soundproofed door right now. To make things worse, I stumble over a cable guard, making a sound that must be audible during the opening headlines. As soon as the title sequence starts, I know I have exactly thirty seconds to find my place manning the phones on set.

There's an embarrassing scraping of chairs as the cops move to help me through to my seat. The title music blasts out of the speakers, I collapse into my chair and sit there inhaling the smell of floor polish, a policeman's after-shave. There's a surprising preference for sweetish cologne among the boys in blue.

A voice near me cuts in above the music, "Oh no, camera on me wrong side again. I told them to shoot my left."

"Speak to my agent about it, darling, and we'll try to do something for you next time."

"Yah, but do tell the fans that I'll be doing me autographs after the show."

Muffled laughter.

"Settle down, gentlemen." The floor manager. "And coming to studio in fifteen. Ten–nine–eight–seven–six–five–four–three–two–one – and cue.

Sitting next to DI Jenkins, Mrs Friedmann puts in a near perfect interview. She's emotional, of course, but still manages to answer the questions and make an appeal for help finding her daughter's killer. It's a kind of balanced performance, that yet again has me wondering. I watch her being led away afterwards, her bulky frame retreating through the heavy studio door.

"So, what did you think?" As we trickle back into the green room after the programme has finished, the two sisters are sitting together, in one corner. It doesn't look as though they've spoken to any of the other guests. In front of them is a tray of kosher sandwiches we've had sent in from Golders Green, still untouched. I remove the cling film.

"She said – the presenter – there has been two calls. Who has called?" asks Mrs Friedmann, clasping her sister's hand.

"You mean the round-up of calls at the end of the show? To be honest, I couldn't really hear much from where I was sitting. The calls are put through randomly, so I didn't take them myself."

"Can we find out?"

"Yeah sure. What did you think of it though? Did it come over as you wanted?"

Yes, was very well done. Very – what was your word? – *moving*," says Leah.

I've offered to send the sisters home in a cab straight after the programme, but they won't hear of it. They want to hang on to find out if there are any other calls. I follow a trolley of coffees and biscuits which is being pushed into the studio. The working lights are on now, casting a flat, uniform blanket of yellow over everything. Phones are flashing red here and there, and there's a low buzz of male voices.

One producer is still patrolling up and down the desks, collecting the sheets filled in for each call, while another sorts them out.

"Hi Julia. How many calls about Stamford Hill?" I ask. "Item eight."

"Er, we've had a few." She riffles through the paperwork, and hands me a pile. "Don't take that anywhere, we need it for the update at eleven-ten." I've got seven sheets in my hand. I browse through them.

"Hi, Sarah?" Julia buzzes up to the gallery on talkback. "Yup, yup. Ten so far on the armed robbery. Thirteen on the newsagents' job." I move away, as she chunters through a list of the calls. DI Jenkins is standing at the edge of the set with some of the other police officers. I show him the sheets. He raises an eyebrow as he reads them.

"Well," I tell the two women back in the green room, "There have been seven calls in total, so far." Two pinched, anxious faces look up at me. "Don't be worried, that's quite good. Remember the phones are still on. And at midnight they are switched over to an answering machine in our office, so if someone wants to contact us later we won't lose their call." They nod.

"And?" says Mrs Friedmann. I look back down at the sheets.

"Four of them describe a man walking down St Kilda's road with a girl who looked like Bruchi. Vague descriptions – jeans, casual clothes." I flick through the sheets, comparing the notes. "These accounts are all a bit different, but seem to overlap. One of the callers even seemed convinced the man was Polish. Not sure why." More nodding. "One of them was certain he was a builder. Another said she thought he lived in a particular road in Tottenham. To be honest, it's all stuff they could have got from the newspapers."

"Why you say that?" asks Mrs Friedmann.

"The others are a bit of a mixed bag. One person thinks they can ID the particular white van. Reckons they can place it parked near a certain address. Might be interesting."

"The Polish. Why they ever let him go? It's him. It's him. I know it," says Mrs Friedmann, wiping a tear from her eye." Her sister puts an arm around her. "We always knew. They should arrest him now."

"But I'm afraid the four people who called to give information, or describing him refused to give their names." There's one thing I haven't told them. In the "any other observations" column, two of the officers have written, "Caller has unusual accent," and "Difficult to identify accent –not English, not foreign." I know that accent.

I've also deliberately skirted round the nature of the other calls. Because one of them has suggested we look close to home. "Caller believes he has evidence that the person responsible belongs to the Hasidic community, and may be a member of the victim's family. Refused to give name and hung up."

On the way home, I notice I've got a text from Dave. "We need to talk." Yes, we do need to talk, about lots of things. But there's no time to call him now, I'm exhausted. I get back to my place in the early hours to find another long, rambling message from Mutti. She goes on and on as though she thinks the machine is her new best friend. Hoping she hasn't downed another bottle of tablets, I wipe the tape and resolve to call her tomorrow.

Chapter 22

There's only one thing on my mind when I wake up. I want to be fit and full of energy to face my first full day as a proper film director without any other distractions. So I hit the gym early in the morning. I set the treadmill for ten minutes, and push the "plus" button at thirty second intervals until I'm storming it, at eleven Ks on a five per cent gradient. I hang in there for two whole minutes, watching the second counter tick over, as the pain slides up my thighs and tightens its grip. I push the air out of my lungs and suck in deeply. My mind goes into neutral, and images from last night's show wash in. I wonder if – the time display ticking the seconds off one by one towards my target – I wonder if – is it possible? Images of Stamford Hill run through my mind, both the real thing and Dave's vivid portraits. They swirl together as I push my legs to keep up the pace. Is it possible that the murder was committed by someone within the Hasidic community?

I can't breathe any more, my lungs are pulling at a void. I grasp the handrail with my left and reduce the speed. With so little spare oxygen I can't think. And I need to think. I'm down to 6km now which should be a comfortable jog, but I'm panting. I guess it's possible that the killer came from within the community, then pointing the finger at Pavel Wiśniewski would amount to little more than a diversionary tactic. But how do I even begin to unpick this one?

The office is almost empty when I get there just after ten. Most of the others are still recovering from a late night entertaining our "colleagues" in Her Majesty's constabularies. I slip off my coat and switch on the computer. But one person has got there before me.

"So, late night then? says Andrew, far louder than necessary.

"Finally succumbed to the attractions of the dashing young detective inspector at Stoke Newington nick?" It's easier to ignore the provocation now that I know Sarah's backing me, but I need to justify her faith in me by getting to grips with the story.

By the time I go for coffee, I've covered four pages of my notebook. Outside Starbucks there's a spare table. I sit there, feeling the morning sun glowing hot on my forehead as I sip my coffee. The dazzling light has fractured my vision, making my squiggles dance around the page with blotches of red and blue. My mind drifts back to last night. Who were those callers? Someone who's got it in for Pavel Wiśniewski, that's for sure. Or is he just a scapegoat? My phone rings. It's Dave.

"Hi, did you get my text?"

"What? Oh yes, something important but good. What's that all about?"

"I've worked out (BLEEP) what to (BLEEP) and it's..."

"Hold on a sec, darling, I've got another call coming in." I put him on hold and switch to the incoming call.

"Hello?"

"Is that Miss Mueller? From the TV?

"Morrie?"

"I wanted to congratulate you on last night's programme. Very well done."

"Thanks, but call me Elizabeth, please." As I'm saying it, a thought comes to me. "Hey Morrie, is there any chance you could meet me for a chat?"

An hour later, I'm upping my caffeine intake yet again, stirring the cocoa powder into the foam on top of a cappuccino. We're on the terrace of what was a grand house, overlooking its former estate. What should be a great view is obscured by a six foot wire mesh fence designed to keep wildlife in or vandals out. Either way, it's a scruffy, or if you like well-used, municipal park café, over-supplied with screaming toddlers.

"I'm torn, Morrie," I say. "Of course I don't want to point the finger of blame at the Hasidic community. But if they know who murdered Bruchi Friedmann…"

"I'm not entirely sure how I can help."

"You can. Tell me about the community. Do you think there's any chance they'd go as far as protecting someone? If they had suspicions?" He purses his lips, putting his head to one side as if thinking about it.

"Well, there have been cases. Not murder, of course. But I think there was something about child abuse. *Alleged* child abuse, I should say. It was a few years ago. Now what was it? A young man was accused of something. Perhaps there was babysitting involved." He sips his tea. "My memory's not what it was."

"Think hard. Can you remember how was the whole thing resolved?" The moustache twitches, as he bites his upper lip.

"I wouldn't want to be seen as criticising the Hasidim. The community has its own way of doing things."

"Meaning?"

"I believe there was pressure brought to bear on the family."

"Tell me more."

"It was suggested that they shouldn't have said anything. They'd committed the sin of *loshen hara* – the evil tongue. "

"So, how exactly was it suggested that they shouldn't have said anything?" He sighs, looks around us, as though he thinks someone might eavesdrop on us. "How, Morrie?"

"There was an incident. Outside their house."

"An incident. You mean some kind of demo? The family did what? Made an allegation, and there was a demo in front of their house?" He nods. "To shut them up?" He nods. "And the young man?"

"A quick flight to Israel. Or maybe New York."

"Why those two places?"

"Big Jewish communities. Easy to lose someone."

Instead of going straight back to the office, I drive up towards Manor House tube station. Just past the traffic lights on Lordship Road, there's a white minibus. It's parked next to the curb. As I slow down to pass it, the driver opens his door and gets out without warning. A *frummer* with floppy earlocks. What is it with these guys? I jerk to a halt and stamp on the brakes as the man spins round looking startled and terrified. And then I see who it is. Nachmann Cohen, Bruchi's odd uncle.

Why would anybody give him a job as a minibus driver? In charge of kids? He's not even on this planet. I'm parking the car at the tube station and thinking does the link between Nachmann and the white minibus add up to evidence? Circumstantial at best, but then so was the evidence against Pavel Wiśniewski from what I can tell.

I get out of the tube at Holborn, heading for the offices of the *Jewish Times*. The lovely old glass doors of a graceful building have become the latest victim of security policy. They've been replaced by wood reinforced with metal strips, and an electronic buzzer system.

"It's me, Betty," I say into the microphone, grimacing up at the video camera. She buzzes me in and waves me through. The papers are stored on old-style microfiches. Each one has to be loaded onto the reader. I have to scroll through them one by one, going back through the years. It takes me the best part of an hour to get through 1997, and gives me a crick in the neck. I manage 1996 in half that, and decide to jump 1995 and 1994, and spin through 1993 as fast as I can. Nothing so far, and it's mid-afternoon. Shit. I should be seen in the office. I'm just about to ditch the microfiches, when I find it.

Family of alleged abuse victim driven from home by mob

A family from Stamford Hill, North London, whose son made claims of sexual abuse against a teacher, are now at a secret address after their home was besieged by a mob. The mother of the boy said her community knew she was telling the truth, but would never admit it. She claimed she had been offered hundreds of thousands of pounds to withdraw the allegations.

I scan down the page. What happened to the boy's attacker? I run down the whole column. There it is. Right at the end.

No charges have been brought. The alleged attacker, Nathan Ginsberg, is said to be living in the Crown Heights area of New York, home to the world's largest Orthodox community.

I scroll through another few weeks as fast as I can, and find a couple more items about the same story. After that, the trail goes cold. I pack everything away order my printouts, and grab them before getting the Central Line to west London. I'll have to pick up the car later.

I'm sweating in the rumbling carriage, and thinking, so they might protect their own when it comes to child abuse – but not murder, surely? Reb Stern seemed keen to point out that his community was made up of law-abiding citizens with a deep respect for justice. But what kind of justice? Ours or theirs?

I dive into the office. Thank God my computer is still on, papers and rollerball pens scattered around my desk. If anyone comes looking for me, it looks as though I've sloped off for a coffee break. The redundant latte I picked up at Holborn has now gone cold, but I put the cup on my desk anyway. It'll add to the general impression I've been sitting here hard at work the entire day.

Anyway, it's time to forget about Stamford Hill. That's the past. I've got to concentrate on my film. "My film," I say to myself over and over again. "My film." It should be my only focus, everything else is irrelevant. I must be mad, dashing out of the office on a wild goose chase. Pavel Wiśniewski's innocence is not my problem. I've done my bit. Time to move on.

But of course there's the little matter of the yellow sticky on my desk saying call DI Jenkins, so I do that. It's a kind of courtesy thing more than anything. I need to keep up the relationship. I should thank him anyway, and well before now. Just the one call, I say to myself, and after that I will be focusing solely on the new film.

"Thought you might like to know," he says, "we've taken another three calls since last night."

"And?"

"Two of them described someone rather like Wiśniewski again. One did give a new name and address, so we'll be following that up."

"The third?"

"Slightly odd. A woman talking rather cryptically along the lines of 'Look in the back garden. There are weeds in the flower bed. Not all grow straight and true.' All very poetic."

"What do you think?" He pauses. I wonder whether he's playing some kind of warped game of double bluff with me. With the whole bloody programme. After all, it's usually the dad or the step-dad who is the prime suspect when kids are murdered, but that possibility has never even been mentioned by Jenkins. That's suspicious in itself. Maybe the film was just a massive smokescreen while they picked apart what was happening inside the family. That's why he's so interested in cryptic phone calls about weeds in the flower bed.

207

"It's definitely worth taking another look inside the community," says Jenkins.

"There's that rather odd brother-in-law of Mrs Friedmann's..." I hesitate.

"Yes."

"So you know about him?"

"I can't say..."

"You do know that he drives one of those crazy, rust-bucket school minibuses. A white one?" A red light is blinking on my phone.

"Can we speak later? I've got another call coming in. Catch up tomorrow?" I switch lines before I hear his reply.

"Hello, I'm calling from the British Embassy in Budapest."

"Yes?"

"Am I speaking to Elizabeth Mueller?"

"Yes, that's me. How can I help you?" My brain must be quite slow to catch up because even as I'm saying this I'm wondering what kind of crime the British embassy might want to discuss with me. What a coincidence, I'm thinking, it's —

"I'm calling because a Mrs Aranca Mueller has been detained by airport police at Ferihegy International Airport."

"Oh Christ. Sorry. What on earth is she doing there?" But of course I know. I know exactly.

"Mrs Mueller was detained on the flight from London."

"I hardly dare to ask you what for." A strained cough.

"I gather Mrs Mueller was reluctant to go along with the No Smoking policy." Why am I not surprised?

"Sounds, er, consistent. And how do I bail her? Do they take credit cards over the phone?"

"I'm afraid not. The airport police seem to be saying that Mrs Mueller will only be released into the custody of a responsible adult."

"She's not a baby." There's a curt silence on the line.

"I think – there's a suggestion that Mrs Mueller may have been – I think you probably—"

"Are you trying to say she was drunk?"

"That does seem to be a possibility, yes, and possibly the Hungarian police will have sought to confirm that with a blood test."

I'm already beginning to weigh up my options. How do I get Mutti home? The guy on the other end of the line has got there before me. "The police seem to feel that there is a safety issue with either releasing her in Budapest or sending her home unaccompanied." Of course she was pissed, I don't know why they are even bothering with the test, it must be pretty obvious. In fact, she's probably been on a month long bender. How could I be stupid enough to miss that? The slurring phone calls at odd hours, the wild plans – what an idiot I am to miss all the signs of Mutti going off the rails.

"So they want someone to come over to get her?"

"A responsible person is what's required."

"That would be me, then." That's great. Absolutely brilliant.

I slam the phone down and as I put my hands up to my face, catching the gleam in Andrew's eye as I do so. I have to get out of the office. The walls are looming in on me. The suspended ceiling tiles are pressing down on my head, the air is as thick as engine oil. It's choking me. I grab my jacket and bag. The carpeted floor is sticky on the soles of my shoes, as though it's trying to slow me down. Hurtling towards the door, I can feel dozens of pair of eyes following me. Smirking. It's only when I tumble out of the lift in the basement car park that I remember I parked at Manor House station, on the other side of London.

The tube is hot and humid. I'm jammed up against the door, with somebody else's bum pushed into my stomach. I let go of the handrail, wriggle out of my jacket, and use it to wipe the droplets of sweat from my forehead. What on earth shall I do? I should leave Mutti in jail until the weekend just to show her. I can't ask for leave now, anyway. Sarah would go ballistic with me, and that would be the end of my frigging film directing career. Game over.

What would Dad do? That's the question tormenting me as the tube rattles along. I just want to pick up the phone and call him, like I used to. There's a physical absence around my right hand and a cold sensation on that side of me because I know I can't just dial their number right now and catch him sitting at his desk working on his invoices. There was a phone extension in the kitchen, of course, which meant the sometimes she got to the phone first when it was him and him only I wanted to speak to. So I'd cut the line because I didn't want my conversation with him to be mediated by her. He was constant, predictable, safe. Gone.

By the time I hit King's Cross station, I've decided to ask Sarah for one day's leave. Just one. I'll book a cheap flight, nip out there, get Mutti and be back pronto, without causing the slightest ripple in my film schedule. At Holloway Road, someone gets out and I collapse into the empty seat. Of course I can't ask Sarah for leave, even a single day. She's just made a massive favour of giving me this great opportunity. It's my last chance, and all the rest of it. She has spotted my latent talent under layers of crap, and all that. It's a big front, power suit and all, but I can't help wanting to be like her, one day when I'm a grown up.

Come to think of it, I can probably get away without even asking for leave. I'll be out on a recce in the Leicester area. Nobody will even notice I'm gone. By now I'm halfway to Dave's place, but that's no good. I stumble out of the tube. It's still only four-thirty. Not sure which way to choose, I set off down High Holborn looking for a travel agent. I find one soon enough. Not part of a big chain, just a scruffy looking office with dayglo posters in the window advertising cheap flights. Long haul and short haul – Jo'burg, Paris, Bangkok, Amsterdam, Delhi, Munich. And Budapest. The whole transaction takes less than twenty minutes. I walk out holding a ticket.

Clasped in my hand, the flimsy paper has a reassuring feel between my thumb and index finger. I get back onto the Piccadilly Line. As the tube chunters along the dark tunnel, I turn the separate, thin sheets, with their self-carbon backs, the clerk's neat handwriting transmitted from sheet to sheet. Each page is parent to the next, the words a bit fuzzier and fainter as they pass all the way to the back of the booklet.

I fall out of the train at Manor House and head home in the car. The flat is hot and airless. I open all the windows, letting a breeze blow through. It scatters all my papers on the floor and makes a mess of my study. I pick up the phone to call the British Embassy back again. I imagine Mutti must be absolutely frantic, banged up in a Hungarian cell, like a bad rewrite of all her worst childhood traumas. I try calling the numbers I've got for the Budapest police, but it seems impossible to get through to the right person. Nobody answers the phone, at least nobody who can speak English. I speak to the Embassy again. The woman I get hold of treats me like someone used to dealing with slow learners in a primary school. No we don't need a lawyer. All that is required is that I turn up with my British passport and the means of paying a fine.

Out on the balcony, I glug down the dregs of an old bottle of wine, watching the neighbours' kids play in their back garden. Kids and parents. Will they grow up to torture each other? I'm haunted by thoughts of Mutti returning to the place where she hid from murderous fascist gangs in a crowded cellar, as her city collapsed under Russian bombardment. Starving and cowering, surrounded by death. And now she's there again, banged up and all alone.

I call Dave. He's a bit abrupt, and I can't even remember whether he's right to be so. I'm in a goldfish bowl, and the sounds coming through the glass and water is thick and muffled. I'm trying to explain myself and what the problem is but it's impossible and in the end I just put the phone down. He calls again and says he's coming round.

While I'm waiting, I decide to go for a walk round the back streets behind Camden Road, leaving the windows open. A burglary would be a pleasant diversion right now. The traffic's backed up. I look at the people stuck inside their hot little tin cans. They're probably on their way to normal homes and families, where people plan a barbecue on the weekend instead of a hopeless quest for restitution in a country only recently liberated from the yoke of communism.

Dave's sitting on the step when I come back, and I burst into tears when he puts his arms around me. We open a fresh bottle of red and sit on the balcony, in the cooling night, watching the lights flicking on in back windows along the terrace opposite.

"The problem," I say, "is that she clicks her fingers and I jump."

"You don't actually believe that, Elizabeth. She's been arrested in the place where she endured stuff we can't even imagine. That hardly counts as clicking her fingers."

"Yes I know, I know. I know what she went through, and I really feel for her – I'm not just saying that I do. But that's little comfort right now because I'm effectively responsible for her. Isn't it usually parents who go and get their wayward kids from police custody for breaking some minor law or getting drunk? This feels uncomfortably like role reversal but the upshot is that I need to go over there and get her. There's no alternative. I'm stuck."

"Why didn't you ask me to go?" I look at him, uncomprehending. "Why did it have to be you?" He insists.

"Well — "

"I haven't got anything I have to do. I've got no films to set up or shot lists to compile for my career altering current project. You didn't ask me. I bet you didn't even think of it." He's right, of course. I'm locked into this metaphorical bloody arm-wrestling match with my mother. But I don't know if I'm pulling her towards me or pushing her away.

"And shall I tell you what?" he says. "You're going because you want to, and you don't want anybody else to take your place with Mummy. Until you stop doing that, you'll never be free to grow up." I feel as though I'm being told off, yet again. I open my mouth to snipe back, but haven't got the energy. Because I know he's right, and when I tell him, he puts his arm around me, accepting that this is something Mutti and I must work out together.

We lie together, spoon-wise, his chin nestling on my shoulder. I can't remember if I dream, but I wake up at five with my pulse racing. I throw some jeans and a summer dress into an overnight bag, and walk down the road to get on the first tube of the morning.

While Dave sleeps on, I'm rattling along to Heathrow, trying to envisage the scene at the airport when Mutti was arrested. The thing is, their police are probably still communist boot boys. There may even be Gulags in Eastern Europe, for all I know.

Chapter 23

The cool of Budapest airport is a welcome relief from the baking tarmac outside. The square, concrete building is haunted by the elusive whiff of old-fashioned cigar. Around the time my colleagues will be beginning to trail into the office in London, I'm using a payphone in the arrivals hall to call to the British Embassy.

Mutti has been taken to a police station halfway between here and the city centre. I get there just as someone in London will be taking orders for coffee and heading for the Italian place around the corner from the production office. I'm going to have to check in with them sometime today. Let's hope they buy the fiction that I'm on a recce in Leicester. But instead of starting a day with East Midlands Police, I'm looking at an officer of the Budapest force. He stands behind a long, black reception desk that's been polished to a high sheen and smells of wax.

Polite but unsmiling, the policeman explains in excellent English how I go about getting Mutti released. There are forms to fill in, and of course the fine. Travellers' cheques, local currency and all major, international credit cards are acceptable. Can't I see my mother, first? I ask. Just to satisfy myself that she's well. The officer's response is to take out a massive pile of paperwork and plop it in front of me. I'll take that as a no then.

I'm hungry and thirsty now, as I slept through breakfast on the plane. There's no sign of a vending machine, and let's not even think about the possibility of a cafeteria. I settle down to complete the forms. It becomes clear that relinquishing communism doesn't mean abandoning a fixation with bureaucracy.

It's disappointing that I never get to see the inside of Mutti's cell, because they bring her up to me. She doesn't look miserable, grubby or even the least bit contrite as I wrap my arms around her. She pats me on the back, and continues chatting in Hungarian to the policeman who has brought her upstairs, as though they are acquaintances who have met at a cocktail party. All she says to me is, "Very good, very good."

Before we can leave, we need to retrieve her enormous suitcase

214

and handbag. And – surprise, surprise – this seems to involve handing over another wad of cash, then signing a further form. The copper calls us a cab, and we head into town. I have a passing thought to ask Mutti to explain why she needs a globetrotter's trunk full of clothes for a couple of days in Budapest, but get side-lined by practicalities. Where are we going? She gives the driver directions with all of her usual hauteur. As we drive along, she also provide a commentary about the many wonderful things we can see and do in Budapest, as though this was just another happy little mother and daughter jaunt. The thermal baths are an absolute must, it seems. And of course the magnificent Buda Castle. I interrupt her flow.

"Are you even planning to say 'thank you'? In fact 'sorry' would be nice."

"Well..."

"You haven't even told me what happened."

"You know what happened."

"I got the briefest possible outline from someone in the British Embassy. Something about lighting up on a non-smoking flight."

"These people are quite unreasonable. It's a three-hour flight, for God's sake."

"Everybody else seems to manage."

"Ah, but they are not *real* smokers."

"And what's that supposed to mean?"

"If you were a smoker, you would know." I can't be bothered to argue the toss over the likelihood that there's not a single *genuine* smoker among the three hundred people onboard a Malev airlines flight. Mutti would always manage to have the last word. "Anyway," she says, "if you had come with me in the first place, as I asked you to, this would never have happened."

"If I had been sitting next to you, you wouldn't have lit a cigarette?"

"Of course not."

"How d'you work that one out?"

"You wouldn't have let me." So it's all my fault. Of course.

By now, it looks as though we are coming into downtown Budapest. Mutti has become flushed and excited, as she looks right and left out of the taxi windows and she's stopped talking. The car bumps over a bit of cobbled road, passing a row of grand, art deco old buildings along an avenue. What's Mutti making of all this after fifty years? Whatever it is must be given an undoubted extra soupçon of piquancy by her night in the cells. A tear is building in the corner of her eye. It wobbles, precarious on the rim, catching the harsh sunlight as we swing round a roundabout, and is dislodged by the momentum. She wipes her cheek, brushing it away, and shoots me a half smile, with the merest hint of apology around the edge.

She says something to the driver, he replies and opens his window. She does the same, then loads her cigarette holder and lights up. Just as I'm about to completely lose it with her, I realise that the driver is puffing away too. Smoking is in the Hungarian lifeblood, then, just like loud conversation and rich cakes. The combined output from the two of them blows back over me, and even though I've grown up with the reek of tobacco, it makes me feel sick all over again.

I look out of the window to distract myself from the wave of nausea, and find we're soaring over an immense river on a suspension bridge. Passenger cruisers glide both ways on the glinting water of the Danube below. There's a disappointing lack of blue in the water. But of course, Strauss was Viennese. The Hungarian Danube is almost black.

I've got the book in my bag, the one I took from Mutti's house. I've read it and re-read it many times by now, wearing down the pages yet further. And I'd say we can't be too far from the place where Arrow Cross death squads did their dirty work.

Hideous things happened in the very streets our cab is trundling through right now. People hid for months in stinking, overcrowded basements, lice-ridden and scrambling for scraps, cowering from constant bombardments. As we swing down a side street, Mutti's looking both ways with a thoughtful expression. But if she's remembering what happened to her back then, she doesn't say a thing.

"Where are we going?" I ask.

"A little guest house," says Mutti. "Very modest." And before I can ask whether we even have a booking she adds, "Civilised policeman let me telephone to say I arrive one day late."

We stop in front of a white-painted building in a terrace of similar houses. It looks not much bigger than the average London family home. Above the door, a sign reads '*Pension Eszterházy*'. A small, cluttered reception area is dominated by an oversized chandelier. There's no response to the brass bell on the reception desk. Nothing. Then a distant shuffling sound, like mice running down a corridor, and finally a small woman with an enormous bosom bustles in on high heels. Gracious ropes of beads swaddle her minimal neck. Improbably red hair is scraped up into an imposing bun above Edith Piaf eyebrows. Though she looks like a brothel madam from central casting, her manner is formal. "*Igen?*"

Mutti says something in Hungarian. The only bit I understand is our names. The formality is dispensed with, something has unlocked a cascade of verbiage, beginning with the words, "*Madame Mueller, szervusz, szervusz!*" uttered in an operatic manner, and continuing without pauses. Mutti looks regal, and very pleased with herself. The two women shake hands, and our hostess bobs up and down in what strikes me as a distinctly pre-communist curtsey.

As Mutti only booked for one, we are sharing a room. It's small and simply furnished, with little more than the Spartan looking double bed and a cupboard, and two unmatched wooden bedside cabinets. The floor space is minimal, and now it is almost entirely taken up by Mutti's massive suitcase. The plain furniture is relieved by a scattering of painted ornaments, and a vase containing dried flowers. The effect is pretty grim and my face must give me away, because Mutti shrugs.

"Very cheap, for good location," she says. I see her quickly pull down the bedcovers, as if checking for bugs, but she doesn't tell me whether she's found any. I declare the bedroom a no smoking zone. Mutti doesn't object, but I suspect she's just deferring the battle.

Downstairs there's a little booth draped with nylon lace curtaining, where Madame keeps her antiquated Bakelite telephone. I sit on a wobbly plastic stool and call Malev to change Mutti onto the same flight home as me. Thank God she's old fashioned enough to travel scheduled. No cut price rubbish for her. We'll both be on tomorrow night's plane to London. Then I dial the office, to speak to Sarah's PA Millie. By now it's mid-afternoon here, so they're probably just coming back from lunch.

"Hi," I say. "Did you get my fax?"

"Yeah. Are you OK?"

"Fine, I'm in Leicester."

"So you said."

"Is everything OK at the office?"

"Why shouldn't it be?"

"Er, no reason. Elizabeth, this line is very echoey, where are you?"

"I'm using a phone in the pub. My mobile's battery has gone flat."

"Right."

"Millie, any chance you could make a couple of calls? I'll ask

Sarah if you can have a researcher credit if you pull in the goods."

"No probs. And Elizabeth?"

"Yes?"

"Be careful. I'm watching your back, but Sarah's got an uncanny sixth sense."

"There's nothing to worry about. But thanks, and everything." I give her the numbers, and tell her what needs doing. My next call is to DI Jenkins.

"I just wondered what's happened with Stamford Hill."

"I've been leaving you messages all over the place. Didn't you get them?"

"Oh. I'm on a recce for my next job. In Leicester."

"Really?"

"Is it that surprising?"

"No, except I spoke to some bloke at your office, who seemed to think you were about to leave the programme. Made some sort of cryptic remark he seemed to think was very funny." Andrew. Fuck. What does he know?

"Sorry about that. The half-arsed researcher who sits next to me. He's got a strange sense of humour. Makes up for being rubbish at his job."

"I'll steer clear of your office politics. But I thought you'd want to know we've arrested a Nachmann Cohen of Stamford Hill."

"Oh my God. Nachmann. Bruchi's uncle? The mother's weird brother? What's he charged with?"

"Nothing yet."

"On what basis have you arrested him?"

"You know I can't tell you that."

"Do you suspect him of being the murderer?"

"Don't push your luck."

"Is there any evidence against him?"

"Do *you* have any?"

"Not unless you count the fact that he is extremely odd, and unmarried."

"If being single over thirty was a crime I could come and arrest you too."

"Is that a police joke? Excuse me for not laughing."

"OK. But I'm just trying to point out that being single is not a crime."

"Of course not, but it is strange for Stamford Hill. I've met enough people up there to realise that different rules apply for the extremely orthodox. The great thing about arranged marriages seems to be that nobody needs to be left on the shelf, however much they lack either social skills or sex appeal. So when it comes to Nachmann Cohen, you simply have to ask why he's not married."

"I can't see a judge going for it on that basis, I'm afraid."

"Which leaves you where?"

Jenkins sighs. "OK, strictly off the record then – he was present, had the opportunity. His alibi is that he was at the party, but no one can remember whether he was actually present all of the time. He could have easily slipped out."

"And if you can't get any more than that?"

"There is some other evidence I can't go into, but I don't think we've got enough to charge him by a long chalk. If I can't get anything else, I'll have to release him by tomorrow morning."

"Shit. Do you have a gut feeling that he's the one?"

"As you say, there's something odd going on." I wonder if I should tell DI Jenkins what I've found out about the community protecting and hiding people suspected of child abuse. If Nachmann did anything, or his family even suspect it, heaven knows what they'd do to protect him. That hardly counts as evidence, though. I put the phone down.

Chapter 24

"What do you want to do, then?" I've found Mutti smoking in the tiny, weed-filled courtyard that Madame refers to in her tangled English as "the garden".

"Well," she says, "I think we take the cable car up to the castle and then later we swim in Gellert baths. This you will absolutely love. I will show you the Liszt Academy – you know this is where I studied the violin – and then the opera house, and the museums." By now she is in full flow. "And of course the parliament building is an absolute must. It has a wonderful Gothic style, with some Baroque and also Romanesque details. In some ways quite similar to Westminster parliament."

"Well if it is like the Westminster parliament," I snap, "we could save ourselves a lot of effort and go to see the one in London." She looks squashed. "Mutti, we've got twenty-four hours, not a week. And I thought the whole point of being here was to pursue the compensation, not some sort of sightseeing jolly. Mad as that sounds, don't you want to at least have a go? Have you got any contacts at all?"

She looks at her fingernails with a petulant moue, picks up her cigarettes, turns them over in her hands, and puts them down again.

"Did you notice the horse-drawn carriages on the way here?" she pleads. "We make a short round trip of the principal sights, no? I'm sure Madame Eszterházy can get us a deal."

"Mutti, get real."

"OK, is OK." She takes a deep breath. "We can meet an old friend."

"Yes?" I'd assumed all her old mates had died or left the country. Most of her cousins and her girlfriend Clari are all in America. She's never mentioned anybody here before.

"Who is she?" She says nothing, but fiddles with her cigarette holder.

"Mutti?" She's blushing.

"He."

"Are you trying to tell me this is – an old boyfriend?"

"Mmmm." She looks away. "Fiancé."

"Don't tell me – one of the two you had simultaneously back in the day?" She looks up to meet my eyes and nods.

"So who is he? Who was he?"

"You know..."

"Let me guess..."

"...nice Jewish boy." That could be a barb. But Dave is far from Mutti's thoughts. "Good family. A lawyer." The nice Jewish lawyer. He wasn't for me at all. Does that mean my father was second best? The one she really wanted got away.

"So what happened?" Her lips move, and her hand gestures in the air. But there is no sound. Then she manages to whisper, "Everything. Everything changed." She shakes her head.

"But you'd like to meet him? Will you be OK about that?"

"*Ja, ja.*"

"Is he definitely still around?" She picks up her handbag, searches through it and pulls out a battered letter.

One hour later, we are on the terrace of Café Gerbeaud, which Mutti wants me to appreciate is the city's most legendary coffee house, but strikes me as being on the kitsch end of baroque. I have allowed her to smoke one cigarette. Then I sent her to the ladies to brush her teeth. You don't want to meet the man of your dreams after nearly fifty years smelling like an ashtray.

At four o'clock, a man approaches our table. He's wearing a jacket over a black polo-necked jumper, like a jazz musician from the 1950s. Steel grey hair has been brilliantined into a corrugated sheet. Mutti gets up. He takes her hand, kisses it and says, "*Szervusz, Editca, szervusz.*" I notice a large gold signet ring on a brown hand. If history hadn't condemned the gesture forever, he would click his heels.

The tooth-brushing was unnecessary, because the first thing Michael does is to take out a packet of Kent cigarettes. He seems surprised when I decline, shaking the packet at me with a twinkle, "They are American, you know. Very good." Mutti and Michael talk in a confusing mixture of English, Hungarian and German. Sentences start in one language and glide into another. Names are thrown in – and ticked off. There is a lot of talk about America – Cincinatti, Chicago, New York. Then Sydney and Melbourne. London seems to be a sideshow in the Hungarian émigré world, let alone Cardiff. Wales is not on the map. I follow some of the conversation. But I'm uncomfortable playing gooseberry to my own mother, so I leave them both to their memories while I go round the block, looking in shop windows. When I get back, the ashtray is full.

"So, *Erzsébet*," says Michael to me, using the Hungarian version of my name. "Excuse us. We have a lot to catch up. I am happy that your mother has such a beautiful daughter." He turns to Mutti, "And to find Aranca looking so wonderful. Almost unchanged."

His ornate compliments make me cringe, but they elicit a coy smile from Mutti, and a dismissive, playful hand gesture. My God, he's teasing her. What a terrible flirt.

"It's nice to meet you, too, Michael."

"You like Budapest? Your first time here?"

"Yes, it's great. It's kind of sad too."

"Sad? What is sad?"

"The lovely buildings looking so run down." He shrugs.

"We are not a rich country. But not so poor as others in Eastern Europe."

"It reminds me of Paris..."

"But," he pre-empts me, "shabbier."

"Sorry, it's obviously not an original thought."

"It's not so bad here – so you know Poland or Latvia? Even

when we had the Iron Curtain we always had more freedom than other countries. Intellectual life went on, more-or-less in the open. Best of both worlds. Communism, but not too communist. And we ate, we always ate. No food queues. And now the Iron Curtain gone, will get better. Believe me."

"It feels like a place you can't escape from history."

"Of course not, but we love our history. The good AND the bad."

"Don't the bullet holes in the buildings just remind you of things you'd rather forget?"

"Bullet holes?"

"So many of the lovely buildings are pock marked by bullet holes. Nobody has even bothered to fill them in."

"Maybe they aren't bullet holes."

I look at him, to see if he's joking.

"OK, maybe they are bullet holes. London's the same. You don't see it because that's the way it's always been for you. You had the bombing, I think."

I smile. It's odd to think this man could have been my father. Then I wouldn't be here. One can't unravel the past. As Michael says, you have to make it work for you.

"Has Mutti told you why we are here?" I ask him. Mutti's shaking her head at me. But I'm going to plough on, whether she wants me to or not. There's no point being overcome by good manners now that we're here.

"I think you come to see old friends and re-live the tragic history of this century. Yes?" says Michael. Very good. I wonder if his irony is born of the *ancien régime*, the communist one or post-communist. It doesn't matter really, I'm not prepared to play games.

"I think you already know there's another reason," I say. All of a sudden, Mutti makes a majestic gesture at the waiter.

"Champagne," she commands. "Very cold." There's an air of

desperation, she'd rather dodge the awkward questions. But now that we're here I want to ask and ask and ask. And champagne, what is that going to cost? There's a big difference in the price of sparkling Hungarian and the real French stuff. The way she's playing dowager duchess, they may well bring us a £100 bottle of Cristal. The waiter buzzes around with an elaborate, free-standing ice bucket, and the cork pops out of the bottle. We drink a toast to our trip. And then another one to the new, re-born Hungarian state. And then, I try to turn the conversation back.

"So," I say, "you were asking about the reason for our visit."

"But Michael," interrupts Mutti , "you must tell me, do you go to the opera? I've heard it is still wonderful." I kick her under the table. Michael doesn't appear to notice.

"The opera is excellent," he says. "And of course, the tickets are very much more affordable than other world leading operas in London, Paris and so forth. You must go."

"Sadly, we are flying home tomorrow," I say, glaring at Mutti. She ignores me. Again.

"*Ach*, I remember my first visit to the opera. I must have been around nine years old. I was so excited about the lovely red dress my daddy bought me to wear, with lots of layers of netting underneath to push out the skirt."

This could go on for some time. Mutti waxing on about the splendid life in pre-war Hungary, as enjoyed by the moneyed bourgeoisie. Michael and I smile at each other.

Mutti beckons to the waiter to top up our glasses, "Isn't this fun?"

"Yes," I say. "And now I'm going to tell Michael about the reason for our trip. Which will also be lots of fun. I promise."

Mutti listens, as I spell out our claim for compensation, nodding at intervals and interrupting with irrelevant points. Michael smiles, but each time he relaxes his face takes on a look which is grave and kind of disapproving.

The waiter brings a fresh ashtray. Michael opens a new packet of Kent and lights one up. "You know," he says, "there are people in Hungary who...are unhappy about the idea of compensation, however limited. Even this $150 you mention, which appears on the face of it to be a sum so small, that it is insulting. So insulting that it has now been raised to $1500. If everybody who is in fact eligible claims, the sums involved could come to – who knows? – many millions. Where is this money coming from?"

"So, you think the principle of compensation is wrong?" I ask. He ignores my question.

"Most of this money will go abroad. As we have said, Hungary is not a wealthy country. We are just emerging from a difficult phase in our political history. State is letting go of many enterprises. New enterprises are forming. Not a good time to lose so much of our capital abroad, when we are just learning about how to be capitalists."

I try to respond to this, but he waves me down. "And if you compensate for victims of Nazi era – not just Jews, but gypsies and people who were called 'sexual deviant' or 'political deviant', what about victims of Stalinism? Political prisoners? What about victims of First War? Where do you draw the line? Why just victims of Nazis get compensation, when there were other victims too? Many Hungarians suffered under communism. People lost homes, businesses, property. Their lives. But our country has to move forward. We can't rewind the clock back to 1944. And why pick out one particular moment in our difficult history to say – the people who suffered then, they should get compensation. The others not."

"Look, Michael, Mutti and I aren't responsible for the whole country and its tortured history. Just ourselves. And our claim is quite simple. My grandfather owned industrial and residential property worth a lot of money. It was confiscated by the

Hungarian government, and he was killed. Now it's payback time."

He picks up his box of cigarettes from the table, lights one and draws on it, looking reflective.

"I understand your mother feels maybe – that she was cheated out of the life she expected. Believe me, I know, I was there. Her family lived in wonderful style. Have you seen pictures of their home? Yes? The height of elegance. Everything was the best. Furnishing fabrics from Paris, glassware from Italy. Tablecloths embroidered with real gold thread. Your grandparents were among the smartest people in town. Is heartbreaking to lose everything. Believe me, I know.

"But was long time ago. Your mother was young when it happened. She was lucky. She escaped to the West. She married a man who was kind and – a wonderful coincidence, he also was an entrepreneur with a factory and lived in just the same kind of milieu that Aranca had grown up in. And they had you, to be brought up with every comfort. At a time when people in Hungary were living with the *dis*comforts of communism."

"Look, Michael," I butt in, "You can't guilt-trip me because I was brought up in the West. It doesn't work like that."

"Doesn't it? You have enjoyed – what do you call it? The Good Life. Is that the phrase? But maybe things are not so good any more? Maybe money is a bit tight back at home?"

At this, I can feel my face turning pink. He's right of course. If my parents hadn't run out of money we wouldn't be here.

"Ah, so I've hit a nerve, I think. Maybe things at home are not so comfortable as they were in the past. Now you have – what do you call it? – a cash crisis? And you want some of ours. Because you have discovered that this country is no longer as poor as it once was. So you come over here and want to take something from us, at the very moment when we are trying to

227

build our country back up. Is that fair? Some Hungarians think that is greedy."

I don't know how much attention Mutti is paying to the conversation. She's been looking disinterested for a while, and fiddling with the bits of foil from her cigarette packet. Now she summons the waiter to pour the last of the champagne. Michael puts his hand over his glass, so most of it ends up in Mutti's. She swigs it back.

"If so many people are against the compensation scheme, then why don't you stop it? Isn't that what democracy is supposed to have achieved?"

"My dear girl, don't be so naïve. We understand very well how necessary a little bit of hypocrisy is to make the world go round. I'm not speaking for myself, you understand. But I want you to know how it will be seen if you decide to go forward."

"Michael, I can't speak for other people with other problems which happened at other times. We'll never bring my grandfather back, but we have a very small chance of getting back the property. I'm asking for your help. If you don't want to give it then we will ask somebody else."

I stand up and reach for my handbag. He takes a sip from his champagne glass, then leans back in his chair and flaps his hands to tell me to sit down.

"Look, I didn't mean to insult you. It is a difficult thing, you ask. Maybe I cannot help you myself. I will see who could help, and I'll call you tomorrow." Tomorrow we'll be on a flight out of here, and he knows that.

Mutti hasn't said anything for a while. She drains her glass, rises to her feet, and stands there swaying.

"Now I know why I left when I did," she says at the top of her voice. "This country is full of cowards, toe-the-line men. Nobody wants to upset the boat," she yells at Michael. "You know exactly what went on. You were there, but now you want to just brush it away, pretend it didn't happen. Let everybody just forget the nasty truth." The other customers on the terrace are craning their necks to see what the fuss is about.

Mutti lurches away, leaving me sitting there opposite Michael. He looks at me as though he thinks I'm about to apologise. Well, I'm not. For once, she's right. And she's perfectly entitled to get pissed. The only thing I am concerned that she's marching down the street without me, and I have no idea where she's going.

I grab my bag and dash behind, trying not to lose her in the crowd of tourists. She takes a sudden right, and I swerve after her, keeping a lookout for the flashes of red jacket up ahead of me. The crowd on the pavement here is bunched up, and I force myself through by dodging right and left, only to be brought to a sudden halt by a red pedestrian crossing light. I'm drumming my foot on the kerb as a wall of traffic passes in front of me. Mutti must be miles away by now.

On green I charge forward, scanning the crowd. Then just a few yards ahead, there's a familiar shape. But that's not Mutti. It's – it can't be – the hunched posture and asymmetrical gait are so particular. Even from behind I recognise that mournful air, that of a woman condemned forever to chase the ghost of a lost child. And the hair, it doesn't move. It doesn't even look real. How on earth could Mrs Friedmann be here, in Budapest? I run past the figure and spin round, coming face to face with a cross looking elderly matron, who looks as though she's about to report me for invading her privacy.

I back off, apologising in English which must make no sense whatever, but hopefully she's written me off as a daft tourist. Maybe it's me who has drunk too much. Now I've no idea which way Mutti's gone, but I rush forward with the crowd, trying to catch another flash of the red jacket. There it is, in the distance. My legs are tired now, and my handbag is rubbing a groove into my shoulder as I chase forward, hoping I haven't made another crashing mistake. I'm getting closer but let's hope she doesn't dive into a shop to shake me off. Finally, I manage to catch up with her in the shadow of a covered arcade. She's managing to walk pretty fast for someone who is half-pissed and can't usually manage the supermarket aisles, barely acknowledging me as I draw level. Where on earth does she think she's heading? I reach out for her arm, trying to get some sense out of her. I miss and pull on her handbag by mistake, and an empty half of vodka topples out and smashes on the pavement.

She yanks her arm away from me and marches onward. By the time we pass the grand opera house, she's beginning to flag. Slowing down, her head sinks, she looks defeated.

"I'm sorry," she says. "Was..."

"You don't have to apologise," I say. "Not at all." She's pink, flushed from the walking. Or maybe she's blushing.

"Silly old woman..."

"You're allowed to meet an ex-boyfriend, you know. That doesn't make you a silly old woman." She looks grateful. "Pity he turned out to be such a dickhead." She gives a wry smile, and puts out a hand to lean on me for support. I stop, trying to work out how to get back to Pension Eszterházy. There's a dark, sweaty patch on my grey tee shirt where her arm has gripped mine.

The high summer air is thick and clammy as we set forth once more, in what I hope is the right direction. I think this is the way to the hotel, though Mutti has refused to bring a map on the grounds that she is at home here. Soon there are beads of perspiration forming on her forehead. One breaks free, and dribbles down her jawbone.

We stop to buy a bottle of soda water, and it's only when I take out my wallet that I realise we left Michael with the bill for the champagne. A feeling of mortification flashes through me, but it only lasts a second. Serves him right for trying to be holier than thou with us. He may think he still knows Mutti, but he really has no idea how angry she is.

As we drink the soda, I scan the street around us and notice something odd – a line has formed along the kerb. People are looking along the road, into the distance. Faint music, coming this way. A boy shoves something into my hand. It's a flag with a red and white symbol. Another boy gives me a leaflet. I can't make out what it's about, and Mutti's not quite with it. If they are trying to sell something, the marketing looks a bit primitive – so much for the onward march of capitalism. I stuff it into my bag, and spotting a bench a few yards away on the pavement, I park Mutti there until the mêlée passes. The footsteps and music come nearer, mixed with the sound of traffic.

The noise is getting louder and louder. I have to crane my neck to see over the people. I can make out what looks like a troupe of boy scouts. But as I'm watching they mutate into fully grown men, in khaki uniforms. The crowd is picking up the tune they are marching to, and starts singing along. Everybody seems to know the words, and even Mutti is tapping her foot in time to the music. It gets louder as the parade comes towards us, in their midst a marching band blasting out the pounding anthem. The man leading the crocodile of uniformed men is waving a large red and white striped flag, with an insignia in the centre. A cross with an arrow on each of its four points. From Mutti there's a sharp intake of breath, I turn to see her face a shade of grey.

The thump of boots marching one two, one two, is competing with the blare of drum and trumpets, and a French horn I now notice for the first time. From the pavement, there are cheers and clapping, as the column approaches. Behind me, a fist beats time into its opposing hand. A small shaven-headed boy waves his flag at the marchers.

But the singing and cheers are mixed with discordant voices shouting to a different rhythm. We've stumbled into a demonstration of some kind, and it has all the hallmarks of an ancient tradition. There are supporters, of course, and dissenters – there is a counter demonstration. The crowd is jeering. They know the routine, it will have been going on for thousands of years. Soon two men will square up to each other, a fight will break out, which will merge into a free-for-all. One side against another. Invaders against natives. Turks against Magyars. Communists against fascists. Austrians against Hungarians. Insiders against outsiders. Everyone against the Jews. Jews against the Gypsies. The music gives way to excited yelling. The crowd are warming up for a bit of fun.

It's time to go, before things turn nasty. I look round to the bench, but Mutti's gone. Well, it's hardly surprising that she's been scared off by jack boots and martial music. Now I'm stuck behind the growing crowd, and I can't see anything through the dense wall of humanity.

A ripple of movement and a familiar looking flash of red. On the road. It's her voice I can hear, rising above the jeers. I push my way to the front, getting jostled from both sides. A handbag swings in and scratches my face. A woman I'm pushing past shoves me back screeching something. I ignore her, and am rewarded with a sharp kick in my calves as I pass.

When I get to the front, I can see Mutti. She's head to head with the man at the front of the column. He's a heavily built twenty-something, with black hair cut so short that it's little more than a shadow on his scalp. She grabs the flag-pole he's carrying, throws it on the ground and stamps on it, ripping the fabric and spitting on it. The crowd jeers. He shouts back, enraged, but though he'd make short work of a man who was his equal in size and strength, the challenge of getting past an elderly woman throws him. In the end, he gives her a half-hearted push. But he hasn't calculated for Mutti's arm-wrestling shoulders and when she resists him, he's wrong footed, and stumbles off-balance. As he re-finds his centre of gravity they come nose to nose.

The column has stopped in its tracks, marchers falling out of line, swirling around the strange old woman in their path. The music falters. Amid the blur, I can make out the head thug and one of his mates grabbing Mutti by the arms. One either side, they pinion her, arms behind her back. If she was a young man instead of an elderly woman they'd have hit her by now. They hold onto her for a frozen moment. She lunges away, taking them by surprise, and managing to free her right arm. But instead of escape, she turns, lashing out at the leader's neck and screaming at him, red faced. This time he's prepared. He coolly grabs Mutti's arm again and twists it behind her back. She squirms in pain. He gives her arm a malicious extra twist. And her whole body judders in reflex. He grins, turning towards the pavement spectators.

The sadistic bastard, enjoying that clenched agony on her face. That's what does it for me. I launch myself from the pavement and tear across the road, dodging a couple of stray leaflet boys. I throw myself onto the boss man, and ram two fingers into his left eye. I'm kind of watching myself do it and thinking where did I get that from? He lets go of Mutti with a roar, but recovers himself quickly and starts towards me. Those self-defence classes I did at uni have must have left a trace element in my brain, because I wait until he's grabbed both my arms. And then I bring my knee up into his groin as hard as I can. I feel him double up, letting me go.

I brace myself for the retribution that's sure to come from one of his mates. I'm surrounded by them. There's a rush of footsteps coming towards us amid a screech of whistling so high-pitched that it stings my ears. A lot of people dressed in black are whirling around, no idea where they came from and whether they are police or some kind of militia. It all happens so quickly I've lost sense of direction and what's going on, but I know one thing. If the marchers grab me I'm in deep trouble for kneeing their boss man. I prepare for the impact. The pain doesn't come yet, but for a moment I'm suspended in time, caught in the eye of the storm where I hang there motionless and untouched while chaos explodes around me.

A myriad scuffles and punch-ups break out. The black clad figures with their screechy whistles launch themselves at the uniforms one-on-one, punching, kicking and pushing. Police sirens. The tap-tap-tap of running feet. I finally get to Mutti, but someone else has got there first, and I'm pushed away by a meaty hand.

"Mutti!" I call. She looks towards me without recognition. "Aranca!" I shout at the top of my voice.

Someone grabs my arm so hard it hurts, and pulls me. I try to resist, but I'm not strong enough. Now he's dragging me by both arms. I try to dig my feet in to the paving stones, I can feel the soles of my sneakers coming away. My toenails are rubbing through thin socks and scraping along the ground. There's nothing to grab onto, and the paving feels slippery beneath me. I'm being yanked along, dragged so fast that I can't get to my feet. Police sirens and more footsteps fast and staccato like a machine gun. Shouting and in the distance now, a plaintive wail from the trumpet.

Around me is a blur of pavements, sky, and towering buildings. I'm turning, or is it the pavement that's moving? I no longer know which way is up. Torn advertising hoardings and graffiti zip past, a girl's bleached smile and a display of medicines. A street sign flashes across my line of vision, too quick to read. Footsteps approach, and there's a dizzy sensation of being surrounded by a crowd of urgent voices like a swarm of flies that gathers and then disperses. Footsteps scatter in different directions.

I'm sitting on the curb, feeling as though I've just got off a merry-go-round. The world looks choppy, my head is trying to make it stop spinning. In the background, I can still make out the noise of whistles, shouting and police sirens. The hands let go of my arms, which feel bruised. There is something sticky on my hands. I hold them away from me and try to focus. Dried blood. I'm covered in small scratches.

"It's OK, don't worry, you are OK," says someone in American accented English.

The speaker is a bearded young man. He's wearing jeans and a tee shirt, with casual black jacket and a baseball cap.

"Mutti. I was with my mother. I need to find her." I pull myself to my feet, feeling wobbly. My voice comes out hoarse and screechy.

"The old lady in the red jacket?"

I nod. "Have they taken her? Those people?"

He nods his head in the direction of the corner of the road. Mutti's limping towards us, leaning on another bearded young man. She's taller than him. Despite the limp, her posture is erect, like a defeated fighter who has acquitted himself well in combat.

"Quite a lady, your mother," says the American. I run forward and she puts one trembling arm around me. Her handbag is still clamped over the other. I'm sobbing and hugging her. She grips onto me, and tries to say something, but her mouth opens and shuts, wordless. She shakes her head. I reach into her bag, and find a packet of cigarettes. I put one into a holder, and light it for her. She takes a deep drag, then looks around.

"I need to sit," she rasps.

"Not here," says the first young man. "Come with us."

"But who are you?" I say. "And who were they?"

"I think your mother has a pretty good idea who they were. Come on, let's go."

We make slow progress, limping our way down a succession of narrow streets. As we walk, the first man passes me a handkerchief.

"You might want to wipe your face."

"Thanks. But I don't normally accept hankies from strange men."

A weak smile.

"Schmulli," he says, pointing at himself. "And that's Aaron." He takes his baseball cap off and adjusts the skullcap underneath.

"I'm Elizabeth Mueller," I say. "That's my mother Aranca. And let me guess – you probably won't want to shake me warmly by the hand." He shrugs.

"Well then, it's jolly noble of your friend to let Aranca lean on him like that, breaking a dearly-held prohibition."

"That's first aid, it doesn't count."

"Thanks anyway. So what are you, some kind of Maccabean paramilitaries?"

"Hardly."

"So?"

"The guys you saw demonstrating belong to a group called New Arrow. They are fascists, as I'm sure you have already guessed."

"Why New Arrow? What happened to the old one?"

"You know what the Arrow Cross was?

"Yes sure, I..." The Arrow Cross, of course. I've read the name so many times without ever trying to imagine what that might look like. The symbol on the banners was a cross with an arrow at each point. Stupid of me not to make the connection earlier.

"So they are some kind of neo-fascists. And that makes you?"

"We aren't anything particular. No group."

"And today?"

"They've been demonstrating every week. They manage to keep

236

one step ahead of the police. Or perhaps the police don't care."

"So how come you knew?"

"We get – information. We have people."

"So, then what?"

"The plan was a peaceful counter-demonstration. Your mother seemed to have other ideas."

We've stopped outside a house. There's a dirty sign over the door. Painted in uneven looped writing are the words "Eva Klein" and next to it there's a large window with a small glass display case containing a meagre selection of lumpy looking pastries. The paintwork on the door is peeling, on the frame a rusty *mezuza* – signifying that this is a Jewish premises, and in the window a smutty *kashrut* certificate.

We've left Mutti and Aaron half a block behind. I want to wait for them, but Schmulli ushers me inside, as though he thinks it's dangerous to linger. Behind a polished wooden counter that looks as though it's been there for decades, there's a woman in an apron. She's caught in the blue glow of a hygiene light. When she sees Schmulli, her eyebrows arch into two mirrored question marks. They exchange a few hasty words. Schmulli steers me out the other side into a backroom, brushing aside loose fringes of coloured plastic that hang down from the top of the doorway.

We sit at a scrubbed wooden table. Mutti and Aaron arrive. One of her eyes looks puffy, her lipstick is smeared. I get up, fling my arms around her and hold her tight, feeling her solid, sweaty body against mine. It's years since I have held her like this, now I've done it twice in half an hour. For too long I've feared being engulfed by her boozy breath and blubbery shape. Often I've felt her hover near me, and even taken pleasure in blanking her. I did it deliberately, to show her I could. But now I want to hold her and hold her, to never let her go, as if that will be enough to save her from all the fascist thugs in Budapest.

"I'm sorry," I say.

"No," she says. "Doesn't matter."

The woman in the café – Eva? – brings us milky coffee in large wide cups. On the tray is also a small bottle of brown liquid and some cotton wool. She pours some of the liquid onto a piece of cotton wool and dabs at my cheek. It stings. Then she hands me the cotton wool to clean up the scratches on my arms and hands.

In the ladies' toilet, I splash myself with cold water. Mascara has streaked down my face and mingled with the remaining traces of blood. I wipe it away. The result is an untidy smear of foundation and eyeshadow. I look like a child who's been playing with her mother's cosmetics case. I clean off as much of it as I can with an old tissue. My eyes are stinging. As I'm rummaging through my handbag to find some fresh make-up. I find the leaflet.

"What's this?" I ask Schmulli, as I sit back down at the table. He smoothes the crumpled sheet onto the table.

"Some of our friends' filthy propaganda."

"And it says?"

"It's about the Jewish hyenas, and their conspiracy to rob the Magyar nation of its hard-earned *forints*."

From the other side of the table, Aaron makes yelping noises, to illustrate the point. Even Mutti smiles, but I'm still seething.

"What can they know about Jews?" I shout. "Even I know that most of the Hungarian Jews were sent to Auschwitz and the few that were left managed to get away after the war or in 1956. Can't they find someone else to pick on for a change?"

He shrugs, but it's probably not the right moment to go into why we are here, I tell them that we've come to Budapest on a sentimental visit. We talk in a desultory way about sightseeing and the Jewish Quarter. By now, Mutti seems more interested in reading the leaflet. When she's finished, she screws it up into a ball, and puts it into the ashtray. Then she pokes it with the tip of her cigarette and it flares up in flames. She turns to the two men, "I want them to pay for what they did to my father. Can you help us?"

Chapter 25

We are booked on a late flight back to London the next day. So at eight-thirty in the morning we rendezvous with the two men outside a building, its neo-classical façade smothered in grime. Schmulli presses the buzzer, and we enter a brightly lit, tiled corridor, off which are several signposted doors. Disinfectant lingers in the air. We enter the first office, to find ourselves in front of a polished, mahogany counter. Behind it, long rows of shelves crammed with files disappear towards a distant wall. To our right are several large reading desks, some of them already occupied. In one corner is a microfiche reader and a photocopier.

A clerk is speaking to a customer. He's wearing a name badge on the kind of brown overall jacket grocers used to wear in 1960s Britain. A woman waits her turn, we sit next to her. The clerk fusses around, bringing one file and then another. The woman looks at each, shaking her head as she gives them back to him. Their conversation seems to drag on and on, the customer increasingly irritable. The clerk looks as though he's taking it all as a personal insult. Then, just when things look as though they are going to turn nasty, the customer snatches a file, and tramps over to one of the desks. The clerk scoops up the remaining ones, muttering to himself. I look at my watch. It's taken him twenty minutes. We'll need to get back to Pension Eszterházy to collect our bags before we head out to the airport. I start tapping my foot on the floor. Mutti nudges me, and shakes her head disapprovingly. The woman steps forward.

Without waiting for her to say anything, the clerk scuttles off and returns with a single file. The customer accepts with a wordless nod. At last.

Schmulli gets up and asks a very long question. The clerk replies in a curt, sullen sentence. Schmulli turns back to us.

"Upstairs."

A flight of stone stairs, another, smaller office, lined floor to ceiling with ancient leather-bound ledgers packed tight into venerable oak bookshelves. Their custodian is another brown-jacketed clerk. Seeing our file, he takes a pair of wire-rimmed glasses out of his breast pocket like a professor of classical history examining a parchment scroll. As Schmulli is speaking, the clerk adjusts his glasses, and examines the documents in our compensation file. He stops at the address of the factory, taking out a battered map book from underneath the desk, leafing through it looking for the right page. Then he stands upright and looks at me and Mutti.

"You come, please," he says in English. We all go over to the shelves. He runs his hands over the ledgers, talking in Hungarian.

"He says these books list all of the property in Budapest," explains Schmulli. "With the names of the owners." He pauses to listen. "It runs up until 1948 when the communist regime took hold." The clerk now walks along the row, stopping at the end, and selecting a volume with 1930 embossed on the spine in black, gothic lettering. He lowers the heavy volume onto a desk, and starts leafing through it, the three of us peering over his shoulder. It's all swirling copperplate handwriting and sepia coloured ink – addresses on the left, followed by numbers and names across the page. He turns over the heavy pages, sometimes going back and forth, and keeping up a commentary in Hungarian, addressed to Schmulli. Who replies every now and then, just one word,

"*Igen.*" Yes. Then they stop. They nod. They look at Mutti and me.

"I think we have something, ladies," says Schmulli.

The brown ink, the lacy handwriting make it difficult to read. But it is there all the same. The address of Grandfather's factory in the Budapest VIII district.

And even I can make out what's written in the second column.

"This," I say, "is my grandfather's name. And this," I move my hand across the page "is the family apartment in *Szent Istvan Korut* – it's the one overlooking the river." I turn to Schmulli, "Does this mean what I think it does?" He nods.

"It means that your grandfather certainly owned the factory in 1939 – it's pretty much proof." He puts a hand up. "But we have to carry on going through the ledgers to see what happened later. Mutti squeezes my hand very tight. Then she rummages in her handbag.

"I go out for a cigarette, *ja?*"

"You want me to come with you?"

"No, I'm fine. Really." She does that thing of pulling herself in which is like she's shaking all the pieces back into the right place. I watch her going along the parquet floor, her tall, bulky frame dwarfed by the room's vast, echoing space. In this setting, she looks small, shrunken, vulnerable. But I'm soon distracted by the physical effort of moving the ledgers about. Together, we heave one, then the next, tracking grandfather's ownership of the property across the years from the 1930s. He's there in 1935 and 1936. In 1937, he's still there, but has been joined by another name, Ferenc Kovács, which is still there with his in 1939.

"Who the hell is Ferenc Kovács?" I ask. Schmulli, and Aaron look blank. "Is there some way of finding out?"

"I think this person," the clerk points to grandfather's name,

241

"is Jew. No?"

"Er, yes," I reply, wondering where this is leading. "This person," he points to Kovács, "not Jew."

"Probably something to do with the anti-Jewish laws," says Schmulli. The clerk nods fiercely. "From years of nineteen-twenties, government make difficult for Jewish," he says.

"Yes," I say, "I know." He ignores me and carries on.

"No vote for Jewish, few doctors, few lawyer. *Numerus clausus*, also in university."

"Academic quotas, and in the professions too," I say. "No cars, boats, trains, radios. I've read about that – but how does that relate to the factory?"

"When they brought in laws 'Aryanising' Jewish property," says Schmulli, "thousands of people could apply for anything owned by Jews, from apartment buildings, industrial plants, even wedding rings."

"That's legalised theft. And people just went OK, here you are?"

"It's a damn sight better than being gassed and burnt in an oven like the Polish Jews, you know, so people just put up with it and I think they hoped one day the tables would turn again. As they always had before."

"So what's happened here? Why the two names in the ledger, and then one?"

"This is just a guess, but maybe your grandfather could see the writing on the wall. A couple of years before the full-scale Aryanisation laws he brings in the non-Jewish partner. Probably he was trying to stay one step ahead of the game. At first, they share the ownership of the business, and then in 1943 your grandfather steps back, and from the outside it looks like an Aryan company. But he's running it behind the scenes."

"But then his luck ran out," I say.

"Do you know what happened to your grandfather?" asks

Schmulli.

"Not really. They hid. Mutti told me he was shot, but never went much further than that. She sort of seizes up and can't get the words out. It's hardly surprising. But I've managed to fill in the picture myself and you must know. Things were pretty chaotic, death squads rampaging around the city pulling people out of so-called safe houses. I just assume..." Schmulli and the clerk nod.

"*Ja.*" I hadn't heard Mutti slip back. She must have heard what I just said. The click of a lighter, the whoosh of air being dragged through a cigarette, and we're all engulfed by a cloud of smoke. "Every night we sat in the cellar, listening out for Russian shells. For footsteps, shouting. In the dark, in the cold. But when they came, it was..." She draws deeply on her cigarette and no one tells her this is a no-smoking zone. "It was early in the morning. Bashed down the door. You, you and..." She falters. "They took him. They... my mother tried to use connections, you see. We knew people, contacts. We had a letter, was supposed to save him. But I didn't find... couldn't see. I left him – to die."

"But you were fourteen, Mutti." She nods. "It wasn't your fault." The clerk crosses himself, and we fall silent.

"But tell me now, who's this?" I ask quietly, pointing at the name Ferenc Kovács in the ledger. The others part to make room for her at the desk. She lifts up the glasses that are hanging on a gold chain around her neck, puts them on and cranes forward to see.

"I can't believe it," she bolts back upright, her face red. "The bastard, the bloody, the..."

"What can't you believe?" She takes another drag of her cigarette.

"My father's chauffeur was Kovács – to us he was *Kovács bácsi.*" She flicks ash onto the polished parquet tiles. The clerk watches it fall. "Uncle Kovács."

"It's not necessarily the same person," I say. "After all, Kovács seems to be a common Hungarian name. You see it all over the place."

"But it makes complete sense, Elizabeth," says Schmulli. "A servant is just the kind of person who you'd choose to put down as the nominal owner of your property. Just the kind of person who might feel some kind of obligation, and who you'd trust to give it back afterwards. That's exactly what people did."

"But I don't think he returned it at all," says Mutti. "Did he?"

We have to turn the heavy pages to see what happens after 1944. The name Kovács continues, year after year until the sequence runs out.

"So that's it?"

"Yes, and I'm afraid though what your grandfather did was a clever move at the time, it leaves you with a bit of a problem," says Schmulli.

"What do you mean?"

"It looks as though the property was legally transferred to someone else and wasn't confiscated. He did it voluntarily, before compulsory Aryanisation came in. You can't really claim it was theft, unless you can find some paperwork in which Kovács undertakes to return the property at a certain time."

"That's ridiculous. Of course he wouldn't have just given it away to some bloody driver."

"But how can you prove intention on the part of someone who is now dead?"

"I'm not giving up on it."

"What else can you do?"

"I'll look through those other ledgers, for a start."

"It's a waste of time. I'm sorry." I turn round to pick the next ledger up, but it's too heavy. The clerk helps me, and together we lever the tome up onto the desk.

The new tome has a repeat of the same information, but has an additional column with amounts of money listed. The clerk shakes his head, unable to explain what they are. We turn the page, and at the bottom of the column there's something new. Another address.

Outside, we're assaulted by a burst of morning sun. Schmulli is leaning up against the wall. I walk towards him, waving my notebook. He shrugs.

"What have you got?" asks Schmulli.

"The address," I reply. "I've got the address for Kovács."

"But it's nearly fifty years old. He won't be there. The building probably doesn't even exist anymore."

From the terrace of a café overlooking a square, we can see leaves on the trees turning dry with the intense summer heat. I heap sugar into my espresso, and gulp it down, craving the caffeine.

"Who says the address doesn't exist?" I say. "We might as well try it."

"And what if he is there? What are you going to say?"

"I'll find out what's happened."

"And then what?"

"I don't know, I'll work it out." I look at Mutti. Impassive, she turns her head to blow smoke away from us.

"I think you have to be at the airport by six, so you probably haven't got enough time anyway. What you should do is find a Budapest attorney who can carry on the search when you are back in London, using the new information." He's right, of course. We thank Schmulli and bid him goodbye. But there's a lot we can do in four hours. We'll sort out the attorney later.

Soon we're on a tram, rattling north along the Danube. Mutti's quiet, gazing over at the water, as if she's trying to see something below the surface. I wonder if the bodies are still lying down there, silted over by fifty years' worth of

245

accumulated debris. Or perhaps the pounding current has washed the bones along the winding river bed towards Romania's border with Ukraine. Where the Danube splinters apart across a vast delta, its separate streams tumbling out into the murky depths of the Black Sea.

"You all right?" I ask.

"*Ja, ja,*" she snaps on a bright smile.

"Tell me what it is, Mutti."

"It would be so nice to go on one of those boat rides on the river. Such lovely views. Nice glass of wine."

"Yes," I say. "It would be lovely." The tram makes a rumbling noise, kerdunk, kerdunk, kerdunk.

"I wanted to stop them, you know. I... I tried my best." Kerdunk, kerdunk, kerdunk.

"You did, Mutti, you did." That's it. We've reached our stop, and stumble off the tram, hands clasped together. We can't find the right bus for the next part of our journey. It should stop here. I let Mutti sit for a while on a bench smoking, while I study the map. It looks as though we need to cut through to the adjacent main road to pick up our connection. We set off, walking at a pace she can manage. The reserves of energy she discovered yesterday have dissolved, and despite her evident determination, her walking is laboured and slow.

"What were you about to say, on the tram?" I ask. We walk on for a few minutes while Mutti is composing a reply. She nods to herself, as though she's trying out different forms of words in her head. She swallows, and looks away.

"I watched them – take my, take my father." Her voice fades away to nothing. "My mother was like a child, paralysed. I had to take charge, decide what to do. I ran to father's old colleagues. If I'd been stopped by the militia they would have shot me too. No good anyway. And then I remembered that *Kovács bácsi* knew them all. He was supplying all the black market nylons and booze for the – those people – he made sure they needed him. He introduced us to some of his contacts, we went round the city from one to another and finally we got a letter requesting my father's release."

We come to a junction and wait for the lights to change before we cross. Mutti looks at me. "I couldn't believe it – I had the precious letter addressed to a Colonel – what was his name? Something beginning with F – *ach* what was it?" She's holding her hand up as though the letter was in it now, she's remembering exactly what it felt like to hold the piece of paper that could spell life or death. "No matter what his name was anyway, I'd never met him, didn't know what he looked like, but he was supposed to be the man with the influence. *Kovács bácsi* still had my father's car, and he took us down to the river. But when we got there we didn't know who to give it to – what to do. We didn't know if we were even in the right place, Anyway, no good. Too late." Her shoulders slump as though she's reliving the impotence all over again.

"It wasn't your fault though," I say. "You were just a young girl – how come you had to bear the responsibility for saving your father?" She shrugs and we walk on until we arrive at the bus stop. Mutti throws her cigarette butt on the floor and grinds her foot into it until it's pulverised into dust. We get on the bus, and sit very close together.

Our journey continues through the traffic-clogged city. As we head north, the streets get narrower and smaller. Elegant old buildings with their ornate mouldings give way to irregular square, modern blocks, blackened with grime, and stacked together. Looming shadows make the road dark, as we bump along. Every now and then the bus catches a slice of sunlight, cutting between the stern edifices.

Mutti wobbles up to the front of the bus to ask the driver if we are near our destination. She comes back waving three fingers in the air. We count the stops, like children on a day trip. Then we're out on the pavement, looking round for landmarks. Grandfather's factory was built in the 1920s, but nothing we can see looks as though it has been here more than about forty years. We are surrounded by squat, Stalinist tower blocks, a crushing memorial to the post-war era.

We scan the roadside, looking for signs, but there aren't any. Along the monotonous road each corner looks just the same. Solid concrete: buildings, satellite dishes and washing bursting from crumbling balconies. A small shop selling cigarettes and lifeless vegetables. I give Mutti the map and hover behind as she goes into the shop and buys a pack of cigarettes as an excuse to ask the shopkeeper for directions. He looks at the map and an ancient business card Mutti has been keeping in her precious folder. He shakes his head, and says something. Mutti turns to me.

"It's not here anymore. The road we are looking for, it's not here, doesn't exist anymore."

"But it's on the map." The shopkeeper is now serving someone else. We wait, then Mutti speaks to him again.

"He says the map must be old." I look at the man in his blue overalls. A black five o'clock shadow on his weaselly face.

"Bastard," I say loudly. He may not speak English, but he'll have got the message.

We pause on a low wall outside the shop.

"It's as though the entire Hungarian nation is against us. They'll do anything they can, even take down the street signs."

"Don't be silly."

"Why don't you sit down here, and let me have a look around?" I say.

"But how can you ask for directions?"

She's right, of course. Mutti is our team communicator, she's already walked far more than she would consider possible on a day at home in Cardiff. I help her up, and she shuffles along, leaning on me.

"We might as well go back to the guest house to get our stuff," I say.

"But we haven't found it."

"And we're not going to at this rate." The return bus stop is down the road, but Mutti's slowed down to a crawl. Looking down, I notice that her legs have swelled up to an alarming size in the heat. They look like great, painful pink sausages, straining out of their skins.

"Maybe a cab?" she says. But the traffic seems to be made up of pick-up trucks and ancient Trabants. Drinkers sitting outside some kind of sawdusty bar stare unsmiling as we creep past. Mutti responds to them with a deep-frozen glare. "Maybe we could sit here for a moment?" She nods towards some empty seats.

"It doesn't look very welcoming," I say. "Are you sure?" She gives me a desperate, doggy look. "OK, but no booze, I don't think that'll do your legs any good."

When the waiter comes, Mutti seems to take a long time ordering soda water for two. He crosses his arms over his chest, expatiating at some length about something. Then she gets out the dog-eared cardboard file and shows him the old business card. There's a lot of "*Igen, igen.*" And energetic pointing one way and then another, as if he's giving directions. Mutti's nodding and smiling.

"He calls us a cab. And he knows where the factory is – it's only a couple of streets away, won't cost much." The waiter comes back with two large round goblets of iced beer, dripping with condensation. I turn to Mutti, but she gets in first.

"Don't make a fuss. Hardly any alcohol. And this I learnt from your Daddy" – she takes a large gulp – "is the most thirst quenching drink on hot day. Better than soda water."

"Yeah. Sure." I take a sip. She's right. It is very thirst quenching indeed.

The cab takes us along to the corner where we got off the bus, and then turns right along a busy main road. There's a shocked look of recognition on Mutti's face as it comes into view. She clasps her handbag tight as we stop in front of a sprawling industrial complex lurking behind a tall wrought-iron fence. A mess of styles, new bits apparently added in different decades. But in the centre, the once-white rendering and lozenge windows suggest sleek art deco origins. A sign whose jagged graphic style suggests it was added in the mid-seventies declares "Feher". With the meter ticking, we buzz the entry phone, and enter a reception area guarded by a suited girl. Cue discussion. Usual thing, highly voluble, lots of hand gestures and some over-dramatic facial expressions on both sides. But oddly enough, quite amicable. Mutti helps herself to a brochure from a pile in a plastic tray on the desk, and gives it a quick glance mid-conversation. Then there's a curt, "*Köszönöm szépen*," and she turns to me. "Come on, we go."

"But aren't we going to talk to somebody?" She shrugs.

"Not necessary."

"How so?"

"No time. And I already know all I need."

"Ask her about Kovács." She looks at me. "Come on, this is our last chance, you said it yourself. Ask her about Kovács." I know that petulant look. It says she knows I'm right. But while she's stalling I get in there.

"Do you speak English?"

"*Leetle*." A fixed smile.

"Can we speak to the boss?"

"Sorry?"

"Head man, senior exec?" I can feel my voice rising.

"Not possible. Must have *appointe-ment*. Please." She picks up a brochure and points to a phone number with the tip of her

250

biro. "You telephone."

"Who owned this factory before?" I make a large hand gesture, as if this will clarify my question.

"Before?"

"Communist time. And before communist time." The girl looks at me with distrust.

"Current ownership since nineteen ninety-one," she parrots as though it's something she's memorised. "Previously owned by Hungarian state, now company *privat* management. Please you telephone."

"Can we speak to someone else? We are flying back to London right now." She's looking at something from the corner of her eye, hand hovering. Oh God, she's got some kind of panic button that'll call a battalion of security men. I grab Mutti and we leave.

I should have more faith in my mother. In the cab she repeats the entire conversation verbatim while I make notes. The name of the company, who owns it, when it last changed hands. Its entire history since the collapse of communism, its turnover, product range of computer casings and even the names of senior executives. Nothing before 1991, though. It's as though that doesn't exist.

By now it's nearly four in the afternoon and we check in at six. We've still got to get back to Pension Eszterházy to get our bags.

"Tell you what," I say to Mutti, "We should go straight for the airport." I've only got a few *forints* left, and I don't think Mutti's got any. There's no time to start hunting for Kovács.

"This is our last chance," she says. "We find the apartment." And in case I'd missed the point. "Kovács's apartment."

"I know, but let's be realistic. That place may have belonged to him back in the 1940s, but what are the chances of him still being there? Virtually nil. We might as well skip it."

"No."

"Don't be stubborn. If we miss the flight, we can't get home, and I imagine you've had more than enough of the airport police." As the car rumbles over uneven tarmac, she sits there brooding like an old toad. Out of the corner of my eye, I can see her fiddling with the map, in that petulant way of hers, folding it one way and another. And then she suddenly yelps something at the driver, and he swerves to the curb.

"It's here," says Mutti, scrambling to get out of the car. "Well, just round the corner. Come on, Elizabeth, please." We take a couple more turnings and then stop. I pay the driver. That's it. Finito. We have now got no cash, no travellers' cheques and just over an hour and a half to get to the airport.

"This had better be good," I warn her. At the corner we check the name of the road. Mutti's right, we are only a few yards away from Kovács's last known address. As we walk along the pavement, noting building numbers and names, each heart beat thuds in my ears. The apartment block is still there, curvy art nouveau lines still evident, despite that now familiar exhausted, tattered look.

"Do you recognise this place?" I ask. Mutti nods, throwing her cigarette butt into a drain, and pocketing the holder, as she marches through the door. Inside, what was once an elegant stairwell has been vandalised by the addition of an old-fashioned cage lift. It clatters to the ground floor, we get in, and it starts hauling us up noisily. My hand finds Mutti's. Hers feels warm and dry, while mine is cold and sweaty. We get out at the third floor. Before ringing the bell, she takes out her powder compact and gives herself a couple of quick dabs. Then she pulls herself up to full height. The door is opened by a young woman in tight jeans and a red jumper. She takes a cigarette from the corner of her lipsticked mouth to say, "*Igen*?"

Mutti says something in a low voice, about Kovács. There's a mention of her own maiden name. The young woman looks doubtful. She makes to shut the door, then seems to have second thoughts and calls into the flat. Leaving the door half-open, she retreats inside. We can hear her in conversation with somebody else, an older woman whose mottled voice echoes down the passage. Mutti flushes, and she nods to herself. A few moments later, an elderly woman in a flowery apron creaks towards the door. She gives us a suspicious look, before asking Mutti a question. Again, I catch the word Kovács, but everything else is just a clatter of Hungarian vowel sounds.

Whatever Mutti has said, it has an amazing effect. The old woman claps her hands together, and lets out a babble of verbiage beginning with the only Hungarian I know.

"*Ó Istenem, istenem.*" Oh God, Oh God. She seems rather in awe of Mutti, taking her hand in hers and bending forward and back in a worshipful kind of way as though she is honoured to bits at our presence. We are ushered into the front room, to sit on heavy, forbidding armchairs while the old lady hobbles excitedly into the kitchen. After a few minutes filled by creaking and jangling as well as a constant stream of chatter, she comes back with a tray of cake and soda water. The china plate stands on a white lace cloth, along with silver spoons and cake forks of exactly the kind Mutti would think *de rigueur*.

It's a long time since breakfast and my hand shakes as I help myself while our hostess chatters away, wiping her hands on her apron while we eat. Mutti keeps up the conversation, turning pink and then pale by turns. Not knowing what they are banging on about is killing me, especially as Mutti is giving me meaningful looks. The moment there's a pause, she turns to me.

"Kovács is her brother. She hasn't seen him for years, but they write." She stops to listen, nodding. "He lives in London. For forty years."

"He what?"

"London."

"Where in London?"

"I don't know, not clear."

"Well, if her letters are reaching him, she must have the address."

The old lady takes a plastic covered book from a bureau, flicking through its alphabetical pages, and showing it to Mutti, and saying, "*Vestempersted.*" We must look blank. She gives us a quizzical look, as if it's us who are stupid.

"Sorry?" I say. Mutti squints at the book.

"W–E–S–T– H–A–M–P–S–T–E–A–D," she spells out. Mutti looks puzzled.

"West Hampstead?" I ask.

"*Igen,*" says the old lady, nodding with pride. "*Vestempersted.*" She turns to a shelving unit in the corner, where some aging post cards are on display, and brings one to show us. Buckingham Palace from around 1960, complete with guards in red jackets and bearskins, the colours faded from years' exposure to sunlight. The old lady points to it, with pride. "*Vestempersted,*" she repeats, nodding enthusiastically.

"The man who took your father's factory lives in West Hampstead?"

"He may not have taken it, we don't know."

"That's not what you said this morning."

The old lady is holding out the plate of cake to me, smiling and urging me to have another piece. It is a cloyingly rich confection, but I need the energy so I tuck in, allowing Mutti more time to prise information from our hostess.

As we emerge back onto the pavement, I check my watch. Apparently Kovács's sister claimed to know nothing about the factory. Ignorance is safer, I imagine, to someone who has spent their adult life under communism, and what I imagine is constant fear of the secret police. It's five o'clock, which means we have just one hour to get back to Pension Eszterházy, grab our bags and leg it. At the bottom of my bag I've found a few coins, but not enough for a cab. We head for the main road, hoping to spot a bus heading roughly in our direction.

Mutti makes a show of setting off energetically, as though she believes positive thinking can get her there. But it's only a few minutes before her swollen legs have pulled her to a halt. Just when I'm wondering how much washing up you have to do to earn an air ticket, she starts laughing.

Then I see it. Coming towards us is a horse-drawn carriage, adorned with brightly coloured ribbons with pom-poms. She waves the driver to a halt.

"We can't go in that. We've got nothing to pay him with, and it'll be no quicker than walking anyway."

But she's already in the carriage. I scramble in to keep up with her as it moves off, getting bounced into the plush, plum-coloured upholstered seat. Opposite me, Mutti sits there like the Queen Mother greeting her people. She puts a cigarette in her holder, looking pleased with herself, and conducting some kind of regal conversation with the driver.

"Don't worry, darling. I make a deal. Will be most reasonable."

Now I'm going backwards along the avenue, and the bumpety motion is beginning to make me feel sick. Mutti points out the Hungarian Academy of Sciences, something called the Gresham Palace, and the glories of the gothic, baroque and Romanesque parliament I've already heard so much about. She turns her face up to the sun.

"Isn't this wonderful?"

"Not if we miss the plane," I say. The driver keeps up a commentary in Hungarian, with Mutti interrupting him now and then, and they share some kind of private joke. When we get to the Pension, we get out. I open my handbag with trepidation, wondering if he'll take a few quid in sterling. He waves his hand at me.

"*Nem,*" he says, shaking his head and then rattling something off to Mutti. She says something back to him, smiling her regal smile and shaking his hand.

"He refuses to accept any payment." I shake the man's hand, puzzled. As he drives off, Mutti says, "Gypsy family." She gives a dark nod implying some kind of fellowhood in suffering.

Mutti persuades Madame Eszterházy to sub us money for a cab to the airport, promising we'll cable it back from London. By the time we hit the departure lounge, the rich cake we ate at Kovács's sister's is churning round in my stomach. Mutti fusses round, getting me water to drink, and dousing me in refreshing travel spray.

Once we're on the plane, I push back my seat, but images of Kovács' sister and the fascist boot boys float round in my mind. I can hear the echoing sound of footsteps on a tiled floor, and "*Ó Istenem, istenem,*" repeated over and over again in my grandmother's voice. I open my eyes to find the air hostess standing there with a tray. The paprika fumes from the hot food make me feel like gagging. But Mutti tells her to put it in front of me, and proceeds to polish off both meals. Then she strokes my forehead like she used to when I was a little girl.

"I phoned him," she says.

"Who?" I ask. My brain grinds slowly, like a machine without oil.

"Kovács." I jolt upright, narrowly avoiding a spillage into my lap. "You phoned him?"

"From the airport. When you were resting."

"You should have waited for me!" I'm fuming. "What did you say?"

"I just asked if we can meet," she says.

"And?"

"*Ja*, he sees us. Tomorrow." She takes a sip of her coffee. "And maybe we take you to the doctor?"

"I'm not that ill – tummy upset. It's been a difficult couple of days. Better tomorrow."

"I think it will take longer than that. Nine months is the usual time." Oh God, *Ó Istenem*. Why didn't I think of that?

"You think I'm..."

"Do *you* think?" I think back over the past month. "I'd better call Dave," I groan.

"*Mazel tov*, darling." She takes a forkful of dessert.

But it may not be that simple.

"You know, I think is best to stick to white or yellow until it is born. Don't you think?" I give her a weary nod, as she continues, "You want that piece of cake?" Between mouthfuls of creamy gateau, Mutti expatiates on the relative merits of different sorts of buggies and prams. Sounds as though she's been researching it for some time. I'm still trying to do the maths.

Chapter 26

I wake feeling sick and shattered. Leaving Mutti to unpack our bags, I drag myself into the office stopping only to buy a coffee and throw up in the ladies' toilet. I make damn sure I'm on the phone to East Midlands police at the exact moment when Sarah sweeps in. My desk is a construction site of files, folders and ordnance survey maps reflecting how bloody busy I've been. But each time I put the phone down, the same question pops into my head. Who is the father?

I work through lunch, so by mid-afternoon I've made a good start on the research and the script is underway. Looking up for a moment, I register a one-line newsflash: Nachmann

Cohen has been relased without charge. Why am I not surprised? I fling off an email to Jenkins and at the last moment decide to cc in his boss. But it's hardly worth expending any more emotional effort on it, I've got bigger stuff on my mind right now. By five in the afternoon I'm making enough headway to slip away without any harm and head home to pick up Mutti. But as I'm driving up Kilburn High Road, there's a niggling thought in the back of my mind. Bruchi's killer is still out there.

West Hampstead is all posh delis and smart furniture shops. We cruise the narrow roads of terraced houses looking for the address while Mutti dabs on some powder. It's not that difficult to find, up some invincible looking granite stairs, and then there's that terrible moment when he opens the door. A distinguished if frail looking elderly man in a cravat. There's a frisson of recognition on both sides, but also a kind of wariness in Mutti. They just stand there looking at each other for what seems ages. And I think what have we come for? To get an old man to sign away rights to a property he doesn't own? Suddenly the whole project seems ridiculous. I want to run away, back to the safety of my flat. But he greets my mother with a stiff "*Szervusz,*" holding her hand for a long time and shaking his head as if he doesn't quite believe she's real. She doesn't resist, but turns her eyes away. Then suddenly he lets go and ushers us in, with a dramatic Prussian-style bow.

In a spacious lounge, the floor is criss-crossed with Persian rugs. A pair of deep sofas face each other, flanked by table lamps on artful ceramic bases. Mutti and I navigate our way round a coffee table piled with large format art books, and sink into one of the sofas. It's the kind of upholstery that doesn't let you sit up straight. Kovács himself chooses instead to sit in a high-backed leather armchair to one side of us.

"So ladies, I must say, this is incredible." He speaks English with hardly a trace of accent. "I don't know where to start. It is a shock."

"Really?" I say. "Maybe it was a shock you've been half expecting." If he catches the anger in my voice, he ignores it.

"When you are my age, you think you've seen everything," he replies. "But to meet someone again after *fifty* years, that is strange and unsettling, when we have all been through such a lot together. No?"

"You remember my mother, then?" He raises a sardonic eyebrow.

"What do you think?"

He says something in Hungarian to my mother, and they both laugh. And then turning to me, "As a young man, I worked for your mother's family for many years. The children called me *Kovács bácsi* – Uncle Kovács"

"So I understand."

"It was a big part of my life." He takes a silver cigarette box from the coffee table, offers them round, takes one himself and makes an elaborate pantomime of lighting up. Still standing, he takes a deep drag, and blows smoke through rounded lips.

"We went through so much, you know. And I did my best to – I think – help your mother's family in very difficult times. Dangerous times. I'm sure she will remember this. And of course, your mother was a very beautiful and talented girl. You must know this. How could I forget her?"

Mutti's expression shifts. She usually loves compliments, but now she looks uneasy. Kovács starts pacing around as he talks.

"Your family survived the war. You know that three-quarters of Hungarian Jews were liquidated between March and July 1944 after Eichmann marched into Budapest? But your mother and grandmother always managed to avoid being deported. That in itself is remarkable, no?" I nod uncertainly, wondering what he's getting at. Mutti's shared very little of this history with me. Every time it comes up she gets drunk or bursts into tears, so I've never really got to the bottom of what happened to her.

Kovács stubs out his cigarette in a large marble ashtray. "And then suddenly I received a call from my sister, describing your visit all these years later. The last time I saw your grandmother and mother was the day before they got on the train to leave Hungary. At first, I thought this was a fantasy or a dream. It didn't seem possible. And then, an hour later, her voice on the phone. Unmistakable. You read these things in the newspapers, but you never expect them to happen in real life."

"But the war and what followed was so – disruptive – in Hungary," I say. "These meetings years later do happen – when people find out by a series of coincidences what happened to their families, friends and..." I trail off.

"Servants?" Kovács finishes the sentence for me. "I must say I find your generation ridiculously reticent about the master-servant relationship. In my opinion it is a very honest transaction. And honourable on both sides."

"But it wasn't something that you pursued once you'd got to London?" I look around the room and its sophisticated décor.

"By the time I got here, I hadn't been in that kind of position for many years. The comrades disapproved of servants nearly as much as you. But it turned out that my former profession was a very useful introduction to the workings of private enterprise. London has an endless appetite for chauffeuring and taxi services, and this was my passport into the world of business. Of course, luck played a large part." He bends over to pick up another cigarette, turning it over in his hands and tapping both ends on the edge the ashtray, as if to allow us a moment to appreciate the lush furnishings.

Mutti colours up, a confusion of emotions rippling across her face, reflecting the internal battle that is taking place. But still she says nothing. He meets her eye with a quizzical glance. And for a moment, I could swear some kind of understanding passes between them.

"I'm not sure what my mother told you on the telephone," I say. "But we came looking for you to discuss another business. My grandfather's business in Budapest."

"Yes, my sister mentioned this to me."

"Do you remember his factory?"

"Of course. I drove your grandfather there every day."

"My mother and I were in Budapest last week, and we discovered something very surprising to us."

"Yes?"

"The ownership of the property was transferred to you in the 1930s."

"Ah, yes."

"So you don't deny it?"

"Why would I want to deny such a thing. It is a matter of historic record, as you say."

"How did it happen?"

"This kind of thing was very common at the time. Anti-Semitic laws prohibited Jews from owning companies, so many people transferred their businesses in name to a friendly gentile. I was trusted by your grandfather, and was happy to take this role on his behalf."

"The problem is that my mother now wishes to re-claim that property. Before we can go any further, we have to establish prior claim." I open the file of documents and photographs and spread them out on the coffee table. "Mr Kovács, I need to prove that it was ours." He pays no attention to my photos, but lights the cigarette he's been toying with for some minutes. He carries on pacing around the room as if thinking through a chain of consequences.

"And for that you need something from me?"

261

"We need you to confirm that the property was transferred to you as a formality. My grandfather did not sell it to you, no money changed hands. So morally, it still belonged to my grandfather, and not you."

"Really?" Kovács gives a theatrical look of surprise. "Will that help? I mean legally it did belong to me, after all." I can't tell what game he's playing.

"But after the war, the property *should* have been transferred back to my grandfather."

"Sadly he perished, like so many others."

"My *grandmother* did not perish. As you say, she survived. You probably know much more than me about where and how, inside the ghetto or out.

"I do know, of course I know. How many times did I intervene to save your grandmother and mother during the war, after the war? What do you think? I knew the right people, I knew what they wanted. I kept them happy, they all seemed to like the various goods I managed to procure. Unfortunately my influence was not enough to help your poor grandfather, and for that I will forever be sorry.

"But why do you think your mother and her mother were never taken to Auschwitz? Have you ever asked yourself that? How did they manage after the death of your father? Where did they get the black market papers your grandmother needed to get out of Hungary with Aranca?"

I'm not getting anything from Mutti, so I say, "I'm sure my family have a great deal to be grateful to you, Mr Kovács. But what did happen to the property after the war?"

"At first we allowed ourselves to hope that the old life would return, but when our hopes were dashed and the communist regime began to take hold of our country."

Mutti looks crushed by the weight of the memories Kovács has stirred up. There's gratitude in her face – it sounds as though our family owes him a lot. But it's at war with something else. I'm in the dark, but as she seems unable to say anything at the moment, I have to speak for both of us.

"I'm sure the family owed you a lot Mr Kovács, but not every last thing they owned. My mother is here now. She is the rightful heir to the property." He shrugs, and sits down on his chair, bringing it close to me.

"Miss Mueller, we have to go back to what happened after the war. The Russians came, you must remember that Budapest was very chaotic for months, years. So much had been destroyed. Towards the end, everything ground to a halt. So many of the buildings were lying in ruins. Nothing was working – the things that we call infrastructure nowadays. Those were not in place. You couldn't just look someone up in the phone book and expect to find them."

"So what happened to it?"

"The factory? Ah yes, a good question. After the so-called 'liberation' things began to get going again, though it was slow. I found my way over to the premises. And there I found things in a pretty poor state. The building had been shelled in a couple of places, so there was wreckage everywhere and a great hole in the roof. Even the sound parts were full of dust and debris. Some of the machinery had been taken by looters. But as I was looking round, I discovered that some of the other former employees were gathering there. They hoped to get the enterprise going again. And that's what we did."

"But my grandfather was dead, so who did it belong to?"

"Legally, as you say, it belonged to me. But we were not concerned with such things. It was more important to get into production. To get things going. We wanted life to get back to normal, as it used to be."

"Did it?"

"By 1948, we were doing OK. It felt like an enormous feat.

To build the enterprise back up from nothing, after what we had been through. And now we were creating something, and providing for over a hundred families. Quite an achievement, don't you think?"

"Yes of course. But what happened after that?" He ignores my question and carries on with his story.

"Soon the Soviets were tightening their grip on the apparatus of state. Our factory was nationalised. No compensation. We were to continue working there, but now we were employees within a vast bureaucracy. And eventually, just as I had helped your mother and grandmother to leave the country – it was possible to get hold of papers if you knew who to pay – I managed to get over the border, and made my way to Paris."

"But at the time it was nationalised, the property still nominally belonged to you."

"Yes."

"It's a long shot. But we are hoping..."

"I understand, you want to claim the property back. I did look into the matter myself some years ago. You are very welcome to inspect the paperwork." At the mention of paperwork, I turn to the documents that I've laid out, and try to pull out the most relevant ones.

"If you would just help us and, yes, any papers you have would be helpful." He doesn't look at the contents of our file though, but carries on.

"Miss Mueller, soon after the collapse of the Berlin Wall, the business was sold off to a Russian businessman, for just over $5,000 in today's money." He pauses, looking bored. "You were recently in Budapest, did you see the factory?"

"Just briefly. It looked very successful – sparkling and spotless."

"Precisely. It is now a very successful enterprise manufacturing computer casings, as you probably know. In today's money it is worth several million dollars."

"But it is rightly ours, and we should be able to get it back, surely we are entitled to something."

"You can't get the property back, you can make a claim for financial restitution – and believe me there are many hoops to jump through."

"It would be justice."

"You would get a very small amount of money, not much worth to you. More of a token really – but it means a state struggling to overcome the dreadful legacy of communism loses just a little bit more? Is that what you want?"

"I've heard all those arguments before and quite frankly that's not our problem. The Hungarian State didn't do much to protect my family. We owe them nothing."

"I see. Well, maybe that's understandable." His face says otherwise.

"Not everybody has been so lucky as you, Mr Kovács. My mother needs the cash, however little it may be." Mutti flashes an angry look straight at me. We're sitting in the sumptuous home of her former servant, and now I've admitted she's broke. Humiliating hardly covers it.

"You know, Miss Mueller – can I call you Elizabeth? Let us not forget that there are many, many people in Hungary less lucky than either me or your mother."

I'm not in the mood for a discourse on relative prosperity, and I'm not prepared to take lectures from this man, there's something creepy about him. By his own admission he was supplying black market goods to the Nazis during the war. That probably makes him a collaborator, and in no position to take the moral high ground. "And what about the sanctity of the master-servant relationship you spoke of so highly," I snap. "Wouldn't my grandfather have wanted you to do your utmost to help my mother?"

265

"We go." Mutti is standing.

"Young lady, there is nothing I can do."

"We go," Mutti repeats, but louder this time.

"But we're just discussing—"

"Enough." She adds something in Hungarian, and Kovács raises an eyebrow. Her face is red, a tear threatening the corner of one eye, her breathing heavy. I pick up my coat and bag, and take Mutti by the arm. She looks fragile as porcelain.

"It's all an act. It's rubbish. He is a disgusting man. A thief, a spy, a liar. You heard what he did during the war – after. He had power, because of who he knew. You ask him. He thinks I don't remember, but how could I forget what he did to. To me. To me." Tears are streaming down her mottled face, cutting a path through her face powder.

"Your mother's memory is playing tricks with her. I think she's confusing me with someone else. I think it is indeed better if you leave."

I start pushing the documents back into their tatty folder as fast as I can.

"You are getting above yourself," screams Mutti at Kovács. I grab onto her to make sure she doesn't fall as I hustle her down the granite stairs. The door slams, and we're on the pavement holding tight onto each other, her body quaking with tears.

"Liar, liar, liar."

I guide her into the car and back to my place as soon as I can. I make a pot of strong coffee. Instead of sweetener, Mutti loads sugar into her cup. She looks shocked. No, it's more than that. She's traumatised.

"What did Kovács do that was so terrible?" I ask.

"*Ach*...what does it matter? There's no point talking about it now." A sour late afternoon sun squeezes its way through the half open curtains. I put my hand on hers. I wish I could read her face, to work out what it is.

"He's a liar," she says.

"But what's he lying about and what really happened?"

She shrugs.

"Mutti, we can't go any further with this if you don't tell me what's going on." She sighs. "It is a fool who trusts his servants."

"What are you talking about?"

"Old Hungarian saying my mother used to use. It means you should always check up on your servants. They watch you and know you. You should watch them too, because they know too much about you. You don't even notice them."

"So that honourable master-servant relationship Kovács was talking about?"

"Rubbish – they are waiting for their chance. That's all. If something's missing, look in the servant's quarters. My father trusted his servants too much. See what happened. My mother knew. She kept the larder under lock and key."

"I think that's rather patronising to people who have to work for their living. Some are trustworthy, and some aren't."

"Their interests are *never* the same as yours."

"Yeah but Mutti, that's the equivalent of the *Daily Mail* saying watch the nanny, she's going to steal your husband."

"*Ja*. You've never had to deal with such people."

"Well, maybe it's lucky that we can't afford servants any more."

She nods.

"What now? How are we going to deal with the troublesome servant?"

"Maybe it's time to stop."

"But we've come so far. We've found out so much."

"Thank you, darling, for coming with me. It was lovely, really. Much nicer than I thought it would be. But I'm tired. I have a rest now." It's true that she looks utterly exhausted and hunched as she makes her unsteady way towards the spare room. Soon I hear her half-snore, half-shout in restless sleep.

It's nearly six o'clock but I drive back towards work anyway, to make up for the time I've lost. Passing through Camden Town, all that stuff about servants is re-playing round my head in a loop. What a different world my mother comes from. What was it she said? Your servants know you and watch you. Well we don't have housekeepers, chauffeurs and maids any more. If only it was still like that, solving Bruchi Friedmann's murder would be as simple as a game of *Cluedo*. It was the butler, in the pantry with the iron piping. Ha. They watch you. Who watches us nowadays? People have cleaners once a week – twice if they're flash. A nanny perhaps, a child minder otherwise. I suppose you could always dial in the man who comes to mend the dishwasher, the service wash lady at the launderette. The modern day servants. I'm not sure if any of this helps. It's about as much use as Mutti's stock of trite Austro-Hungarian proverbs.

When I get home late that night, she's doing a crossword at the dining room table, and finishing off the last of the coffee. The gargantuan suitcase is still there in my spare room. I was rather hoping to get her on her way to Cardiff, now that we've seen Kovács and there's not much else to do. I'm going round to Dave's later, there's so much to catch up on.

"Come on, Mutti, if you really want to get home, I could drop you off at Paddington tomorrow morning on my way to work. How about it?" She's smiles a bit too broadly. "Do you want me to help with the packing?" She fiddles with a bit of the foil from her cigarette packet, flattening it out on the table.

"I can't go."

"What do you mean? Aren't you feeling up to it?"

"Nowhere to go to."

"Don't worry about the house, it'll be fine when you get there. Might be a bit dusty, but you can spend tomorrow straightening it out."

"I've let it out."

"You've done what?"

"How do you think I got the money for Budapest? I've let out the house for six months."

"So where are you going to live?"

She looks at me.

"Here? This is the only place you've got to live? For the next six months?" She nods. Of course. The outsized suitcase, with its ample array of sartorial options. Not even my mother takes such a comprehensive wardrobe for a weekend.

"Why didn't you tell me?"

"Wasn't the right moment."

It turns out Mutti's let out her house to a friend of a friend. The rent will allow her to live comfortably for the next six months. In practical terms, I have to congratulate her. In emotional terms, it's a complete disaster. My adolescent nightmare has returned.

I haven't got the heart to tell her off. In her place I'd do the same. I leave her getting ready for bed and head for Dave's place. There's no reply so I let myself in.

I look around the empty loft. Camera bags are stowed to one side. The sleeping space is neat, candy-striped duvet cover fluffed up and spread across the bed, the four pillows leaning, in symmetrical piles next to the headboard. But where is he? And why hasn't he been answering the phone?

The answering machine is flashing red. I hesitate for the merest fraction of a second before pressing play.

"Hi Darling." It's me calling from the airport. "Are you there?" I delete it, not wanting to hear my voice prattling on in the echoing studio. Beep.

"Hi Dave," a woman's voice. "It's Naomi here." I don't know a Naomi. Neither does Dave. As far as I know. "Is six o'clock any good for you?" For what? I play the message again. On his desk there's also a note on a filing card. "Naomi" and a phone number. Probably the picture editor of that women's magazine who was going to give him some work. Hold on a sec, wasn't she called Zizi? The phone rings but I don't answer. The answering machine clicks into action,. I stand there, feeling like an eavesdropper. But whoever it is doesn't leave a message.

Any moment, I tell myself, he'll be back. I wait and wait, wandering round the dark, echoing warehouse, staring into the gloom. A police siren wails in the distance, getting louder as it passes the window. As it recedes away, there are footsteps on the stairs, but like the siren they go past and disappear into the night. By the time I decide to quit my vigil, the late summer sun is dropping behind the scruffy Dalston skyline. I get back in the car and go back home, creeping up the stairs and trying to open and lock the door without too much noise.

It's ten-thirty and Mutti's snoring is loud enough to be heard from the door of the flat. I can't imagine where her head's at after the encounter with Kovács. Oddly enough, I'm not tired, so I start pottering around in an aimless way. The horrible nausea that has stayed with me since Hungary is welling up in my throat. Throwing myself down on the sofa, I find my face is wet, though I didn't realise I'd been crying. My face is burning, my eyes swollen. I bury my head into the cushions and blub as quietly as I can. I don't know how long I'm there on the sofa, but it's pitch dark outside when I get up. Tea tastes metallic and foul, and I end up eating three stale digestive biscuits. While they are in my mouth, the nausea abates, but soon after I've swallowed, it comes back, worse. The musty taste lingers. I look out at the grey traffic backed up on Camden Road, under a lugubrious sheet of cloud that skims the rooftops.

The pregnancy. My pregnancy. I think the words and they sound strange. I haven't even stopped to think about it until now. The fact is that *I don't know who the fucking father is*. How could I be so stupid, so feckless, like some silly teenager? I've got myself into a god awful mess like a character from a soap opera. Meanwhile, my mother is asleep in the spare room, an unwelcome semi-permanent guest. It feels as though I'm stuck. Still umbilically tied to her. Story of my life.

My child is now just a microscopic bunch of multiplying cells. What will she think of me in eighteen years' time? I run my hand over my abdomen. It's usually tight and toned. If I ever find a suggestion of bulge I do another hundred sit-ups. But now it feels tender, and there's a hint of a curve. She's under there, my child. And if she judges me as harshly as I judge my own mother, then she'll leave home as soon as she's old enough and never want to speak to me again. At least Mutti has an excuse. What have I got? Raised by middle class (though dotty) parents in apparent financial security, with no greater threat to my existence or theirs than an attack of the measles. Yet I've still managed to mess things up.

I've spent years seething about Mutti's madness. Decades. How self-indulgent that now seems. OK, maybe it's true she hasn't been the perfect mother. She cooks and cleans as though it'll be her salvation, but the drink made her impossible. Well, maybe it's not just the drink.

Isn't it about time I forgave her for being a crap mother, now that I'm about to become a crap mother myself? I barely even know who the father is, and you can't have a worse start than that. I was arrogant enough to stand in judgement in her, just because I was the one picking up the pieces and carrying her handbag. Maybe it's she who should be forgiving me. For disloyalty. For being patronising and superior when I had no right. It's hot and sticky in here.

And then, as I unlock the French windows, I notice a lithe figure in jeans, walking downhill towards the flat. I go out and meet Dave on the stairs.

"Your eyes are red," he says.

"Jet lag."

"It's only a two-hour time difference. You can't get jet lag."

"I mean I'm just tired. You would be too, if you'd spent forty-eight hours being dragged round Budapest by my mad mother. Listening to her ranting on about the servant problem."

He empties a bag of food out in the kitchen and puts on some whispering jazz track which won't wake Mutti. I'm not allowed to get up or help, while Dave tidies up and makes a late supper. He warms up the soup Mutti has left on the stove while we talk in undertones about Michael and the fascist demo, and about Kovács. We creep around like parents with a sleeping child in the next room.

While he's taking out the rubbish, I take a sly look at his phone and see he's made three calls to Naomi in the past two days. I manage to chuck it back onto the coffee table just in time when I hear his footsteps coming back through the hallway.

"They sound like a couple of cool guys," he says, wiping his hands on his jeans as he comes back into the flat.

"Who?"

"Those guys Schmulli and Aaron."

"Oh yeah, they are," I say.

"I'd like to meet them."

"Really?" After we've eaten the soup with the cheeses, fresh crusty bread and creamy French butter, my exhaustion returns.

"I'm going to turn in," I say to Dave, who is clearing up. "I'll be fast asleep by the time you come to bed."

"Well, I may go home, actually."

"Why?"

"I wouldn't want to upset your mother by putting in a surprise appearance at breakfast. Anyway, you'll sleep better without me. "

"No I won't. I missed you. I want to know you're there even when I'm dreaming. And we can have breakfast together tomorrow."

"I know," he kisses me on the back of the neck. "Breakfast for three. Very romantic. But I've got stuff to do tomorrow, and I imagine you'll be heading for the office at the crack of dawn."

"What stuff have you got to do?"

"Just stuff."

I wake up early with my mother's voice jangling in my ears. I can see her again, face to face with the fascist thugs on the Budapest street, and there she is, sitting in the ridiculous horse-drawn carriage looking radiant and smug. There's something in this whole thing that's not right. It's like a crossword clue I should know the answer to but clangs around in my head. Where's that red velvet photograph album? I find the ballet girl shots, and study her face, watching her grow as I turn the heavy pages. Silk dresses, and sleek plaits.

"Liar, liar, liar." What did she mean ?

I'm looking for a shot of Kovács in his chauffeur's uniform. I can't be imagining it. I'm sure I have seen that before but there's nothing here. Instead, I find myself looking at an image of a young Mutti playing with a dog inside the apartment. It's all carefree innocence. She's so painfully beautiful, with shiny auburn hair tumbling down her back. And that's when I spot it.

I go into the spare room, where she's still asleep, and shake her by the shoulder.

"Mutti, wake up. I've just noticed something a bit odd."

"What is it?" She turns over and rubs her eyes. "What's the time?"

"Never mind the time. In the photograph album there's a shot inside your family apartment in Budapest."

273

"*Ja*. Mmm, lots."

"Yes, but on this one you can see some paintings on the walls."

"*Ach* darling, we had so many." She's sitting up in bed, rubbing her eyes. "Have you made some coffee?"

Chapter 27

I'm on the way to work when Dave calls.

"Will you come round to dinner at my place tomorrow?"

"Are you sure you want me to? You didn't exactly hang around last night. I started wondering whether I had BO."

"I had stuff to do."

"So you said."

"Don't come over all spiky with me."

"Well, I've been away, even if it was just a couple of nights. You come over, cook dinner then disappear. What's going on?"

"I was preoccupied. Tomorrow, I want to cook you a lovely meal, and talk."

"Are you sure? I mean, I can open a can of beans and watch TV with Mutti if it's too much trouble. She seems to have taken up permanent residence, so no worries about me getting lonely."

"Don't be stupid. Be there at seven-thirty."

"Do you want me to bring anything?"

"No, nothing. But you could wear a dress if you like."

"A dress? Is anybody else going to be there?"

"No, just you and me."

"Is it something sexual?"

"No."

"Any kind of dress? I mean, should it be a ballgown? Or will my usual cocktail dress do?"

"Just be there."

After work, instead of going straight home to change, I detour via Stoke Newington nick. DI Jenkins meets me at reception and takes me up to the station canteen for a cup of tea.

He understands that this is personal, and that not a word must get back to my office. He's friendly but guarded. I explain the business about the factory in Budapest and the family history as briefly as I can, and how the trail has now moved to West Hampstead. I then explain my new suspicions about Kovács. He says it might be possible to get an opinion from the specialist art squad. It all sounds like a bit of a long shot.

As I'm getting up to leave, he says, "By the way it appears that Mr Nachmann Cohen has left the country."

"Oh sh— dear. Where to?"

"Flight to Tel Aviv, in the first instance. After that, who knows?"

"Does that mean you can't get him back?"

"Not if we don't know where he is. But all that's pretty immaterial unless we get some more solid evidence against him."

Later that evening I go round to Dave's, as promised, leaving Mutti happily watching some kind of cop show on TV. The air in the road outside his place feels like a ripe fig, ready to burst. The heat of the pavement percolates through my thin sandals. As I enter the stairwell, I'm hit by a wall of cool air. Then, further up it melds with notes of roasting meat twisted together on the breeze with saxophone riffs. The sounds and smells intensify across the canvasses and mannequins, and past the space heaters that fill the loft. On the dining table is a fresh, white cloth, and in the middle a lovely old painted jug overflowing with the bulbous heads of pink and red ranunculus. A pair of silver candlesticks complete the tableaux. It's an oasis of order amid the arty assemblage of junkyard trophies. Dave's wearing a blue and white-striped chef's apron, as he labours over the antique gas stove.

"This looks romantic," I say. "What's changed?"

"You'll find out."

"Don't be so mysterious. Tell me what's going on."

"Be patient. Good dress."

"I try my best."

"Sit down and relax. There's a packet of posh crisps in the basket."

"Are you sure you don't want any help?"

"Sit down and do what you're told."

"Shall I light the candles?"

"Don't you dare."

I flop into an armchair, and check my phone. There's a voicemail from DI Jenkins. He's been in touch with the art squad. They'll call us next week. I switch it off, and wander over to the studio space. On the desk are a pile of fine photographic prints. The portraits of Hasids from Stamford Hill. I leaf through them. They are formal, seated or standing – fur hats, black dressing-gown style coats, lapels gleaming. Full length ones showing guys wearing tall black leather cavalry boots, and others with white stockings and knickerbockers. The full range of perplexing and mesmerising variations of Hasidic dress. They all look into the lens, direct and frank, individuals and pairs, men, women and children. One family spreads up the stairs, children of ascending ages grouped around the parents. Enough pictures here to make a good show, almost enough for a book.

"I get the long lens stuff, fair enough, you don't have to ask for permission," I say. "But how did you persuade people like Stern to let you – to let you take photos and all that? Isn't it against everything they stand for? It's taken a massive diplomatic broadside for me to get into the community. How come you just walk in and they are ready to pose for you?"

"Who says I just walked in? I spent a lot of time talking to people about what I wanted. And it's all about context, Elizabeth. I think you can overdo the secrecy thing about this community. I'm not asking them to go on network television to talk about some kind of horrible and highly sensitive murder. No fingers are going to be pointed. I asked respectfully about portraits, talked to them about showing the pictures mentioned a gallery, maybe – don't get your hopes up – a book one day. All quite low key. And of course not everybody wants to be photographed, but that would be the same anywhere. As it happens, there seem to be enough who actually wanted me to show their community *at its best*. They love it."

A sweet, yeasty smell infuses the warm air, as daylight begins to fade. I put the photos back, and return to the dining table. Dave brings over a heavy breadboard with two large loaves on it. The baking smell is intense. The music has stopped.

"Two whole loaves for the two of us seems a lot. Gosh they're plaited. Like *chollah*. Nice touch, where did you get them?"

"Grodzinski's in Stamford Hill."

"The real McCoy then? Can I have a bit, I'm starving." I pick up the bread knife.

"Not so fast, there. Hang on."

"What's the problem? We're not going to run out, are we?" Dave puts down an ornate salt cellar. "Is there some butter?"

"No butter. Behave yourself."

"C'mon Dave, be a *mensch*."

"That's exactly what I am trying to be." He brings over a bottle of wine.

"Have you got some glasses?" I twist round the bottle to see what it is. The label is familiar. Palwin No. Ten. Hold on a second.

"Kosher *kiddush* wine? Are you mad? You know this stuff tastes like cough mixture? It's not designed for pleasure. It's not the Jewish equivalent to Rioja, you know." If he's trying to latch on to some tasteful ethnic buzz, he's got it wrong here. But Dave's gone through the gap in the furniture, to the kitchen. Opening a dresser door, he takes out a goblet. Just the one. He brings it back to the dining table, and sets it down. It looks newly-polished, its solid silver and engraved Hebrew letters gleam in the fading light.

"Why have you got this stuff?"

"It's Friday night," he says.

"You aren't answering the question. What's the *kiddush* wine for?

"Now let me think," he says. "What's *kiddush* wine usually used for?"

"Who's making *kiddush*?"

"I am."

"But you can't. You're not even Jewish." He takes a *kippah* out of his pocket, and puts it on his head, with a defiant flourish. "Not *yet* Jewish."

I gasp. It's the worst thing he's ever said to me.

"Is this it? The big thing you wanted to tell me, that I was going to be so happy about?"

"What if it is?"

"Don't be stupid. What happened to my romantic, candlelit meal?"

"Don't be so insulting. It's not stupid, and this is your romantic candlelit, traditional Friday night meal."

"Why on earth would anybody want to be Jewish?"

"That's a bit rich, isn't it? I've spent nearly two years being made to feel like an ignorant heathen by your parents because I'm a *goy*. Meanwhile Mutti's lining up a succession of more suitable candidates behind my back. You think I don't know?"

"But you can't just convert. That's not going to suddenly make her happy."

"It's not just for her."

"You just said it was."

"That's how it started. Not any more." He takes a packet of matches out of his pocket with shaking hands. The box is covered by an ornate mother-of-pearl cover decorated with a Star of David. He places it next to the candles.

"And let me guess," I say. "Has somebody called Naomi got something to do with this?"

"How do you know about Naomi?" It's difficult to explain this without admitting that I've been nosing into Dave's stuff.

"Well it wasn't exactly hidden."

"You've been poking round – you don't trust me."

"It's not like that. I was looking for something else."

"No you weren't. You were checking up on me." There's an angry silence. I'm trying to think my way out.

"What did you find?" he asks.

"A note. And a phone number."

"So what? I have loads of phone numbers and messages."

"A woman's name and a phone number. Why do you think that seemed significant?"

He bangs his fist on the table, so that the breadboard judders. "Nice to know you trust me, then." It's dark now. I sit in the dense silence feeling the weight of my own hypocrisy. And praying that even if Dave knows about Mutti's matchmaking schemes, he has no idea about what really happened with Jon. Because of course it's not *he* who has been unfaithful. I'm sitting here pregnant with what could easily be another man's child. But why do I feel as though I'm the one who's been betrayed? Because he's becoming a different person from the one I signed up for. And that seems far worse.

"OK," I say, "So you haven't been seeing someone else. But you have been sneaking off behind my back to – to change yourself. That's just as bad. Why did it have to be some big secret?"

"It wasn't a secret at all. I've been trying to tell you. But it's beginning to feel as though I'm the least important thing in your life."

"That's not fair."

"Oh no? You put me on hold and then forget about me while you are running round Budapest and Stamford Hill. You don't return my messages, and can't seem to find a window for me in your busy schedule. I'd love to know what it feels like when you really decide to ignore someone."

"So turning all Jewy on me is a ploy to get my attention, is it? Well I'm sorry to spoil the party." I pick up my bag and grab my jacket. I stumble down the stone stairwell, catching a spiky heel on one of the steps. I manage to catch the banister soon enough to stop myself falling, but end up twisting my ankle, so that by the time I get to the bottom I'm hobbling. I can hear Dave calling my name down the stairwell, where the usual smell of rancid urine has now reasserted itself. The echo bounces off the tiled walls and stone steps as I plunge out into the dark of the high road. It's pouring. The heat has burst, releasing a torrent of water from the skies. I hobble my way to the car, splashing my strappy sandals into the puddles that have formed in the dirt-caked pavement. My hair is dripping, and my dress is soaked by the time I've walked the few yards to the car, and there are filthy splashes up the backs of my legs.

Staring out between the swishes of the windscreen wipers, I can't believe I missed all the clues. Dave's interest in the prayers at Dad's funeral, discussing theology with the rabbi. The lunch at Leah's when he knew so much more than he should. It's like one of those pictures that start with a few lines that don't look like anything and then suddenly take shape with the final flourish.

Back at mine, Mutti's doing crosswords in her dressing gown, the television blinking silent in the corner. While she makes me a cup of tea and a cheese sandwich, I towel dry my hair. Outside the rain is gushing down with naked energy, bringing a crash of thunder over our heads.

"He thinks it's so simple," I fume as I change into my dressing gown. "He doesn't realise that it's not possible to *become* a normal Jew, the kind that eats bacon butties at a football match on Saturday afternoon. The only way to convert is by becoming some kind of religious nutter. You can't become *a bit* Jewish."

"So, why don't you find someone who's already Jewish? Enough with all the nonsense."

"I don't need him to be Jewish at all. That was his idea. And he got it from you."

"You'll be happier with someone Jewish."

"No, *you'll* be happier. I don't care."

"You'll have more in common."

"I'd have plenty in common with someone who likes Bob Dylan's songs and Jackie Mason's *shtick*. Better still if they read Phillip Roth and cook Evelyn Rose. You don't actually have to *be* Jewish for any of that."

"So, are you going to tell Dave that?"

"I think it's already gone too far."

"Hasn't he heard about anti-Semitism? What about the persecution? Does he realise what he's getting into?"

"I think that's one of the attractions."

"That's not funny. Not everything is a joke, Elizabeth."

I'm about to answer, but nothing comes out and she gives me one of her looks. I've been found out. It's not as though Mutti's always been Dave's greatest fan, but she knows loyalty when she sees it, and I suddenly feel ashamed. In that moment I have a sudden overview of my relationship with him – on-off, up-down, warm-cold – it's always been about my needs not his. I've given him mixed messages, used him for emotional support when I needed it, dipped in and out of his life when I felt like it, and when he's going through something big, I'm just not there for him. I feel shallow, but don't really know what to do about it. I should apologise, just not tonight. I don't know where to start. So I just snuggle up on the sofa with Mutti, who puts a big, meaty, comforting arm around me. At least she forgives me.

An hour later we are still watching television when the doorbell rings. Or rather buzzes, as the flats are all equipped with an entry system that comes with an angry-sounding beeper. Today it sounds more furious than usual.

"Are you expecting anyone?" asks Mutti.

"At ten o'clock on a Friday night?"

"You know who it is. You can't keep him waiting out there, it's pouring."

I walk over, pick up the handset, and without listening to see who's there, press the door release button.

Dave is sopping. His hair is wet, his tee shirt soggy, and his jeans are the kind of dark blue that denim only goes when it is quite, quite saturated. He comes in, making a damp trail on my cream carpet. He stands there, looking at Mutti and me, silent, belligerent and soaking.

"I get you a towel," says Mutti.

When she's gone he says, "Well?"

"Well what?"

"Why did you just leave like that?"

"I'm sorry, you ambushed me."

"Yeah sure, I ensnared you with roast chicken and *chollah*. Must have been terrifying."

"But why?"

Eyes raised to the heavens. To the god he has found salvation in. "Because I love you, and I want you to be happy."

"You don't need to *convert* to make me happy. I liked you the way you were." He shakes his head, spraying a fine mist of water droplets around him.

"No you didn't. It was when we were in the church I saw it. You said you were scared your parents might be right. That's what did it. I thought yes, OK, if they are right, what can I do about it?"

"But my parents aren't right. You don't have to be Jewish to marry me, I thought we'd established that. I was cool with the quaint country church and the row of podgy bridesmaids. "

"Who are you trying to kid? I saw the look on your face, Elizabeth. That's what made me go back and ask myself what both of us want."

"But it takes years to convert."

"Absolutely. We've got to both live as observant Jews – keep kosher, go to synagogue on Shabbat, the works – and then after two years or maybe more we'll be a happy, Jewish family. And what I've discovered is – it's wonderful, meaningful, rich. And you will too."

"But I don't want to do that. And I can't wait years for you to be Jewish. I'm having a baby. You need to be Jewish now." There, I've said it.

"A baby?" You're not! You are? I can't believe it." Dave's next to me, clasping me in his strong, soggy arms. He's cold and wet to the touch, and he makes a sodden imprint on my dry clothes.

"Careful, don't squeeze the baby."

"Oh God," he lets go suddenly. I laugh, despite my fury.

"It's not that delicate. I think. But it's not going to wait for you to convert."

"Well, it's going to be Jewish anyway, because you are Jewish."

"So it'll be a little Hymie or Rachel anyway."

"B'ruch ha shem."

"You can drop that *B'ruch ha shem* stuff right now. I don't mind you being Jewish, but I'm not marrying some mad *frummer*."

"Please God that our baby will be a little Hymie or Rachel. Am I allowed to say 'Please God'?"

"Certainly not."

Mutti's come back with a towel, and a fresh shirt and pair of jeans from the drawer of Dave's stuff that he keeps here. She puts it down on the coffee table, then stands there as though she can't decide whether to sit down. She perches on the edge of an armchair, and fiddles with an empty cigarette holder.

"David," she says in a voice so quiet it is little more than a whisper. He looks up at her, still beaming. "Is not so easy to become Jewish."

"I know it's not *easy*. But it's straightforward if you observe and study."

"I don't think so."

"I'm very sorry, Aranca, but I think you'll find Rabbi Levi—"

"Rabbis." She interrupts. "What do they know?"

"That's the whole point isn't it? Rabbis, teachers, leaders..."

"No."

"In Jewish law, a convert is just the same as a person born Jewish. No different at all. That's the *halacha*." It sounds as though he is making a huge effort to keep his voice steady.

"They say that, but it's a trick. Nobody believes this." Now Dave has gone white, and starts to tremble as though he's just realised he's standing in cold, wet clothes.

"*You* don't believe it, maybe," he says. Mutti is standing, anger flashing from her dark eyes.

"I don't," she says, shouting now. "Is a – a – a, what you call it? A con. A trick. Is not real."

"You don't know what you're talking about. You're just desperate for a reason to decide I'm not right." He starts pacing up and down the room, gesticulating and spraying drops of water around. "Not good enough for your daughter. That's been the story from the start. And I was stupid enough to think it was just a matter of faith. I've done everything anybody could reasonably expect to accommodate your – your whims. And to

show my love for your daughter. Why is that not good enough?"
He's screaming at the top of his voice. She shouts back.

"Because nobody really accepts a convert." She spits the
words between her teeth. "They whisper behind their hands.
They 'forget' to invite you to their son's barmitzvah. They tell
their daughter not to play with yours. As if it's catching. And
you can never, never, never overcome this. You are tainted for
ever," she screams at Dave, then shuts her mouth, as if appalled
at what she has just heard herself say.

"But," she adds, limp and defeated, "when the anti–Semites
come, you are Jewish just like the rest of them." Blinking hard,
she turns and leaves the room.

We look at each other. "I think you'd better go," I say. "I'll
call you in the morning. I'm sorry." The towel and dry clothes
stay untouched on the table.

Chapter 28

The weekend hangs heavy. Mutti and I circle each other like
cats staking out territory. By Sunday morning, I've read too
many newspapers and drunk too much coffee. I get into the car
and drive up to Stamford Hill.

The Victorian terraces of St Kilda's Road look empty minus
the police tape and paparazzi, let alone all their peripheral
vehicles, silver boxes and step ladders. I want to see what it
looked like here on the day Bruchi was murdered. Not exactly
quiet, from what I can see. Cars whizz up and down the cross
streets. Out of open windows, boys' voices float down to the
street, chanting prayers in unison. There's something sterile
about it. A young orthodox woman pushes a buggy past me in
a tearing hurry. I track her as she heads towards me on the
pavement, to see if she'll make eye contact. No. What about this

older man with a bushy grey beard that matches the cardigan under his long black coat? I try a tentative smile. Nope, I may as well not exist. I'm a ghost. If Bruchi's killer was walking along instead of me, no one would want to notice.

I scan around 360 degrees, suddenly spooked by the thought that I'm being watched. I am. In an upstairs window a girl in a navy and white-striped jumper is peeking out from behind greying nets, but the moment she sees me looking she pulls the curtains back together and shrinks away. It's like a throwback to the fifties when respectable people minded their own business. That's why somebody could whisk a child away without being challenged.

I feel as though I ought to be looking for clues as to what happened. But of course, there's nothing to see now. Just small signs that this is not like every other street in North London. The huge number of rubbish bins, all overflowing with bulging black bags and surrounded by piles of other detritus – cardboard cartons, old toys – the amount of waste tells a story about the sheer number of people there must be crammed into each house. There's something about the concreted over front gardens that give it an air of concealment.

The warm breeze blows around some empty crisp packets, and with a lull in the level of activity, it reminds me of one of those desolate towns in cowboy movies. In that silent moment before the guy in the black hat rides into town.

Who knows what's lurking inside. I scan from house to house, but those nylon nets keep a thousand secrets. If anybody's spying on me now, as I clumsily survey what was the crime scene, they are well hidden. This is it, number eighty-eight, with its estate agent's board listing in the light breeze. I go quickly up the path and ring the doorbell.

"Any interest yet?" I ask Mrs Friedmann, pointing at the For Sale sign. She nods me in. We go into the kitchen, where there's a big bag of carrots, half of them peeled. She picks up a vegetable knife.

"Yes. A couple came yesterday to see." She peels as though it's a life sentence.

"I've got something to ask you, Mrs Friedmann. It might sound odd, but have you got anybody working for you?"

"I'm not that, well... you know. I receive money." I know that she's bringing up the children on benefits, which doesn't worry me but she seems to embarrassed to spell it out. "I get a little money from my ex-husband. But I can't afford..."

"Do you have any help at all around the house? A childminder, a cleaner?"

"A cleaner, she comes once a week," she concedes. I wish I could afford more often." She sighs, throwing a carrot into a glass bowl full of murky water, where it sinks onto a pile of others.

"How long have you had the same woman?"

"About a year." The cleaner is a woman called Danuta who seems to have escaped Mrs Friedmann's blanket condemnation of all Poles. The only other person is a window cleaner. Mrs Friedmann doesn't know his name, only that he comes on the first Tuesday in the month and charges nine pounds for front or fifteen for front and back. I wonder if he drives a white van.

It's Monday, a week later, when I wake to the sound of the coffee grinder. It's still dark in the flat, but out of the French windows, I can see the sun rising over a misty Holloway. A few straggling rays, pulling their way up the sky. We sit on the balcony at the back of the flat, so that Mutti can smoke. And for once, I don't complain about the wind blowing it all my way.

"You don't have to come, you know," I say. "You might find it – upsetting. May not be the moment of triumph you are expecting. It'll be an anti-climax, after all the build-up."

"I come. I want to see the look on his face."

Mutti looks like an ancient film star on her way out to meet her fans on a tribute night, in her best grey suit, high heels and a fur wrap. I dress as I would to doorstep any other crook – jeans and boots, and lightweight black hiking jacket. DI Jenkins arrives in a marked police car. He introduces us to an academic-looking woman police officer from the specialist art squad. In her hand is a large manila envelope containing large-scale blow-ups of the photographs from Mutti's album.

As we're driving up Holloway Road, crackly radio traffic comes in from an unmarked car parked outside Kovács' place. At eight-thirty this morning, an elderly man in sports jacket and cravat has left the premises, returning just before nine with a newspaper and a loaf of bread. He has entered the house in Lancaster Road, and unless there's a rear exit, he's still there. Mutti holds my hand and squeezes it tight. The journey continues in silence, interrupted only by the occasional radio update from the other team, and the sound of Jenkins' fingers drumming on the arm rest.

Another message crackles through. A man aged about thirty with dark, curly hair and casually dressed has left the house. The elderly man is now alone.

"Let's get there before he decides to go walkabout, Ben," says DI Jenkins to his driver. The junior officer bangs on the siren, and the car lurches forward at speed. I'm sucked into the car seat as we accelerate up Tufnell Park Road, and have to steady myself on the handle above the door. It's thrilling the way other traffic stops to let us through. We pause for the briefest moment at traffic lights. The seat belt cuts into my shoulder, and coffee swills around in my empty stomach.

Messages come through on the radio as we draw closer to the house. The postman has delivered. Someone has arrived. A woman in leather jacket. We pull up. It's bumper to bumper along the pavement. But DI Jenkins and Ben jump out of the car and swing up the steps to the front door. Another officer appears from nowhere to slide into the driver's seat. He sits, foot poised over the gas pedal. The front door of number twenty-seven opens. A young woman. Jenkins is speaking to her, showing her the search warrant. They talk for what seems ages. But then, Jenkins turns and beckons.

The driver helps Mutti out of the car. She's wearing her dowager duchess's disdainful expression. She doesn't look at me, or the officer, but mounts the stairs. Inside the house, Jenkins holds up a hand to tell us to be quiet – shouting can be heard from upstairs, then a pause. It's one half of a phone conversation in Hungarian.

"Can you make out what he's saying?" He asks Mutti. She listens for a moment then shakes her head. There are footsteps on the stairs, and Kovács appears, patting down his oiled, iron-grey hair. A hint of irritation ruffles his previous crisp demeanour.

"Gentlemen, I have no idea what you can be looking for, but please go ahead. I apologise for any delay." The woman from the art squad takes out the photos. She goes around the room, bit by bit with Jenkins, comparing the blow-ups from Mutti's photograph album with all the paintings on the walls. Jenkins turns towards us.

"Could you point out where you thought you'd seen the suspect pictures, please Miss Mueller." I look at the wall opposite the sofa. The striking yellow abstract with russet swirls that I noticed last time we were here is there in the middle. I look either side of it. There are several portraits and some landscapes, most of them contemporary. But the picture of a woman sitting at a table with a bowl of fruit is not here. Neither is a modernist, attenuated portrait of a girl I remember very clearly. The whole arrangement looks different. I think. I check the photograph of my grandparents' apartment in Budapest, and then the wall in front of me again. I look carefully for any lighter or darker patches on the paintwork, or marks from picture hooks that have been moved.

"I think it was here," I say. "Something's changed."

"You have a fevered imagination," spits Kovács.

"Liar," shouts Mutti from behind me. She's stayed near the door. I don't think Kovács has noticed her until now. But suddenly she launches into an avalanche of Hungarian, bearing down on him from across the room. Jenkins and his mate look uncertain.

"Now, Mrs Mueller," protests the DI. I grab onto her arm to stop her getting too near Kovács. He's a slight man and with her arm-wrestling shoulders she could easily throw him to the ground.

"You think I'm going to do something to him? Huh? An old woman like me. But I wasn't always old."

"Mutti, this isn't going to get the pictures back."

"You think I really care?

"You know what he did to me, him and his Russian cronies? You ask him. They were brutes. Nobody cared then, and nobody cares now." She turns to Kovács. "You tell them, you tell them. You think money is the only thing he took from me. Mother couldn't even look at me for a week." She breaks back into Hungarian, a torrent of words rising on to a hysterical pitch. And tears are streaming down her face. Now she is inches away from Kovács, and the words are still flying out of her. He stands his ground, his chin jutting out. He's turned grey and I am now the only thing standing between him and Actual Bodily Harm.

DI Jenkins is by Mutti's side now. "Come on, Mrs Mueller, this isn't helping." He's about to steer her away, when she breaks free and raises her arm. It's as if we are all holding our breath, waiting for her to hit him. But she goes limp, and she just jabs him in the chest and spits. A great gob of saliva hits him just above the eye. He doesn't try to wipe it away.

"I was sixteen. You animal," she says, then screams, "Animal." He stands there, unflinching, just shutting his eyes as the saliva drips down his face. Mutti clicks open her black patent handbag, the one that matches her shoes. She takes out a lace handkerchief, sniffs, and wipes her eyes. Now she pulls herself to her full five-foot-ten, and swishing the fox fur around her shoulders, leaves the house.

As soon as she's out of the door, Jenkins turns to Kovács. "We are now going to search the rest of the property for stolen goods depicted in these photographs," he says.

"Very well," replies Kovács. But his tone has changed. "You will excuse me if I don't assist you."

"And if we subsequently discover items that are relevant to our enquiry, Mr Kovács, we will add obstructing justice to the list already on the sheet."

"I can assure you, that I have been threatened with far worse than that in my life. Ah." He turns to the open front door, where a younger version of himself has appeared, wearing jeans and a cashmere sweater. And a well-cut head of thick, dark brown hair threatening to curl at the ends. "My son, Andris," he says by way of explanation more than introduction. And before Jenkins can ask the younger man to leave, he adds, "As Andy is also my legal advisor, I presume you will permit him to stay."

Andy hands out smart, designer business cards, showing that he is a partner in some kind of upmarket City legal firm. And while he is examining the warrant, the search continues upstairs. Jenkins, Ben and the art lady are joined by two more officers. At first, I follow them round, watching. But as their punctilious search drags on, I go back down.

"So," says Andy, as I reach the bottom stair, "You are the daughter of the legendary Aranca. I heard about your last visit." It's a struggle to maintain my hostility towards someone so absurdly good-looking.

"I wish I could say it's a pleasure to meet you," I mutter.

"Look," he says. "It's not surprising that my father should find this all a bit intrusive. However, I want you to know that I have advised that the best policy is complete openness."

"That's very big of you, Mr Kovács," I say, turning my back on him and walking out of the house, feeling petty. The officer in the car directs me to a café on West End Lane. Mutti is sitting on the terrace with both an espresso and a glass of wine, even though it's still only nine-thirty in the morning. I fan away the cloud of cigarette smoke that is billowing around her, and order a cappuccino.

"That stuff with *Kovács*. Why didn't you say anything earlier?" She shrugs, and takes a deep gulp of the wine.

"How much earlier? When you were a child?"

"Of course not."

"I was waiting for the day you would be old enough to understand."

"And?"

"It never came." Right in the guts. I've been legally entitled to vote for a decade and a half, and she's still the one person in the world who knows just how to make me feel like a crummy little girl.

"And now?" I ask. "Am I old enough now?"

She purses her lips and looks away. "The night the Russians came to us, there were three men. *He* showed them into the apartment, then he disappeared. That would have been enough. One grabbed my mother and another pushed me into the bedroom and forced me onto the bed." She's breathing heavily, as though pulling this all out is an immense physical effort. "He hit me in the face. I think it was just a bit of fun for him. He was shouting at me in Russian, and while my head was reeling he did his business as though I was just a sack of potatoes. If I said no he would shoot me. Nobody would care. Maybe the

Germans had gone, but I was still just a Jew. In fact, worse than that. A Jew bitch."

Another pull on the cigarette, flick of ash.

"I could hear my mother screaming from the other bedroom, and the soldier shouting at her. I tried to get to her, but the soldier grabbed me. He was heavy and rough, laughing with his filthy breath all over me. He didn't even let me take my dress off, just ripped it and forced his way into me. I thought I was breaking in half, my skin is tearing, bleeding. And then..." She looks down, stirs the sugar in its blue bowl, watching the spiral patterns in the white. "I lost control. I wet myself. That made him angry, so he hit me again. And he was laughing and hitting me, and pushing into me again and again. Seemed to go on for hours. I was lying in my own piss and blood, hurting everywhere and I couldn't stop crying. Then I saw Kovács had come back to the apartment. I thought thank God, he will tell them to stop now, to leave us.

"He brought me a glass of water and some schnapps. He was my saviour. He helped me clean myself up and put a clean blanket on the bed. But then he shut the door. He came to where I was lying. And he said 'Now let's make you better.' I – I realised what he wanted and I said, 'No, I can't. Please leave me.' And he just changed suddenly, 'There's another guy out there – you want him or me?' It was that power, you see. He was enjoying it. Turning tables on the boss's daughter.

"Then he changed again and came over friendly. It was all about how he could make life so much easier for us with his connections and his black market goods. I should just lie down and enjoy it. Sixteen I was.

"And I was still bleeding, bruises all over my face. He was saying so many disgusting things about how he'd been watching me grow up, seeing me become a young woman. Each time he'd taken me to the tennis club, and to parties. All the time he'd been leering at me. I felt sick that he'd been there looking at me like that all the time. He was a disgusting viper, my *Uncle Kovács*."

She empties her glass of wine.

"Enough now," she says. "I suppose he's hidden the paintings?"

I shrug. "They'll never find anything."

The squad car is going to drop Mutti and me back home. If I leave straight away I'll get to the office in time for the coffee round and nobody will be any the wiser. But I need to get out of my practical gear, and make sure Mutti's comfortable first. As we approach the flat I stop. There's something wrong. The glass in my French windows at the front of the building is broken.

The squad car is speeding off towards Holloway by now so I race ahead of Mutti and up the steps, open the door, and scan the front room. The stereo's still there, and the TV. Did we scare them off?

I stumble over to have a look at the damage. A more-or-less even, round hole has been made in one of the panes of glass. There's a bit of cracking round the edge, but that's all. It's an odd place to go for a break-in. You'd have to be an amazing athlete to leap from the forecourt to the balcony. Any sensible burglar would try the back first, surely?

Inside, I check the carpet to see where the glass fragments have gone. There are bits on the floor next to the window and scattered across the dining room table.

"Be careful," says Mutti. "Don't cut yourself."

"It's OK, I'm not going to touch anything."

"What's that?" She's pointing at the floor on the other side of the table. Amid the splinters there's a half brick.

"Why would anybody want to break my windows?" I ask. She shrugs. I go to phone a glazier. While I'm speaking, Mutti puts something in my hand. A dirty, crumpled bit of paper with what looks like Hebrew writing on it. We try to decipher what it says, but it's smudged, and Mutti's hazy recollection of the contents of Hungarian prayer books certainly isn't going to help us with it. So, is this some kind of warning? I arrange for the window to be replaced later this afternoon.

I don't want to scare Mutti, but I suggest that instead of staying here alone she might finally like to avail herself of the glories of the British Museum. The stones there pose no threat. She agrees surprisingly meekly, and we leave the flat together. She'll come back at five to meet the glazier.

I'm still feeling wobbly by the time I hit the office, though thank Christ it's not eleven yet. There's a yellow sticky on my desk in unmistakable pointy italics, "*See me.*" It's from someone who knows that a signature is unnecessary. I knock on Sarah's door.

"Come in and tell me how it's going with Leicester," she beckons, with the kind of efficient smile that doesn't overuse her cheek muscles. I slide into the chair opposite her, flip open my notebook, and give her an update. It's all beginning to come together surprisingly well, especially as I've been in Budapest for at least half the research period. She asks lots of questions, pointed and perceptive ones, making sure I've thought about all the angles. OK, it's true I do have to blag my way through it just a teeny bit, but I also realise that in a strange way I've been thinking through a lot of the issues even when so much else has been going on. We talk about shooting styles, and I make some tentative references to movies I like, hoping I don't sound like that pretentious plonker Andrew.

I'm just about to go when she says, "And I gather you've already been on a recce. Fast work."

"Er, yes. I just had a bit of a look round."

"You are in Leicester for two days, and yet you didn't see fit to contact the local police. That seems like a surprising oversight for someone who has been so meticulous in other ways."

"No, er, well I was just looking at the locations. Trying to get them straight in my head."

"Yup. And is the University Hospital of Wales by any chance one of those locations?" I have got no idea what she is talking about.

"Let me remind you. On Saturday the fifth of July, you took a cab from the hospital to an address in the Rhiwbina area of Cardiff, using the programme's account. Does that ring a bell?" Oh shit. Mutti's bloody taxi. I forgot to sort it out with Millie.

"Yes, *that* cab. Elizabeth, I need hardly remind you that misuse of company expenses is a sackable offence."

"It was personal, for my mum – I couldn't get to her because I was working but I was going to pay the money back, honestly Sarah. I've been so busy I forgot."

"And what else have you forgotten? The fact that you haven't been anywhere near Leicester, maybe? I bumped into DI Braithewaite at a conference last week. He was surprised to hear you'd been on their patch because he most certainly hadn't seen you."

It all tumbles out. She knew about my father's death, of course, but Mutti's suicide bid, her claim for reparations and our adventure in Hungary is all news to her. Once I've started talking, I can't stop.

"Look," I say, getting up. "I'll clear my desk and give my notes to Andrew. I'm sure he'd appreciate a chance to direct a film. It's nearly ready to go. The schedule and scripts are so detailed it'll be like colouring by numbers."

"Sit down," she says. "I'm not about to give that idiot the job you've earned. And I don't want to hear any more about you trying to throw it away either. You should be fighting to keep it with every sinew in your body.

"Considering what's been going on, I'm amazed you've done so much. According to Braithewaite you've got a fabulous phone manner, and all the paperwork you've sent them is top notch. Sounds like you're in good shape for a shoot next week."

"But aren't you going to sack me for fiddling my expenses? Not to mention lying about the recce."

"Just because it's a sackable offence, doesn't mean I have to. In case you haven't worked it out, Elizabeth, I'm on your side. Pay the money back, and do me a favour – try to get to the end of the month without any secret trips to Budapest, Kiev or Warsaw. The film sounds fine. I look forward to the viewing. Now piss off."

That evening, we don't want to hang around in the flat, so Mutti takes me to the Cosmo for a *Wiener Schnitzel* and a glass of wine (I permit her just one, and myself one too). Now that the house rental is coming in, her bank account is off its death bed. She wears her unseasonal fur stole, and I open the door for her, so that she can sweep in and be grand.

We behave like actors in a black and white film from the 1930s, sitting with straight backs, and making short, witty remarks instead of having a proper conversation. But by the time the apple strudel arrives she's starting to look tired. I put a hand on hers.

"We'll get them, in the end," I say. "Don't worry." She gives me a sceptical look.

"Doesn't matter any more." She strokes her fur, pensive. "You know, it was for you."

"What was?"

"All this rubbish – claiming the money."

"But you need it to live on."

"I'm OK. Get state pension, small savings. I can sell house, no big deal."

"So why have we been doing it?"

"Say sorry."

"You want the Hungarians to apologise. Well, they bloody well should."

"No. It's for me. I need to say sorry too."

"What are you talking about?"

"To you. I wasn't great mother. I loved you but it wasn't enough."

"You did your best."

"Sometimes that's not enough. You will do better." She thinks the poison gets diluted through the generations. I wish it was that simple. But you can't unstitch the past that easily and put it back together. I'm the product of her damaged childhood, just as much as she is.

"You don't need to say sorry, and I don't need your money. We'll be OK." She squeezes my hand. "Though to be honest, I will be glad to get my flat back. I hope you don't mind me admitting that."

Mutti goes to bed, while I sort through the compensation file late into the night. There must be a loophole, a clue, something. When I stop, it's nearly midnight and the shared hallway is dark. All my neighbours are safely locked in their flats.

Before turning in, I put my trainers back on and go outside. The front of the property looks secure, bathed in the glow of the street lights. All of the windows are sound. At the side of the building it's dark and the security light with a movement sensor which should go on automatically, doesn't. I wish I'd brought a torch. I scan the side and back of the house in the gloom, it all looks OK, but I still can't shift the horrible feeling that we are being watched. Of course, I should let DI Jenkins know what's happened, but that'll wait until tomorrow.

I'm just pulling my pyjamas over my head when I notice there's something on my pillow. It's one of those little plastic snowstorm shakers, featuring a tiny model of the admirable

Hungarian parliament with its Romanesque, Classical and Gothic architecture. And underneath it, a bundle of letters tied up with a stained silk ribbon. I untie the bow, and release a wad of paper sheets so thin they are almost transparent. Letters with several different dates, the pages criss-crossed by crease marks where they have been folded and folded. Though the ink has faded to brown, and there's a scattering of blurry splodges from tears or snow, the words are still clearly legible. If only I could read Hungarian.

There's one other sheet with the bundle. It's torn from the type of lined, ring-bound reporter's notebook that Mutti uses for her shopping lists. In pencil, in her favoured capital letters is written:

December 1943
My dearest girls, Be happy for me!

I compare it with the top letter in the bundle which is headed December 1943. Mutti's note continues:

I have managed to come by a greatcoat from one of our fallen comrades, when so many others are left with nothing but rags. By night we lose several of our number worn down by the cold, the meagre rations and the endless marching. The officer in charge of food supplies is an old friend from university days. He favours me with extra bread. So you see, my situation is improving, and I am strong. You must not worry....

Who is this from? *My dearest girls.* From my grandfather to whom? Mutti and my grandmother I imagine. In the margin, there's a pencil scribble. The word *Munckaszolat,* I've seen that before. Of course, the forced labour divisions of the Hungarian army. If my grandfather was conscripted he must have got back to Budapest. He was shot in 1944. That would be ironic. In a bad way, a truly appalling way. He escapes the horror of the front line, only to be shot by fascists when he manages to get home. There's a line, and Mutti's written the word *MORE,* and then,

> *I miss you both so much, my two lovely girls. At night, I think about what we will do when the war is over. We will travel to Paris and Perugia. We will eat the greatest delicacies, the tenderest meats, the most delicate pastries. All that matters now is that we get through, and find each other once more when this hell is over.*

It peters out there. It's a fragment of a fragment. I shake the snowstorm and look at the letters again, the wobbly attempt at copperplate. While the flakes are settling on the miniature architectural marvel, I finger the worn sheets, where they are coming apart on the creases. These letters have been eroded by handling, the pages ripe with love and grief. I read it and read it again into the early hours, running my eye over the puzzling Hungarian sentences flecked with accents, and try to imagine the grandfather I never met.

Chapter 29

I must drift off, because I'm woken by the phone ringing. I jerk myself up and lunge at the bedside table, but when I get the receiver to my ear, all I can hear is dialling tone. This is getting creepy, but I don't know what to do. Hoping that the noise hasn't woken Mutti, I sink back on the pillows and watch the pink-tinged daylight breaking over the rooftops. I put on my dressing gown and drift into the lounge, gazing through the new pane in the French window across the dense maze of terraced houses and council blocks that stretch away, till scruffy

Lower Holloway gives way to leafy Tufnell Park. I won't tell Mutti for now.

The nausea is still there, but it's accompanied by a ferocious physical energy. The only way of getting rid of any of it is the gym. The place is humming with the kind of successful people who have to exercise early in the morning, because that's the only 'window' they have left in their busy diaries. I'm not even sure whether pregnant women are supposed to run on treadmills, but I don't care. I hide myself among them, hoping nobody will spot that I'm a fraud, running until my thighs are seizing up and sweat has saturated my bra. I heave weights above my head, watching in the mirror as my muscles contract into sinewy shapes, lifting and lowering again, and again, until I lose count. At home, Mutti's is probably just shaking off the sleeping tablet fuzz. I hope she's OK. Make mental note to call DI Jenkins about the stone through my window.

Leaving my kit in a locker, I walk the pavements for miles until I reach Holborn. It's mid-morning by the time I'm standing outside the office of a smart legal firm. It's a cliff face of glass and steel, refracting a dazzling broken jigsaw of the building opposite in the morning sun. A receptionist with a painted-on smile and geometric hair looks unblinking at me.

"Mr Andris Kovács, please."

"Is Mr Kovács expecting you?"

"No, but I think he'll want to see me." She picks up a phone and dials a number.

"And who shall I say is calling?" Before she's had a chance to write down my name, I've pushed through the turnstile with a girl in high heels and am hurtling up through the atrium in a glass lift. When I get out, I find myself facing a long glass wall with a row of offices. Helpfully, there are name signs on each door. Less helpfully, there's another dragon with savage red lips outside the office of Andris Kovács LLB, partner.

"I'm sorry, you don't seem to have an appointment."

"I don't need one," I say and walk past her open mouth. I'd like to bang the door shut in her face, but it's got one of those hydraulic mechanisms which makes it shuffle to a silent close. He's wearing a pin-stripe suit every bit as well cut as the jeans he was wearing yesterday and has a phone tucked between ear and shoulder.

"Er, you might have to bear with me one moment," he says into it, and turning to me. "Miss Mueller, this isn't at all convenient."

"It's convenient for me," I say, sitting down in a chair opposite him, putting my bag on my lap, and looking him straight in the eye.

"Look, I'm sorry about this," he says into the phone, "but something's come up." I wait for him to put the phone down. He straightens his blue silk tie. In any other situation, I'd be too overwhelmed by his devastating looks to even say hello.

"Mr Kovács," I say, "or should I call you Andy? Anyway, I'm fed up of playing games of cat and mouse, and pretending to be pally. It's all a front, and I want to know the truth."

"I'm sorry?"

"The pictures, Mr Kovács. Where are they?"

"I have no idea what you are talking about."

"Really? I reckon you and your father would make quite good mug shots for our rogues' gallery on *The Crime Programme*. Or maybe you'd like to see yourself in a dramatic reconstruction film telling the story of a major art theft."

"Don't talk such rubbish."

"I'm serious."

"And I am too. I presume there are professional guidelines even for your tawdry profession and barging into my office has got to be breaking every rule in the book. Not to mention making wild allegations without an iota of evidence." He picks

302

up the phone. "What's the name of the person in charge there?"

The thought of Sarah hearing what I've said takes my breath away.

"Well?"

"The series editor's name is Sarah Phillips," I say, trying to look as though I don't care whether he calls her or not. I dictate her direct number, one digit at a time. He scribbles it on a pad. And looks at me.

"First I'm going to phone my father."

"There's nothing he can tell you that you don't know already."

"I'm just trying to find out what's going on."

"Really?" I say. "Either he or my mother is lying, and I know who I'd put my money on." I'm on his side of the desk now, trembling with anger.

I grab him by the lapels, and I'm shaking him, spitting in his face as I shout. "My mother trusted your father!" – by now I'm blubbing out of control. "And he took advantage of her in the vilest way possible." I shake him, screaming at the top of my voice, "And now you are both trying to fuck us over again."

Andy tries to push me away, but I'm gripping him with superhuman strength. "Have you got any idea," I yell, "what it's like growing up with a mother who is so disturbed that she's got to anaesthetise herself with booze all the time? Have you?" My nose is an inch away from his. "So that you couldn't count on her getting through any routine event without completely losing it? Not a school play, not a birthday party, not a trip to the swimming pool."

Out of the corner of my eye I see somebody else enter the room, and as that happens Andy pushes me again. This time I lose my grip because by now I am shuddering and crying, my strength vaporised. One push is enough to put me off balance. I stumble backwards and hit the floor with a thud, jerking my head back. A bolt of pain shoots down my neck. I'm struggling to get back onto my feet, but somehow it's difficult. I feel as though I'm at the bottom of a swimming pool with Andy towering above me, and the other person looming into view. I struggle to focus. Shiny brass buttons on a blue jacket. I feel a big hand clamp round my arm and pull me. But I'm not sure who it is.

"That's enough now. Come with me, please." I can hear snatched bits of conversation, but none of it makes sense.

"Hold on... her head..." The voices are muffled. Nobody finishes a sentence. It's like a bad edit, with shots cut in half and spliced together randomly and stray bits of audio popping up out of sync. I hear a groan, and realise it's my own voice. Then, "She's bleeding..." I flop back down, the ground swinging beneath me.

The next thing I know, I'm sitting on a sofa holding a wet compress on the back of my head. And Andy's there with a cup of hot, sweet tea. He's terribly solicitous and, of course, still fantastically good looking.

"I'm sorry", I groan. "I didn't mean—"

"It's OK, just forget about it."

"What I mean is I just got a bit carried away."

"It's understandable."

"It is?"

Andy excuses himself and lets the first aider take over. She examines my head and checks my reflexes. My hair is wet with congealing blood at the back, but the cut is small, perhaps I haven't got concussion after all. She gives me some painkillers and puts some liquid plaster on the cut. After she's gone, the red-mouthed dragon puts her head round the door. And gives the sweetest smile.

"Mr Kovács is just finishing his conference call. He'll be with you in a minute." She disappears, leaving me alone. I look around. There's lots of white light, and it's hurting my eyes. I take a make-up mirror out of my bag and clean up the smears of mascara. Then I put on my coat and find my way back to the lift.

I start walking down High Holborn, feeling hot and limp. It's still quite early, the morning is clouded but close, and heat is radiating up from the pavement making me sweat. That constant queasiness pursues me, as though I'm trapped in a rocking boat. And now I'm exhausted too. I look round for a cab. The paracetamol must be wearing off because my head's beginning to throb again, and now I've got stomach cramps as well. Where on earth is a taxi when you need one? I keep walking, with an eye on the traffic. I see one, but as it comes closer I can see it's full. Then there's another, empty and coming straight towards me. I step out into the road, just as it sails on past. The backdraft slaps me in the face. There's a tight spasm in my stomach.

I crouch on the edge of the curb holding my tummy. I think I'm about to be sick. There's a tap on my back. I turn to see a policeman.

"Are you OK, madam?"

"It's nothing," I say. He helps me to my feet, and scrutinises me. Oh God, he thinks I'm drunk. How loud do I have to say that *I am not like my mother*, for Christ's sake.

"Officer," I say, speaking as clearly and unslurringly as I can, "I don't suppose you can help me find a cab?"

I tell the driver to take me home. I'll just clean myself up and lie down for a few hours. Everything will be fine. Then we hit a pothole and my stomach sends out another spasm. I feel my pulse shoot up. Something disgusting and wet creeps down the inside of my leg.

"Tell you what," I call up to the driver. "Take me to the nearest hospital."

On the pavements of Farringdon Road, girls in neat little suits and pumps are rushing between offices. They weave their way through the stationary traffic carrying loaded cardboard coffee cup holders. There's a billboard advertising a new film, an *Evening Standard* vendor shouting out the headline news. We've trundled under the railway bridge, towards the traffic lights before I've clocked "Arrest in Stamford Hill murder" on the newspaper placard. That is what it said, isn't it? I crane my head round, but it's disappearing behind us. There don't seem to be any more newsstands, along the miles and miles of pavement. I call Jenkins, but his number's on voicemail.

At the hospital, I lever myself out of the cab, thighs pressed together and trying not to breathe. No sudden moves. Hurrying as slowly as I can, it's an agonising waddle from the forecourt into Accident and Emergency. I reach the main entrance through a curtain of cigarette smoke. Inside, I pass a fat woman bursting out of a minidress with her head bent over a grey cardboard bowl. I steer a wide circle around her, fearful that the odour of vomit is going to make me heave too.

"The current waiting time is three hours," says the receptionist. "As you can see, it's very busy." Really? I can only see a only few people sprawled out over the metal benches.

"I'm bleeding."

"The triage nurse will come and see you," says the girl with a flat, impassive expression that makes me want to slap her. On TV medical dramas they seem to get very excited about people who are actually bleeding. They run around "resus" looking concerned, and put up drips, measure blood pressure and exchange many meaningful looks over the patient as they are working. It doesn't seem worth pointing this out to the receptionist.

A man with an impressive cut on his forehead makes space for me to sit down. I sit there for a long time, listening to a woman in stiletto sandals and tight jeans complaining in a screechy voice about "that Shaylah", and how she "turned round and told her what she thought of her".

The stomach cramps are still there, though at least they don't seem to have become any worse. There are a few ragged old magazines lying around with straplines like "My cross-dressing son murdered my daughter" and "Five-year-old's ten foot tapeworm". My eyes settle on a television that is suspended high up on the wall. It's playing some kind of game show.

After just one hour, a nurse calls my name, but it's a false alarm. A further hour and I'm ushered into a cubicle. I lie on the bed because there is nowhere else to sit. And as I do so, the cramps worsen. Over the next twenty minutes, the pains get more and more intense, and there's still no sign of a medic. Then the curtain is pulled aside, and a nurse puts her head through.

"Do you think I could have something for the stomach ache?" I ask. She gives me a disparaging look, as though she knows that I'm suffering the morning-after effects of too many pints of lager and a curry.

"The doctor won't want you to have anything until he's seen you," she says.

"How long do you think that might be?"

"I'm sorry but we're very busy," she says, as she disappears.

As the curtains swing back together I get a feeling as if someone has plunged a screwdriver into my guts. Churning cramps. My knees pull themselves up to my abdomen of their own free will. Sweat has broken out on my forehead, but my mouth is dry. The sense of loneliness is desperate.

I can't imagine a baby surviving inside me now. It would seem like an earthquake for her. And after the earthquake, the tsunami. I can feel a large, gelatinous bulk slide into my pants, and as it does so, the pains begin to subside. A feeling of disgust overwhelms me and I try to drag off my underwear, to get the fearsome, disgusting, alien mass away from me. I'm scrambling up the bed, dragging and ripping at it, just as the sharp sound of metal rings swishing along the curtain pole announce the arrival of the doctor.

A confusing swirl of images, mixed through with the white glare of ceiling lights. And breaking through it all, a familiar face in a white coat is looking at me, with an expression of shock and concern. I can't quite focus on who it is. Don't care.

"Something's come out, it's come out. Get it away," I shriek.

"Lie down, just relax and let us do this," he says, pressing me back onto the bed, and shouting out, "Nurse! Now!" The nurse appears in moments, and holds me round the shoulders while the doctor eases my knickers down with latex-gloved hands. He wraps the thing into a large piece torn from the roll of sterile blue paper, and leaves the cubicle with it. The memory of it coming out plays over and over again in my mind. I'm shaking and shouting, and pushing it away even though I know it's gone really, but it feels as though it's still there. The rational side of my mind can't take control and stop me juddering and scrambling back along the bed.

"It's OK, it's gone. Stay still." I can feel the nurse holding me down, and the sharp prick of an injection. Bit by bit, the shaking stops, and the replayed sensations grind to slo-mo and then a freeze frame. Even with the fluorescent lights piercing my eyelids, I can feel my breathing and pulse subside, and I must drift off. I don't know how long I'm out for. The nurse shakes me.

"I've got a cup of tea for you here, if you feel up to it." I'm still trembling, so she holds it and lets me sip the hot, sweet liquid until I'm calm enough to grasp it myself. Another swish of the curtains and the doctor is back. Recognition kicks in. It's Jon. With a stethoscope. I jerk with surprise and spill some of the tea on the surgical gown I seem to be wearing. He puts out a hand to steady me, and helps me hold the cup level.

"How are you feeling?"

I shrug but don't manage to say anything, because I'm shocked how lovely he is, and how pleased I am to see him. I scrutinise his face for the arrogance I saw there before.

"So you *are* a doctor then," I say.

"Yes, sorry about that."

"No, I didn't mean – it's OK, it's fine. It's good." He smiles a disarmingly charming smile.

"And in my medical capacity there is one good thing I can tell you. You won't need to have any further surgery."

"I suppose that's something."

"But it might take a day or two before you are back to normal." He's folded his arms, with one hand on his chin and a worried look.

"Sorry, I didn't mean to be rude," I say. "Bit of a shock. Is there something else you wanted to say?" He looks embarrassed.

"Nurse, would you give me a moment, please?" She nods and steps through the curtains. He sits down on the bed next to me. "I do need to ask you something," he whispers. "Were you – um? When we, I mean... am I just jumping to conclusions when I wonder? "

"I'm sorry, this is going to sound very irresponsible," I say. "But I don't know."

"What exactly don't you know? Were you pregnant before – when we...?"

"Oh, no. At least I don't think so. I only realised a few days ago."

"So who is the...?"

"That's it. I don't know." I'm bracing myself for him to be judgemental, with every possible justification.

"So," he says. "It is possible?" And he points to himself.

"Possible that it was yours? Yes. But it's not what it looks like."

"What does it look like?"

"Well, as though I'm... What I mean is – there is one other person. Possibly."

"I see." He nods. "The hapless *goyishe* photographer?"

"Yes." I expect him to say something nasty. But he doesn't. He just stands there looking at me.

"I'm sorry," I say. "I should have got in touch."

"Would have been nice and all. Even if I was only in with a fifty-fifty."

"Are you trying to say that you would have *wanted* me to have your baby?" His redness intensifies, and I'm sure I'm not imagining that I can make out a certain wetness in his eyes.

"Look, forget about it." He turns to go, then seems to have second thoughts. "This is all totally unethical, and I'll probably get struck off if anybody finds out, but can I give you a call later on? Maybe we could have that coffee?"

Chapter 30

Mutti's shocked to see what a state I'm in when I get back home. She wants me to go to the doctor's although I assure her there is nothing whatever wrong that a couple more painkillers, a cup of tea and some chocolate biscuits won't fix. She knows I'm lying. Not one of those casual lies I tell every day about where I've been and who I've been with, but a big huge massive lie that I'm telling myself as well as her. That I don't care. That it's for the better. That it wasn't really a proper baby yet, just a bunch of cells.

Of course it wasn't just a bunch of cells. And now that it's gone, I realise for the first time how curious I am...was...about the baby and whether I'd be any good at all as a mother. But now I'm gripped by a terror that I'll never, ever be able to get pregnant again. After all, I deserve to pay the price for being such an idiot.

Mutti knows all this without asking. She doesn't want me to talk about how I feel, just wraps me in a big fluffy blanket and sits there holding my hand. The following day she's still treating me like an invalid. She's even phoned work on my behalf. I don't protest.

We've got an unspoken pact not to discuss the broken window and what is now an unsettling series of silent phone calls, because it spooks us out. I need to find out what was in that scribbled Hebrew note, and the best hope for that has to be Morrie, but I haven't got the energy to call him now. I'm hoping that the new arrest for Bruchi's murder will have sorted the problem, but when Mutti's not about I can't help stealing the occasional furtive glance out of the window. And I'm screening my calls again. I really will have to talk to Jenkins. When I'm ready. For now, I lie back on sofa while Mutti fixes foul smelling herbal tea that must have been in the cupboard for years. I'm sniffing the steam rising from the cup when there's a ring on the doorbell.

"Are you expecting someone?" she asks, pressing the intercom. We look at each other, and in that instant I regret not calling Jenkins. I most certainly am not expecting anyone. Who on earth is it?

"Delivery ma'am." I haul myself up and go to the speaker.

"Have you got ID?"

"Yes, ma'am. But first, you might want to take a look out the front." There's a van on the kerb inscribed with the logo SINCLAIR SPECIALIST DELIVERY, and then in smaller letters underneath "Transport you can trust". I open the door to find a man in blue overalls.

"Miss Mueller?"

"I haven't ordered anything."

"Larry mate," he calls out. "Young lady says she hasn't ordered anything. Check the docket, will you?"

"Look," I say, "I'm sure it's a mistake. Do you want to come back when you've sorted it out? I'm really not up to this today."

"It'll only take a minute, Miss. Hang on." As he says that, the driver gets out of the van, holding a clipboard, the edge of its paperwork fluttering in the breeze.

"Nope, mate, it's all kosher. I spoke to Ed, and it's the right place." I'm still musing on the fact that he's got no idea at all what "kosher" really means, when he rolls up the back of the van. The two men start unloading a picture covered in many layers of bubble wrap.

"Where do you want them, Miss?"

Mutti's gone back to her crosswords. She gets to her feet when she sees the men in overalls coming into the room carrying a substantial canvas.

"Bring it here. On the sofa."

"I don't advise putting an artwork on the sofa, Madam. How about the table?"

"*Ja*, good. Put it down." He lays the painting flat. Mutti starts fumbling at the bubble wrap with shaking hands.

"Hold on now, madam. That's no way to handle an oil painting. Do you want me to remove the packaging?" She nods. He takes out a Stanley knife, and neatly snips the sellotape on the package. Layer after layer falls away, until the gold frame pokes out of the wrapping. Then the painting itself emerges. It's the woman next to the table, with the bowl of fruit. Mutti groans.

By the time the men have finished, there's a row of pictures of different sizes, arranged in a careful row along the wall of the lounge, still in their bubble wrap. As he puts down the last one, the delivery man asks me to sign a document on his clipboard. He unclips an envelope from underneath it and gives it to me. It's heavy, laid paper, the kind you get in old-fashioned stationery shops. Mutti's name is written in elegant handwriting on the front, by someone who uses an expensive fountain pen. I look round, but she's not there. I find her on the balcony, breathing heavily and swaying.

When I give her the letter, she just looks at it as though she's forgotten how to read. So I open it for her. The card is headed ANDRIS KOVÁCS in small, square black embossed capitals. The content is brief. No "dear" anybody, not even "For the attention of". But in the middle of the page are the words,

I know 'sorry' doesn't really cover it. Kindest regards, Andris.

When the men have driven off in their delivery truck, we sit on the bench together, watching the darkness eat up the back garden. Rush hour traffic grumbles on Camden Road. We've left the paintings in the front room still swathed in their layers of wrapping while we enjoy this moment of calm. One by one, lights come on in neighbouring flats, as their owners return from office, studio and workshop. Whirring, banging and grinding tell us that kitchens have come to life once more. And discordant chorus of voices chatter and hum from televisions, radios and CDs.

"Don't you want to have a look at the rest of them?" I ask. Mutti looks surprised.

"*Ja*, why not?"

We unpick the bubble wrap, bit by bit, dropping layer upon layer onto the floor. As the last piece drops away, a curlicued gold frame emerges, and finally the canvas itself. A magnificent likeness of a lady, looking as though it dates from the mid-nineteenth century. The regal blue gown is corseted at the waist, skirts spread over a vast crinoline, with silk fabric looking soft enough to touch, each fold and scallop catching the light in a different way. Mutti nods.

We unwrap the next and the next. There are landscapes and portraits, interiors and still life, like a potted history of the styles and techniques of European art through the nineteenth and early twentieth centuries – impressionist, expressionist, and even one abstract. A nod to Picasso there, to Degas there. After we've looked at them all, we carefully replace the bubble wrap, and leave them stacked against the wall.

"They probably aren't worth anything, anyway," I say to Mutti.

"No," says Mutti. "Nothing at all."

"But there's a lot of sentimental value."

"*Ja*," says Mutti. "Very much sentimental value." And she flicks a long pillar of ash into the ashtray.

When I catch up with Jenkins, he tells me that they've arrested a man called Germaine Jones. He was working for a local estate agent.

"He was just the guy who went round putting up the For Sale signs. He had a heap of them in an old white minibus." I gasp.

"I saw him!"

"You didn't say anything. When?"

"Well I had no idea – I mean I didn't suspect... It was the very first day I came up to Stamford Hill to have a nose around. I'd gone into an estate agent to see if I could get any information about the area, and that bloke was bodging about there, coming and going. It must have been him."

"I bet you didn't give him a second thought."

"Not one. He was just in the background. But how did you work it out? I don't remember him being on your list of possible suspects." Jenkins looks momentarily embarrassed. Hardly surprising if there's stuff they don't want to – or can't share, I suppose.

"In the end, the white van was the clue. You think there are dozens of them in the area, but each of them criss-crosses the same streets a couple of times a day, so you think there are far more than there really are. It wasn't all that difficult to track them down, and that was it, really."

"So no real link to the community, nothing sinister there?"

"Just opportunity, I imagine."

I congratulate DI Jenkins, and we shake hands. I'd like to give him a hug, but that would be unprofessional in the extreme. Walking out of the station into "Stokey" High Street, it's still going round in my head. It was just some regular guy. Well, a regular weirdo anyway. That's real. Not like a TV drama where the killer turns out to be one of the cast members who you've already been ploddingly introduced to, and whose motive is suddenly revealed by a clever twist of the plot. But this is real life. You couldn't have guessed. There was no conspiracy. Just one of those awful things that happen, and Bruchi was just in the wrong place at the wrong time, stupid bloody cliché that it is.

Chapter 31

The following week I'm out in Leicester, directing my film. Let's say that again, *I'm directing a film*. The armourer is scarier than his guns, and the actors really do ask me about their motivation. I don't get a minute's sleep in my hotel bed, because I'm so busy working out my shot lists for day two. Despite exhaustion, I manage to stumble towards the wrap and Bill says he's sure it's all in the can, "Well done, kid."

Six months later, I find time to slip in to the opening of Dave's new show. He's found this little gallery space in Stoke Newington for his photographs of the Hasidic community. It's a little shop front. Where the greengrocer used to sell cabbages and carrots from stands covered in artificial grass, they've painted the walls brilliant white. The stills are set on cream mounts in aluminium frames, several of which bear little red stickers meaning they've been sold. There are a handful of *frummers* there, and the kind of arty crowd Dave's always hung out with. It's perfect synthesis of both the worlds that he inhabits now.

I told him about the miscarriage, and about Jon, as soon as I could. That's not why we split up though. Well, not the only reason. He tells me about the classes he's doing, and the way he manages to fit daily religious observance round his work. And as he walks away, I notice the white tassels hanging down from under his shirt. It's not for me, it's for him.

Mutti has moved back in to her house in Rhiwbina. When she's had time to settle in, I go to visit. As the engine stills, I catch some faint notes of violin music floating in the atmosphere. I open the car door, and sit listening. Street sounds, a front door banging closed, birdsong and the distant bark of a lawn mower. Then a rising arpeggio cuts through the static, a fragile wisp of a thing, clinging on to the air. I think that's Mendelssohn's violin concerto. Can't be Mutti, surely? It stops, and then starts again, repeating a phrase several times, before sweeping on. But she hasn't got an instrument.

I let myself into the house, and the playing gets louder. Coming from upstairs. Then it's suddenly interrupted by a noise from the kitchen. The staccato whirring of an electric mixer, in short compulsive bursts. I find Mutti at the Kenwood, surrounded by flour, butter and piles of rich yellow apricots.

"Who's playing the violin?" I ask, as she kisses me hello.

"I'm making B&B. I told you."

"Yes, yes, Mrs Llewellyn is helping you with the advert. You told me, but that doesn't explain the music."

"She tells me special place for advert, WNO."

"What is WNO?

"You know. Welsh National."

"Welsh National what?"

"Opera. What you think? Opera!"

"But don't their musicians have a home already?"

"Guest artistes for violin section." She scrapes cake mixture off the side of the bowl with a large red spatula, and sweeps a fingerful into her mouth.

"Mmm delicious. Needs drop of vanilla. Must practise four hours a day." As she bustles into the larder, there are footsteps on the stairs, and a young man with a blond beard appears.

"Hi, I'm Hugo." I shake his hand as gently as I can. I don't want to be the person who mangles his virtuosity.

"Can I help with something, Mrs M?" he asks as Mutti emerges from the larder.

Hugo and I lay the table together for late lunch, as he has a performance tonight. Mutti insists on an embroidered tablecloth that was part of her trousseau. While she is kneading the *galuskas*, and fine-slicing the cucumbers, she begs him to bring down his instrument. He demurs. Mutti begs him.

"Please. Would make me so happy."

He says, "Look, I'm sorry to disappoint you, but I must think of my performance." And I think, oh no, let's not be responsible for ruining tonight's recital. Let alone tomorrow's. Think of all the people who have paid exorbitant sums for tickets. Can this man really withstand the rigours of Mutti's hospitality? Let's hope she doesn't decide he needs a spot of arm-wrestling as a warm up. But he suddenly caves in, "OK, OK," and I realise it's an elaborate game they've been playing with each other.

He's teasing her and she's lying there on her back having her tummy tickled. In the metaphorical sense. Hugo sets up his music stand in the middle of the kitchen, playing a ravishing mazurka, with Mutti singing along and conducting as she scatters dill over the cucumber salad in time to the music.

"The auction's next Wednesday," I say. "Are you coming down to London?"

"Of course," she replies. "I wear my mink."

"Don't get your hopes up, sweeping in dressed to kill and ending up disappointed. You know what the lady at Sotheby's said. It's impossible to predict what kind of price we are going to get for any of them."

"I don't care. Maybe I don't sell after all. I have paintings all around the house. I make special artistic B&B with priceless art collection." She flourishes the salad server around her head in time to the music.

One painting has been hung in pride of place in the dining room. It's not going to the auction – an oil painting of a beautiful young woman in a red silk dress, playing the violin. A portrait of a young Mutti. It watches over us as we eat dinner.

Hugo eats with enthusiasm, complimenting each dish. For Mutti, that would be reward enough. But, to my astonishment, he appears able to discuss the finer points of Hungarian cuisine. That's something even Dad wasn't up to. He wonders if Mutti favours the sweet paprika or the strong one for a *gulyas*. What is her view of caraway seeds? She glows, as I have never seen her glow before.

For dessert, Mutti carves out three generous tranches of apricot *kuchen*. Through the ripples in Hugo's beard, I discern a look of satisfied anticipation. She dollops a heavy spoonful of *schlagsahne* on top of one piece, and hands it to him. She cuts another slice, sinking the silver ladle back into the cream and scoops it up. As it is poised over the cake, she turns to me.

"So," she says. "How's Jonathan?"

"He's fine," I reply. "Jon's fine." And you know what? It's not code for anything.

ABOUT HONNO

Honno Welsh Women's Press was set up in 1986 by a group of women who felt strongly that women in Wales needed wider opportunities to see their writing in print and to become involved in the publishing process. Our aim is to develop the writing talents of women in Wales, give them new and exciting opportunities to see their work published and often to give them their first 'break' as a writer. Honno is registered as a community co-operative. Any profit that Honno makes is invested in the publishing programme. Women from Wales and around the world have expressed their support for Honno. Each supporter has a vote at the Annual General Meeting. For more information and to buy our publications, please write to Honno at the address below, or visit our website: www.honno.co.uk

Honno, 14 Creative Units, Aberystwyth Arts Centre
Aberystwyth, Ceredigion SY23 3GL

Honno Friends

We are very grateful for the support of the Honno Friends:
Jane Aaron, Annette Ecuyere, Audrey Jones, Gwyneth
Tyson Roberts, Beryl Roberts, Jenny Sabine.
For more information on how you can become a Honno
Friend, see: http://www.honno.co.uk/friends.php